He dreamed of a wolf, its coat more dazzling than the whitest snow, its eyes as fierce and golden as his own. The Spirit Wolf padded closer, but when he looked into its magical, golden eyes the dream became all tangled. A woman came to him, silver-haired and silver-eyed, her hands held out to him. From her fingers a small object dangled: the medallion with the heart pierced by seven swords. He reached out to embrace her, but she dissolved into mist. He heard a voice crying out in fear and loneliness.

He awakened with it ringing in his ears, and knew it was his own.

Also by Marianne Willman

Silver Shadows

Available from
HarperPaperbacks

ATTENTION: ORGANIZATIONS AND CORPORATIONS

Most HarperPaperbacks are available at special quantity discounts for bulk purchases for sales promotions, premiums, or fund-raising. For information, please call or write:
Special Markets Department, HarperCollins Publishers,
10 East 53rd Street, New York, N.Y. 10022.
Telephone: (212) 207-7528. Fax: (212) 207-7222.

YESTERDAY'S SHADOWS

MARIANNE WILLMAN

HarperPaperbacks
A Division of HarperCollinsPublishers

If you purchased this book without a cover, you should be
aware that this book is stolen property. It was reported as
"unsold and destroyed" to the publisher and neither the
author nor the publisher has received any payment for this
"stripped book."

This is a work of fiction. The characters, incidents, and
dialogues are products of the author's imagination and are not
to be construed as real. Any resemblance to actual events or
persons, living or dead, is entirely coincidental.

HarperPaperbacks *A Division of* HarperCollins*Publishers*
                  10 East 53rd Street, New York, N.Y. 10022

Copyright © 1991 by Marianne Willman
All rights reserved. No part of this book may be used or
reproduced in any manner whatsoever without written
permission of the publisher, except in the case of brief
quotations embodied in critical articles and reviews. For
information address HarperCollins*Publishers*,
10 East 53rd Street, New York, N.Y. 10022.

Cover illustration by Elaine Gignilliat

First printing: May 1991

Printed in the United States of America

HarperPaperbacks, HarperMonogram, and colophon are
trademarks of HarperCollins*Publishers*

10 9 8 7 6 5 4 3

For Melissa Ellen
Emily Marie
Amber Lynn
Jeffery Ky. II
and
Alexandria Louise
Willman

—Who are all much too young to read this book—
with loving wishes that you will all find adventure,
fulfillment and love
by following your own bright, shining stars.

Prologue

Clarksville, Pennsylvania: 1826

"Just for a few weeks, ma'am. No more than a month at most."

Miss Olmstead folded her hands upon her desk and looked up at the handsome stranger. "I'm afraid you are under a misapprehension, sir. This is not a boarding school, but an orphanage."

He ran a quick hand over his forehead, pushing back the lock of heavy dark hair. The silent child at his side, a girl of four or perhaps five years, crept closer and hugged his leg.

"I understand that, ma'am. But you see, my wife is . . ." He glanced quickly at his daughter. "I'm a widower, new in town. There's no one a'tall I can turn to, and this is a life-and-death matter, like I said. And it's just for a few days."

Miss Olmstead eyed him appraisingly. There was a tension about him, an air of suppressed excitement in his bearing. Not a fugitive, she decided. There was nothing frightened or furtive in his manner. Her keen mind pierced the mystery. He was running, not away from something, but toward it. An adventurer, always chasing the rainbow that shone over the next hill.

Her gaze fell upon the girl. A thin child, with startling gray eyes that mirrored her every emotion, and hair so pale a blond that it looked like threads of polished silver. Those wide gray eyes were fixed upon Miss Olmstead, filled with

1

a knowledge of sorrow and loss that was too adult, too profound for the pointed little face.

There was something else in them, too, something the dour spinster had never seen in any of the frightened or sullen or dull-eyed orphans who'd been brought to her before: a desperate longing that here, within the plain and unadorned walls of the Susquehanna orphanage, she might find a place to belong—at least for a little while.

"What is your name, my dear?" Miss Olmstead asked in a soft tone that would have made the older girls of the orphanage goggle in surprise.

"Bettany."

Only good Christian names were allowed at the Susquehanna Home for Girls, but Miss Olmstead rolled the word around in her mind. *Bettany.* A wildflower name, an elfin name. It suited the girl with her otherworldly face, that moonlight hair. The headmistress considered a moment. The poor mite had nothing but her father—no great shakes in Miss Olmstead's mind—and her unique name. It would be cruel to take it from her now.

"Bettany. That's a lovely name. Would you like to stay here with me, Bettany?"

There was no direct answer. Not in words. But Miss Olmstead recognized the passionate hope staring out at her from those wide gray eyes, heard the unspoken wish as surely as if it had been said aloud. The intensity of the girl's response dazzled her. It was like staring too long into the heart of the sun.

Miss Olmstead blinked and switched her gaze to the father. "How long has it been, Mr. . . . ."

"Howard, ma'am. Samuel J. Howard. And this here's my daughter, Bettany Anne."

"How long, Mr. Howard, has it been since Bettany has had a permanent home?"

He recognized the change in Miss Olmstead and pressed his advantage. "Nigh on a year, ma'am. We never stayed more'n a week in one place since then. It's been hard on her. Real hard. A girl needs a woman's touch."

Miss Olmstead struggled mightily within herself.

"We are full to capacity since the flood, and our resources are limited. I'm afraid that the trustees would not—"

Sam Howard scented victory. "No need to burden the trustees." He reached a hand to his pocket and jingled the silver and gold. "I can pay for her board in advance."

While Miss Olmstead calculated rapidly, Bettany fixed her attention on the matron. She liked what she saw. The lady's eyes were brown, and her eyelids crinkled when she smiled. Her hair was auburn, but she smelled of Camellia Lotion, just like the vague blond creature who floated through her memories and was called Mama. Much as she loved Papa, it would be so nice to stay here with this lady— it was scary to sit alone in a hotel room night after night, listening to the strange sounds. And sometimes, when they didn't have a hotel, she had to sleep in the open wagon, tucked under the seat with a rug over her. Wondering where Papa was and when he was coming back. Wondering if, like Mama, he had gone away forever.

Those nights were the worst.

But once Papa found them that special place he was looking for, she wouldn't have to worry ever again. They would go to sleep and wake up each night in the same beds, and she would never be lonely again. Papa had promised.

She stared up at the lady and wished hard. *Please let me stay with you. Just for a while. Just until Papa can find a place for us to stay. Oh, please!*

The heat of Bettany's passionate prayer had a profound effect on the headmistress. Something inside Miss Olmstead, something that had been frozen for decades, thawed and melted. Her bleak, wintry face softened into spring. She smiled at Bettany, and Sam realized that she was younger than he'd thought and that she must have been quite pretty once upon a time. Miss Olmstead nodded.

"Very well, Mr. Howard. In view of your advance payment, there can be no great objection, but as I said, we are filled to capacity. There is, however, a little storage room beside the dormitory. It is snug and sound, with a window facing west. I will have a bed put there for her."

Sam Howard smiled the smile that had won him hearts from the green lawns of Richmond, Virginia, to the rocky shores of Rhode Island. "You have a kind heart, ma'am, and God will surely bless you for it."

But, Miss Olmstead knew, the trustees would not. Well, the decision was made, and she would abide by it. She would cope as she had always done. Somehow.

Sam knelt down beside his daughter. "There's something I gotta do, Bettany, and I can't take you with me. I'm gonna leave you here with this kind lady until I can get us settled in a real home. A home of our own."

The little arms twined trustingly around his neck. "And then you'll come back for me."

"'Course I will, Button." He gave her a quick hug, and his face looked solemn. "I'll come for you around sunset. You keep a watch, and one evening when that first star is just a-peeking out you'll see me ride up the road to fetch you."

"All right, Papa."

He hugged her again and rose, his eyes so like her own, aswim with bright moisture. He paused in the doorway and looked back. "Don't forget, Button. Don't forget to watch for me, now."

"I won't, Papa. I promise."

Bettany kept her word. She adjusted quickly to the routine of the orphanage. Two weeks went by, then another, and every evening—no matter how tired she was—she waited at the window for that first sight of her father riding up the road. The headmistress found her asleep by the window more than once. And each night, when Miss Olmstead said her prayers, she added one to bring Sam Howard safely home to collect his daughter.

The third time it happened, as she carried the child to her bed, Bettany rested her head against her shoulders. "Papa's been gone so many days. How long does it take to go to California and back?"

"California!"

That night, and in the weeks that followed, Miss Olmstead, who had never cursed before in her thirty-eight years, learned to curse silently. Fluently.

Every night she watched Bettany waiting at the head of the stairs, her little white forehead pressed against the narrow window until darkness fell. Every night Miss Olmstead felt the knife twist in her own indignant heart and wondered what greater pain Bettany felt in hers. When Mr. Howard returns, she thought heatedly, I shall give him a good sound piece of my mind.

Though Bettany eagerly awaited it, Miss Olmstead began to loathe and dread the nightly appearance of that first bright evening star.

One night, two thousand miles away, a Cheyenne warrior sat before the campfire, waiting for the first star to appear against the darkening sky. Buffalo Heart loved the moments before twilight when the sun's rays softened and did not dazzle his rheumy eyes. Now, in the mild glow of the fire, he could see most clearly the faces around him and the beauty of the land.

The others in the circle waited patiently, some glancing from time to time at a wide-shouldered youth who stared into the fire as if he had never seen it before. Already Wolf Star showed signs of becoming a great warrior. He could best the young men of the camp in wrestling, riding, and throwing the lance, and he led them all with bow and arrow and in daring. Only during the telling of the story each year did they remember that Wolf Star was not Cheyenne by blood, but born of the *ve-ho-e*—the pale, white-skinned ones.

When a single star glimmered against the deepening sky, Buffalo Heart began. Into the gathering dusk he spoke the customary prayer of pardon before telling the sacred story of *E hyoph' sta*, "The Yellow-Haired Woman," which must be told only at night. Wolf Star had heard it many times before. He wondered if Yellow-Haired Woman was like the Silver Woman who came to him in dreams. Each time, just as he was about to learn why, she would dissolve into the early morning light. Each time he felt bereft.

The others listened closely, awed by the magic of Buffalo Heart's ancient tale. When he was finished, the old man stirred the fire and began another.

"It was at the Time of New Beginnings, the time that is with us now," Buffalo Heart began, as he had for the past ten years. "Game was scarce, and we sent out many hunting parties to feed our starving People. A group of brave warriors were cut off from the rest of their party."

The others leaned forward, immersing themselves in the story, which was as familiar to them as their own lodges. Buffalo Heart continued:

"Without warning a great storm of snow and wind came out of the northern sky. A man could not see his hand before his face, or the frost of his own breath. There had been no sign of such a storm, and the hunters knew it was sent against them by Winter Man. Out of the whirling whiteness, the keening of a wolf rent the air, unlike any they had ever heard before.

"The snow diminished as they stumbled toward one another, and a great silver wolf materialized out of the forest. The men were frightened, yet felt compelled to follow it, for they knew it was no ordinary wolf. The Spirit Wolf led them to where a female wolf lay at rest, her eyes glowing like golden embers. Resting between her forelegs, warmed by her breath, was a child of two moons or less. A child with eyes as yellow as the wolf's.

"Angry and unafraid, the babe filled its lungs and cried out with all its might, and the great Spirit Wolf went over to where it lay. The man-child, for such it was, laughed and grasped the fur of the wolf's ruff, and the creature nuzzled him gently. Then Wind came again, blowing the loose snow into a great cloud that settled slowly, like drifting feathers. When the braves could see again, the wolves, male and female, had vanished, leaving the babe behind.

"Notched Arrow, the great war chief, came forward and took the child up respectfully, for he knew its Medicine was great. 'This child I will take, and raise as my own. He shall be son to my wife, and brother to my son.'

"The moment he spoke those words the snow ceased and Thunder banished Winter Man to his icy northern realms. Warm rain came during the night and melted the snow. In the morning the barren forests were filled with creatures, and the hunting party took many deer and other game back to the People. The boy grew to manhood in the lodge of Notched Arrow, as son to the war chief's wife, and as brother to his own son."

Buffalo Heart finished his story in a low chant. "And that," he said to the stars and eager listeners, "is how Wolf Star came to the People, bringing many blessings with him."

The light of the gods dimmed in his eyes, and Buffalo Heart returned to his body. The old storyteller looked from face to face around the circle, but the one he sought most, the one he loved above all others, was missing.

"Where is Wolf Star?" he asked, but the boy had gone off alone, and no one could answer him.

One

Clarksville, Pennsylvania: 1840

For Bettany her eighteenth birthday was like every other day, busy from moment to moment yet never-changing. She sensed nothing special in the air as she stepped outside the kitchen door; but when the breeze feathered her cheek, whispering the tantalizing invitations and elusive promises of spring, she was eager to listen.

Maud, a buxom blond who was almost her own age, followed her to the dooryard. "Slip around to Miss Olmstead's parlor. If you listen outside the window, you might hear what Elder Gebbermann is saying. It's about the overcrowding, I'll bet. They'll try to get rid of some of us."

Bettany pretended not to have heard. Listening at windows and keyholes was Maud's way, not hers. If Miss Olmstead's visit from the elder affected them, they would know soon enough. In justice, however, Maud did have reason to be concerned. The elders had always placed the girls in service or as apprentices when they reached the age of fourteen, but for the past few years they had not had great success. The mill had burned down and was just now being rebuilt, and as a result the trade in the Clarksville shops had fallen off. With few openings for apprentices in town, the Susquehanna orphanage was bursting at the seams.

Still in the grip of spring fever, she carried the pot to the well. Even the children seemed infected with it: the words of a familiar nursery rhyme floated over from the packed-dirt play yard where the girls skipped rope.

8

Pussycat, pussycat, where have you been?
I've been to London to visit the Queen...

Bettany smiled to herself as she drove the handle up and down, but her expression was a bit wistful. At the Susquehanna Home for Girls, time flowed like a river of molasses, pushing some forward and trapping others in place. She was afraid that she was becoming one of the latter. Would any of the orphans in her charge ever go farther than the new mill they were building up the river?

Would she?

She glanced over at the girls in their plain jumpers, indistinguishable one from another except by height and hair color and the size of the scabs upon their knees. Some were clever, a few dull, and most of them good—but what kind of life awaited them with no family and no dower?

A muffled snapping came from the river beyond the line of willows, and two great birds flew up above the feathery branches. Bettany pumped water into the bucket, her eyes on the white herons winging west against the blue spring sky. She wished with all her heart that she could follow them. It didn't matter where.

When she returned for a second bucket of water, the elder was just riding away and one of the younger children was waiting for her by the well, her face pink with excitement. She opened her palm to reveal a handful of translucent pink quartz pebbles. "Look what I found."

"They're beautiful, Phoebe."

"They're wishing stones. You throw one over your shoulder and you make a wish. Like this."

The girl closed her eyes and tossed one behind her. The stone skipped and vanished. Smiling, she held her hand out to Bettany. "One is for you."

"Why, thank you."

Bettany started to slip it into her pocket, but Phoebe stopped her. "You have to throw it and make a wish—but don't tell, or it won't come true."

Bettany didn't want to hurt Phoebe's feelings. "Of

course." Shutting her eyes, she threw the pebble over her
shoulder as hard as she could. When she opened them,
Phoebe was skipping away to rejoin the other children.
Bettany shook her head. If only it were that easy.

> Patty-cake, patty-cake,
> Patsy had a stomachache . . .

The piping voices lifted and fell as the cold water splashed
into the tin-lined boiler. The days when Bettany had played
in the yard and skinned her own knees seemed very far
away to her now. The memories of her father had grown
almost as dim and distant as those of her mother. She could
hardly remember his face, except in dreams. But on warm
summer evenings when the first star appeared in the sky,
she would hesitate by a window and look out, as if still
expecting him to come whistling up the road for her.

There might be dozens of reasons why he'd never returned. Time after time she had considered them: illness,
infirmity, captivity, loss of memory, loss of limb. Loss of
life.

No! If anything had happened to him, she would have
known. He was alive somewhere. She was as sure of it as
she was of her own existence. And someday she would find
him. That was what she'd wished for.

Cold well water splashed across her hand from the overflowing bucket. Bettany came out of her reverie with a start
and realized another visitor had drawn up in the front yard.
The sounds of the arriving wagon had been obscured by the
rattle and squeak of the pump and the gushing water.

The man clambered down, stopped, and looked around
intently from beneath the wide brim of his hat. For just a
moment hope streaked through her like a bolt of summer
lightning. His height was right, and over the span of years
Papa might have put on some weight. Then he turned, and
even in the gathering dusk, his profile was all wrong: heavy
rather than fine-boned, more plebeian than patrician.

She had been familiar with disappointment for so long

that she had thought herself inured to it, but today it had hit her with the sharp pang of her first weeks at the orphanage. Struggling to contain it, Bettany carried the pot back into the kitchen and placed it on the freshly blackened iron stove, then removed her apron and slipped into the corridor that led to the front entrance hall.

Outside, Axel Vandergroot hitched his wagon carefully in front of the red-brick building and paused to give the building and grounds a long and critical examination. He didn't like what he saw. The Susquehanna orphanage did not fit his idea of what was seemly for an institution of charity. It was nestled too comfortably beneath its canopy of budding elms, and the window curtains were edged with ruffles—a waste of time and good material, he thought; the work of idle hands that would have found better use in performing proper chores. It did not bode well for his purpose. He went up the front steps thinking that perhaps this was not such a good plan after all.

"May I help you, sir?"

Bettany had opened the door to admit him. Afternoon light streamed in through the open doorway. Despite the prim dress she was luminous in the pale sunshine, her fair hair and gray eyes gleaming like silver. Axel Vandergroot blinked. He did not approve of her, either. Still, he removed his hat.

"I am here to see the headmistress."

"Miss Olmstead has just stepped upstairs. If you will follow me, I'll take you to her private parlor."

She led him across the hall to a door on the opposite side. There was a bowl of wildflowers on a small chest. His frown deepened. Ruffles and wildflowers and silver-eyed girls. Again he had misgivings. Again he didn't leave.

Bettany stepped aside for him to enter. "Miss Olmstead will be with you shortly."

When he was alone Axel scrutinized his surroundings. The room reassured him. It was plain and impeccably clean, with a dark wood desk, a long bench against the wall opposite, a tall cupboard, and two straight-backed chairs. There were no colorful carpets, no sentimental pictures, and only a framed certificate upon the white walls.

He took the chair facing the desk. It creaked beneath his weight, for he was a tall man and big-boned. The chair held solidly. Good workmanship. Solid. No fal-lals.

Axel approved. In fact, his doubts were considerably alleviated. A child raised in such tidy surroundings would not develop frivolous habits or attitudes. Perhaps his trip had not been in vain after all.

Not many minutes passed before Miss Olmstead arrived, neat as wax and briskly efficient. She was rather pleased with the interruption. Anything to put off the unpleasant task she had to face later.

The introductions over, she seated herself and eyed him across the desk. She knew his type well: a hard worker who rose with the dawn and worked until dusk, never questioning his lot in life or his place in the universe. A man who could express himself in pride or anger yet remain inarticulate about his deepest feelings. It was always the hardest for them.

"Perhaps you would care for tea, Mr. Vandergroot?"

He shook his head and began twisting the rim of his hat slowly between his hands. "My wife of six years, she died this morning, suddenly."

So recently! Miss Olmstead's sympathy was genuine. "Please accept my condolences."

"I have two children . . ."

The silence returned, thick and heavy. Gently, Miss Olmstead led the way, as she had so many times before.

"I understand, Mr. Vandergroot. Although it is difficult to part with your children, you wish to have them make their home with us until such a time as you might be able to, ah, make other arrangements?"

He looked at her in blank surprise that turned to ruddy indignation. "You think I have come to put my children in an orphanage? *Ach*, no! Axel Vandergroot takes care of his own. I have come," he said firmly, "to replace my wife."

Now it was Miss Olmstead's turn to stare. "To replace your wife?"

He shifted impatiently. "Tomorrow I leave for Missouri, and from there, west to California."

He carefully unfolded a broadside and plunked it down before her. Miss Olmstead quickly scanned the top lines:

Looking For Freedom and Free Land
in
CALIFORNIA
Captain Angus McGrew's
Escorted Wagon Party
Leaving Westport, Missouri May 15th
EXPERIENCED GUIDES PROVIDED

There was more, but she didn't need to read further. "The fifteenth of May is not that far away, Mr. Vandergroot."

"Yes, and there are many arrangements to make, both now and later. You will understand why I am in need of a wife to look after the children and cook and mend."

Miss Olmstead didn't understand why at all. Surely it would be more natural for the man to stay and mourn his wife in the bosom of his community, where there were friends to support them in their loss. Perhaps, she reflected, the wanderlust that was known to come over even the most doting of husbands and fathers was too strong to resist. As for herself, she had never wanted more than this small place and the opportunity to aid unfortunate children.

Axel retrieved the broadside, folded it neatly, and replaced it inside his pocket. "If possible, I would wish not too large a woman. My wife—my late wife had purchased a good deal of cloth and made up several outfits for the journey west, and I would not like to find that money wasted."

Miss Olmstead's sense of seemliness was outraged. Practicality was one thing, but such stony indifference to his loss was quite another. While she sat frozen in silence, he began ticking off his requirements on his thick fingers.

"Healthy, you understand, and strong. Sound of limb and tooth. Hardworking and God-fearing. And she must be plain. I do not want a pretty woman. They are nothing but trouble to an honest man."

Miss Olmstead's brown eyes frosted with indignation. His wife not even cold in her grave, and he spoke of replacing her as if she had been nothing but a harness mule that had dropped in its traces. She sat up a bit straighter.

"I am not quite sure, Mr. Vandergroot, of how you think I might help you."

He kneaded his big red hands impatiently. "My neighbor is an elder—John Gilmartin. He said you were looking to place some of the older girls as servants. I can give one of them something better. A wedding ring and an honest name. And children, God willing."

It would have given Miss Olmstead great satisfaction to send him away with a flea in his ear, but she mastered the urge. Her personal opinion of the man aside, she could not lightly toss away a chance at marriage for one of her charges. She swallowed her chagrin.

"There are three young ladies here who are of marriage-able age, and it is true that I am trying to place two of them. But any such arrangement would have to be the girl's own choice. Frankly, I don't know if any of them would even consider your offer, with so little time to weigh the matter."

He dismissed such qualms with a wave of his hand. Axel had no doubt of the outcome. A woman's place was beside a man, and honest bread earned with sweat was better than milk and honey taken in sin. He leaned forward and clamped his hands on his knees. "Bring them in."

Any orphan girl, with no better future than laboring as a kitchen maid, would be happy to have a fine, upstanding husband and the respectability of the wedding ring he had in his watch pocket. No need to tell her it had already been used once.

"Very well," Miss Olmstead said after a brief but intense

struggle with herself. "I will send for the young ladies and you may interview them in my presence."

He nodded, pleased by her brusqueness. "Good. I am anxious to be on my way."

Light footsteps came hurrying down the corridor outside the door, and Maud hovered on the threshold, honey-blond braids bouncing behind her shoulders. "Oh! I didn't know you had anyone with you, ma'am. I certainly didn't mean to intrude."

The bold blue eyes took in Axel Vandergroot from top to toe, noting his apparent age, health, and level of prosperity. The girl was an incurable snoop, and Miss Olmstead knew that she'd manufactured an excuse in order to examine the visitor. "Yes, Maud?"

The girl's blue eyes widened ingenuously. "I was wondering if I might put a bit of flour in the stew. It's rather watery."

Axel shifted and eyed Maud. Despite his stolid appearance, he was an impatient man. "Is this one of the girls Gilmartin spoke of? She looks well fed."

Miss Olmstead couldn't tell whether the remark was a compliment or a hint that he felt the orphans ate too well. "Maud, please fetch the other senior girls."

Bettany and Hilda came to the parlor, curious and apprehensive respectively. The headmistress introduced them to Axel, then asked him to leave them for a few minutes. His face reddened, and he shuffled his big feet in irritation. Bettany thought he looked like a bull, deciding whether to charge or retreat. Prudence won. With reluctance, he turned and went out into the hall.

Miss Olmstead saw that Hilda was holding a towel over a cut on her hand. "You look pale, child. How badly did you cut yourself?"

"It's all right. I alus' get sick at the sight o' blood. Ever since Pa cut hisself open butcherin' hogs."

"Then if you will take a seat with the others, I would like to explain the situation to you all." She folded her hands before her. "My meeting with the trustees this morn-

ing did not go well. We have too many mouths to feed—
and too little money to do it. I petitioned the board last
year and they were able to make an exception, but now,
since the six Guderman children came, we are already well
over the mark the elders feel they can afford. I have just
been apprised of their decision."

She braced herself. "They have decided that the Abbot
twins and two of the others are old enough to take over
most of your duties. I can only keep one of you on past
Easter."

Hilda began to sniffle. "Oh, Lordy Lord, what will become o' us? I never thought we'd be thrown out in the
cold."

Bettany felt just as stunned. She reached out and covered
Hilda's hand with hers. "We'll try to stay together. There
might be work for us in Skilton."

The tip of the matron's nose grew suspiciously red, and
she blinked her eyes furiously before continuing. "The Johnson family is willing to take one of you in to help with the
chores. Milking and cheese making and looking after the
younger children. Mr. Vandergroot also has a proposition
that might be of interest to one of you."

Hilda sniffed noisily and wiped her nose with her hand.
For once it didn't call down a reprimand. "Not me, Miz
Olmstead. I don't wanna work fer him. I expect I know *his*
type—work my fingers clear to the bone fer a pittance an'
make me sleep in the hayloft, he would."

Maud laughed and tossed her curls over her shoulders.
"A lot you know, Miss Fraidy-cat. I know why he came
here. He's looking for a wife."

Miss Olmstead gave her a stern look. "Eavesdropping
again, I see. I am sadly disappointed in you, child."

"But it is true."

"Hush, now, and listen to me. Mr. Vandergroot is indeed
in need of a wife. He leaves tomorrow for California."

Hilda toyed with a corner of her apron, completely un-
interested. Bettany was startled. California! Only a short
time ago she'd stood by the well, wishing she had a means

of following her father's trail to California—but the stolid Mr. Vandergroot hadn't been included. It wasn't until Miss Olmstead got to the crux of the matter, though, that Bettany's interest was suddenly and fully engaged.

"Mr. Vandergroot has two small children, orphaned by their mother's death only this morning and . . ."

Bettany felt a pang of pity for the children. Motherless and homeless, left to the care of a father who had no notion of a child's needs or fears. A flood of emotions came back, carrying her along in its swift currents. The sensations of confusion, loneliness, and abandonment were as real, as immediate, as they had been so many years before. Poor, poor children.

She realized she'd missed a part of Miss Olmstead's explanation. ". . . and Elder Gilmartin sent him to us, with a written recommendation. I know it is sudden, but if either of these alternatives appeals to one of you, I will do whatever I can to help you."

Maud broke in breathlessly. "Bettany isn't strong enough for all the milking and fetching and cheese making. It's heavy work. I will go to the Johnson farm. I grew up on one, and it would suit me perfectly."

"I cain't go nowhere," Hilda wailed. "Who'd want me? I cain't never learn nothing like Maud and Bettany do. And I don't never want to git married. I seen what men are like." She shuddered. "I know."

Bettany put her arm comfortingly around the girl's thin shoulders, trying to understand what she should do. Her heart went out to the two children, motherless and about to be uprooted from their home. But at least they were not alone, as she had been. At least they had each other.

Yet, Bettany wondered, if she stayed on at the orphanage herself, what would become of Hilda? She was a good little soul and hardworking at chores she understood, but there had been no good fairies present at her birth. Hilda was homely, exceedingly timid, and a bit simple. Her mind could grasp routine facts, but she seemed incapable of learning anything new. There was no place for her on earth except the Susquehanna orphanage—and she was kind to the children, who loved her dearly.

Lifting her head, Bettany looked to Miss Olmstead for guidance.

The headmistress was unable to answer the silent question in those gray eyes, although she read it quite clearly. If Bettany left, she would lose more than a dear companion whose mind was as quick and lively as her own; she would lose her spiritual daughter, the child of her heart. "I can't fathom the ways of the Lord, Bettany. You must do what you think best."

She rose. "Mr Vandergroot needs an immediate answer. I'll check on the progress of the stew and let you discuss it among yourselves."

The minute the door closed behind her, Hilda turned to Maud. "The Johnsons will work you like a big ol' ox. Why ever would you want to go there?"

A cream-pot smile creased Maud's broad face. "The Johnson farm is prosperous. Every one of them is plump and happy, and they've got decent clothes and shoes to wear for church on Sunday."

"Huh! Do you think they'll treat you like one o' them? A serving girl? You won't be no better off there than you are here."

Maud tossed her braids. "I won't always be a serving girl. You'll see." Her face grew sly. "Ole Johnson has a strapping boy of almost sixteen. I'm only seventeen. We'll be together a lot. And if he doesn't take a liking to me, I'll make sure one of the younger ones does. There are ways."

Bettany was shocked. "Marriage is a sacrament, a covenant between a man and woman. . . ."

"Take away the courtship time, and marriage is just a business arrangement. A man needs a wife to cook and mend and tend the sick, to preserve food, make medicines, bear children, and work along beside him. A woman needs a man to provide her with a home, protection, and children. But don't worry," Maud said with another sly look. "The one who marries me will get more than he bargained for. I'll prove my worth."

Bettany had no desire to be the Johnsons' maid-of-all-work, but neither did she want to marry a total stranger, even though he offered her a way of getting to California. She paced to the front window and glanced out. Two white faces peeked over the side of the wagon. She hadn't even known the Vandergroot children were out there.

The little girl clasped her brother around the neck. The boy, although built along his father's sturdy lines, looked frightened and painfully vulnerable. Seeing her, they ducked behind the wagon's sideboard like sparrows hiding in a nest.

Years later Bettany would look back upon that instant. How strange that that one small action could change lives irrevocably—if the wagon had been parked on the other side of the entrance, if she hadn't looked out the window at that moment, if the children hadn't peeked out at that very second. If she hadn't known, too well, every one of the emotions that she had just read on their wan, tear-streaked faces. But at the moment she wasn't concerned with ifs.

The deep-rooted strength of the female instinct to nurture and protect caught her completely off guard. Her response was immediate and overpowering. She wanted to rush out to the children, to gather them in her arms. Hold them and reassure them. To smooth the hair from their foreheads and ease their fear. The future became clear. Maud would go to the Johnsons and eventually marry one of their hapless sons, Hilda would stay within the sheltering walls of the Susquehanna orphanage—and she would find her own fate in California.

When Miss Olmstead came back with Axel Vandergroot, Bettany was ready with her answer. He took the news stolidly and looked her up and down as if she were a brood mare at auction. She fought the urge to ask him if he'd care to inspect her teeth and hooves.

"I had hoped to get the sturdier girl," he said as if she

could not hear or had no feelings to consider. "Well, get
your things together and I'll go fetch the preacher. Hurry.
It will be dark soon."

His brusque manners had offended her, and Bettany had
to remind herself that he had buried his wife only that
morning. Biting back a retort, she hurried up to her room,
pausing a moment on the landing, remembering. Her arrival
at the orphanage was still incredibly clear in her mind.
Almost fifteen years had passed since her father had left
her at the orphanage to follow his California dream. She
hadn't known then that California was a continent apart.
As far apart, for all the good it did her, as the moon and
stars.

Papa had said he was coming back for her in two weeks,
and she'd never doubted it. The weeks passed and still she'd
kept her faithful evening vigil, never losing heart. A letter
had come from a place called Bent's Fort along the Santa
Fe Trail. Things were looking good, and as soon as he was
settled, Papa would come for her. But the seasons turned,
and the months had chained into years. Miss Olmstead's
auburn tresses had gone gray, and Bettany had grown to
young womanhood, leaving behind her cherished childhood
fantasies.

As she turned to the window, she caught a single glimmer
of light in sky. The evening star. She took it for an omen.
I'm coming, Papa. If you're alive, I'll find you, she vowed.

A mere hour later she was a wife and stepmother. The
children were clean, neatly dressed, and silent as stones.
Nils was six, Hannah just two years old. They stared at
Bettany as if she were some exotic animal, intriguing yet
possibly dangerous.

In a matter of minutes it was all over, and Bettany left
the Susquehanna orphanage forever. The reins snapped,
and the team took off at a steady trot. Nils sat in back of
the borrowed wagon on an old blanket, looking as if he
wished he were not too old to suck his thumb. Hannah
shivered on the seat beside her new mother, trembling
between excitement and fear. Bettany's insides were doing

the same. Only Axel seemed controlled and indifferent, as if being a widower and bridegroom in one day were in the natural order of events.

At the bend of the road Bettany looked back for her last glimpse of the orphanage. The last rays of sun turned the windows to gold. They shimmered and blurred with the tears that stung her eyes. A few hours ago she'd stood by the well and thrown Phoebe's pebble. Her wish had come true, although in a way she could never have anticipated. She turned back and faced the road before her. The road west.

She must not look behind, but forward. A new life was beginning. Tomorrow she would start out on the long road to California, with two bewildered children—and the stranger who was her husband.

Medicine Bow Mountains

He could smell the smoke for miles. As Logan rode toward the ridge, the faint acrid tinge carried down through the cool green pines and across the shimmering turquoise lake. The wind lifted a strand of dark hair from his forehead, and his eyes narrowed. Smoke on a fine spring day, and far too much to be from a single cook fire. The scent of tragedy bled down through the trees.

The dun gelding whickered and laid its ears back nervously, but the rider sat still, his bronzed face taut and grim. Only the eyes, a deep and disturbing amber, were alive. Keen, observant. Watchful as a wolf. Noticing every significant detail. Nothing looked out of place, nothing seemed wrong—except for the instinct that prickled between his shoulder blades, and too much smoke on a fine spring day.

For a moment Logan didn't want to go on. Didn't want to meet the nameless evil that awaited him. The feeling had been growing all day, one that he knew well: a black emptiness that curled around the edges of his heart and left it numbed with cold. The moment passed. He urged his mount out of the clearing and into the dappled shadows of

the forest. With his sun-browned skin and dark hair, Logan
might have passed for a French trapper, a man of Spanish
descent, or a half-breed Indian—and in fact he had passed
as all three at various times when it suited the situation.
Now he blended into the background, completely at home
in his environment, keeping below the crest of the switch-
back as he moved toward the valley.

Toward the smoke.

The tip of his right index finger stroked the long scar
that ran from his jaw to beneath his buckskin shirt. His
quarry had more than two weeks' head start, but in the
seven days Logan had been tracking them, he'd gained
ground with every passing hour. Four white men, careless
now in the vast empty landscape. And dangerous. Maddened boars, blood-lusting through the untouched Eden of
sunset.

And he'd been the one to set them on their rampage.

As the sun lowered toward the rim of hills, he reached
the plateau that stretched out above the crumpled valleys.
There were dozens, large and small, scattered through this
section of country, but he rode unerringly toward one.
There were only two dwellings ahead that he knew of, old
Jed McCoy's place at the valley's entrance and the rough-
hewn cabin cupped in the green bowl of land. The source
of the smoke could be either—or both.

Logan slipped from his mount and became one of the
deep shadows along the ancient rock face. Gliding with
practiced grace, he moved so deceptively that he seemed
to be standing still. One moment he was here, the next
there. A gray squirrel blinked its eyes curiously, then went
about its business. A smudgy yellow haze drifted up to the
achingly blue sky, and Death rode the rising columns of
air.

All along he had known he'd overtake them. It was just
matter of patience, endurance, and time. Now, it seemed,
time had run out. He slid down a vertical stone surface for
a clearer view. McCoy's shanty was only a smoldering pile
of blackened ash, and the thick air clotted in his lungs.

Below, the cabin seemed untouched, but a sense of forsaken melancholy surrounded it.

Logan made his way back to his gelding and rode down the trail, no longer trying to remain invisible, only attempting to control the sudden surge of hope he knew was doomed. He'd thought they'd be safe as long as old Jed McCoy was there to keep an eye on them. A chill settled in his bones. As Logan passed the shanty he almost gagged at the stink of burned flesh. There was no sign of other violence. If McCoy had been sober—an increasingly rare occurrence of late—he'd have blasted at least one of them with his double-barreled Sharps.

Logan grimaced in remembrance. The Irishman had always prophesied that whiskey would be the death of him. It had, but not in the way the poor old bastard had expected. There'd be no more songs of Connemara floating in the firelight on long winter evenings.

Leaving the somber scene behind, he descended into the heart of the protected green valley. What terrible whim of fate had led the murderers here, to a place that had known only peace? The sun meadows were thronged with early wildflowers, splashes of crimson and gold against the canvas of leaves. But here was no birdsong, no rustle of animals in the brush. He reined in a hundred yards from the doorstep.

"Cassie?"

The woman's name echoed briefly. He called again, knowing she would never answer. Logan had brought her the news, as he'd promised his cellmate. Cade had died in his arms, not from the flesh wound he'd suffered in the jailbreak, but from the consumption that had riddled his weak lungs. Logan had merely come to deliver Cade's dying messages; he had never meant to stay.

He dismounted and walked to the cabin. Soot streaks showed around the window opening on his right, where they had tried unsuccessfully to fire the cabin. The door hung ominously open on its leather hinges. With every step his feet lagged and his heart grew heavier.

This place had been one of warmth and gentle laughter, after Cassie had adjusted to her widowhood. The winter had been harsh, and Logan had found her invitation to stay a few days a welcome one. His prison-racked body, all sinew and bone, had fleshed out with Cassie's good cooking.

He would have been on his way then, if she hadn't fallen ill; but the pain in her right side left her so weak, she was unable to lift a hand until long after the punishing cold came. Even then she had never regained her vigor. Logan had taken on the responsibility of keeping the woman and her daughter alive with fresh game and firewood. Before the days grew longer, Cassie had invited him into her bed. The respect was mutual, and the need was there, greater on her side. Logan had accepted, more for her comfort than his. One day had stretched to another, one week to the next.

Cassie had been good to him, and if she hadn't told him about her past in the beginning—well, he hadn't told her everything about his, either. They'd respected each other's secrets and fallen into an easy pattern as the weeks wore on, one that seemed comfortable for everyone. Still, except for one thing, he would have been gone with the spring thaw.

It was the child that bound him to her, with her innocent eyes and eager heart. Anna's undemanding devotion was something he had never known or expected, balm to his scarred and wounded spirit. His affection for her had grown to a love Logan had not known he was capable of feeling. Over the long winter, while Cassie's care had helped to heal his body, her daughter's love had helped to heal his soul. And he hadn't been here when they'd needed him.

Vain regret was a heavy burden. It weighed upon Logan like a cross of stone, slowing him down with every step. If he hadn't gone down to the fort that day. If the soldier hadn't recognized him. If . . . if . . . if . . . He stopped on the threshold, his high moccasins planted firmly on the rough plank that formed the sill. "Cassie? Anna?"

His eyes grew accustomed to the dim interior. To the

right a mound of bedclothes drew his eye, and he forced himself to enter. The air was still and heavy, and the smell of death was very strong. The droning of flies drew him reluctantly closer. Cassie lay on the bed, her torn clothes strewn around her. She had fought valiantly—the cuts and bruises proved it—but in the end she had lost.

Her face was turned away, her eyes closed. He was glad of that. Gently he pulled the quilt up over her ravaged body, up to her chin to hide the dark, jagged wound. Some people looked peaceful in death; Cassie's cold and silent form reflected the violence of her passing. All her life she had been forced to struggle against the odds. This time they had been overwhelming. Logan stared silently down at the woman he had laughed with and made love with in this small cabin. His strong fingers brushed the hair at her temple once, before he turned away.

He had to find Anna.

Logan called for her, inside and out, without results. Next he searched the cabin—every place she had ever hidden in their endless games, every place into which a child of two could squeeze her small body. Then he went out and began again, circling around the cabin in ever-widening swaths until he found her in a stand of trees.

She was lying huddled on her side in a blue print dress. Her feet were bare and dirty. At first he couldn't find a mark on her. She might have died of hunger or thirst or eating a poison plant, but he didn't think so. She might have died of terror and loneliness, wondering what had happened to her mama and why Logan had not come back in time to soothe her tears. He touched her hair and found a swelling near her temple. Had she fallen or been struck?

He smoothed her hair away from her face, then picked her up and held her to his breast, fighting back the rage and grief. It descended upon him, a dense cloud that was black with hate, red with bloody wrath and the need for violent reprisal. Nothing existed but those three overwhelming emotions.

It was much later when Logan came to his senses again

to find his muscles rigid with tension, rusty with disuse. Anna was still in his arms. The sun had dipped, and its dying rays threw gold-pocked shadows on the valley's eastern flank and filled its hollow with lurid carmine light. Logan realized how much time had passed while he'd been lost in the heat of his madness. It was gone now, leaving behind a deadly chill that permeated body and soul.

He rose stiffly and carried the child into the cabin and laid her in the crook of Cassie's arm, the way he'd seen them so many times. Trying not to think of it. Trying not to think at all.

He knew Cassie would have wanted them to be buried beneath a leafy tree, but he couldn't force himself to do it. He couldn't bear the thought of the two he had held in his arms, closed away from the warmth and light beneath the cold ground.

Logan splashed oil from the lamps across the quilt and mattress and all around the bed. He splattered every surface he could, then poured out the remainder in a generous trail to the door. Ribbons of oily liquid streamed across the scored puncheon floor. The sunset lit them prematurely, flaring orange and red from the glistening streaks and spreading puddles.

Outside, the cool breeze swept his hair away from his sweaty brow. He twisted long dried grasses into a crinkly knot around a bundle of dry sticks. Standing back, he set the desiccated stems afire and threw them into the cabin. The small red flames lapped eagerly along the flows of lamp oil and erupted into an inferno. The crackle and roar drowned all other sounds, except the beating of his heart.

Cassie, I'm sorry. Anna . . . oh, Anna!

He wanted to say a prayer, but he didn't know any. Not the kind a parson could have said. Fists clenched, eyes dry, Logan watched the first glowing bits of ash rise to the sky. Let them go free. Let them dance on the wind. Let them soar like clean bright sparks until they merged with the light of the stars. And let their killers know, by this blaze of light that would be visible for miles against the indigo night sky, that their deed had been discovered—and would be avenged.

Logan was impatient to start out on the vengeance trail, but something compelled him to stay. The log walls were fired at last, and the cabin was engulfed in a dazzling ball of fire. The heat was intense, and his skin glowed gold with the light of that terrible, false sun.

When the roof fell in with a roar and a great spout of flame, something almost physical released inside him and he was free to go. Logan turned and climbed up into the hills, moving as silently and swiftly as the clouds across the moon's bright face. At the top of the shallow valley he turned once more to watch the conflagration below.

The cabin was a beacon of writhing orange flames that reflected in his pupils. His eyes shone in the captured light, a bright and bitter yellow like no other man's eyes in all the world.

But very like a wolf's.

Two

Westport Landing, Missouri

Bettany tied on her new straw bonnet and examined her reflection in her landlady's hall mirror. It wasn't reassuring. Her dress was an unpleasant shade of brown, with the dull, dusty appearance of accumulated hair in the bristles of a brush. Just looking at it made her itch. The fabric was heavy and more suited to cold climes and winter months. It had been made by Axel's late wife, and Bettany thought it made her look like a member of some austere and very odd religious sect.

Well, beggars couldn't choose, as Miss Olmstead had often said. There had been no money to purchase material to make others, and in any case Axel would have thought it wildly extravagant of her. He considered Porter Renfrew, who would be making the journey with them, a profligate wastrel because he'd bought his young sister-in-law another bonnet when she already had one to her name. Bettany walked past the mirror, averting her face. Ah, well. Frugality is not the worst vice a husband can have, she decided.

Outside, she found Hannah ensconced on the settle beside Mrs. Cummins, the kindly landlady. She had offered to look after the children while Bettany ran some errands. She was knitting a shawl of unbleached wool, and the thick yarn seemed to fall from the needles, row upon row. Hannah was fascinated by the process. Meanwhile Nils was galloping about with a broom for a hobbyhorse and making the hens squawk. Bettany put on her plain tan gloves. "I won't be more than a few minutes, Mrs. Cummins."

"Take your time, dearie. I'll keep an eye on the young-un's."

"Thank you." With a wave to Nils, Bettany opened the gate and went out. He rode along the low fence, brandishing a stick which she mistook for a chivalrous knight's sword. She would have been less sanguine if she'd known he was playing a Pawnee brave, about to scalp his squawking victims.

She hurried beneath two old elms in new leaf and crossed from the rutted street onto the weathered boardwalk. In the distance a row of trees shaded the bluff, and below that was the great Missouri River, marking the westernmost boundary of the United States. Beyond it lay the adventure of the Unorganized Territory and far California under Mexico's rule—and perhaps the answer to what had happened to her father so many years ago.

She came abreast of the bank just as a man exited the building. Despite his well-tailored suit and elegant hat, he had the lean, burned look of a frontiersman. She felt a small ripple of satisfaction. Her timing had been perfect.

"Good Morning, Captain McGrew. It looks to be a fine day."

"Morning, Mrs. Vandergroot." He tipped his hat, but the warm May sunlight sparkled coolly in the depths of his blue eyes. "A fine day indeed."

She smiled at him, hoping the friendly rapport they'd already established would dilute some of the bad feeling that had arisen between the organizer of the wagon party and her new husband. She'd hoped it would blow over, but apparently the captain was still offended. He touched the brim of his hat again and seemed about to continue on without stopping. Bettany's heart sank. Evidently he was still angry because Axel had dared to question his knowledge of their proposed route. She put her hand on McGrew's sleeve.

"I hope that you didn't misconstrue my husband's ques-

tions at the meeting yesterday." She reached into the deep
pocket of her cloak and withdrew a square of folded paper.
"You see, he was going by this map that he bought from a
trapper back in St. Louis."

McGrew took the map she placed into his hand and
opened it, scanning quickly. "Quicksand. Poisoned water.
Barren deserts and dead-end canyons. Poppycock!" He
thrust the paper back at her. "I tell you the trail west is
almost as flat and level as a tabletop, with plenty of sweet
water and good grazing from here to California. I've sworn
my oath to it."

"Yes, I . . . I was very relieved to hear you say that yesterday."

"Well, I can understand your concern, with people going
about selling fraudulent maps like this." He bade her good
day in a voice that was much more cordial than his initial
greeting and went down the boardwalk, his boot heels
echoing back from the wooden slats.

Bettany was relieved. She had managed to mollify the
captain somewhat, and now if she could put the map back
before Axel noticed it was missing, everything might turn
out well after all. She'd been more worried about McGrew
than she'd realized. A former army officer, he had laid down
strict rules at the very first meeting of the overland emigrants. He'd warned would-be emigrants that teamwork and
cooperation were vital to their success and that discord and
strife were more of a danger than the vagaries of nature or
attack by hostile Indians.

The California-bound pilgrims had taken the captain's
advice to heart, and tonight the group as a whole was going
to vote on the acceptance or rejection of each individual
family seeking passage west. Bettany was still anxious about
the outcome. Axel, with his inflexible opinions and ag-
gressive stubbornness, was not a popular man among his
fellows.

Bettany drew out a long list her husband had made. The
writing was very like the man himself, plain and determined. Beyond that it revealed nothing. Bettany would

have been grateful for any further clues to his character. They had been married six weeks now, and she was still a virgin.

Axel was giving them time to become better acquainted, she had concluded at first, surprised and touched at this unexpected consideration. She had felt that she'd badly misjudged him and had been embarrassed at not recognizing that his hard practicality was just a veneer over his more sensitive feelings. Yet over time she'd begun to realize that Axel was purposely avoiding her company. Since arriving at this outpost on the banks of the mighty Missouri, he spent his time away from the family, making arrangements and consulting with the other westbound men. Meanwhile she had employed herself in getting to know her stepchildren and the other twenty families that would make up their small party of fifteen wagons.

Miss Olmstead had never encouraged vanity among her charges, and Bettany, surrounded by females in a place that emphasized spiritual worth, had never dwelled much on the importance of physical beauty. She knew her features were regular, she kept her person neat, and others found her appearance pleasant enough—and Sean O'Connell, Captain McGrew's assistant and second in command, had made it plain in his cheerful, rough-edged fashion that he felt a degree of admiration for her that Axel apparently did not. Bettany was distressed by the one, embarrassed by the other.

That night, her chores done, she attended the social at the livery barn that Angus McGrew had arranged, two warm pies in her basket. Axel had gone somewhere on his own business but hadn't objected to her attending the festivities.

The area outside the livery was filled with the smell of new-sawn wood and the aroma of the roasting beef that Captain McGrew had supplied. Inside, long tables were set up at one end with benches and crates lining the other walls. The fiddlers struck up the "Yorktown Reel," and soon the floor was filled with two lines of dancers, more eager than expert. Bettany helped out by ladling punch to fill the empty cups.

Mamie Ebbersoll came over. "I'll take your place," she said briskly. "You run along and get a bite to eat before the menfolks wipe every single platter clean. You'd think they hadn't eaten for a week, the way they're carrying on."

Thanking her, Bettany came from behind her station and wandered over to the "serving table" made of planks set on sawhorses and covered with a red-checked tablecloth donated by one of the women. The dumplings were cold and stuck together in a solid lump, the sausage and sauerkraut gone, and a few chicken legs lay congealing in their own fat. She took only a biscuit and a spoonful of preserves. Her stomach had been unsettled since morning when she'd eaten a plate of her landlady's hash of beef.

"Sure and you'll waste away to nothing," a low voice said in her ear. "I'd advise you to eat hearty while there's plenty available, for 'tis a long way to California."

Sean O'Connell was standing at her shoulder, his hazel eyes capturing and holding the reflected light. "It's beautiful you are tonight..." He tried to call her by her married title but couldn't. What did a man like Axel Vandergroot, with no more poetry in his soul than a dried-out crust of bread, know about a woman such as this one? A woman full of life and passion that had not yet been awakened?

He touched her wrist. "I've a mind to take a stroll in the moonlight, and I was wondering if I might persuade you to accompany me?"

His smile was warm and more suggestive, more disturbing, than his words; but it was his frank admiration and the sense of a kindred loneliness that unnerved her. Bettany stepped away, suddenly breathless. "Thank you, Mr. O'Connell, but if I take any moonlit strolls, they will be in the company of my husband."

"Ah, now, but if you go waiting for him, you might wait a long time, *alanna*. He doesn't exactly buzz around you like a fly on honey."

People were approaching the other side of the table, and Bettany drew away, leaving O'Connell to stare after her wistfully. Porter Renfrew and his genteel, sad-eyed wife appeared at her elbow. They were an oddly mismatched couple. Renfrew was bluff and given to coarse comments, his wife a pale wraith of a woman with delicate features and a fragile, distracted air. Letitia Renfrew smiled her faded smile. In her gown of off-white muslin, she looked even more ghostlike than usual.

Renfrew's big laugh boomed out when he saw the contents of Bettany's plate. He pushed his thick brown hair away from his forehead.

"Why, that bite wouldn't feed a bird, Mrs. Vandergroot, much less a grown woman. Give me that plate and I'll get you some real food. Rare beef is what you need to put some meat on your ribs. You know the saying: 'A woman's got to give her man something to grab hold of in a thunderstorm.'"

As he walked away Letitia Renfrew flushed. Much as she disliked the man, Bettany didn't want to add to his wife's embarrassment. "Are you enjoying the dance, Mrs. Renfrew?"

The sad eyes grew wide and dark with emotion. "I hate it. I hate everything about this place."

Her vehemence was as out of character as it was unexpected. Bettany thought that it was like plucking a flower and hearing it scream. "Then you must be eager for the wagon party to set out."

Letitia Renfrew stared at her as if she were demented. "I wish I was still back home in Maryland. I . . . I wish to God I had never come out to this terrible place."

Renfrew returned in time to overhear. "Now, Letty, I told you not to carry on so." He handed Bettany her plate. "Here you are. Don't mind the missus. She's been a little upset. Heard about the Pawnee massacre of those missionaries last month."

A sly young man named Phillips strolled over shaking his head. "I heard 'twas the Cheyenne. Kilt a family o' missionaries just north of Fort Laramie the beginning of May," he declared. "Scalped 'em and peeled the skin off'n 'em, too. Even the dog."

"No," Renfrew said, scratching his chin. "It was the Pawnee that slaughtered the missionary families. 'Twas the Cheyenne that attacked the trade wagons last year. Cut their victims' tongues off and scooped their eyes out like they were poached eggs."

There were several horrified gasps, the loudest from Letitia Renfrew. "That's right, I recollect it now," Phillips replied. "Nailed their hides to the sides of the wagons and gnawed their limbs like they was chicken drumsticks."

Bettany stared down at her plate, where a thick slice of very rare steak swam in its own blood. Her stomach turned over with a lurch, and she dropped the plate as the room went topsy-turvy. Without stopping to pick it up, she pushed her way past the sweaty throng and ran outside.

Porter Renfrew's laughter followed her out into the night.

"Miz Vandergroot?"

She recognized Mamie Ebbersoll's voice but wasn't able to answer.

"Poor thing. Maybe she's breeding. I mean, dropping her food like that and all. I remember when I was having my fifth, or was it the sixth one, now?"

The woman's loud tones faded as Bettany went along the rutted road toward the stand of elms. Gasping in great gulps of fresh air, she tried to keep her queasy stomach from rebelling. It was difficult, but she succeeded. Dear God! What kind of dangers were they traveling toward? And what kind of inhuman monsters would do such terrible things to innocent men and women—to children?

She turned at the sound of quick footfalls behind her. Captain McGrew had heard and come after her. "Now don't pay any mind to Porter Renfrew. He just likes to have a little fun now and then, and gets carried away."

She clung to his arm weakly. "Do you mean it isn't true?"

"Little lady, I've heard ten versions of the same story, and each time it's worse. Idle stories are like weeds, you know, and grow like Jack's beanstalk."

"But why?"

McGrew rubbed the back of his neck. "I reckon some of

the trappers mean to keep settlers out with that pack of lies. There's been hundreds of trade wagons gone out in the past years, and I swear before God that every one of them reached their destination safely. There's been no Indian attacks on organized parties."

Bettany had recovered her composure. "I see. Then Mr. Renfrew meant to frighten me, hoping I would return to Pennsylvania, taking my husband and family with me."

The captain's mouth firmed. "I reckon you're right, Mrs. Vandergroot, but Porter Renfrew doesn't run my outfit. Tell your man we're pulling out across the river tomorrow to spend the first night camped on the other side. If he hasn't changed his mind again and means to join us, you should be at the ford early in the forenoon."

"Thank you. We'll be there." Refusing his offer of an escort, she set off for the rooming house. McGrew didn't try to dissuade her.

Bettany made her way back to Mrs. Cummins's place without incident, but the captain's assertions couldn't allay her fears. It was probably true that the stories she'd heard had been embroidered beyond recognition, but there was another truth that Bettany recognized.

A great oak did not grow unless first there was an acorn.

Logan followed his quarry through the rugged hills and canyons, making camp only when it would have been foolhardy to go on. Now that less than a mile separated him from Halsey and his men, now that it was almost over, it seemed as if hours had passed rather than weeks. His enemies were bedded down for the night somewhere just beyond the next ridge. If he'd wanted, if he were that kind of man, it would have been easy enough to slip among them, silent and deadly as a gliding owl, and slit their throats one by one.

But that wasn't Logan's way. He purposely postponed the meeting. Let them see him in daylight, let them know he regarded them as cowards and had no fear of them.

Imagined success had made them careless, and at the

beginning fate had seemed to side with his quarry. Logan
had been delayed by a lame horse, then by one of the sudden
spring floods that could roar down from the mountains
without warning—but the thought that Halsey's gang might
outrun him never once entered his mind. Day by day, hour
by hour, he had narrowed the distance. Only blood for
blood would blot out the horrors engraved on his memory.
Only when his dead were avenged could he go on with his
own life.

The night was cold, but he built no fire. The burnished
flames and glowing coals would be too filled with memories.
In the chill hours of the mountain night, he lay awake for
hours beneath the sharp, bright stars, imagining them as
fiery sparks, fixed forever in the heavens.

As Bettany approached the boardinghouse, the parlor
light shone warmly through the curtains, casting lacy shadows across the porch. Inside, she found Mrs. Cummins in
a flannel robe and cap, reading her Bible. She insisted that
Bettany leave Nils and Hannah with her, since they were
sound asleep on the truckle bed.

"After all," the landlady pointed out, "it will be their
last sleep in a proper bed for many a long month."

Bettany thanked her and hurried up the stairs to the
silent second floor of the big house. The other boarders had
left earlier. It was a big room with a slanting ceiling and
two plain beds covered with blue-and-white quilts. The
night was humid. Stripping to her shift, she sponged off
with tepid water from the pitcher of thick, blue-banded
china.

Tomorrow the real adventure would start. Tomorrow she
would be heading west, to California. Axel had told her
that the enormous lands were crisscrossed by only a few
major trails. It was possible she might be traveling over the
same ground that her father had taken. Perhaps at the end
of it she would have some answers to the questions that
had haunted her all her life.

She stood before the mirror, running the brush through her long hair. Suddenly her hand stilled.

Realization chilled her like a cold rain. This was also her last night with Axel in the privacy of a bedroom, and it would be the only night alone since they'd exchanged vows. Dear God, what had she done?

No matter that she wore Axel's ring on her finger or that their marriage lines were packed within her trunk. He treated her as if she were a servant rather than a wife, and in the busy weeks of their travels Bettany had almost come to accept her status. She had absolutely no desire to change it now.

For several crucial seconds she debated the prudence of fetching Nils and Hannah up to the room. She was sure there'd be no question of any . . . any *occurrences* with the children sleeping nearby; on the other hand, would that be a shirking of her marital obligations? Apprehension won out over duty. She was reaching for her robe when the door opened without warning.

She whirled around to find Axel standing in the doorway. He didn't move, just stared at her as if he were really seeing her for the first time. He closed the door quietly, his gaze never leaving her, and leaned against it. His breath came in odd gasps.

"Axel? Are you ill?"

There was no answer to her question. As he stumbled toward her, Bettany felt a shiver of alarm. Was he drunk? She'd seen men too far gone in liquor during their travels, but Axel had always been there to shield her from them.

Who would shield her now, from him?

As he advanced toward her she retreated until the edge of the marble-topped dressing table stopped her. "The . . . the children are with Mrs. Cummins for the night. I . . . she thought it better not to disturb them from so sound a sleep."

He wasn't listening. His hands clamped down upon her shoulders so roughly, she exclaimed in protest. He didn't say a word, just held her like that until the wind blowing in the open window caught her hair and set it swirling around her shoulders. Axel groaned and dug his fingers into her arms.

"You're hurting me." She tried to pull away, but there was no room to move.

"Why . . . ?" he asked thickly, and shook his head as if he were shaking off cobwebs. "Why are you doing this to me?"

"Doing what? I don't know what you mean."

Bettany was afraid. There was such raw emotion in the face that had always seemed so stolid and inexpressive. She hardly recognized Axel. Was it loathing or hatred she saw?

It seemed it was neither. With a terrible moan he pulled her against his body in a smothering embrace. While she struggled to get free, he bunched up her shift. The touch of his hands upon the backs of her thighs was as much a shock as the hardness she felt rising in his loins.

He buried his face against her neck and held her so tightly, she was unable to pull away. Her face was squashed against his chest while his thick fingers kneaded her flesh. The angle of his neck was strange. She realized, with a jolt, that he was facing the mirror, looking at her nakedness as his hands wandered over it.

Embarrassment overcame her. "Axel! Axel, please . . ."

His touch grew more urgent. The hairbrush slipped from her hand and thudded against the windowsill. In the heat of his arousal he shoved her back against the dressing table and she lost her balance. Paralyzed with reaction, Bettany found herself lying sideways across the dressing table, impaled on a shaft of moonlight. The moment she had dreaded was here. In the mirror her bare legs gleamed white as milk against the darker shadows of the room.

Axel's breathing was ragged, coming in great sobbing gasps. Suddenly he reached out and pulled her shift down, pinning her arms to her side while exposing her breasts. He cupped them in his palms, ground his hands against her chest, making queer groaning sounds that frightened her. Bettany steeled her nerves. This was her sworn duty, the seal of marriage and the beginning of intimacy between a man and woman. And something was very wrong with her, because she felt nothing but fear and forlorn resignation. If she could have erased her vows then and there, she would have done so without any hesitation.

Axel was unaware of her feelings. As his big hands roved over her body, her fear grew, not of Axel, but of the act that would forever take away her innocence and exchange it with the secret knowledge of womanhood. He lifted her up, knocking his shaving gear to the floor, and took her to the bed.

Now it would begin, she thought, the kisses and caresses and words of endearment that were part of the courtship and marriage; instead he rolled over atop her and lay there unmoving, his chest heaving. It took her a while to realize that the gasps she heard were really sobs. Her surprise and revulsion changed to pity as they grew deep and racking. She had never heard such anguish. Instinctively she put her arms around him in the same mothering manner that she used with Nils and Hannah.

Axel broke free and rolled away, scrambling to his feet. In the moonlight his face was swollen and blotchy, distorted into a horrible mask. Bettany sat up, pushing the heavy mass of hair away from her face. In the mirror she caught a glimpse of herself, a half-naked wanton with a disheveled cloud of hair and her shift twisted around her waist.

"Have you no shame at all?" Axel grasped the edge of the quilt and threw it over her. "Cover yourself," he said sharply.

Bettany pulled the blanket over herself. She couldn't keep pace with the changes in him. A moment ago he'd embraced her with rough passion. Now there was only abhorrence in his eyes. "What is wrong, Axel? Why do you look at me like that? What have I done?"

He averted his face. "Bind up your hair and keep it bound. A woman's hair is the devil's net, meant to trick an unsuspecting man into the sin of lust."

"Sin?" What was he talking about? "But . . . we have

been married before God these six weeks and more. I am your wife."

His voice was filled with loathing. "You are a stranger to me. My wife is the woman I buried in the Susquehannah churchyard—or do you think I have forgotten her already?"

Tears of mortification filled Bettany's eyes. Axel's previous referrals to Nils's and Hannah's mother had been so unemotional, she'd thought it was the other way around: that he had already forgotten the poor woman. "Of course I don't. But I don't understand you in the least, or have any clue as to what you think or feel about anything." She ran her hand over her face. "I thought you wanted a wife. A . . . a helpmeet."

Axel's face was cold and bleak. "What other choice was open to me? I could not set out for California without a woman to look after things, to prepare the food and tend the children."

Bettany's humiliation was complete. "You wanted nothing more than a cook and laundress and nursemaid? I wish," Bettany said bitterly, "that you had been honest enough to tell me that. I would have been far happier as your hired servant. In fact, I would not have even asked for wages, only for my passage to California."

His disbelief was patent. "No decent woman would journey unchaperoned across the continent in the company of a man who isn't related to her by birth or marriage." He turned his back and paced to the window. "I meant this to be a marriage in name only. I thought you understood that."

It was the longest speech Bettany had ever heard from Axel, and it hit her with the force of closed fist.

His eyes narrowed with sudden suspicion. "Or maybe you did understand, after all. Why else would you go arranging so we'd be alone like this, waiting for me in front of the window with the light shining through the cloud of your hair."

For just a moment that same light blazed in his eyes, and he made a move as if to come to her again. Bettany pulled the covers up to her chin and shrugged back into her shift.

"My only plan was to brush out my hair and braid it and get a good night's sleep. I have as little wish for you to be in my bed as you have to be in it."

"Then bind your hair up or keep it covered. Hair like yours incites a man to lust, and I will not fall victim to your wiles again so easily."

He turned to stare steadily out the window, and Bettany snatched up her dress and slipped it on. Axel saw her womanliness as something evil, a temptation he must resist as much as possible. She shook her head wearily. What a terrible mistake she had made. Working as a tavern wench would have been preferable to this travesty of a marriage. There was nothing to salvage from it. What kind of life could she create from such fragile building blocks? She hadn't expected love, but she'd certainly expected respect. Instead her husband treated her with the scorn he'd show to a common whore.

The thought of annulment flitted briefly through her head but was almost instantly banished. Bettany had been abandoned in childhood herself and could never inflict that deep, particular pain on Hannah and Nils. Not so soon after they had lost their mother. Not when she had already grown to love the adventurous boy who brought her wildflowers and bashful smiles or the docile little girl who cuddled so trustingly in her arms. Yes, she would build her life around Nils and Hannah. They would be enough.

They would have to be.

She pushed the hair away from her face. "I understand now, Axel. We will be father and mother, not husband and wife. I'll fetch the children."

He didn't reply. After slipping on her shoes she hurried to the door. As she reached for the handle the muted light shone on the plain band on the finger of her left hand— not the circle of trust and fidelity that she'd imagined, but a thin golden shackle.

Before dawn Logan was on his way again, keen-eyed and alert despite the lack of sleep. He didn't need sleep or food;

his purpose sustained him. His concentration, his entire being, were focused on one thing. He rode briskly through the swirling ground mists as if their trail were a wide road blazed through the wilderness. He was a tracking wolf, following the scent of evil to its lair.

When the morning sun streaked the low-hanging clouds with bloody fingers, Logan knew it was time. Leaving his horse picketed in a grove of pine, he moved like a ghost down the crumpled slopes, his eyes gold as a wolf's. There would be no more women and children left to die along their trail, no more cabins turned to blazing funeral pyres against the twilight sky.

Logan came upon the three men he had sought so long, camping beside a stream. A lanky red-beard was readying his pinto for travel, in a careless jingle of harness. The other two—younger but hard-jawed and thin-lipped—were drinking coffee, mumbling to one another as they rubbed the sleep from their eyes. They were at ease, feeling safe and secure in the midst of their familiar morning routine, until Death walked in, a Colt revolver in his hand.

Logan took his stance, gun ready. The hammer clicked, spinning the chamber and locking it into place. The sound startled the others. There'd been no sign of his coming.

"Jesus-Gawd-A'mighty!" Scalding coffee poured over one outlaw's hand. He didn't seem to notice.

The other man choked and coughed on a hot mouthful. "Halsey, it's Logan!" It was difficult to understand him through the chattering of his teeth.

Logan didn't have to say a word. His finger tightened on the trigger, and the three men froze. They knew that he had tracked them down and what he meant to do before he left.

And why.

The red-beard, the one called Halsey, turned around slowly, hands held carefully away from his body to show he carried no sidepiece. Sweat broke out on his ruddy face as he bargained for time. "Lookit, we din't think you'd take it so personal. The boys was jest lookin' fer a good time,

and got a leetle carried away. No need fer you to git sore—
Jezuz, it was just a woman."

Again, rage flared like a fiery blossom, spreading through
Logan's chest. He smothered the flames until once again
only an icy core remained. The other two sighed softly in
relief, but Halsey wasn't reassured. He knew that ice would
burn the unprotected skin, that cold could kill.

He sidled closer to his horse, casually moving his arm
within reach of the plains rifle slung through his blanket
roll. The horse shifted and tossed its head, sensing the
tension. Halsey kept his face toward Logan while his fingers
slipped smoothly toward their goal.

"Nothin' we can do ter bring her back. She knew where
Cade hid the gold from the other bank job. That's where
we're heading now. Twice as much as from the one you
got sent away with us fer. And we ain't averse to sharing
it with you, no sir. Let bygones be bygones, is what I say."

Logan didn't answer, but his trigger finger tightened.
Halsey jerked like a marionette with tangled strings. Every
blotch and broken blood vessel stood out on his suddenly
ashen face.

"Hold on now, Logan. Friends shouldn't be fightin' over
a dead woman."

"We're not friends, Halsey, and we never were. I just
helped with the jailbreak to get out myself before they
finished that gallows."

"C'mon, Logan. There's eighty thousand dollars in gold
bullion hid up in the mountains, and Cassie had the last
clue to it. We'll split it, the four of us. Now, I don't know
what hold she had on you, but hell! With all that gold,
you kin buy yourself a better woman than that worn-out
whore. God, you should've heard her. . . ."

As he spoke, Halsey suddenly blurred into rash movement. Logan's mind took the moment and split it a dozen
ways, until every action seemed separate and distinct: Halsey's freckled hand swinging the rifle into position as he
dodged behind the pinto's rump, the line of light along the
rifle barrel before it turned its ominous dark eye upon him,

the steady thumping of his own heart, the heft of his revolver and the feel of its satin-smooth handgrip.

Halsey's thick finger curled around the rifle trigger while the pinto snorted and rolled its eyes. Words ran in circles through Logan's brain. Halsey's words.

"Hell, with all that gold, you kin buy yourself a better woman than that worn-out whore. God, you should've heard her. . . ."

"Heard her" what?—weep? pray? beg? Logan wondered as he squeezed the trigger.

The explosion of the outlaw's rifle shattered the silence just as Logan's bullets, passing beneath the pinto, shattered Halsey's knees and sent him tumbling and screaming to the ground. The horse reared in fright, loosing the reins that were looped over a branch, and bolted. The men by the campfire didn't move at all. They knew that the Paterson Colt revolver held only five shots—but they also knew Logan. Two of them, and three bullets left; the odds were much too high.

The shots echoed from the hills beyond in diminishing waves. In the stillness of the camp, Halsey's low moans and curses sounded eerie. They brought Logan out of his suspended state. Time took on its normal shape and texture. The pain came flooding back.

The men huddling by the fire were gray as the ash that rimmed its edges. Fear, of Logan and of what they had brought down upon themselves, held them immobile. They didn't reach for the guns so near, only a reach, only a motion—only a miracle away. They stared as he drew closer.

"Fer Gawd's sake, Logan, have mercy!"

Logan moved in, eyes as cold and shadowed as his heart. "Men like you don't deserve mercy. They deserve justice. And I'm here to see that justice is done."

Later, when the sun was lowering, Logan cleansed himself in a cold mountain stream, washing away his rage and bitterness with the blood. Halsey had first set events in train by trying to implicate Logan in the bank robbery.

That had been his first mistake, but not the one he had paid for. That had been for Cassie and Anna—and it had not been enough.

The clear, cool water flowed through Logan's hands like a baptismal fountain, washing away the stains. Now it was all ended. His work was done. Vengeance had been taken, the dead appeased.

He reached into his medicine pouch and pulled out an oval of cast metal. In boyhood he'd found comfort in the special talisman. Buffalo Heart had told him it was the answer to the riddle of his past. It had been found sewn into his clothing when Notched Arrow had found him among the wolves, but what its meaning was he didn't know.

The talisman burned in Logan's palm. It was oval, framed in gold, and cast in silver. On one side was a mother and child, on the other a garnet heart. A heart pierced by seven swords.

In his youth he'd felt that the talisman marked him for something special and he had dreamed that it would help him uncover the secrets of his past. It had been his most treasured possession. Over the years, when he understood all the ramifications, his feelings about it had changed.

He kept it now, not as a keepsake of his unknown parents, but as a memento of his cruel abandonment. A reminder that they had conceived him and given him birth—and then, without a qualm, had left him in the snow to die.

Logan watched the sun set in a sea of color and thought again of sparks flying high. He buried his face in his hands. Slowly the ice facade cracked and broke apart, until he couldn't tell whether his face was bathed with melting water or with tears.

He had cared for Cassie. Cared deeply in his own way. For a short while he had found a haven with her and with Anna. He had never once forgotten that he was an exile, but in that little cabin the edges of his loneliness had softened and warmed. Now he was alone again.

More alone than ever.

Three

Mexico City: 1840

It was unseasonably warm. Hot enough within the high, guardian walls to bake tortillas on the colorful courtyard tiles. Inside the thick walls of the Convent of Our Lady of the Seven Sorrows it was almost as bad, but the woman lying upon the bed felt cold. So cold.

While the others were at prayer Dona Ysabella lay alone, with only the comfort of the crucifix upon the opposite wall to sustain her. A bar of light fell upon the figure on the cross, turning the racked body and agonized features from bronze to gold. Motes danced in the sunbeam, highlighting a shred of delicate cobweb and the design carved into the prie-deux, of a heart pierced by seven swords.

Dona Ysabella knew much of hearts pierced by sorrow and pain, her own among them. Her thin fingers clutched the hem of the sheet with surprising strength, as if by holding on to the white cloth she could hold on to life as well. But the effort could not be sustained much longer. The priest must come soon, before it was too late.

She drowsed part of the time, floating in and out of restless slumber, and her breathing became irregular at times. It would have been so easy to let go, to drift away on the next ebbing of consciousness; yet Dona Ysabella never lost her grip upon the linen sheet. She forced her eyes open, and her pallid lips moved slowly.

"*Kyrie eleison. Christe eleison. Mater Dolorosa, ora pro*

nobis, ora pro nobis. . . ." Lord have mercy. Christ have mercy. Mother Most Sorrowful, pray for us. The mingled Greek and Latin phrases were dry whispers, like the rustle of gathering wings. The cold had sunk into her marrow. She became one with it, sinking deep, deeper. . . .

Dona Ysabella was suddenly back in the past, fighting the diminishing snowstorm that had swept down upon Santa Fe in the spring of 1812. Ten inches of wet snow followed by violent winds that had killed the newborn lambs and calves and left shepherds frozen among the huddled remnants of their flocks. Suddenly she was running, running through the drifts, scarcely able to see or hear over the wind and dancing snow.

Cold, so cold. Her breath was a ragged cloud before her face as she stumbled, alternately praying and cursing. It was only when she heard the bells tolling that she realized it was all in vain. She had blundered in a circle and ended up back where she'd started. Quinn would leave, and it would be too late.

And then what would happen to the baby?

Tears stung her eyes. She had vowed on her immortal soul to help save the child. Nothing must stop her from fulfilling that vow, not even all the frozen fury of the storm. Pulling her cloak around her more tightly, she stumbled on. *"Mater Dolorosa, ora pro nobis. . . ."*

The sound of her own voice roused her to the present, and the door opened on the dying echo of her prayers. She remembered where she was as the padre entered, a strange sight in this bastion of women. He was tall and stooped with the face of an abstracted saint. His eyes seemed to focus, not on his immediate physical surroundings, but on the world beyond.

He made a small sound of sympathetic distress when he saw Dona Ysabella. The yellow waxen skin, the sunken eyes and hollowed cheeks, all spoke of death's imminence. He did not know her. She had been a lay sister at the convent for decades, attending daily mass but never taking Communion, working hard at whatever tasks the nuns required of her yet

never taking her vows as a bride of Christ. Bending over the
bed, he took her thin, cold hands in his.

She roused at once, and her dull eyes took on a feverish
light. "Thank God you have come. There is something I
must do before . . . before . . ." She took a deep breath. "I
cannot die until I right a grievous wrong. I did not know
what to do. I waited for guidance. I waited too long. . . ."

For a while the room was silent except for her wheezy
gasps. "It has grown cold," she murmured at last, "and the
room is very dim. A cloud has come over the sun."

But to Father Ignazio the room was still filled with heat
and warm, golden light. With his free hand he pulled the
stole of confession from his pocket and placed it around his
neck, and he brought out the container of blessed chrism.
Dona Ysabella summoned her remaining strength.

"There is a packet of papers in the wooden coffer. I never
sent them, but they will tell the story. You must read them
and decide what is best to do, after all these years. I solemnly
swear on my immortal soul that every word in them is true."

Without further preamble she launched into the opening
words of the confession that she knew so well, although
she hadn't spoken them in decades.

"Bless me, Father, for I have sinned . . ."

Before the rambling confession could commence, her
voice trailed off into a gusty sigh. That was all. It took the
priest a moment to realize that her soul had slipped gently
away. Whatever her sins were, and Father Ignazio guessed
that they were few, Dona Ysabella must confess them now
to God Himself.

He closed her lids gently and opened the container of
holy chrism and began the final prayers and anointing. Only
afterward did he remember her parting injunction. The
wooden coffer stood on a small, open table and was
unlocked. Inside, worn from much handling and spotted
with puckers that could only be dried tears, were several
sheets thickly crossed with spidery writing and a small
medallion fashioned of gold and silver.

Father Ignazio took out the first letter and scanned the

lines of faded ink. He frowned. People and places were named, including one he recognized: Don Miguel Alvarez de Medina, a powerful man whose influenced stretched from Mexico City to Santa Fe.

He read further, lost in the shadows of decades past. His expression was no longer abstracted. Now he looked like a disoriented saint, yanked from tranquillity of God's glory into the reality of human anguish. Insulated in his holiness, he had never experienced the depth of suffering that the letters revealed; but Dona Ysabella had written into them all the terrible passions of her past, and so vividly that he felt like a voyeur.

Father Ignazio glanced from the yellowed paper to the still form upon the bed and back again to the faded lines. The incriminating words were still there, the stark outline of events with the ghosts of tears and tragedy whispering between the faded lines. Whispers that could turn to shouts if the revelations of these letters were ever made public and their accusations proven.

He understood now why she had remained silent so long and why she had never taken her vows but remained a lay sister instead. He could also understand why she felt the need to see the old wrongs redressed, the sins punished.

Father Ignazio looked suddenly much older than his years. "God in heaven!" he murmured, rubbing his forehead. "What am I to do? What am I to do?"

Four

THE PAIN DROVE LOGAN INTO THE HEALING
reaches of familiar places. He spent a week on Spirit Mountain, mourning the woman he had respected but not loved and the child he would always carry in his heart. He could not ease the agony that burned within him, consuming him. He had no purpose, no roots, and no real will to live. Slowly the beauty of the land seeped into his heart, and the solitude soothed his soul.

On the seventh night he dreamed of a wolf, its coat more dazzling than the whitest snow, its eyes as fierce and golden as his own. The Spirit Wolf padded closer, but when Logan looked into its magical, golden eyes the dream became all tangled. A woman came to him, silver-haired and silver-eyed, her hands held out to him. From her fingers a small object dangled: the medallion with the heart pierced by seven swords. Logan reached out to embrace her, but she dissolved into mist. The mist became fog, the fog became snow, and the world was blotted out by the blizzard's fury. He heard a voice crying out in fear and loneliness.

He awakened with it ringing in his ears and knew it was his own.

He felt a powerful sense of loss as the dream faded away. It had been many years since he'd dreamed of his mysterious Silver Woman. The dreams had come all his life, but no one had been able to tell him their full meaning, not even Buffalo Heart, whose medicine was the ability to interpret signs and visions. The day wore on, and still the illusive images haunted him. To understand their message became an obsession with him. He must pierce the illusions of the world around him to the invisible world beyond.

Fasting, he built a sweat lodge in the way he'd been taught in his youth, knowing it was what he should have done from the start. He must purify himself after his stay among the *ve-ho-e* and hope for a vision. He didn't dare to hope that it would answer the questions that had burdened him all his life: Who was he? Where did he belong? And why, as a helpless babe, had he been wrapped in blankets and amulets and then left to die in the snow?

Despite the lapsed years when he had wandered through the white man's world, he remembered everything he must do: the correct way to dig the hole and roof it with the proper branches, the building of the fire and the sacred prayers that must be sung at each stage. Inside the lodge, with sweat pouring off his naked body, he sang the ancient chants.

Heat and hunger made him light-headed, but he poured more water on the rocks, and a silver wolf materialized out of the cloud of steam. It came to him carrying something in its jaws, and he saw it was a Cheyenne arrow fletched with striped turkey feathers, banded with black-and-yellow stripes. Logan recognized the arrow. It was one that Small Eagle had made, marked with his sign. He looked at the wolf, waiting. It met his gaze steadily until it dissolved. Logan searched the floor of the sweat lodge, but there was no wolf sign, only a pattern traced into the soft earth. It was a large square, balanced on one corner, with a straight line pointing out from each side. The Cheyenne symbol of the Morning Star.

Logan stared after it for what seemed like mere seconds, but he realized that the fire had been out so long that the sweat lodge was cold. He'd asked for direction and received an answer that he didn't like. Yet in the morning, when the sky was a rosy seashell and dew beaded the grass, he headed toward their summer hunting grounds. There he would find the secret of the Silver Woman.

Nothing occurred to disturb his journey. It was after sunset several days later, as he prepared himself for sleep, that Logan heard the short barking cough of a fox. This was Cheyenne territory. He listened intently, but the bark was not repeated.

Wrapping himself in his blanket, Logan lay down. There was no moon, and the stars were streaked with layers of sooty cloud. The soughing of the breeze through the pines and aspens soothed him. A short time later he heard the vixen bark again, this time from a greater distance. Soon his breathing deepened. An hour passed.

Out of the trees a shape crept slowly, almost invisible against the blackness. It drifted toward Logan like a wind-blown leaf and made less sound. Beside him, the silent form folded down and in upon itself, and extended a hand with a lethal knife.

"You sleep soundly and unwisely," a voice whispered in the Cheyenne tongue. "Your throat is slit, and your life-blood runs out upon the forest floor."

"You are wrong, Small Eagle."

The Cheyenne started as Logan spoke from somewhere behind him. "And if I had not recognized you," Logan continued, "it might be your own blood staining your moccasins at the moment."

The moon glanced out through a spangled veil as Small Eagle jerked the blanket away from the arrangement of saddlebags and mounded brush. He rose, chuckling, and sheathed the knife. "I should have been prepared for one of your tricks. How did you know me? I was silent, a feather on the wind."

Logan came out of the shadows, his eye gleaming gold as coins in the reflected light. "More like a bull elk in rut. Only a man with no ears would not have heard you."

"No. Only one with the ears of a wolf could have heard me. Only my brother, Wolf Star." Small Eagle stood very still. "I heard your call and came to meet you."

So, Logan thought, the old bond still held. Since child-hood they had had the ability to reach out to one another across long distances, to "call" in times of trouble or need; but he had thought it had been severed on the day he'd left the Cheyenne camp in bitterness. Not once in the years of his lonely wandering had he heard it.

Small Eagle watched him intently. "I knew if you called to me, that the past was set aside. I have waited many years for your return."

Logan's face hardened. "I might have returned long ago—if the choice had been mine to make."

Small Eagle digested this, running his gaze over the scar that curved from Logan's jaw to his collarbone. "I thought it was because of me that you have stayed away all this time. I thought you had not found it in your heart to let your anger die."

"I was in a white man's prison. Twice." Logan didn't go into detail. Small Eagle would not understand a man giving up his freedom to protect the honor of a Kiowa woman. Not after the Kiowas had massacred a hundred and fifty Cheyenne of the Bow String Society. As to the other thing, well, that was part of the past.

"There is no need to forgive, Small Eagle. It was a boy's trick, and we are men now."

Small Eagle relaxed. "It is good, my brother. Now you come home to us. Home to the People. And you will not leave us again."

A sigh shuddered through Logan's lean frame. "No. I will never leave."

"My heart rejoices, Wolf Star. Welcome back, my brother."

The wagons rode abreast, like great beasts lumbering through the tall prairie grasses that were the height of a mounted man. The sun was strong, and like the other women of the wagon party, Bettany was hot and tired. Unlike the majority, she was also exhilarated. She was living the adventure she had always craved and never expected to experience. It was worth the discomfort.

Captain McGrew rode past them, ordering the wagons

into single file as they approached Ash Hollow. "The most difficult part of our journey is over. From here on, the way to California is easy, with fresh water and fair game in abundance. Ash Hollow lies ahead, the gate to the land of milk and honey."

Ash Hollow. As the drivers followed McGrew's directions Bettany forgot her aching feet and the dust they would have to eat from the wagons ahead. The Hollow was said to be a beautiful place, much like the woods and flowering meadows of the United States, now so far behind them. The endless, treeless horizons stretching away from the Platte River were too open and lonely for someone raised among the green hills of the Susquehanna.

A trio of sandhill cranes flew like arrows across the water, followed within seconds by thousands upon thousands of their flock. They rose in a churning, flapping cloud over the shallow river channels that twisted and braided in long, silvery plaits.

"Oh, if only we could fly so swiftly," Bettany exclaimed aloud.

Axel was too literal-minded. "Mankind will never achieve the speed and ease of travel that is inherent in birds. It is not what God intended, and it is ungodly to aspire to it."

She didn't debate him. Axel could find an answer in his Bible to support any of his arguments, but that didn't mean his interpretations were correct. And the fact that Adam and Eve hadn't journeyed from Eden in the comfort of canvas-covered wagons didn't bother her husband in the least.

The lead wagons pulled up on the bank in preparation for the crossing. When the sunlight struck the surface of the meandering channels of the river, they looked deep and wide, but up close the Platte was shallow, silt-laden, and filled with treacherous quicksands. Bettany was relieved that the river crossing was finally behind them. It had been far more arduous than they had anticipated, and Abraham Carter had almost lost one of his oxen.

By the time the emigrants were all safe on the south bank, the animals were as drained as their owners; and only total exhaustion—and a sharp slap from her exasperated husband—had ended Letitia Renfrew's attack of frenzied weeping. Several of the men cheered. Bettany could scarcely blame them.

Nils, tired and dusty, swung up on the lazy board that ran along the off side of the wagon. His face was flushed with early June warmth and liberally smudged. "My feet hurt." Walking to California was not as much fun as he had expected it to be. "How many more days before we get there?"

Before Bettany could give him the bad news, Axel called her to lead the oxen and took off in search of the captain, muttering, "By God, the man is either a damned liar or a damned fool."

When they reached Ash Hollow she understood. The lovely valley below them was bounded by lofty cliffs to one side and rich in trees and water. Wild roses bloomed in profusion, perfuming the air; but the way down seemed impossibly steep, almost perpendicular. Only an angel with a fiery sword would have seemed as formidable a barrier as the descent into Ash Hollow.

Porter Renfrew came striding up and whistled when he saw the steep angle. Axel nodded grimly. "We'll have to turn back. The wagon will run away down that incline and smash to kindling wood. McGrew should have listened to me when I tried to show him my map."

"Be damned to your map, sir." The captain came roaring up, followed by several of the men. "We'll winch the wagons to the trees and lower them down. Take the wheels off first, if we have to. I've seen worse."

Axel eyed him grimly. "You've seen worse. But you've never seen this particular place before in your life, by God."

McGrew's skin darkened with a rush of blood. "I never said I'd personally walked every step of the trail, but I knew about this place." He shot a threatening glance around the assembled crowd. "This is the testing ground. The real men will go forward. Those who are afraid can turn back here and now."

His challenge fell on chastened ears, and everyone pitched in. The rest of the day was a nightmare of exertion as the ponderous wagons were lightened and winched to the trees, then lowered bit by bit down the precipitous grade. By the time the last wagon was angling down the sheer slope, the only casualties were a few rope burns and Letitia Renfrew's nerves. A sharp word from her husband and a dose of Mamie Ebbersoll's smelling salts soon had the situation under control.

Once the Vandergroot wagon was down in the hollow, Bettany settled Hannah down for a nap. The girl's eyelids drooped, and her fingers curled around a piece of her stepmother's skirt. Smoothing a wisp of hair from Hannah's forehead, Bettany felt her heart fill with tenderness and love. Hannah seemed very young for her age, but perhaps that was a reaction to the sudden loss of her mother and being uprooted from the only home she'd known. Bettany was determined to make a good home for the children in California. A home filled with love and laughter and song, like the one in her dimming memories.

Axel came back, muttering beneath his breath. "That fool McGrew will be the death of us all." He held out his map. "Look here. This is the incline above Ash Hollow, just as we found it. And there is a notation that there is no wood from here on for a hundred miles."

"What does Captain McGrew say?"

"That fool! He claims there's plenty of wood for cooking and any repairs, all the way from here to California."

Bettany sighed. "Then we'd better gather as much wood as possible now."

Axel folded the map and put it inside his inner vest pocket. "You have a lot of common sense for a woman."

She smile wryly. Misguided as it was, that was the first compliment he'd ever given her. Marriage was much more difficult than she'd anticipated. She'd envisioned herself working hand in hand with her spouse, discussing decisions and exchanging opinions. The only decisions thus far had been made by Axel, and the only opinions he wanted to hear were his own. At least there had been no repetition of that last horrible night at Mrs. Cummins's boardinghouse.

Hannah made a soft snoring noise. The child could sleep anywhere. Worries nagged at the back of Bettany's mind. Hannah was sweet-tempered but passive. At times she seemed more engrossed in a leaf or a button or the pattern of clouds overhead than with the people about her. On the other hand, Nils was active and curious about everything. Since they'd left Westport Landing he was alternately boisterous and outgoing or withdrawn and secretive. The task of helping them survive their grief was more difficult than Bettany had ever imagined.

Nils came around the back of the wagon on the heels of her thought. He stopped short when he saw her, and a shiny disk, like a large coin, fell from his hand. It rolled to the edge of the blanket, and Bettany retrieved it for him. It was a medallion with a profile of Thomas Jefferson on one side, clasped hands upon the other.

"It's mine! I found it in the dirt by the river, when we stayed at Mrs. Cummins's boardinghouse. Finders keepers!"

"Of course." She put it into his outstretched hand and watched as anger changed to bewildered gratitude.

Nils took the medallion from her and stuck it in his pocket as if afraid she would change her mind. He scuffed a toe in the dirt and looked up from beneath his brows. "I found something else, too. The top of a sword." His dark eyes brightened. "Probably from a pirate. It would have to be from a pirate, don't you think?"

She heard the wistful note in his voice. This was no time for history lessons. "I'm sure you are right."

"You are? Golly!" He flashed her a blinding smile and ran off in a burst of boyish exuberance.

Bettany smiled after him. She was making some progress in gaining his acceptance, but his mother's death had wounded him deeply. He was old enough to feel abandoned, yet young enough to be confused by it all. It would be some time before he would be able to trust again—longer before he felt safe enough to love.

Over the next weeks the land changed gradually from the familiar greens and rich earth browns to shades of bronze and sun-bleached buffs and tans. The creak of the wheels, the sounds of the oxen and horses, and the tinkle of harness became the music of Bettany's days. Nils hung the medallion he'd found from the back of the wagon for luck. It shone bright as a star, leading them westward.

One night she was wakened by a dull and constant thunder. McGrew came along the wagons, reassuring everyone. "That's the sound of a buffalo herd, running across the prairie. There'll be fresh buffalo steaks tomorrow for everyone."

The following day she had her first glimpse of a mighty buffalo herd, a plume of dust many miles long, flowing across the distant landscape like the waves of a dusty brown ocean. McGrew and four men were able to bring down one of the beasts, and they dined heartily. For all of two days and two nights the herd rumbled past in a thunder of hooves that shook the earth, and still they filled the land to the horizon. Only the fact that the wagon party followed the river and the buffalo followed their own instinctive drive eventually separated them.

Thirty miles farther on they passed a curious formation of weathered stone. It suggested balconies and pillared porticoes, surmounted by a great dome.

"The Acropolis of the West," McGrew proclaimed grandly. "Carved by Mother Nature."

"A cathedral," Letitia Renfrew said solemnly.

"No, more like a courthouse." Her husband laughed. "And see that smaller 'building'? Why, that's the jailhouse." He slapped his knee in high good humor. "Just goes to show we're not all that far from civilization."

From their night camp they saw Chimney Rock, a needle of stone trusting up from a mound of fallen debris. The grand scale of their surroundings made Bettany feel very small and insignificant. The wagon party was a mere speck on the immensity of the land. If disaster struck, they could only look to one another and God for help.

The next twenty miles took two long days, with Scott's Bluff looming like a blue smudge on the horizon. The entire wagon train cheered when they got close enough to recognize it, for it meant they were nearing Fort Laramie, a rude fur-trading post where they could replenish their supplies. Firewood would be a luxury, one they could ill afford; meanwhile the plentiful buffalo chips made an excellent and nearly smokeless fire. Bettany and the others no longer minded. The important thing was to have hot food and a warm fire on cold nights.

Only Letitia Renfrew, the one woman among them who put on white gloves to gather an apron full of chips, disdained the ready fuel. She had lost considerable weight on the journey. "Knowing what the food is cooking over takes my appetite clean away."

After reaching Scott's Bluff, they stopped to make their midday camp. Once the animals had been unyoked and watered, several of the men and boys and a few of the younger girls planned to set out on foot and carve their names upon the rock. "These landmarks are like trail letter boxes," McGrew said. "Anyone comes by and leaves a message, the next ones along the trail will carry it on. People traveling from Maine to California or Oregon will stop and see our marks for years to come."

Bettany wanted desperately to go, but Hannah was asleep beneath the wagon. Mamie Ebbersoll came over. "I can tell you and the boy want to go along, and I've no mind to go traipsing any farther than I have to. I'll stay with Hannah, if you like."

Bettany smiled her thanks. "That's kind of you."

While crossing over to Captain McGrew, she was hailed by Josie Carter, a shy young woman a year older than she. Over the weeks she and Bettany had struck up a friendship. Josie, who had been married at fifteen to a much older man, had not been blessed with children yet, and her affection for Nils and Hannah had proved an added bond.

"I think I'll go along with you and Nils," she said. "I'd like to see the view."

The group of explorers set off at a brisk pace. In the deceptively clear air, Chimney Rock looked less than a quarter mile away, but it was well over two miles to the base of its rocky talus slope. They'd taken no water with them and arrived hot and thirsty but determined to make their mark upon the land. Indian signs were painted or cut into the rock, stick figures that looked like children's drawings to Bettany and others of animals that were lifelike miniatures, so vitally drawn that they seemed about to leap right off the surface.

Less imaginative, but more informative for her purposes, were the names carved into the surface along with dates and places of origin: "H. Ketcham, New York bound for Oregon, Lord have mercy," "Alkali wtr. ahed, bewar," and "Rbrt. W. Take s. trail 6 miles. Archie."

The one name she hoped to see wasn't there. Finding some trace of her father's journey wasn't such a remote possibility, since the tracks followed Indian paths as old as time and had been used by white men since their arrival in the New World. Bettany knew that these trails blazed in ancient times were still the highways across the vast continent. Where they converged, trading posts or towns and villages had sprung up, and a traveler's passage could easily be traced. Only the Indians and isolated trappers wandered freely across the land. But if Sam Howard had come this way, he had not taken time out from his quest for gold and California to mark his passage.

Bettany scratched her own message into the weathered rock:

> Bettany Anne Howard 19 yrs.
> Penn. to California, 1840.

Josie puzzled over it but was too much of a lady to comment. The red in Bettany's face was only partly from the reflected sunshine. "I . . . I used my maiden name, since my husband is chiseling his own over there."

She brushed the dust from her sweaty hands and stepped back to examine her handiwork. The letters weren't deep, but they were clear. Clear enough for Sam Howard to see them if he ever came this way. If he was still alive. And when they came to Register Rock, a day's journey past Fort Laramie, she'd leave her name again. In fact, she intended to leave her mark somewhere along the trail all the way to California. Miss Olmstead had always said that God helped those who helped themselves. At this point God seemed very far away, and Bettany was taking no chances.

By late afternoon the wagon party reached the delta formed by the meeting of the North Platte and Laramie rivers. To the west the Laramie Mountains seemed to be stacks of hazy blue clouds, and the blue pyramid of Laramie Peak shimmered beneath its summer cap of snow.

Fort Laramie was an unprepossessing conglomeration of stockade walls and weathered log buildings, but plans were already under way to replace it with a new and enlarged adobe structure. Bettany cheered with the others to see the American flag snapping in the breeze over the square turret.

The open plain was dotted with knots of people and horses. Bettany was surprised. "I didn't think there were this many people in the territory, much less in one place."

Hannah had been clinging to her skirts but let go to stare at a brown-and-white dog racing along with a naked Indian boy. Suddenly all eyes of the wagon party were on the group of Indians mounting their spotted ponies not a hundred feet away. Bettany scooped Hannah up in her arms and looked around for the child's brother and noticed the clusters of tipis here and there.

Nils was fascinated by the Indians and had to be kept from straying. He thought he could manage one of their sturdy ponies just fine, for they were smaller than Captain McGrew's gelding. The Indians were dressed much like the traders, in buckskin breeches or breech-clouts and leggings with fringed shirts. Many were bare-chested. He wanted to get a closer look at their bright necklaces and see how they afixed the feathers to their long black hair. But every time he managed to get near, some grown-up spoiled it by calling him back.

Outside the stockade, one of the braves was having an archery contest with two white men. The Indian won every time, spearing the target with his iron-tipped bow.

A drunk loitering nearby watched. He wore the buckskins of a frontiersman with a red-checked shirt and an incongruous bowler hat. After another volley of arrows he took a pull from his bottle and shook his head.

"Christ, you'll never beat him at his own game, Murray! There's only one way to settle a match with an Injun."

He pulled out his sidearm and shot at the target, but his aim was wide. The three arrows, clustered so tightly, were sheared off in midshaft.

The Indian was furious, and so was Nils. "You shouldn't ought to have done that. That wasn't fair." He gathered up one of the feathered ends that had splintered near his feet, his face crimson with indignation.

"Shut your bone-box, kid." The drunk picked Nils up by the collar until his feet dangled off the ground and shook him like a dog shaking a rabbit. "Fair is for white men, you stupid little bastard. It don't count with no Arapaho."

The three men laughed while Nils struggled and kicked to get free. Suddenly a shadow fell across them. The Arapaho brave stood beside him, the tip of his knife tickling the drunk's ribs.

"Leave go," he commanded in accented English.

Nils felt himself lowered to the ground so abruptly that his teeth clacked together and he bit the side of his tongue; but the dirty paw still held him by his now torn collar. The Indian prodded a little more forcefully with his blade.

"What the hell's going on out there?" One of the trading company men hurried out and summed up the scene. "Michaels, turn the kid loose and go crawl away somewhere till you're sober. Go on, git!"

The drunk slouched away with a black look over his shoulder. The other white men stood tensely, hands near their weapons. The trader stood between them and the Arapaho. "You'd better light out, too, Cloud Man. I don't want no trouble with women and children here."

The Indian's mouth stretched wryly. By women and children, McCorkel meant the white women and children of the wagon train. If there'd only been Arapaho and Cheyenne present, it would have been another matter. As he walked away Nils ran after him, holding out the broken arrow shafts. "Here. Maybe you can fix them."

Cloud Man looked down at the boy, noting his youthful dignity and the smear of blood at the corner of his stern little mouth. The Arapaho smiled suddenly. The arrows were beyond repair, but some of the damage done by Michaels had been erased by the boy's courage. "You are a brave warrior for one so small. A warrior needs an eagle feather to show his bravery to all."

He plucked one of the feathers from the leather thong that bound his hair and presented it to Nils, who took it with as much awe as if it had been the Holy Grail.

"Thank . . . thank you, I mean . . ." but Cloud Man was already gone, drifting through the throng toward the gates. Axel came by and saw his son's trophy. "Throw that dirty thing down."

But Nils only pretended to, and he took his treasure away and hid it inside the wagon beside the broken sword hilt he'd found half-buried along the shores of the Missouri. It might look old and useless, but he was convinced in his six-year-old mind that it had belonged to a pirate. He ran his fingertips over the fancy scrollwork. It wasn't just a pretty decoration, he'd decided, but a cleverly disguised map to where the pirate had buried his treasure. Someday he'd find it and dig it up.

Unless, of course, he decided to become an Indian brave and live in a hide tipi. That certainly held more appeal for him than his father's plans of farming. A farmer couldn't wear war paint or have sword fights on the high seas.

When he came out, still filled with visions of gold coin spilling from a sea chest, a man was examining the wagon. He was short and wore a gray hat with a bullet hole through the brim. "Where you bound for, young fella?"

"California."

"Zat so? This here's the first load with women and children I've seen,'cept when the Whitman party came through a few years back."

"There'll be lots more," Nils said, eager to show off his knowledge. "Once he proves that it's safe to travel overland, Captain McGrew's got hundreds and hundreds of people he's going to bring over the trail. My pa says there'll be thousands more in a couple of years."

The man touched the hole in the brim of his hat. "Then they'd best watch out for Injuns. Party of Cheyenne caught me unawares one day. Lost part of my scalp, but at least I got away in the nick of time."

With a chuckle he strolled away, leaving Nils burning with curiosity as to what lay beneath that battered hat. Had the man really been scalped? What did it look like? And what did it feel like? After thinking it over, Nils ducked back inside the wagon and retrieved the eagle feather. If they met any Indians along the way, he'd pull it out and show it to them as proof that he was a brave warrior, too.

While Nils daydreamed, Bettany was catching up on the news. Great Britain had recognized Texas's independence, odds were that William Henry Harrison would be the next U.S. president, and an Indian brave, riddled with bullets but still alive, had been found last week not twenty yards from where the Renfrew wagon was drawn up.

The last bit of information rattled her. She wouldn't draw an easy breath until they were safe in California.

The night before they left, one of the men brought out his fiddle and played some ballads and some rollicking tunes. Even the happy ones seemed poignant so far from home.

It was during a group singing of "Shenandoah" that the

door opened and two figures came in. One was a mountain man, dressed in worn buckskins with two Bowie knives strapped to a belt around his waist. His companion was an Indian woman with a sleeping baby on a cradleboard. They took up a place on the edge of things, and while the trader exchanged comments with the man, his wife drifted over toward the women of the wagon party.

She moved up behind Bettany. "What will you give me if I tell you your future?"

Bettany turned around in surprise. "What do you mean?"

The woman smiled and bobbed her head. "If I cast the herbs and stones, I can tell you what path lies ahead."

Intrigued but a little frightened, Bettany racked her brain. She had no money, but there must be something she could give the woman in exchange.

The squaw startled her by guessing her thoughts. "I would like a spoon," she said softly. "A metal spoon. Or a red ribbon."

Bettany had no spoon to spare, but she did have a red ribbon threaded through the neck of her dress. She pulled it out and dangled it from her fingers. "Very well."

Letitia Renfrew pushed her way through. "I will give you a spoon," she said in a tremulous voice. "A silver spoon. I . . . I *must* know what lies ahead."

The woman took out a small bag of heavy brocade, much worn, and spilled its contents into her hand: a twig, a bit of rusted metal, a smooth blue stone, a circle of copper, and flakes of pungent herbs. She looked at them, then at Mrs. Renfrew. "Ask me a question."

"Will I live to old age?"

"You will live so long you will be weary of life."

While Letitia sighed in relief and went to tell her husband, the woman put the items back in the bag, shook them and spilled them out once more. She took the ribbon from Bettany. "What is your question?"

"Will . . . will I find what I am seeking?"

"You will know great love and great sorrow. You will feel the eagle's wings as well as its claws, and steal the heart of the wolf. And yes, you will find what you seek."

Bettany wasn't satisfied with such a cryptic response, but the woman was finished. She bundled up her things and put the brocade bag back inside her bodice, refusing to say any more. Disappointed, the other women drifted away.

Bettany was curious. "There must be other things you want besides a spoon and a red ribbon, and the other women wish to hear their futures, too."

The squaw's eyes were hooded. "They have no futures," she said softly. "They are only shadows dancing in the flame."

Five

"INDIANS!" NILS SHOUTED, RACING ALONG BESIDE Bettany. "Over there! Three of them!"

Every head on the wagon train turned, but there was nothing but the bunched grasses swaying in the wind and the sharp-edged knolls that were half scrub and half stone. Soon they would be able to feast their eyes on the green slopes of the Laramie Mountains, which were so dark with juniper, cedar, and other vegetation that they were known and marked on maps as the Cheyenne Black Hills. But as for Indians, the traveling party had seen only those at the fort and, when they'd first set out, a few Pawnee who had wanted to trade fresh game for trinkets and calico shirts. But here in Cheyenne country there were—as far as Bettany and the others could see—no Indians.

Axel strained his eyes. "Where, son?"

Nils pointed toward a ridge of high ground, but Bettany spied only a tuft of wild grass and some low-growing sage. Indians wanting to trade made themselves known: only hostiles would lurk in hidden places. The wagons had been moving four abreast, but at McGrew's shouted order the lead wagons began to pull into a tight defensive circle. Bettany helped Nils into the wagon, made sure Hannah was safe, and reached for the Kentucky rifle that she'd learned to load and shoot.

After a very tense hour with no disturbances, a scouting party was sent out. They returned hot and dusty and very annoyed. McGrew rode over to Axel and Bettany. "If that was my boy, I'd give him a hiding that'd peel the bark off a hickory tree."

"I did see Indians! I did!" Bettany put an arm around Nils. His shoulders were shaking with indignation. "I wouldn't make up something like that."

McGrew didn't answer him directly. He looked Axel up and down. "The apple never falls far from the tree. The boy's a born troublemaker. If it wasn't for your wife and all the help she's been to us, I'd cut you loose of this party right now."

He whirled his horse about and gave the orders to make noonday camp. Although the nights were cool the days were uncomfortably hot, and the wagon party prudently rested during the worst of it.

Axel disagreed with the captain. "If there are Indians about, we are foolish to settle down here like ducks on a pond."

"Let me remind you, Vandergroot, that I'm the captain of this party, not yourself."

He trotted off, and while Axel fumed, Bettany tried to comfort Nils. "You don't believe me, either," he said accusingly. "I thought that *you'd* believe me!"

"I do."

Josie Carter came up beside them. "Nils is right. I saw something, too. It looked like several men up along the rocks. I reported it to Captain McGrew, but he said it was only an antelope. I suppose he thinks I was being fanciful."

Bettany tried to reassure her. "If it was Indians, perhaps they were just watching the wagons. I've heard they are quite curious about us—more so, I'm sure, than we are about them. Nils, fetch the kettle, if you please, and fill it halfway with water from the barrel for me."

Nils dropped the sharp stick he'd been poking into an anthill. He was fascinated by Bettany's wealth of myths and fables gleaned from Miss Olmstead's small personal library. "When it's on to boil will you tell us another story?" he asked.

"Of course."

Throwing away the stick, he hurried to the wagon.

"You're winning him over," Josie said.

"It's difficult for him to see me in his mother's place. Where Hannah clings to me for comfort, Nils turns to me only for necessities." Bettany sighed. "I can understand that. It all happened too soon. They lost their mother in the morning and had me thrust into her role by nightfall."

"Where is Hannah?" Josie had taken a shine to the quiet little girl. "Sleeping again?"

"Curled up on a pile of quilts as if it were a featherbed." Unlike Nils, Hannah never got travel sickness inside the swaying vehicle. She much preferred riding under the curve of canvas, secure in her own private world, rocked in the wagon's womb.

Nils came galloping back with the kettle, water sloshing with his haste. Bettany thanked him, and he scuffed the ground, embarrassed. "It's not a proper boy's chore," he said. "But rabbit stew is my favorite."

He doubled his small fists at his sides and scowled fiercely. "But if that Sean O'Connell teases me again about doing girl's work, I'm going to punch him right in the snout."

Sean swaggered over, laughing. "Is that the way of it? I'd think before trying it, me boyo. I'd hang you upside down from a cottonwood and let the buffalo nibble on your ribs, I would."

With a grin and wave he passed the women by, his gaze lingering longer on Bettany. She headed off Nils's frustration. "Well, now. What story shall it be today?" She gave him a quick sidelong glance. " 'Sleeping Beauty'? 'Cinderella'?"

He leaped to the bait with a young boy's disdain. "Hah! Those are *girl* stories. I want to hear about Alexander the Great or Jason and the Argonauts or Ulysses and the Cyclops, not baby stories like you told me back in Pennsylvania."

"Back in Pennsylvania"—a few short weeks ago. Bettany smothered a smile, and Josie ruffled the boy's hair. "My, you are an adventurous young man, aren't you? I'll leave you to your bloodthirsty tales and see to my own dinner."

Bettany pondered a moment as she jointed the rabbit carcass. Nils was much older than his six—almost seven—years: an intelligent child who enjoyed boyish games yet was more comfortable in older company than with his peers. She'd soon realized that he wasn't much for tales of magic wands or good fairies who rescued foolish mortals from their problems. Her stepson had inherited some of Axel's more practical nature and liked tales of adventure and daring where the hero's own strength or cleverness helped him outwit his adversaries.

"I have it, now," she said. "I will tell you all about Cuchullin, the Great Hound of Ireland."

Nils frowned. "A dog story?"

"No. The Hound of Ireland was a very brave boy who was given the name of Cuchullin by the High King of Ulster, and later became his country's greatest hero." She saw that she'd caught him now. "You see, his real name was Setanta, and he lived long, long ago, far across the sea . . ."

Nils sat wide-eyed and silent as she related tales of Setanta's early days and how he came to the court of Connor MacNessa, the High King of Ireland, and earned the name of Cuchullin. She had the natural storyteller's gift, shading her voice dramatically and making the ancient heroes live again through her. When she finished the stew was beginning to bubble.

She adjusted the fire while Nils frowned thoughtfully. "What happened to Cuchullin? Later, I mean, when he was all grown."

He added a few more sticks on the fire. "Was it like the fairy tales? Did he find a beautiful princess and live happily ever after?"

"No, I'm afraid not." Bettany couldn't very well tell him that Cuchullin had gone on to slay his best friend, Ferdia, in battle and had died later from an enchanted spear, still mourning him. She chose her words carefully.

"Living happily ever after didn't matter much to the old

heroes," she said slowly. "To people of Cuchullin's time and place, it didn't matter much how it all ended, as long as a man lived and died bravely. What the people then admired most were courage and cleverness and the gifts of music and poetry."

"Poetry! Huh!" Nils stuffed his hands in his pockets. "Poetry's for girls, and music's for sissies. I'm gonna go see if Mrs. Svenson will let Jan get out the checkers set."

Half-amused and half-exasperated, Bettany watched him head toward the Svensons' wagon, kicking stones as he went. She didn't know that in his mind Nils was Setanta, the great Gaelic hero, scattering imaginary enemies with every outward lash of his steel-toed boot.

Logan didn't like the looks of the sky. They were heading across the plateau, their destination the river plain far below and then the Cheyenne encampment another day's ride south. To the northwest massing clouds spread out in a thick dark line, and the air held the peculiar sense of gathering tension that preceded a major storm.

"If we take the cliff path instead of the roundabout route, we might reach camp before it hits."

Small Eagle frowned. He had dreamed more than once that he would die in a volley of thunder. Although he had shared nearly every aspect of his life with Wolf Star, this was one of the rare things he had never told him. "That way is more treacherous, Wolf Star. We might be caught along the cliff face."

"We can shelter behind Old-Man-Pointing-Rock and exchange stories. We have a lot of catching up to do."

With one wary glance at the approaching storm clouds, Small Eagle fell in behind his foster brother. The cliff path rose steeply upward along a rise for several hundred feet, then passed back down through gentler country to the stretch of meadowland below. Halfway up the track provided a clear view of it, and the strange cast of light and clear air magnified every detail. On the horizon Logan spotted fifteen tiny wagons inching their way across, tiny stick figures walking along beside them.

He reined in sharply. What in the hell were they doing so far off the trail? Hadn't they realized that they'd wandered from it, and were following instead a track laid down by some recent buffalo run? Frowning beside him, Small Eagle made a sign to ward off evil. His people, the Tsistsistas, had been warned of the coming of the white men and the evil they would bring.

Sweet Medicine, hero of the Long Ago Time, had fore-told the arrival of a new people, who would bring new animals that the Tsistsistas would ride, and in time the white men had brought the horse to the buffalo plains. Next Sweet Medicine had prophesied that the newcomers would cause the buffalo to go away. After that, the new-comers would also cause the Tsistsistas to vanish from the face of the earth. Although the buffalo were still as nu-merous as the stars in the night sky, the ever-growing pres-ence of these *ve-ho-e* made Small Eagle uneasy.

Logan was thinking along different lines. As he watched the wagons fall in and form a long line for the canyon approach, he felt something twist in his chest. Cassie had come this way across the plains, hoping to leave her past behind and find a new life. Instead she had found a lonely and terrifying death. "The white women should stay back east," he said aloud, "safe in their snug parlors. They are not of this land, and it will kill them."

Small Eagle made a low rumbling sound in his throat. He had seen white women at the fort and trading post and been curious about them, until he'd seen a trader's wife up close. She'd been sitting outside the post on a wooden crate, fanning her shiny pink face with a bit of stiff paper. She'd looked, he thought, like a slug without its shell, naked and exposed.

"How pale and ugly their women are," he chuckled, "their hair and eyes so faded. It is a wonder that their men can even mate with them."

For a moment Logan looked out from Wolf Star's eyes.

"When you know them," he said abruptly, "they can be very beautiful."

Small Eagle was not a man to search for hidden meanings in another's words, but something alerted him to the underlying tension in Wolf Star's tone. Whatever adventures his foster brother had experienced, they had not all ended happily. "Come, Wolf Star. Let us go around to the Red Fox trail and avoid them."

His companion hesitated. The part of him that was still Logan couldn't turn away from a last look at the people among whom he had lived for the last few years. Before settling permanently into his Cheyenne skin, before forgetting forever that his blood was wholly white, he wanted one last chance to turn his back upon what might have been. He squinted into the sunlight.

Already the tall rocks grew long shadows. The narrow wedge of meadow below was not a good place. He could tell by the tingle at the base of his neck and the prickling up and down his arms. The wagonmaster had made a very bad choice of route. The overlanders would not be safe until they came out of the narrow gorge and into the open plains beyond. The storm was gaining on them all now, darkening the sky to a dull, dirty green. Even so Logan rejected the roundabout trail, nudging his mount due south. "Let us take the cliff path. It is quicker, and I am eager to be among our people once more."

Small Eagle nodded, following the path Wolf Star had chosen—the path that would change their lives forever.

Bettany watched the sky anxiously. By midmorning the wind had picked up and the sunlight soon altered. The rich gold became wan and tinged with green. The farther west they went, the more ominous she found the terrain. By noon the moss-colored clouds were rapidly filling the sky, blotting out the misty shapes of the far mountains.

The lead wagon slowed down, and McGrew came riding back toward them, his bullwhip wound round his saddle-horn. "We're pulling up. Camp in that wing of land ahead. Storm's coming in fast."

Axel started to argue. "Let us forge ahead until we reach the gap between the outcrops."

"I'm wagonmaster here. We're pulling up."

"That makes no sense," Axel started again. "There'll be better shelter from the storm between—"

McGrew threw him a disgusted look. If not for Vandergroot's wife and kids, he'd have cut him from the wagon train by the third day. "Likely to be rock slides," he muttered, more to shut Axel up than to explain his decision.

Bettany flushed. Axel's constant head butting with McGrew—and with several of the others—put a constant strain upon her. McGrew's patience was wearing dangerously thin; one infraction of rules or breach of discipline on Axel's part, and he might throw them out of the wagon party. How they would ever manage to get across the continent alone was something she feared to contemplate.

They pulled into the angle of land, and while Axel unhitched the team she got the children settled and made sure the canvas was drawn tight. She took a bar of wax and began to run it over the inside of the seams to ensure that they stayed as water-resistant as possible. The day had been unusually warm, and she'd plaited her heavy silver hair in a loose braid which hung down her back. When she went outside again, the stiff breeze pulled the ribbon free and whipped her long hair loose about her shoulders. The smell of rain was strong in the air.

Axel returned, his face red and set in a mulish expression, and her stomach plummeted. Had he gotten into another altercation with McGrew? Thunder rumbled, and a bright flash ripped across the darkening clouds. "What is it, Axel?"

"That damned fool McGrew and his shortcuts. For once he admits he made a mistake, for all the good that will do us. He said the south cutoff would save us some hard miles. Instead we've gone on a wild goose chase down into Cheyenne territory. It will take us at least three days to get back on the trail."

Axel blotted his brow with his wadded kerchief. His homespun shirt was patched with perspiration, his forehead glistening. For the first time he looked at her. "Bind up your hair," he said angrily. "You look like a harlot with it streaming down your back."

She flinched and reached back to catch at the long, loose strands. He didn't like her hair, the one thing about her that she felt wasn't plain and ordinary. It was ironic that the one feature she valued was the one that Axel least appreciated. But then, he hadn't married her for her looks. Axel had married her for her strong limbs and sound health and, mostly, for the convenience.

To him a wife was a necessity, like a rifle or horse or cow: something meant to be useful rather than decorative. Someone to use, not someone to love. How fortunate her own parents had been, at least in the early days. Even now, after so many years, Bettany could still hear the laughter in her mother's voice, see the glow in her father's eyes, as the three of them walked together hand in hand through the meadows. Odd, but she didn't even know where those meadows had been, although every hill and tree and bend of the meandering stream were etched forever in her mind.

The sky opened and the storm that swept over them all at once was like nothing Bettany had ever seen before. Everyone dashed for cover. Rain fell in blinding sheets, accompanied by hail the size of oranges. The ice balls pelted the wagons, ripping canvas covers, shattering wheel spokes, and spooking the cattle. If not hemmed in between the wagons and the rocks, they would have stampeded, stranding the overland party.

Bettany and the children huddled beneath several quilts for protection in case their canvas was breached. Nils was stoic, but his lower lip quivered in the half-light. Axel sat apart with a harness that needed mending in his hands. "I'll not cower like a woman," he'd muttered to her; but when the storm passed over them, howling like a cloud of banshees, she found him leaning against a chest for support, the harness grasped tightly between his two hands. His face was streaked with sweat, and his eyes were glassy and unfocused.

"You are ill," she said, hurrying to his side.

He waved her weakly away. "It is nothing, wife. Leave me."

She heard emotion in his voice for the first time since she'd known him. It took her a moment to recognize it as fear. Fear was not something she expected to find in a man as stolid as her husband. Her blood turned to ice. Axel was desperately ill and trying to cover it up.

He saw his own fear reflected in her eyes. "It's not the cholera or typhus. I've had pain in my stomach these past three days." His breathing was shallow, his voice hoarse. "It grew worse this afternoon."

"Oh, Axel I'll get Mr. McGrew at once, and—"

Axel grasped her arm with clammy fingers. *"Say nothing,"* he hissed between clenched teeth. "The others must not know. If they do, they will turn against us for fear of contagion. And McGrew will leap at any chance to abandon us."

Bettany knew he was right. Even the shadow of suspected illness would be enough to send the rest into a frenzied panic. They'd all heard of entire settlements wiped out by disease in a matter of hours. The rules were clear and strictly enforced: The good of the entire party took precedence over the needs of any single wagon. If Axel was truly ill— if his indisposition became evident to the others—they would be left behind or condemned to follow at a great distance, alone.

Alone, in the country of savages so vicious they scalped and skinned families. Bettany shivered.

"What shall we do?"

"Nothing. Act as if all is well. We'll have to stay here until morning. By then it might have passed."

She helped him stretch out on the quilts. Hannah reached out to one of his shiny buttons. Axel's face twisted in pain. "You must take them both outside. Keep them there."

Pretending nothing was amiss, Bettany shooed the children out of the wagon. As she helped them down she caught a strange expression on Axel's face as his gaze rested upon Nils and Hannah, and it frightened her terribly. It was as if he were taking one last, long look at his children.

The ground was muddy, and she spread an oilcloth for Hannah beneath the wagon and gave her a cloth doll to play with. Nils ran off almost immediately, squelching his boots through the mud with great glee. For once Bettany didn't try to stop him; he might notice too much.

The rest of the camp had come through with only a few injuries. Sean O'Connell had been knocked out by the hail, but except for a sore head had recovered his Irish spirits rapidly. Josie Carter had sustained a severe bruise to her arm, Curtis Ebbersoll's horse had broken its leg and was subsequently shot, and Letitia Renfrew was suffering one of her frequent nervous attacks. Everyone seemed to feel they had all escaped disaster by the skin of their teeth. The wheels would be repaired by morning, the canvas patched where possible, and the wagon party off at first light.

Bettany slipped back to dose Axel with willow bark tea, but there was no improvement. He had neither vomiting nor dysentery, so she was sure it was neither cholera nor typhus. Bettany tried not to think of other dire conditions, like the fatal colic that had carried off Jenny Morehouse at the Susquehanna orphanage. Axel lay curled up on his side, grunting with pain and barely able to respond, but he rallied enough to order her away from him.

The others imagined Axel was sulking because McGrew had humiliated him publicly, and Bettany kept the children outside and occupied while she prepared their meal. Each time she checked on him, she found his condition had worsened. Axel's face was pasty gray, his breathing labored. The only respite he got was by curling up on his side with his knees drawn up to his chest. She did what little she could to make him comfortable and gave him some laudanum, hoping against hope that it would help. Remem-

bering that this was how Jenny had been in the hours before
she died.

Through the opening Bettany saw Letitia Renfrew drifting wraithlike toward the wagon, apparently recovered from
her hysterics. She knew she had to keep Letty away before
she heard Axel's moans. Since leaving Westport Landing,
Mrs. Renfrew had fastened on Bettany in the way the weak
often did to the strong, inundating her new friend with an
unending deluge of complaints, worries, and minor catas-
trophes. Although Bettany felt sympathy for the troubled
woman, she had begun to dread the daily sessions: as Sean
O'Connell had told her more than once, it was a long way
to California.

On this occasion, however, Mrs. Renfrew had come not
to seek advice, but to offer it.

"I hope you won't take this amiss, Mrs. Vandergroot, but
. . . there are ways to make it easier. I don't mean to be
indelicate, but . . . but we women must look out for one
another. Think of curtains. That's what I do."

"I beg your pardon?" Bettany turned startled eyes toward
the woman. "Curtains?"

"Oh, dear. This is so awkward, but I feel it must be said.
I was speaking of when . . . when you're with your man."

Letitia leaned down, her thin fingers writhing and twisting together like snakes. There was a strong odor of something that might be cough elixir on her breath, but Bettany
suspected she'd been at her husband's gin supply. There'd
been whispering to that effect, coupled with others about
Porter Renfrew and his pretty young sister-in-law. Bettany
had dismissed the second as pure malice, but the other
seemed sadly true.

Those writhing fingers reached out and caught her sleeve.
"Even the best of men become . . . ornery, if their needs
are not met, so you might as well give over and make up
to him before you're pushed aside. Put it all . . . all out of
your head and think of something nice that makes you
happy. That's what I do. Think of curtains, I mean."

Bettany stared at her, bewildered. "Red velvet ones,"

Mrs. Renfrew continued. "With fancy gold ropes to loop them back, and French lace undercurtains. Just like the ones I had back home." She giggled, and Bettany detected a twinge of hysteria in the woman's voice. "Look at me now at my age, setting out for California with not a piece of velvet nor a single stick of furniture to call my own."

A bubble of mad laughter followed, and Letitia's hot breath fanned Bettany's face. "So you see, nothing matters. Make your peace with your man and get through this hellish journey as best you can."

"I'm afraid you're under a misapprehension," Bettany said when she had mastered herself. "I haven't quarreled with my husband. He's sleeping inside the wagon tonight."

"Oh, you're brave. Far braver than I. But you don't have to pretend with me. Take my advice, or you'll find yourself alone and unwanted, your place at your husband's side usurped." Her voice broke in a ragged wail. "I know. Dear God, I know."

Pity filled Bettany. "Come, I'll take you back to your wagon."

"No!" The woman whirled around and stumbled over the sandy soil into the darkness. Bettany would have gone after her, but Porter Renfrew caught his wife. "Here, here, Letty. No need for that."

Bettany saw the way the woman recoiled from her husband. Poor, poor Letty Renfrew, ripped away from all she held dear and forced by the vows of marriage to emigrate to a foreign territory. Perhaps forced by fear and loneliness over the line of sanity into madness.

Nils came running toward her suddenly, shouting and waving his arms. "Come quick," he hollered in a voice that carried disastrously on the brisk breeze. "Pa's moaning and talking out of his head. He's been taken mortal bad!"

McGrew looked grave. "I'm sorry, Mrs. Vandergroot, but rules are rules. I can't risk the entire party when I don't know what's ailing your man."

"But you can't abandon us," Bettany protested, remembering the horrid stories she'd heard back in Westport. "This is Cheyenne territory. And it's your fault we're here in the first place."

McGrew colored. "The Cheyenne haven't bothered anyone in these parts in years. You can follow the train if you keep back a goodly distance. If your man recovers and no one else in the family falls sick, you can rejoin us in a few days."

Despite her attempts to sway him, the captain reyoked the oxen himself and led the Vandergroot wagon away from the others. Panicked and angry, Bettany had no choice but to follow with the children. Mamie Ebbersoll's eyes filled with tears, but she was afraid for her family. Only Josie Carter came running after them.

McGrew waved her back. "If you come too close, Mrs. Carter, I'll have to leave you and your husband behind, too. We can't take a chance."

Bettany sent Josie a grateful look. "It's all right. Please do as he says. I'll manage."

Grim-faced, holding Hannah in one arm and taking Nils by the hand with the other, she marched after the wagon. The others watched them leave. "I'm tired," Nils complained. "I don't want to walk any more today. I want to ride in the wagon."

"This is what your father wants."

McGrew selected a site protected to the north by a V of enormous boulders. "To keep the wind off you if the storms come on," he explained, but Bettany knew the real reason: to keep them out of the direct line of sight of the wagon train and ease his own guilty feelings.

McGrew mounted his horse and started back toward the others. "If you need fresh game, tie a piece of cloth to something. We'll leave some along the way for you."

Bettany didn't bother to answer. She knew how to use their Kentucky rifle. If they needed game, she'd get it herself.

After sundown Axel's condition worsened. She hurried through her usual evening routine, checked the cattle, and arranged the children's bedding beneath the wagon. "You may have your wish tonight, Nils." She patted the soft quilts invitingly. "Your father will sleep better alone in the wagon."

Nils was thrilled. "You mean we can sleep here tonight? Hannah, do you hear that? We can pretend we're Indians, sleeping in our tipis." He wanted to stay awake and savor the experience, but fell all too quickly into the deep sleep of childhood.

Only Bettany lay awake through the hours after midnight with the Kentucky rifle loaded beside her, hearing every sound and imagining an array of dangers to account for each of them. Suddenly she was startled by a faint, hoarse cry that made the hairs rise on the nape of her neck. Her fingers curled around the rifle barrel. Then the eerie sound repeated, and she realized a trick of the wind had made it seem to come from far away. Axel was calling her name.

She climbed inside the wagon in the bright moonlight. Axel lay back against the pillows, his arms flung up as if to protect his face. He stared at her as if she were a stranger, and then his eyes cleared. "Bettany . . ."

"Yes. I'm here." It was the first time he'd ever called her by her name. She sponged off his face and gave him sips of water. His lips were puffy and cracked, and he had great difficulty getting any down. Bettany got a spoon and fed it to him, drop by drop.

"You've . . . been . . . a good wife," he said.

His words and they way he said them frightened her. "You're going to be all right, Axel. You're getting better."

"No . . . ," His fingers closed around her wrist. "I'm dying . . . I want to tell you . . . everything."

His eyes closed and she thought he'd fallen asleep, but his hand still held her captive. He began to talk, without opening his eyes, and she knew that he was reliving the events as he described them. There was a tavern outside Clarksville that he'd always avoided until he heard about the monthly wrestling matches and the prize money for the winners.

Axel struggled against the pain. "I was . . . always a strong man. I entered in hopes of winning a stake . . . so Elsa and I could emigrate to California. . . ." His hand clutched hers, hot and papery, like onionskins. "I did it for Elsa, for the family. . . ."

Bettany listened, filling in the blank spaces. Axel had won the big purse, and the men who'd won wagering upon him had insisted that he join them for a victory drink. Flushed with success, he had succumbed to the temptation. Bettany could readily imagine how the strong drink had gone to the head of a man unaccustomed to it.

"There . . . there was a girl. A tavern wench . . . pretty . . . with long shining hair. No pretty woman . . . had ever noticed me before." He closed his eyes tightly. "She teased me and made me laugh. Made me feel proud of myself. . . ."

The whole story came out in agonized bits and pieces. Axel, with a wife at home in her eighth month of pregnancy, had been intoxicated by his triumph as much as the liquor and flattered by the attentions of a flirtatious tavern girl. Bettany covered his hand with hers. "It's all right. You don't have to tell me."

His eyes opened, and his voice grew stronger. "I must. I must! They told me to meet a man named Barnaby behind the stables. I went out. There was no man there, only the girl." He paused again to catch his breath. The pain was relentless, but so was his need for confession. "Her hair . . . it was loose and hanging down her back . . . and her bodice was open. I could see the fullness of her breasts, and lust filled me. I . . . I fought it. I wanted to run away from the temptation. . . . I wanted to, but I didn't. I was too weak and sinful."

The admission was obviously painful, yet there was something in his voice as he relived the events that told Bettany things about her husband she had never guessed; the animal hunger and feverish urgency came out with every word.

"She was so beautiful. Her waist . . . so small. Her hips swayed when she walked. We went to the grove of trees beyond the tavern. I touched her hair. It was like silk . . .

like your hair. It maddened me. I tore her bodice away and
. . . filled my hands with her breasts. I pulled her to the
ground and took her there. Later we went up to her room
over the stables. . . . We spent the night in sin."

Sweat beaded his upper lip. Bettany sponged his face
again. Confession might be good for the soul, but it was
having a devastating effect on her husband's body. "It's
over and done with, Axel."

He grew agitated. "No . . . I have to make you understand. . . ." He squeezed her wrist so hard that Bettany's
hand went numb. She couldn't believe there was still such
strength in his fever-racked body. Taking a deep gulp of
air, he continued. "I drank too much and was sorry for
what she'd made me do. I beat her for leading me into
adultery. When I woke up the sun was high. The girl was
gone . . . and so was all my money. What I'd won and what
I'd had from before.

"I went home . . . Oh, God! Blood everywhere. Elsa was
dead, and the baby with her. She'd delivered the child and
hemorrhaged to death . . . alone, while I was with that
wicked, wicked girl. That girl with the long, shining hair.
. . . And despite my shame I still think of her. I remember
how it was to lie with her, and my loins ache for a woman's
body beneath mine.

"I wanted you, wife. . . . Night after night I ached to take
you, and when we were alone in the boardinghouse I almost
did . . . but I can no longer act the part of a man with a
woman. . . . Remorse comes and kills desire. . . . I am no
longer a man . . . it is my punishment from God."

He burst into low, agonized weeping, and his grip slackened. Bettany rubbed the circulation back into her wrist,
understanding so much more now of the complicated man
she'd wed.

After unburdening himself, Axel's restlessness eased, and
in a few minutes he fell into a deep, profound slumber.
Near dawn Bettany went outside to check on the children.
They were stretched out on the quilts side by side, and the
temptation to join them for a few minutes was too much

to resist. She lay down on the quilt, vowing to close her
eyes only for a moment, and awoke with the sun just above
the horizon.

It was the lowing of oxen and the sharp, high whinny
of a horse that had roused her. Bettany sat up hurriedly,
rubbing her eyes, and was suddenly aware of other sounds:
the clink and soft jangle of harness, the creak and rumble
of many wagon wheels in motion. The wagon train was
already on the move. The failure to notify her was deliberate. Fear of contagion had sent them fleeing west, abandoning Bettany, Axel, and the children along with all
human principles of charity and compassion. She threw
back the corner of her blanket and rolled out from beneath
the wagon.

To her dismay, what had awakened her was not the start-
up of the wagon train, but the echo from the walls of the
canyon it had entered. The lead wagons had already been
swallowed up between the sheer rock faces.

"Cowards!" she cried after them, caught between hot
fury and cold awareness of their predicament. "Cowards
and fools!"

She ran for her own team's harnesses. "Nils! Wake up!
We must hitch up the oxen before they leave us behind."

If they lost sight of the wagon party in the labyrinthine
countryside ahead, it would be a death sentence. She ran
for the lead pair and hadn't gone more than five or six steps
when she heard sounds that stopped the breath in her throat
and set her heart hammering wildly: the echo of rifle fire
from the canyon, a tattoo of pounding hooves and whooping
war cries, approaching rapidly.

Indians were attacking the wagon party.

Six

SOMETHING WAS WRONG. LOGAN AWOKE WITH IT prickling between his shoulder blades. It was still dark in the shadow of the rocky outcrop where they'd made their night camp, and Small Eagle was still asleep, but the faint rosy light coloring the hills beyond told him the sun was just over the horizon. The horses were grazing peacefully, so the danger wasn't immediate. A few years earlier he'd done a stint on the Erie Canal and had experienced the same sense of presentiment one fine morning. On that occasion it had been a broken lock gate a few links ahead of them that had sent thousands of gallons of water rushing through the canal in a wild torrent, swamping barges and sweeping men to their deaths. This was the same kind of feeling. He climbed the rocks.

From a ledge twelve feet up he had a wide view of the plains below and the place where the wagon party had settled. The lone wagon remained isolated behind an angle of rock, but the main party was already under way between the high rock walls of two eroded plateaus. They'd been foolish enough to leave the main trail in the first place; the present route could prove disastrous for more reasons than one.

Something moved in the periphery of Logan's vision, and he saw the armed riders break from cover far below. Smoke and flame burst from their rifle barrels, visible long before he heard their thunder. Small Eagle jumped up and joined him. Both men came to the same conclusion: despite their

85

Cheyenne garb and war paint, the attackers were not of
the Tsistsistas.

"Renegades," Logan said angrily.

Small Eagle made a sound of disgust. "Our people will
suffer for this. We will be blamed."

Logan was already on his way back down. "Not if we get
there in time."

The chances were slim, but they had to try. A moment
later they were mounted and riding down the steep trail,
taking the perilous shortcut to the plain below.

Nils jerked awake and Hannah began to cry, aware with
an instinctive prescience that something was dreadfully
wrong. Bettany froze, the harness dropping heavily from
her shaking hands. The rear wagon had just entered the
wedge of meadow between the escarpments, and a band of
Indians—perhaps twenty-five or thirty—had closed off any
hope of retreat. Grabbing the rifle with one hand, the
children with another, she urged them into the wagon.

"Get inside and stay there until I tell you to come out.
Nils, see if your father is awake."

Bettany made sure her ammunition was in order and then
looked up. Gunfire echoed sporadically, then stopped.
Flames licked at several of the wagons. Five horsemen had
broken away from the others and were riding in her direction. She was sick with fear. *"Nils? Nils!"*

He poked his head out the back in panic. "Something's
wrong with Pa. He won't wake up. He's awful cold."

Dear God in heaven! There was no time to check for
herself, no time to mourn. "Get Hannah. Hurry!"

As Nils ran for his sister, Bettany saw that the Indians
were covering the ground rapidly. Their shrill war cries
carried over the screams and gunshots from the other wagons. It was difficult to keep from shooting as they closed
in, but they were too far out of range. Waiting, waiting,
her nerves screaming for the release of action, she forced
herself to lift the rifle and take aim.

She fired at the lead rider, and the recoil numbed her

shoulder. Her shot missed the man and hit his pony instead. The beast shrieked, stumbled and fell so quickly, its rider was unable to hurl himself clear. The others plunged on toward her as she reloaded and fired again.

Nils caught Hannah by the hand and ran to Bettany. "Run!" she ordered. "Hide in the rocks and don't come out for any reason. And keep quiet, for the love of God!"

Nils was angry and frightened. If only he were Cuchullin, he would stand and fight the Indians; but he was only a six-year-old boy. Picking Hannah up, he ran into the maze of tumbled rock, seeking a safe haven. When he grew up he would have his own rifle and no one would dare shoot at them.

The cries of the Indians drowned out Hannah's wail and sent a chill up the boy's spine. Pa was sound asleep, and his new ma was just a woman. It was a man's job to defend his family. Nils filled his pockets with smooth stones and got out his slingshot.

He found a hiding place and gave Hannah a stale bit of barley candy from his pocket. "Suck on this and don't make a sound. If you do, I'll smack you."

Nils had never hit her, but the look on his face was enough to silence Hannah. She watched, big-eyed and for once jolted out of her own private world. Nils crept around a boulder, slingshot in hand, like Setanta facing his enemies with only stones and a sling for weapons. He put a stone in his sling and whirled it over his head. He was no longer Nils, but the Great Hound of Ireland. He would save them all.

Bettany fired again and he saw one Indian fall backward from his mount, his shoulder dripping blood. Perching between two rocks, Nils took aim once more. The first stone went wide, but the second struck a spotted pony in the withers. The horse reared, almost throwing its startled rider. As Nils loosed another missile, the man brought the animal back into control and turned to face his unseen enemy.

"Ludo! Get a move on! Get that goddamned kid!"

Nils slipped another stone into place and shot it. This

one caught his adversary in the neck, just above the collarbone notch. He fell, clutching at his throat, and was trampled beneath his horse's hooves. A flush of victory raced through the boy. His next stone went wild, and as he groped for more ammunition, he spied a warrior close in behind him. The club came down glancingly on the back of his skull, and the world blinked out.

"I've got the boy," the renegade called out, slinging Nils's body under his arm. "C'mon, Ludo! Grab the other one. The Comanche pay good for young children."

On the far side of the wagon, Bettany was trying to hold off the attackers, unaware the children had been taken. Then she saw a brave riding away with the screaming girl in his arms. The shock was severe. For a moment she couldn't move, couldn't believe what her eyes were telling her. Then she mobilized her reserves.

"Hannah! Hannah!"

She stumbled after the horseman carrying the struggling child, unmindful of her own danger. He was getting out of range. She aimed and fired. Her hands shook so badly that the shot went a little wide, striking the pinto of the Indian beside him. The beast stumbled and crashed to the ground, pinning its rider beneath it. The other kicked his mount into a blistering gallop and thundered away. An arrow fired the canvas covering of the wagon, and acrid smoke filled the air.

Stunned by her failure, deafened by the beating of her own heart, Bettany didn't hear the third horseman riding up behind her, club raised to come smashing down upon her skull. His shadow fell across her and she dodged too late, taking a glancing blow across the right shoulder. The force of the impact slammed her into the wagon wheel. Blinded by pain, she crumpled beside it, her arm limp and temporarily useless. She tried to rise, but was filled with disabling nausea.

While she gasped and retched, her assailant turned his horse and came at her again. A pretty young woman was an unexpected bonus. Six feet away he jumped down, preparing to launch himself at her. His knife blade flashed in the light, and Bettany knew her last moments had come and that they would be shameful and agonizing.

Suddenly he grunted and spun awkwardly to the side, then dropped to the ground. His eyes opened wide, outraged and surprised. Bettany didn't realize what had happened until she saw the arrow protruding from his neck. The iridescent blue-and-black feathers, the symmetry of the shaft's striped banding, the scarlet bubbles that burst into runnels of blood, were all etched upon her brain like a copper engraving. Years later she could still see it clearly.

Bettany looked up to see her saviors—and saw two more Indians bearing down at her from the ledge. "Nils! *Nils?*" There was no answer. She prayed that he was hiding but feared that he was dead.

Then she saw him, thrown limply across the neck of another pony that was fast disappearing from sight. For a moment she was completely empty of emotion. Then grief and fury filled her, so hot and fierce that it overflowed. There was no way she could save the children now, and it didn't matter what happened to her. But, by God, she'd take a few more of them with her first.

As Logan raced to her rescue, he saw Bettany reload the rifle. Her actions were awkward as she fought off the effects of her injury, but her aim was true. There was no time to explain. Logan rode down upon her, snatching the rifle up and away as she pulled the trigger. The shot whizzed past his ear and cracked against the rocks in an explosion of sound and splintered stone.

Logan leaped from his mount and caught Bettany around the shoulders. "Easy," he said against her ear as she struggled. "We won't hurt you."

Half-mad with terror, Bettany was deaf to his words. He pinned her arms against her sides and glanced back over his shoulder. Small Eagle had pulled up by the wagon and was peering in. He shook his head.

"A man," he said. "No wounds, and not dead long." As he came up to them he made a hasty sign to ward off evil.

Logan and Small Eagle understood why the single wagon had been isolated from the others: fever. The one enemy that all men feared. The evil that could not be seen or defeated by strength and courage. The stealer-of-breath, who could slip into a camp by night and leave nothing but corpses behind. And the woman might be carrying the disease. Logic said to leave her here among the carnage. But Logan couldn't do it. Cassie had died alone, and Anna.

Bettany still struggled futilely, hysterically. She kicked out at Logan's shins with her steel-tipped boots and connected, hard. He gave her a shake that rattled her teeth like stones in a hollow pot. "Calm down. We're trying to help you."

She couldn't even hear his words over the roaring in her ears. All she knew was that the wagons had been attacked by murdering Indians who had stolen Nils and Hannah, and now one of them was trying to drag her away to his horse. Visions of rape and torture blotted out everything else. Logan had his hands full trying to soothe her hysteria and made a split-second decision: at this rate she'd get them all killed. He drew back his hand and administered a smart slap that brought her out of her panic and into a state of stunned immobility.

Small Eagle called out to him in a spate of rapid Cheyenne. "Leave her. She might be tainted with the fever."

"I can't abandon her to these renegades."

"What is she to us? We cannot travel with the woman, and we have much ground to cover today." The Cheyenne gave her a hard look. "She is too thin and ugly to be of much use. Leave her. Someone will find her, or she will die. It is not ours to decide."

"I would no more forsake her in such circumstances than I would forsake you," Logan snapped. He was about to add something when realization hit him like a kick from a mule. His eyes narrowed in disbelief. Silver hair. Silver eyes. Was this the woman he had dreamed of? If her face were serene rather than terrified and tear-streaked . . .

"Look at her. The Silver Woman."

His voice was harsh, and when Small Eagle frowned in surprise, Bettany thought they were arguing. She couldn't understand their rapid Cheyenne and drew her own conclusions. It seemed plain to her that the mounted Indian wanted his companion to let her go. Holding her breath, afraid to hope, she glanced away and again saw Nils being carried off by his abductor. The boy's cries carried faintly on the wind.

"Pa! Help me, Pa!"

Bettany tried to run after him but was stopped by Logan's unyielding arm. Horse and rider vanished behind the wall of rock, and Bettany turned blind eyes to her captor, choking on her fear. "Please. Let me go. They've taken the children. Oh, God! They've taken Nils . . . and Hannah!"

The grief in her voice broke open the bleeding wounds of Logan's own loss, and the name she whispered echoed another: *Hannah. Anna . . . Anna . . .*

Logan had to go after them. "Take the woman," he told Small Eagle. "I will go after the children."

The adventure appealed to Small Eagle, and his eyes lit. "I will go with you."

"No. Those renegade *ve-ho-e* will come back with reinforcements."

Logan looked up to the escarpment. The main body of the renegades had gone ahead through the meadow to the far side, but where the trail forked west and north, two smaller groups broke off.

"Damn it. They're splitting up."

Small Eagle grimaced. "Do not bother with the girl-child. Get the little warrior. He is more valuable."

Logan released Bettany. "I'll get them both. They're riding into a blind canyon. Take the woman back to Fort Laramie. I'll meet you there."

He swung up onto his mount, and the animal picked up his urgency. As Logan urged it forward the horse took off in a burst of power, scattering dust and clods of dirt.

Bettany drew back as Small Eagle alighted, but he made no threatening moves. Beyond him she saw the bodies of two of the men who'd assaulted the wagon train. An arrow protruded from the bare chest of one, and the other's eyes were open in death above painted streaks of black and crimson. Even in the midst of her turmoil, Bettany noticed the difference. The two newcomers were not painted for war and that they were dressed in buckskin shirts and breeches, frontier style. They were not hostiles, then, but riders from some neighboring tribe, sent by chance.

Small Eagle held out his hand, made a dismissive gesture toward the ruins of the wagons, and indicated that they should depart before the others returned to finish their evil work. She let him lead her past the wagon but stole a quick glance over her shoulder at all she was leaving behind: the bodies of her husband and friends, the flaming remnants of the wagon party, and the secret hopes and longing that had burned as brightly in her own breast. She spotted a bloody corpse sprawled beneath one of the wagons: Sean O'Connell. He'd been right. The road to California was long, and a lot of things could happen on the way.

The canvas of her own wagon was already blazing, and the wood of the wagon was beginning to smoulder. Axel would go up with the funeral pyre and not be left to the scavengers, like the others. There was nothing she could do for him now, except offer up a prayer and hope that his tortured soul had found peace.

The prayer was interrupted by Hannah's shrieks, carried by the fitful wind. Bettany screamed and began running desperately, futilely, in the direction the abductors had taken. It was hopeless. The men and horses were out of sight. "No! Oh, no!"

Weeping with fear and fury, she stumbled after them, but Small Eagle caught her and held her firmly. When she struggled to get free he gave her a shake that rattled every bone in her body and every tooth in her head. Then he pointed to the horsemen bearing Hannah and Nils away, to Logan racing after them, and finally to Bettany. Releasing her, he positioned his arms as if rocking an infant in them, then repeated the pointing.

She remembered his short, sharp exchange with Logan and viewed it through the distorted mirror of hindsight. She thought she understood. This Indian was telling her not to worry, that he'd sent the other man to rescue the children and bring them back. Bettany smiled.

Small Eagle was amazed at the change in her. He had thought her slight and pale and unattractive, like all women of the *ve-ho-e*; but as she turned to him now she seemed suffused with light. He could scarcely meet her eyes for the lightning that struck out, blinding him. The earth shook and rocked beneath his feet, but after a moment he realized it was not ground that had moved, but his own perceptions.

He remembered Wolf Star's words: *When you know them, they can be very beautiful.*

It was true. He stared at Bettany: that moonlight hair, that luminous skin, and her eyes . . . *her eyes!* They could steal a man's soul from within him. The thunderstruck sensation eased when he finally tore his gaze from Bettany. Once again he was in command of himself, but something had changed inside, and he would never be quite the same as he had been before.

The Cheyenne struggled with himself and lost. She was the Silver Woman of his brother's dreams. Wolf Star had told him to take her back to her own people at Fort Laramie; instead Small Eagle headed west with Bettany, toward the crumpled folds of the foothills and the distant Cheyenne camp.

Seven

LOGAN RACED AFTER THE RENEGADES. THE BOY was struggling wildly, kicking and flailing so violently that his rider was controlling his mount with difficulty. A brave boy, but likely to be knocked senseless or thrown into a broken heap from the back of the galloping gray pony. He couldn't see the girl, who was shielded by her captor's back, until they angled to the east. She was strangely passive. Frightened to death, Logan thought, and the thought was like a spike through the heart. Had Anna looked like that? Had she been frozen with fear, or had she cried and tried to run away?

The horse caught his rider's sense of frantic urgency and fairly flew over the rough ground. As the boy struggled, Logan saw the rider raise his arm to deliver a blow. The glare from the river and rock was blinding. For a few precious seconds Logan could scarcely see. Cursing and squinting into the sunlight, he saw the boy was slung crosswise over the neck of his captor's horse, obviously unconscious. There was nothing Logan could do to stop or slow them, but when he reached the turn and the sun was no longer in his eyes, he could do something about the other three fleeing across the open ground to the east.

Logan raised his rifle and took aim. The rifle butt recoiled against his shoulder, the acrid smoke blew past his face, and a figure toppled from the back of a paint pony. The renegade's rifle went off as he fell, catching the pony behind the eye. The beast didn't even have time to scream. When

94

Logan went past, both lay still in a spreading scarlet pool.

Although his mind, like his body, was fixed on rescuing the children, a disconnected part of it registered certain facts about the fallen man: skin much darker on face and throat and hands than chest and arms, and wide hazel eyes fixed in a death stare. A white man beneath the war paint and the feathered band. This was no time to question why. He tucked it away for future examination.

Hope and hatred spurred him on. Logan laughed when they veered between two buttresses of rock, thinking to escape him. His eyes came alive with that gold flash that Small Eagle—or the late and unlamented Halsey—would have recognized. The renegades didn't know the country-side as well as he did. There were dozens of ridges and wrinkles leading up to the plateau above, and they looked very much alike. Only someone who grew up exploring them would know that this one was a blind canyon, walled by treacherous talus slopes and blocked after the second turn by a great wing of stone.

A child's frenzied cry echoed from the rocky maze. A cry so desolate and hopeless that it tore Logan's heart out. He flew after them like a man possessed, and there it was, a thin shoulder blade of the plateau, glistening white and smooth as a buzzard-picked bone.

The renegades discovered the dead-end too late. One rider gestured to the other. He wheeled his horse about and rode at the steep slope at an oblique angle. His mount's hooves skittered into the unstable ground, shaking loose shards of weathered sandstone. Puffs of dust blossomed with every step. The second rider followed suit and was less successful. His pony laid its ears back, nervous and much less sure of its footing. A trickle of dirt and stones gathered speed and collapsed upon itself as horse and rider scrambled upward. If they reached the ledge above, they might still escape him.

Suddenly the mass trembled and shifted, throwing the lead horse off stride. The pony's right near leg sank deep in the perilous scree, and it tossed its head in panic. As the rider struggled for control, his little captive wriggled free of his grasp. Hannah fell and rolled downslope with a shriek of pure animal terror. It was a miracle that the slashing hooves missed her.

Logan dashed toward her, leaning down from the side of his horse to swoop her up. He never got the chance. Everything happened at once. Loose stones rained down in a dusty hail, and the ground trembled. A sound seemed to start in his bones, changing from an dry, whispery murmur to a deep-pitched, threatening growl. The growl grew to a bellow that overpowered the child's frightened screams and reverberated from the canyon walls. Logan's ears itched and rang with it, became so full they felt as if they were bursting. As the pressure grew against his eardrums, he was gripped by a nauseating dizziness.

The earth slide peeled tons of rocky debris away from the stone. It might have been the thrashing horse and rider above him who'd started it—or it might have been the shot he'd fired himself—but Logan had no time to think about the cause. In a split second the towering talus slope above him shivered and writhed like a living thing. It curled outward in a tidal wave of stone and sand and hung, impossibly suspended, before collapsing inward upon itself.

And upon him.

Choking on dust and dirt, pelted by stinging stones, Logan tried to outrace it. Only three feet separated him from the sobbing Hannah. He leaned down from the saddle, prepared to snatch her up. Just as his fingertips touched her fragile wrist, the incline lost its solidity. They were torn from each other, swept downslope in the shifting brown cloud that billowed around them. The horse lost its footing, and Logan, sacrificing his own slim chance of safety, hurled himself free of his mount, reaching out with searching, desperate hands. Blinded, suffocating, his fingers brushed over a small warm limb and grasped it. He dragged himself closer, shielding Hannah with his body. Then the landslide crashed down upon them in a dark, smothering wave.

•   •   •

Small Eagle reined in on a ridge overlooking a wide and fertile plain. Bettany was too numb to appreciate the view below. The sun cast long shadows, but beyond the line of trees that bordered the copper-colored river, the Cheyenne tipis spread out in double line. This was Place of Plenty, a site favored by Small Eagle's particular band for its bountiful wood and water and abundant game.

The Cheyenne raised his arm and indicated the camp to the silent woman at his side. Behold my people, his proud gesture said. Behold their greatness and their strength.

Bettany, reeling with worry and fatigue, straightened and squinted her eyes against the dying sun. At first she saw nothing but sky and trees and endless rolling plains. Gradually, as her eyes adjusted to the immense scale of the view, the outlines of the Cheyenne camp became visible in the far distance. Her heart sank. There were at least sixty or seventy tipis there and only God knew how many Indians.

She closed her eyes for a fraction of a second, willing herself away from these sandy hills and bone-colored rock and back among the verdant green ridges of Pennsylvania. It didn't work. When she opened them she was still atop a horse, accompanied by a ferocious-looking Indian, and weary and frightened to the core.

The ride had been an endless purgatory, torn in two as she was. Part of her—a mere physical shell—rode south with her Indian companion, but she'd left her soul left behind with the shattered remains of the wagon train and the children. Her children. Hers, not by blood, but by love. Her terror for them was so intense, she'd felt none for her own predicament. Until now.

The journey that had seemed too long had ended too suddenly, and for the first time since the attack had ended, she felt deep personal fear. Riding along with one Indian, who had thus done her no harm, was difficult enough; to be alone and defenseless and surrounded by hundreds of his people was unimaginable. The sunset blurred in the shimmer of tears on her lashes. Overcome by weariness and reaction, she swayed again. Small Eagle's hand reached out to steady her, lingering a moment as if for comfort.

Bettany tried not to flinch from his touch. The wagon-master had told her the Indians admired strength and despised weakness, therefore she must be strong. For Hannah, for Nils, and for her own sake. Lifting her chin defiantly, she shook his hand away.

Small Eagle smiled inwardly. A strong woman, and proud. A warrior's woman. He stole a glance at her. She was so pale, as if her skin had never known the sun, yet he found even that beautiful, like the piece of translucent white stone he kept in his medicine bag, or the pearly sheen of a shell held up to the light.

The others of her kind that he had seen didn't bring such pictures to his mind's eye. Their exposed skin reminded him of slimy things that hid from the sun's brightness. Things that skittered out from beneath overturned rocks and burrowed into the earth. Small Eagle's curiosity was piqued. Perhaps the white-eyes folk had come from the underground world in the beginning of time and never adapted to the world of light. He thought of the men in the valley of Rainbow River, their many guns and wagons and strange machines, and wished they would go back to their dark underworld and leave the valley in peace.

But this woman he did not want to go away. It was no wonder that his brother had dreamed of her, this shining Silver Woman who had drawn him also into her spell.

Bettany was aware of him staring at her. What was he waiting for? She gripped the reins of the horse that had once belonged to the wagonmaster and concentrated on showing no fear. When she turned to face him coolly, Small Eagle nodded in appreciation of her courage. He motioned for her to go forward and nudged his own pony along the ridge and down the trail that led toward the river.

The tipis were arranged in a double line on the far side of the water, their lodge poles just a few feet lower than the tops of the tall cottonwoods. As she drew nearer Bettany could make out various designs painted on their hide covering, horses and antlered creatures, rayed circles that must represent the sun, and dozens of other symbols that meant nothing to her at all. Only the yelps and squeals of playing children were familiar.

A group of them played a curious game along the riverbank. Some straddled sticks and rode them in the same manner that white children back in Pennsylvania rode their hobbyhorses, brandishing rods of sharpened wood as if they were swords or lances; but the way the others were acting was as alien to Bettany as their nakedness and bronzed skin. These Cheyenne children held out long sticks with thick green ovals attached to their pointed ends, and they thrust them at the "horse riders," who dodged and feinted in return. She realized the fleshy pads were prickly-pear plants stuck to the ends of the poles. It seemed a barbaric and potentially deadly game.

At her side Small Eagle was pleased that the woman would see how brave even the children of his camp were—all but the youngest learning to hunt by attacking mock buffalo and learning also to avoid the three-inch thorns that represented the buffalo's mighty horns. Surely the predictions of Sweet Medicine must have been misunderstood by his ancestors, for the bravery and strength of the Tsistsistas would never be overcome.

He glanced at the woman from the side of his eyes. Her face was still pale, but two spots of color bloomed like flowers in her cheeks. *He-ha*, but this silver-haired woman of Wolf Star's blood grew upon a man.

He wondered if Wolf Star found her desirable. Since childhood, suckled at the same breasts, he and his foster brother had run side by side in everything—and more often than not, in every kind of contest, Wolf Star had been the winner. Perhaps Wolf Star would want her for his woman. But Wolf Star was not here, and he was. The corners of Small Eagle's mouth tightened.

They had come to the water now, and both horses lowered their heads to drink. Small Eagle let them slake their thirst, but not too deeply, for there was still the river to ford, and the currents were swift. As the horses splashed

into the water, stirring up eddies of silt, a cry went up from
the opposite bank. Small Eagle was recognized, and curiosity brought many Cheyenne to the riverbank. Some
stared, others spoke and gesticulated, and several women
drew their youngest closer to their sides. Who was the
ve-ho-e woman riding beside him, and why had he brought
her to the camp?

Their ranks parted as the two riders brought their horses
through the shallows. Bettany kept her eyes straight ahead.
She was aware of the sudden silence, crystal drops of water
flying away in bright arcs from the horse's hooves, the cool
breeze blowing her damp hem about her ankles, the faces
turned to watch her progress.

Then they were across. Cheyenne crowded around her,
but Bettany didn't meet a single glance: to do so would
have unnerved her. As they rode into the camp hands
reached out to touch her calico skirt, but she kept her head
high. Small Eagle was gratified that she hid her fear. It
reflected well upon him.

A proud woman, this white-eyes creature. Fit to be any
man's wife and to warm herself at his fire. But she had come
into Wolf Star's dreams in company with the Spirit Wolf,
and her medicine was strong. She was for Wolf Star, not
for him. The sudden wave of jealousy hit him by surprise.
Small Eagle had been sure he'd put it behind him and was
ashamed. He raised his own head a fraction higher. He
must not let such unworthy emotions cloud his mind.

Originally Small Eagle had planned to take the reins from
Bettany and lead her as his captive; instead he let her ride
beside him as a mark of special favor. She was unaware of
his intentions and her apparent change in status, but the
Cheyenne were not. There were murmurings among them.

They rode past the lodges until they reached the one
that was his. Small Eagle dismounted, signaling for Bettany
to do the same. She wasn't used to so many hours in the
saddle and got down stiffly, to the amused contempt of
some of the onlookers. Young boys ran up to hold the
horses, and a woman came out of the tipi. Her body was

thin and frail, and her hands were knotted with rheumatism, but there was strength in the bones of her face and pride in her bearing.

"My son, what is this?" she exclaimed. "Why have you brought this white-eyes creature to our camp? Her people will follow and make trouble for us."

Small Eagle let one of the eager youths lead the horses away and greeted his mother respectfully. "Her people are dead. The woman will help you. She will take over your chores so that you may rest and ease the soreness in your bones."

Her son meant well, but Blue Morning Flower was ill pleased. She did not want a *ve-ho-e* woman sharing her lodge. Small Eagle didn't notice. Instead he turned away, satisfied, and left the women to their women's business.

Bettany didn't understand the language, but whatever fate awaited her later at the hands of the Cheyenne, her introduction to them was familiar: Blue Morning Flower pointed to a basket of roots to be scraped and chopped and then to the skinned rabbit carcasses hanging from a pole. Her meaning was clear enough. A pot was already simmering on the cook fire nearby. It had been no different on the wagon train or back at the orphanage. There were always meals to prepare and woman's work to be done.

Taking the stone scraper the Indian woman handed her, she drew the wrinkled skin off in long, thin strips. Underneath, the flesh of the roots was firm and yellow. Bettany's stomach growled, and she realized she hadn't eaten since the previous evening. It amazed her that such a basic need could intrude upon her grief. She chopped the roots viciously, venting her rage upon the pithy vegetables, when it was the attackers she wanted to slash to bits; then suffered for it when her bruised shoulder muscles protested. She was still glad she'd done it.

While she was occupied, Small Eagle joined the men. Smoke Along the Ground, the elected head of the band's council, was not pleased to hear of the slaughter of the wagon train. "This is an evil day. More white men will come to avenge the death of their kind, and they will drive us from these lands."

"Since early times our people have met here at the hunting grounds. No man can deny us. If they try," Small Eagle said grimly, "we shall war with them, and we shall drive *them* back."

The young warriors nodded, eager to test their mettle and determined to defend their people against the encroachers. Even alliances with previous enemies could be embraced, if they would hold back the white men and avoid the outcome of Sweet Medicine's ancient prophecy.

In the midst of their martial plans, old Buffalo Heart spoke up from his place of honor. "I had a vision in the night." The rest fell immediately silent.

Small Eagle was jolted. Did the old warrior know that Wolf Star was returning? Buffalo Heart had many powers. Could he look into his heart and see the confusion there? He glanced away.

"In this vision," the seer said, "a warrior came each day to his tipi with fresh game, and life was good. But one day, after a long hunting trip, he returned and found the carcasses of many slaughtered deer lying all about his lodge, and he knew they had been killed by a giant bird that nested in nearby valley. This warrior, he grew angry that the bird had played such a trick upon him, and he dragged the carcasses into the woods and left them there, but he did not leave." The group looked at him expectantly, waiting to hear how the hero had revenged himself upon the bird; but Buffalo Heart frowned and fell silent.

Small Eagle was gratified. "This must speak to our meeting with the Kiowa and Comanche," he said. "It is a good story, and we must learn from it. We will not be driven away from this place."

Buffalo Heart interrupted. "It is an evil story, and I have not related all of it to you. In the vision this warrior remained in his lodge, ignoring the giant bird, but while he slept the bird came into his lodge, and with his sharp beak he ripped out the warrior's heart."

Shock and anger followed his words, but Smoke Along the Ground raised his hand in command. "Buffalo Heart has spoken. The fate of the woman does not concern us, and Small Eagle will follow his own mind in the matter, but we must hasten our plans to ally ourselves with the southern tribes, as we did long ago with the Arapaho and the Lakota."

The men nodded in accord. "Very well," Smoke Along the Ground announced. "At first light we will break camp and move down toward Deer Creek Meadow."

While the men conferred, the women of the camp gathered in small knots or went about their business, pretending to ignore the newcomer. No one approached Bettany, but she was very aware that dozens of eyes were fixed intently upon her. She was disjointing the rabbit carcass when a small stone struck her on the shoulder. She blinked away tears of anger and pain and went on with her work. Another pelted her, from the same direction. The third was larger and hit with dangerous velocity. If it had struck her head, she might have been severely injured. Bettany had read in the Bible about people who had been stoned to death, and she wasn't prepared to die that way. Spinning around on one knee, she confronted her tormentor.

A thin boy, no older than Nils, with a handful of stones. The absurdity of her fears and the small, dirty face of reality made her laugh aloud. The boy, so belligerent a moment ago, gave her a startled look and ran off. The women of the camp watched from the corners of their eyes. Bettany resumed her task as if the interruption hadn't occurred.

She took down the second rabbit and prepared it for the cook pot. She didn't know why she'd been brought here or what fate awaited her; but if they saw that she could make herself useful, they would be more likely to keep her alive. She had to stay alive, for there was no other person in the world who knew or cared about what happened to Hannah and Nils. If she died, they would be lost forever with no hope of rescue. The thought was intolerable.

She wept then, softly and silently. Wept for Mamie and

Curtis Ebbersoll, for Josie Carter, who had wanted to help them, for swaggering Porter Renfrew and his mad, pathetic wife, all lying dead among the carnage of the wagon party. When she looked up from her work, dusk was rapidly devouring the sunset colors, and a few stars shone like lonely beacons in the sky. She wiped her eyes surreptitiously as if she could wipe away the terrible images or obliterate the foolish dreams that had brought her to such disaster.

A point of light glittered through the sheer veil of clouds, cold and bright and distant. Pennsylvania and the Susquehanna orphanage seemed just as far away. Oh, Papa! To come all this way in search of you and have it end like this!

Four hundred miles south, in Mexico, a priest made his way along the trade road beneath those same stars. Father Ignazio was weary with traveling, and *banditos* roamed the hills by night, but he trusted that they would not attack a man of the cloth. Another hour and he could rest, but there were still many days of travel ahead before he reached his destination. He wondered if Dona Ysabella had guessed what havoc would be unleashed once her letters were made public—and how many other lives would be touched by the shadows of yesterday's sins.

Eight

Hacienda de Medina, Mexico: 1811

"In your mother's day, Dona Ysabella, you would be preparing now for your presentation at court."

Manuela's face flushed just thinking of it. She smoothed back her young mistress's hair and pinned it in an elegant knot at the nape of her neck. What a sensation Dona Ysabella would have created with her perfect features and skin like the petals of a white rose. "There would be grand balls, receptions—such gaiety that it would make your head whirl."

Ysabella shrugged with the disdain of almost fifteen summers. "I have no interest in kings and courts, Manuela, and neither should you. Ramon Fernandez says we are Mexicans now, not Spaniards. And someday our country will be free of Spain's dominations."

"Ah, but royal blood flows in your veins, and you know the old saying: 'One's blood cannot be denied.' And you should not repeat the things you overhear. Leave government matters to older and wiser heads."

Resigned, Ysabella let Manuela rattle on. Her affection for her former nursemaid was deep and abiding, but she had no interest at all in Manuela's social aspirations. Let her chatter of dances and parties, and let her own father talk of marriage contracts and the merging of properties. It would be to no avail. In her heart Ysabella was almost sure that God had spoken to her and that she was meant to be a

105

bride of Christ. In fact, she had been quite sure until her chance meeting with Ramon Fernandez.

She had known him all her life, although their contacts had been few, for he was the unprepossessing son of a commonplace merchant, while she was the daughter of a wealthy and influential man. But in the years since she had last seen him, Ramon had grown from a gangly boy to quite the handsomest young man she had ever seen—and he had whispered that she was the most beautiful woman in all of Mexico.

A woman! That had pleased her greatly, for although many girls of almost fifteen were already married, or at least betrothed, Ysabella felt that her family still looked upon her as a child. They certainly treated her as one. But that night at the reception, Ramon had made her feel like a grown woman, sophisticated and desirable. He didn't care that her eyes were a deep, rich topaz and not the liquid black so much admired. "Like raw honey in the comb," he had told her when they'd stolen a few private seconds together.

He had kissed her hand, his mouth warm and lingering against her skin. She had gone home in a state of high excitement, stimulated by his admiration as much as by the sense of power it had given her. Since then she had seen him twice, always in company and strictly chaperoned. He had spent the time sending her ardent glances and at their last meeting was able to pass a note to her, tucked among some roses. But that had been many weeks ago, and he had not been at the bullfight Don Enrique had arranged in honor of his saint's day.

It was hardly enough to base romantic fantasies upon, but Ysabella was young and bored. Her father had been away for several weeks, and there was nothing to do. Tía Estrella was her father's hostess and managed the entire household, leaving Ysabella's hands and thoughts idle. Although she really didn't think she should like very much to be a merchant's wife, it was certainly better than the alternative her father had hinted of—an espousal with Don

Enrique, the wealthy neighbor who had lost his front teeth in an accident and had two daughters older than she.

Yes, all in all, Ysabella was inclined to think her true vocation would be found in the service of God. She gazed at her reflection, imagining her face framed by a starched wimple—much more suitable than the red silk flowers Manuela was pinning over her ear. She wiggled, and the sharp hairpin slipped. "Oh!" The saintly vision vanished, leaving only an imperious young face.

"Do be more careful, Manuela. And that reminds me. I wish you to brush out Pepito again. He ran out this morning after a rabbit and returned with burrs in his coat."

Manuela smiled inwardly. She put no credence in her mistress's fine ideas of entering a convent and dedicating her life to God's service; who then would arrange her little dove's hair or brush the burrs from her dog's silky coat? No, Ysabella would fall in love with a dashing young man like Ramon Fernandez—*!Qué hombre!*—and have many fat babies. And she, Manuela, would be their doting nursemaid, with a strong young girl, of course, to do the heavy work. It was all planned out in the maidservant's mind.

The door opened unceremoniously, and Ysabella's aunt entered in a rustle of silk. Her elbow-length sleeves and high-necked gown made no concession to the weather or Mexican fashion. Not for Dona Estrella the full flounced skirts and ruffled blouses that were so popular, and which her niece wore to such stunning effect.

"You have a visitor, Ysabella." Her elegant face was disapproving, yet there was no trace of it in her voice. A Mr. Quinn Logan."

Ysabella turned and frowned. "I know no one of that name."

Her aunt raised her brows. "Perhaps you've forgotten. Although I do think the gentleman is . . . rather memorable. He is in the parlor."

Manuela twitched her charge's skirts into order and then watched her exit with her relative. The maid was perplexed. Dona Estrella was up to something. Of that she was sure, and who would know better than she, who had known Don Miguel's sister since childhood? But then, who could really say they knew poor Estrellita? She had been a plump, sunny-dispositioned girl but had grown into a thin, brittle woman with shadowed eyes. Impossible to believe that she was just past her twenty-third birthday.

How sad that Don Miguel's sister had no husband or children of her own, for she would have made a loving wife and mother. Shaking her head, Manuela cleaned the bristles of the ornate silver hairbrush. Ah, Dona Estrella should have married one of her many admirers in the past, for there were certainly none in the present. She had bloomed like a rose until just past her fifteenth birthday and then wilted too quickly. Instead of her own *niños*, Don Miguel's sister had no one to vent her maternal instincts upon except her niece—and when Dona Ysabella married and went away, as she must one day, what would her poor aunt do?

The maid folded a lace shawl and placed it inside a beautifully carved chest. This no was no time to dwell on the past. There was work to be done and—she smiled again—a small dog to be brushed.

Ysabella followed her aunt down the tiled corridor, wondering who this American could be and for what reason he had ridden out to the hacienda. It was well known that her father had no use for Americans. There would be trouble not only in Texas, but throughout the territory of New Mexico, he said. The war with Spain had drained the Mexican economy, and the upstarts east of the Missouri had their sights on the lucrative Santa Fe trade. Although Ysabella was tired of the endless political strain, she accepted her father's assessment. Don Miguel was God within the walls of his own house.

She paused inside the doorway of the *sala*. Unlike the rest of the hacienda, this long room was furnished in brooding Spanish style with deep colors, dark wood, and embossed leather. Even the vigas of the ceiling were heavily carved with intricate designs. Against this unlikely background the visitor rose to greet her, a rangy, broad-shouldered giant with straight dark hair gleaming with deep red highlights.

Ysabella was quite sure she had never seen him before in her life. He certainly didn't match her red-haired, pale-skinned idea of what an *irlandés* would look like. His skin was dark as a mestizo and deeply weathered from years of summer and winter sun, and instead of the bright blue eyes she'd expected, his were mossy green and gold. He came forward a few steps, stopped with awkward suddenness as he noticed Dona Estrella's presence in the doorway behind her, and made a brief, unpracticed bow.

Cautiously Ysabella glanced back at her aunt, who had taken a chair near the doorway, just out of earshot, and busied herself with the alb she was embroidering for their new chaplain. Tía Estrella was being very discreet today. Relaxing a bit, Ysabella turned back to the giant with a question in her eyes and seated herself. He obeyed her indication to do the same, and she noted the tiny triangle of folded paper he held in his left hand.

A little smile played about Ysabella's rosy mouth. Despite her father's displeasure, Ramon was growing bold. "I think, Señor Quinn Logan, that I do not know you. Is it perhaps that you have come with a message for me? From a mutual friend?"

Quinn stared at her like a man bedazzled by a merciless desert sun. So this radiant little coquette was the beautiful princess his young friend Ramon had raved on and on about. There was no need to ask why. From her sleek dark head to her dainty feet she was an exquisite thing, and beneath the aristocratic facade he sensed all the smoldering passions that were yet untapped. That was, he decided, the strongest part of her appeal. It would take a man of stone to turn away from the chance of being the one to awaken her slumbering womanhood. For the first time Quinn sympathized with the girl's father. Who could blame him for reaching far higher for his daughter than a struggling merchant's son?

"Well?" Ysabella's imperious little voice snapped him out of his musings.

Quinn sent a quick glance across the room to where the girl's aunt was plying her needle. There seemed little resemblance between this haughty, vital creature and the juiceless spinster intent on her embroidery. He saw no threat from that quarter and gave Ysabella his full attention.

"I do indeed bear a message for you, señorita." He paused and frowned. "I am afraid it is not a pleasant one. My good friend Ramon Fernandez is bound for California, where he will be learning to manage his grandfather's business near Santa Barbara. He asked me to give you this."

She took the folded paper he thrust into her hand. "Gone? Ramon Fernandez has gone?"

"Not yet. He sets out tomorrow."

"Without even saying good-bye!"

Quinn had been prepared for tears, not for the hot indignation that greeted his news. It was his turn to be taken aback. He had steeled himself, most reluctantly, to be the bearer of sad tidings and perhaps offer a few words of comfort. He hadn't been prepared for a fit of girlish pique. No grief, no longing, no symptoms of dashed dreams. Only a smoldering fury that would have been funny if it hadn't been so touching.

Ysabella trembled with a rush of anger but managed to keep her tongue. After all, she was the daughter of Don Miguel Alvarez de Medina. She flattened the note open upon her lap, read the protestations of undying love and the pleas to wait for Ramon, no matter how many years it took. Her mouth turned down in scorn. How could she have ever thought she loved such a . . . such a . . .

Slowly, carefully, Ysabella folded the note neatly once more. It took great willpower when she wanted to tear it into a hundred pieces or wad it into a crumpled ball. She schooled the muscles of her face but could not hide the contempt and outraged pride that blazed in her eyes. Her thick lashes swept down to cover them.

"It was kind of my old friend Ramon Fernandez to write

to me at such a busy time, and most kind of you, Señor Quinn Logan, to deliver his note. I will ring for a servant to bring you refreshments."

It was clearly a dismissal. Quinn was torn between amusement and chagrin. What a spoiled little minx; and in a year or two, what a devastating woman she would be. All in all, the long ride out to the hacienda had been worth the trip. He rose and bowed.

"No need to bother, señorita. I can find my own way out." His eyes twinkled. "And I'm happy to see that your heart isn't broken—or even bruised in the least. And now, you heartless little coquette, I'd best be on my way before your father arrives and finds me mixed up in your silly shenanigans."

Ysabella went rigid with affronted dignity. *Silly shenanigans!* How dare he! And how dare he call her a vulgar flirt! Her heart *was* broken. It was! Why, her entire life was blighted!

Quinn leaned over her hand and grinned. "You're a lovely little baggage, but you won't fool me with your play-acting. And if I was your father and had caught you flirting with Ramon Fernandez, I'd have sent him a bit farther than California—I'd have sent the young pup to China."

Ysabella's eyes opened wide. "You are a hateful man! I hope I never have the misfortune to set eyes upon you again."

"Your wish is my command." He bent over her hand and kissed it, a breach of etiquette so flagrant that it robbed her of all ability to respond. Quinn left her sitting there like a statue of wounded vanity.

On the way out he paused to bow to her aunt, who seemed astonished at his quick departure. Quinn was still surprised that she had let her niece visit with a man who was a stranger to herself and had come without a proper introduction. Although still young, she seemed a proper dried-up spinster, all the fires of passion long burned out. Certainly not the kind of woman to further her niece's romantic intrigues.

But Estrella's face had come startlingly alive, and Quinn was surprised by her peculiar expression. For just an instant her eyes were eloquent with unguarded emotion.

Quinn could almost swear that it was disappointment.

Estrella was picking dead flowers from the vine that rioted over the *portal* and thinking of the American named Quinn Logan. It had been a long time since a man had looked at her with admiration in his eyes. Longer since she had done the same. He had a nice face. A good face, if not devastatingly handsome like . . .

She suddenly shivered and turned her thoughts in another direction, but the uneasiness persisted. All day she'd been filled with growing trepidation, a sensation of storm clouds gathering on some unseen horizon. Although the sun was bright, thunder rumbled in the distance. Ah, it is really a storm blowing up, she thought. What a foolish creature I am to fall prey to my morbid imagination.

The thunder grew without a break. Estrella straightened and listened. Not thunder, but approaching riders. She crossed the court, entering the one beyond that served the stables. Her brother had returned from his journey sooner than expected. He would be angry, Estrella knew, when he learned of the American who'd paid a call on his daughter, but she wouldn't be cowed by that. These were difficult years for a young girl, and someone must stand by Ysabella.

It was essential that her beloved niece have someone she could confide in. Estrella knew that her own life would have been very different if there had been someone to whom she could have turned. She entered the house and directed a servant to send refreshments to Don Miguel's *sala* and returned to the *portal* to meet her brother after his long absence.

Estrella was startled to see another man with him. Even though she'd known the day would come soon, the sight of the newcomer's handsome, fine-boned face was a great shock after so many years. "Don Luis!"

The man came toward her with athletic grace and enfolded her hands warmly in his. "So formal, Estrellita?" He leaned down and kissed her cheek. "Are we not family?"

She had no answer. Miguel clapped his brother-in-law on the shoulder. "I told her I would bring a surprise when I returned, and you see she is speechless. Come, Estrella, where are your manners? Have you no welcome for Luis?"

Avoiding their eyes, Estrella stammered out a greeting. Miguel was surprised that even now his sister could be tongue-tied in his brother-in-law's presence. Several years ago he had suspected that Estrella had a developed a young girl's romantic attachment to his wife's brother, the dashing *caballero*. Miguel had nipped any pretensions Luis had indulged in before they grew out of hand.

True, a matching of the families would have consolidated their holdings, and his influence might have been enough to gain a dispensation from the church, but there would have been talk. The de Medina name was an old and proud one, and Don Miguel would have cut off his arm rather than tarnish it. Luis had been made to understand his point of view, and had eventually made a good enough match of it with the granddaughter of Gaspar Torrejon, and surely her rich California lands made up for her lack of beauty— at least in Miguel's eyes.

A door opened and Ysabella came dancing out and threw herself into her father's arms. "How I have missed you! You must never leave us for so long again!" She noticed the man with him. "And Tío Luis! Oh, what a wonderful surprise! Is Tía Pilar well? Did you bring the shawl she promised to send for my saint's day?"

They all laughed indulgently as Ysabella rattled on. She was so excited, she forgot that she was angry with him until they were settled around the long table eating chicken with rice and drinking goblets of cool lemonade. It was when her father mentioned California that she suddenly remembered. Ramon Fernandez was even now on his way to California at her father's decree, all because he had dared to give his heart to her. It was most unjust. She'd meant to pout and brood over it but was much too happy to have her father home—and Tío Luis as well. But she did manage to show her disfavor by suddenly withdrawing from the animated conversation.

Estrella was distracted by her own thoughts, and Don Miguel was never one to pick up on his daughter's rapid changes of mood. Luis noticed first, and his eyes, so very like her own, glowed with deep golden lights. Ysabella thought that she had never seen him look so handsome. There was a softening of the square line of his jaw as he leaned forward.

"Ah, what is this? A cloud marring that perfect white brow? This must not be, Ysabella. Tell us at once what is troubling you."

"It is nothing," she said shortly.

Don Miguel frowned. "Mind your manners, Ysabella. That is no way to speak to your uncle."

She scowled and stared at her plate. Her father was seriously displeased. "You are not a child, Ysabella, to make such grimaces. What distresses you?"

"I am too old, Father, to be chastised like a small child. I think that you know very well what has distressed me." She pushed her chair back and flounced out of the room.

Estrella was about to go after her, but Luis put his hand over hers and smiled. She was unable to move. "Leave her be, Estrellita. We all know that girls on the brink of womanhood are prey to odd humors. I will speak to her later."

"That will not be necessary. I shall attend to it myself."

Luis's smile widened. Estrella would have given anything to be able to throw off the weight of his hand. The light touch seemed to press her back into her chair and render her incapable of movement. Luis had always had this effect upon her. She wished with all her heart that he had stayed forever in California.

Luis found Ysabella in the walled garden. "What a cold welcome I have received at your father's home, *querida*. Your aunt ignores me and you flee my very presence."

Ysabella tore the petals from a scarlet flower and let them

drift to the ground. "Tía Estrella does not approve of you, I think. And I do not approve of my father. He treats me as if I were a lapdog with no mind of my own."

Brushing a handful of blood red petals from the bench, he sat down beside her. "Your father loves you very much. He would never do anything to harm you."

"But you don't know what he has done."

"If you are speaking of young Ramon Fernandez, I believe I do. He is a handsome weakling who could never have tamed a passionate creature like yourself. Your father, in his wisdom, has saved you from throwing your affections away on a most unworthy object."

Ysabella had risen to take an agitated turn about the garden. Now she whirled dramatically to face him. She had worked herself into a fury. "You don't understand. I was . . . I *think* I was truly in love with Ramon."

Luis caught her by the shoulders, laughing softly. "I think not. I think, *mi corazón*, that it is your pride that is wounded, and not your foolish little heart. Someday you will learn to love a man—a real man—and you will not even remember this one's name."

Although his words dismissed her feelings for Ramon as mere infatuation, the tone of his voice told her that he understood. The calm confidence and the smile in his eyes had a strange effect upon her. Ysabella's anger fizzled out, and she felt like a silly child, only dimly aware of great forces that were beyond control.

She pulled away and looked at him through the screen of her lashes, testing him. "You all think I am only a tiresome child."

He put a finger beneath her chin and lifted her face up to his. "No, Ysabella. I see quite clearly that you are a woman."

Smiling and blushing, she backed away. A moment later she turned and vanished through one of the doors that opened on the *portal*.

Luis laughed and entered the house from the opposite side of the courtyard in search of his brother-in-law. Don

Miguel was in the parlor with Estrella. "What, have you quarreled with Ysabella so soon?"

"No, no." Luis chuckled. "But I fear I have offended her dignity by not taking her 'broken heart' as seriously as she had hoped." He stopped before the portrait of his late sister, and the laughter went out of his face. "Do you know, it takes my breath away that Ysabella is so much like Julianna. She has the very look of her."

A cloud passed over the sun, and the room, inside its thick adobe walls, felt suddenly cold. A cold wind played over Estrella's skin. She was familiar with the same proverb as Manuela: "One's blood cannot be denied."

Don Miguel's thoughts ran in the same vein. "Yes. I see that she has suddenly blossomed into a young lady. Fortunately I did not let her fill her mind with books and studies as I did with you, Estrella. Education, except in the domestic sphere, ruins a woman for marriage."

Dona Estrella stiffened, and Luis shot her a swift, laughing glance. She ignored him. A pensive look had settled over Don Miguel's aquiline features. "Ysabella has her mother's beauty, and I fear that she inherited her passionate nature as well. I think I should talk to Don Enrique very soon. The girl is ripe for marriage."

Luis's eyes met Estrella's in a slow, mocking glance. "Ripe as a summer plum."

Nine

Cheyenne Territory: 1840

Bettany was mortified. She'd prepared the food carefully but had turned her back on the roasted rabbits—just in time to see a camp dog make off with one of them in its jaws. Exhaustion made her clumsy, and next she knocked over the pot of stew, spilling half the contents in the dirt. While the old woman scolded, the other squaws laughed behind their hands or shook their heads.

"This woman that Small Eagle has brought with him is useless," they said to one another, "either from stupidity or laziness." Bettany understood as clearly as if they'd spoken in English. Her face burned with embarrassment and suppressed anger. With Axel dead, Hannah and Nils taken away, she had more important things to think of than the preparation of food.

Not that she meant to really be of use; Bettany hoped that in the hubbub of milling children and dogs and horses, she might be able to slip away unnoticed. She would have tried to escape earlier on horseback, but the Indian who'd brought her to the camp had kept her reins in his hands and led her along. She hadn't expected to travel so far. Fort Laramie was at least five days' walk from here.

It wasn't wishful thinking. After trudging almost seven hundred miles alongside the wagons, she was fit enough to attempt it without difficulty. It helped that she could follow the river for a while, but there was a vast stretch of land where she would have to use the sun and prayer to guide

her. Once she reached the canyon the trail of the doomed
wagon party would lead her back to the trading post. She
wasn't anxious to see what remained of it.

She'd already managed to steal some jerked meat from
the line where it had been hung to dry, and there would
be water ahead. The two things she lacked were a weapon
for protection and something to keep her warm during the
cool nights. There had to be blankets inside the lodge or
one of the painted buffalo robes like she'd seen Pawnee
braves wear.

The old woman began to scold, and Bettany jumped up.
Oh, dear! She'd left the rest of the meat too near the fire
and scorched it. Now she was sure to be in for it. Rapid
movement, seen from the corner of her eye, provided a
distraction for everyone.

A rider in buckskins came down the line of lodges at a
fast clip. Her heart skipped a beat. A white man! She cried
out to him to stop, but his head was turned in the opposite
direction. He didn't hear her, and he didn't see the small
boy who'd stumbled directly into his path. Years of caring
for young children galvanized her to action.

Reacting instinctively amid the shrieks and cries, Bettany
thrust out the stick she was holding to alert the rider,
simultaneously launching herself at the Cheyenne child
across the intervening space. It was too late for the man
to pull up, and there wasn't much room to maneuver. The
stick touched the horse's flank and he managed to swing
away by scant inches, passing in a flurry of dust and flashing
hooves. As Bettany rolled away with the boy in her arms,
one hoof clipped her shoulder. It still ached from the bruising she'd taken in the wagon party attack, but that had
been nothing compared to this. The whole upper half of
her torso felt numbed by ice, then seared by fire, and her
arm hung useless at her side. She tried to move it. Agony
erupted and overwhelmed her: for the first time in her life,
she fainted.

Small Eagle heard the commotion and raced up from the
river. He saw his nephew pale and chastened, the rider

surrounded by angry women, and Bettany lying unconscious on the ground. "What is this? What has happened to her?"

Blue Morning Flower helped the shaken boy to his feet. "We have been spared a calamity. Your woman has risked her life to save Three Reeds from the white man's carelessness."

Small Eagle knelt beside Bettany, who was sprawled at his feet, senseless. Others crowded up to see what was going on. His mother gave the boy into the care of a family member and examined the *ve-ho-e* who had risked her life and suffered for it.

She placed her hand over Bettany's face and felt the tickle of warm breath against her palm, while Small Eagle watched, his body rigid with tension as he awaited the prognosis. Blue Morning Flower addressed her son. "Her *tasoom* has not gone. She will live."

He relaxed. Blue Morning Flower was skilled in the healing mysteries. "*Ipewa.* It is good."

"Yes, it is so. When you first brought her into your lodge I was not pleased, but I have misjudged your woman. I see now that she is a warrior as you are, my son."

Spirit Walker, a young woman with wise and merry eyes, pointed at the Trapper, who had listened anxiously to the rapid exchange. "Blue Morning Flower speaks the truth. Your woman, she saved the boy—and counted coup on the *ve-ho-e* as well. He has been shamed. It is good that this warrior woman was here to save Three Reeds."

Her joke and the brave act had swayed public opinion in Bettany's favor, but she was totally unaware of it. While the trapper dismounted she lay pale and unmoving in the dust. Small Eagle's mother opened Bettany's dress to expose a massive bruise and a dislocated shoulder.

"I will need your strength to help me set this back in place, my son. It is best to do it here, before we move her."

Bettany fought her way up through a fog of pain and felt a worn hand placed gently upon her brow. "Rest easy, Warrior Woman," Blue Morning Flower said. "Soon you will be put to rights."

Small Eagle did what was necessary to set the shoulder, even though Bettany fainted once more during the process. Her flesh was as smooth beneath his palm as a river-washed stone, but soft and warm. His pulse quickened, but no one watching would have guessed it from his calm face. When it was over he lifted her in his arms and carried her into the lodge. He was proud that she had not cried out and gratified at the names the women of the camp had given her: Warrior Woman. She Counts Coup.

Ipewa. It was good.

Blue Morning Flower had dosed Bettany with an herbal remedy, and she fell into a much needed slumber. In her dream she lay drowsing against the grassy bank on the west side of the orphanage, sunlight shining warm and pink through her closed lids. A light breeze fanned her cheek and stirred the squirrel grass. One of the plump tassels tickled her ankle. She moved her leg and resettled herself.

Vague awareness of an ache in her shoulder penetrated the dream, but she was too tired to open her eyes and find the cause. It was so peaceful that she didn't want to be disturbed. A cloud passed over the sun, and the whimsical breeze fluttered her skirts higher. The squirrel grass bent before the wind and brushed over the skin just above her knee, and—

She woke with a start to find herself in a shadowy lodge with a throbbing shoulder, with Small Eagle blocking the firelight and his hand upon her bare leg. Enraged and frightened, she pushed him away.

He grinned and stepped back, then hunkered down with his back to the fire, watching her with the intent concentration of a cat before a mousehole. A wheezy voice chuckled from the opposite side of the tipi. "Don't fancy him, eh? A woman could do worse. Small Eagle, he's a mighty important fellow among the Cheyenne."

At the English words, Bettany looked around the lodge quickly. The old woman who'd set her to cleaning the roots was sound asleep a few feet away, wrapped up in a warm buffalo robe. The voice had come from a lanky figure sprawled in the darkness beyond the flames. With his long hair and buckskins, he might have been an Indian, too; but when he leaned forward the light gleamed on grizzled yellow hair and a beard to match. Her heart lurched with excitement. The white man from whom she'd rescued the boy.

"Thank God. My prayers have been answered. . . ."

Another wheezy laugh interrupted her. "If I'm the answer to your prayers, missy, they must be mighty queer ones." He rose and came toward her. "Folks're more likely to think Ole Thorson's been sent by hell than by heaven."

Bettany's spurt of hope died in a blast of whiskey fumes. Now the weather-carved lines and deep cynicism were evident in the broad, mocking features. Instinct warned there would be no help from this quarter, but still she had to ask.

"Please, sir, you must help me."

"Well, now . . ." The man took a long pull of raw whiskey from his canteen. "I don't think Small Eagle'd appreciate my interfering. I learned to mind my own business and let the Injuns mind theirs. That's how I've kept my scalp."

She clutched at his arm, and her words came out in a breathless rush. "Our wagon train was attacked, and my husband is dead of fever, the children abducted by Indians. . . ."

His eyes sharpened. He didn't look very pleased. "They're here? In the Cheyenne camp?"

"No. They were taken by others—I don't know why— but this one brought me here. I *must* find them. Please, sir. Please help me."

Small Eagle eyed the big Swede. "What is it that she says to you?"

Thorson grinned and replied in the Cheyenne tongue. "Says you're a fine-looking warrior. Brave, too."

So, Wolf Star's Silver Woman found him desirable. Once Small Eagle got over his surprise he almost preened with satisfaction. Modesty was a great virtue, but he was pleased. It was true that he was a noted warrior, much admired by the Cheyenne, but he hadn't thought that a *ve-ho-e* woman could appreciate his qualities. He, in turn, was equally intrigued by her.

Bettany had tried to follow their swift exchange. Thorson's sardonic smile seemed to bode no good. "Please . . ."

"You're asking the wrong man. Can't help you. But you might try cozying up to Small Eagle." He scraped at a tooth with his fingernail and gave her a considering look. "Play your cards right and you won't have to worry about your own skin."

"It's not mine I'm concerned with."

"No? Well, you're a mighty fine looking gal. Seems like he's taken a shine to you, too."

She swallowed her anger. "Sir, for the love of God, you must not turn your back upon me."

He took a swig of gin from the metal canteen beside him. "There's nothing I can do. If there's any other Injuns in these parts, they'll likely be Arapaho. They're allies of the Cheyenne. But Kiowa or Comanche now, that's a horse of a different color." He shrugged a shoulder in Small Eagle's direction. "I don't meddle in Small Eagle's business. He's a healthy young buck. Needs a wife to look after things. Play your cards right and see what he'll do."

"You are not serious." Her indignant look amused him.

"Worth a try." Thorson turned to Small Eagle with a gleam of mischief in his eye, and spoke in Cheyenne. "The woman asks that you get her children back for her. Says she'll give you anything you want in return."

Small Eagle's heart raced. Once Wolf Star returned, he would claim the woman for himself. Jealousy burned inside him. He took a deep breath and drew himself up. "Tell the woman I will bring her children to her if she will be my wife and lie with me."

The trapper rubbed his jaw. "I think you just got yourself a wife, my friend. In addition, she says that you must give me that gray pony you got from the Arapaho, for being the go-between."

"So be it."

Bettany waited nervously during the exchange. "What did he say?"

Grinning, Thorson rose. "Oh, Small Eagle will bring your young'uns back, safe and sound. For a price." He winked at her. "Not a bad deal, since you've only got one thing worth bartering. I told him you'd think about it." He laughed, a short, sharp bark like a fox's cough, and went out, well pleased with himself.

Small Eagle was glad Thorson was gone. He wanted to be alone with his new wife, yet he knew he must go gently with such a nervous creature. His gaze locked with hers and he fought the urge to stare into her eyes until he could pass behind them and know all the secrets of her mind. Brave as he was, he didn't dare. They could drag his soul from his body.

Bettany's mouth was dry. He towered over her, the firelight outlining the naked muscles of his chest and arms, accenting his sinewy strength. A shiver ran up her back. She couldn't do it.

The Cheyenne noticed Bettany's tremor. Did she feel the same thrill that ran through him? Did she desire him as he desired her? He stepped closer until his flesh brushed her breasts, then reached out and covered them with his hands. They were warm and firm, and her heart thundered beneath his palms.

Bettany understood now why animals froze when threatened. She could not force her limbs to obey, and her throat was too constricted to scream.

Slowly Small Eagle pressed closer, until she felt the strength of his arousal. The blood drained from her face as she jerked away. Her thick-lashed eyes seemed to grow larger and darker, as if their light had been extinguished.

Small Eagle was both shamed and angered. He was drawn to her so strongly that he was in danger of losing the discipline instilled in him from birth. A Cheyenne warrior must be the master of his own emotions and actions. A man who acted hastily or foolishly, out of no other reason than pure sexual desire, was not a man. His fiery need ebbed.

Bettany watched the flush fade from his high cheekbones, then return again as anger shone in his eyes. She was sure her last moments had come, and that they would be humiliating and painful, but she refused to weep or grovel. Summoning all her determination, she lifted her chin bravely. If he tried to harm her she had no weapons to defend herself with other than her hands and teeth, but she would bite and kick and scratch at his eyes as long as she had life and breath in her.

To Small Eagle, the defiance in her features looked more like disdain. He had no intention of earning her contempt. When her nerves were ready to snap like a plucked bowstring, he dropped his hands and stepped back, then swung away from her and left the lodge.

The relief that flooded her being was as shattering as the fear had been. Bettany's whole body shook, and her legs were no longer able to support her. Sinking to her knees, she bent over, gasping in great gulps of air, trying to quell her nausea. Her hands were smeared with blood. She had fisted them so tightly that the short nails had broken her skin.

Fighting back panic, she wiped them carefully on the hem of her dress. She mustn't lose control. Self-command was her only hope, for there'd be no help from Ole Thorson or anyone else in this heathen camp. Giving way to her emotions would only make things worse. She needed time to ponder her situation and consider her alternatives. Too much had happened, too quickly, without any time to think. There seemed to be only two courses of action open to her: she could try to escape and strike out alone and unequipped through the wilderness, hoping to make her way to Fort Laramie—or she could take Ole Thorson's advice.

Small Eagle—she thought that was the name the Swede had used—hadn't treated her badly. He'd shown lust and then retreated. Perhaps the Indian didn't find her desirable.

Or perhaps he'd expected some sign of gratitude for rescuing her from the massacre. It never crossed her mind that he had wanted a willing partner.

What should she do if he approached her again? She trembled so hard that she had to clutch her hands together in her lap. To trade her body for gain was harlotry, a scarlet sin. Yet hadn't she traded herself to Alex in exchange for a set of empty marriage lines and the opportunity of going to California? Surely that was as much akin to harlotry as what she was contemplating now in hopes of saving Nils's and Hannah's lives. And her own.

The girls in the Susquehanna orphanage had been strictly raised to follow the Ten Commandments, and she would rather die than jeopardize her soul; still, wouldn't abandoning even the slightest chance of rescuing Hannah and Nils be the greater sin? Bettany prayed she would not be put to that test. But a nagging, insistent voice within her asked: What will you do if Ole Thorson is right, and the Indian can help you rescue the children? If it comes down to it, will you— can you—trade your honor for Hannah and Nils, two children who are not yours by blood, whom you've known for less than three months? Who might even now be dead?

There was, of course, only one answer to that question. Bettany's teeth chattered. She huddled closer to the fire, but despite the heat it gave out, she could not get warm.

Nils flew across the broken ground in a desperate, stumbling run. There was no plan or direction to his flight, only the need to escape. He had imagined himself as a smaller version of one of his bold heroes, facing danger and death bravely—in fact, always victorious against overwhelming odds. Instead he was only a small boy, fleeing for his life through the falling dusk. A small boy who was tired and hungry and very, very frightened.

He jumped over a rotting log, cast up on the riverbank by a forgotten spring storm. The ground was sandy and crumbled easily. Nils slipped and slid back toward the water, falling in with a splash. The river was low and came up only to his knees, but it was cold and swift. When he struggled up it grabbed him by the ankles and dragged his feet out from under him.

The force of the water carried Nils along on his back like an overturned beetle for five yards. He fetched up against a boulder, bruising his thigh painfully. At least it had stopped his helter-skelter travel downriver. He scrambled to his feet and clawed his way back up the bank trying not to whimper. The wind was brisk and chilling, and at first he felt as if he were burning. Then the sensation of heat ebbed, and he felt as if he were encased in ice.

He had been cold before, but never like this. He had been out in the night darkness before, but never alone. Nils wiped his nose with his sleeve and panicked when he couldn't feel either his arm or his nose. His fingers were curled into claws, numb and almost useless. It was too much for a boy of only six years. Why didn't someone come to help him? Where was Pa, and where was his new ma? Didn't anyone care that he was ascared and tired and hungry and cold?

Tears spilled over his lower lids, warmer than the cheeks they ran down. He began to run again, blindly, into the deepening gloom. The exertion warmed him. Soon it was so dark he could hardly see. Luck led him into a niche formed in an irregular outcrop of rock. He wriggled his wiry body inside. Sheltered from the wind and near exhaustion, he sat huddled with his head cradled on his knees and wept softly. He sobbed until he was sick with it, but no one came to help him. Nils pictured his new ma asleep in the quilts below the wagon, pa snoring beside her. He knew suddenly that no one was looking for him or for Hannah. No one at all.

Anger replaced tears. From now on he would have to look after himself. His breath came in labored gasps, and his stomach ached badly. A twig snapped, but he didn't hear it. Lost in his misery, torn between hopeless despair and a wordless, childish rage, Nils was unaware he'd been followed until a figure loomed up over him, framed against the starry sky. He sucked in a breath, and the sound gave him away.

"Hungry, boy?"

He recognized the voice. The man called Ludo, the one who'd carried him on his horse the last part of the way. The bearded man, Kearns, had hit him in the jaw, and Nils still ached from that blow; but Ludo had been more gentle all along. Nils lifted his head, too terrified to speak.

Ludo's voice came persuasively through the dark. "Them wood pigeons should be about roasted by now. Yessiree. Can't you just taste 'em? All crisp and crackly outside and full of hot juices inside? Makes my belly rumble, just thinking of it. Yours rumbling, too?"

It sure was. Nils felt hollow as a scooped-out pumpkin, and his mouth watered. He thought of the birds cooked to a tempting golden brown over the open flames. He could almost smell and taste the meat. He hadn't eaten since the previous evening.

Ludo sensed his near capitulation.

"Yessiree, the grease'll be dripping off 'em into the fire. Um-umm! C'mon, boy. We'd best shake a leg and get back afore Kearns thinks we're lost and decides to eat 'em all hisself. Won't be nothing but a few bones left if we don't get a move on."

The thought of the warm food so near and in apparent jeopardy was the final straw. Nils wriggled free and took the hand that reached out to him. Ludo had come looking for him when no one else had. Ludo wouldn't hurt him.

Ludo was his friend.

A week later Nils had his first chance to sit around a fire with a real Indian—a Comanche, Ludo had said. Thrills of excitement and fear chased each other up and down the boy's spine. Everyone was afraid of Comanches and Apaches, and here he was, sitting only a few feet away from one.

Antelope Chaser's thoughts engrossed him as his guests took portions of the steaming food. The small warrior was alert and showed no fear, but the Comanche war chief was wary. He did not understand why these men wanted to sell the boy.

Ludo sniffed at the chunk of cooked meat speared on the tip of his knife. "Prairie dog."

Kearns chewed his own bite ruminatively and swallowed. "Un-uh. *Dog* dog."

"Dog!" Nils choked and spit out his mouthful.

The two men who had brought him laughed. Antelope Chaser's face showed no sign that he understood, although he spoke their language well. The wolf did not reveal his den to the coyote, nor did the hunter warn away his prey.

Folding his arms across his chest, Nils watched the others with disgust. Ludo stabbed another piece of meat and offered it to him. "Go on and eat. We were just having a bit of fun with you."

"I'm not hungry."

"Suit yourself."

Nils retreated into wounded dignity. He didn't see why Ludo had to side with Kearns. He didn't like Kearns. Neither did the Indian; Nils was sure of it.

Through all this, Antelope Chaser had been weighing their offer. The little warrior's mouth watered for hot food, but his pride would not let him take it. Pride was a good thing in a warrior. It made him brave.

"Hey, boy," Kearns said sharply. "I've got a powerful thirst. Fetch me that can of eyewash."

Nils got up and went around the fire to where the man had left the canteen of pungent gin, dragging out every step as slowly as he could to make his adversary wait. He hoped the gin would rot a hole right through Kearns's stomach, like Ludo had warned his partner it would. His forehead puckered. Would the hole be just on the inside, or would the gin burn a hole clear through the outside of Kearns's belly?

While Nils ruminated on the matter, his abductors were talking together in low tones. "Seems to me like this redskin isn't too keen on taking the kid off our hands. If that's the case, we'll have to get rid of him when there aren't any witnesses around."

Ludo turned on him. "Shut your bonebox. He'll take the boy all right. The Comanche won't care what color his skin is. Antelope Chaser will treat him like he's one of his own."

The Comanche addressed Ludo: "What place does this small warrior come from, and who are his people?"

Kearns answered hastily. "Comes from Santa Fe, but his people were wiped out by a fever. He's kin to my partner, here."

So, Antelope Chaser deduced, the boy came from the north or east. Men like Kearns always covered their tracks. But the last part was likely true. There seemed to be a bond of trust between him and the man called Ludo. "Why do you not take him with you, then?"

"We ride hard and far," Ludo said in halting Comanche. "The boy slows us down too much."

While the bargaining went on, Nils stared into the campfire. The dance of the flames tired his eyes. He leaned back against Kearns's saddle and fought to keep them open. Once he roused and saw the Indian shake the contents of a small pouch into Ludo's hand. The irregular pebbles shone gold in the reflected firelight. Ludo stared down at his palm, then nodded and tucked the nuggets into his pocket. Nils's eyes flickered shut, and when he opened them again it was dawn and the fire was out.

He sat up quickly. Ludo, Kearns, and their horses were gone. He couldn't believe it. At first Nils thought he was all alone. He stumbled to his feet, trying to swallow the lump that constricted his throat. There was nothing left of the night camp but the ashes of the fire, already scuffed over, and two diagrams scratched into the ground. He turned and almost ran into Antelope Chaser, who was standing among the lacy willows.

"Where are they? What did you do to them?"

Nils hadn't expected an answer, and Antelope Chaser's reply startled him. "I have done nothing to them. They rode away of their own desire at first light."

"Ludo wouldn't go without me."

The Comanche approved. The small warrior was frightened but hid his fear behind a shield of fierceness. "You no longer belong to them," he said firmly. "They have sold you to me in exchange for knowledge of the soft metal your people prize so highly."

"You can't sell people," Nils retorted, but his voice quavered. He remembered the gold pebbles in Ludo's hand and looked again at the drawings Antelope Chaser had made in the soft earth. He knew that what the Indian said was true: they had traded him for a picture scratched in the dirt. The hurt of Ludo's betrayal was intense.

The terrible events of the massacre had blurred in his mind. That first night Ludo had given the boy the impression that he had rescued him from hostile Indians, and gradually Nils had come to believe it. Had wanted to believe it. Ludo had saved him. Ludo had been his friend.

But it was all make-believe. A dull ache settled in his chest, but he tried hard not to cry. Nobody wanted him. His ma had left him to go to heaven, where there was no trouble or sorrow and the angels sang all day. That's what Pa had told him. It didn't seem right for her to go to a nice place and leave him and Hannah behind. And then there was Pa. He'd just stayed asleep in the back of the wagon and let his son be carried off. He hadn't come after him, so that meant Pa didn't want him, either. Almost worse was his new ma's betrayal. She'd been the only one to ever say she loved him. At first he'd been embarrassed about it, and later he wasn't sure that she'd really meant it; but by the time they reached Westport he'd believed her. Bettany had lied to him. And Ludo had lied to him, too.

Nobody wanted him.

He ate the food Antelope Chaser gave him and settled into sullen misery. By the time they rode into the Comanche camp that afternoon he had isolated himself in a hard shell of anger and rage.

He let Antelope Chaser lead him into a big lodge where

an old man leaned in pain upon his painted backrest. "*Nei mataoya*, Grandfather. How are you?"

"*Nei chat.* I am well." The invalid struggled up the moment they entered, feigning a strength he no longer had. It cost him dearly to do so. "Who is this *tohobt nabituh*, and why do you bring him to this lodge?" he demanded.

"I have brought you my new son, for your blessing."

The old man thought a while in silence. Antelope Chaser's wives had borne him no children since he'd been marked by the spotted disease, and the old man himself longed to see a young face again in the lodge of his eldest son. He gave a grunt that signified acceptance.

"It is well for you to have a son again. *Suvate.* So be it."

The younger brave put his hand on the boy's shoulder. "From this day forth you will make your home with me. You will grow tall and strong within my lodge, and Medicine Bow, who is my father, shall be grandfather to you now."

His words, and the fact that they were in English, finally registered upon Nils, who'd been too tired to think about it last night, too shocked to notice this morning. He surveyed the Comanche brave with a frown. "You can *talk!*"

Antelope Chaser smiled. Did the boy think the only language was the one he had learned to speak? But he was young, and there was much he had yet to learn.

"I can 'talk' and do many things, and I shall teach them all to you." The Comanche had divined the deep loneliness that scarred Nils, and he chose his phrases carefully. "You will live in my lodge and be my son, as if you were born of my loins. You will become one of the People, and I shall teach you to be a great warrior—and you will never be alone again."

Never be alone again. The shell surrounding the orphaned boy cracked and fell away, leaving his soul naked and vulnerable. Nils felt his chin begin to tremble and fought to control it. He must not shame himself with tears. He believed that Axel and Bettany had abandoned him and knew that Ludo and Kearns had sold him as if he were an animal for trading, with no worth but what he would bring at market. Now, just when he was lost in the current of dark betrayal, Antelope Chaser offered him a secure refuge. A place of value in the world.

A warrior's life.

Although Nils didn't understand the emotions welling up inside him, he had a child's instinctive yearning to be safe. And loved. The hot anger he had felt toward Axel and Ludo and Bettany had changed into something cold and dead. But Antelope Chaser wanted him. He had even given away gold for him.

The Comanche watched the flicker of thoughts play over the boy's face and pressed his advantage. "Do you wish to do this? To have me for your father and to become one of my people?"

Not knowing what else to do, Nils stuck out his hand as he'd seen his father do when sealing a bargain. "I do," he replied solemnly. "And . . . and you won't be sorry. I'll be the bravest warrior of them all."

Antelope Chaser translated, but Medicine Bow already understood. The boy had pride and courage. Yes, this was a good thing that his son had done. While Nils shook hands with his adopted father, the elderly brave said a few words in his own tongue.

"He asks your name," Antelope Chaser said.

Nils turned to his new grandfather and drew a deep breath. "My name," he announced, "is Setanta."

Ten

THE WHIMPERING OF A SMALL, FRIGHTENED ANI-
mal impinged upon Logan's uneasy dreams. He wished it
would stop. He was much too tired to chase it away, his
body too heavy and earthbound. To drift away and lose
himself again in nothingness was all he wanted. The cries
persisted. He must stop them, somehow. Sluggishly he tried
to shake off his weariness and found himself unable to move.
The weight of centuries seemed to burden him, press him
deeper into the world of sleep and forgetfulness.

At last the pitiful sounds grew softer, less frequent. He
should have been glad, sinking gratefully into the tranquil
nothingness from which he had been drawn. Instead the
silence triggered a sense of desperation. With a supreme
effort he broke free, surging violently upward toward consciousness.

He groaned with pain and opened his eyes, aware for the
first time in many hours. The morning sun pierced his eyes
like bright spear points, and they closed in a spasm of agony,
but Logan had seen enough to orient himself. He lay half-
buried beneath the rubble of the collapsed talus slope. There
was no need to examine further. His bruised body marked
the location of every major stone and every sharp pebble,
and his skin was covered with fine ocher dust. Grit clogged
his tongue and ground between his teeth.

But he was alive.

He half dug, half dragged himself out from beneath the
debris, and small stones trickled loose with small nick-

ticking sounds. It reminded him of the sound a disturbed
rattler made. Then it happened again, when nothing moved
at all. He slid his glance sideways, in the direction of the
sound. An ugly coil of earth-colored muscle and venom
tensed in the sun less than four feet away. Logan froze,
weighing the accessibility of his Colt and the odds of it still
being serviceable, over the throbbing of his brain. If the
barrel and firing mechanism were as crammed with dust as
his mouth, it would prove more lethal to him than any
snake.

In the next split second he realized that he was not the
intended target, and that he was not alone. Hannah! She
was lying on her side with her back to him, unmoving; but
the light wind caught at strands of her hair and tousled
them carelessly. Dangerously.

The movement of her hair had attracted the rattler, and
that could prove fatal—if she was still alive. He couldn't
tell from his vantage point, but the nape of her neck was
fragile and vulnerable beneath the streaks of dirt. Logan
realized he'd been hearing her cries through the night and
that it was the sudden silence that had finally roused him.
The snake gave another dry rattle, loud and angry. Logan's
right arm was bent up alongside his head and felt as stiff
as a piece of wood. He tried to close his hand over a fist-
size rock. The numbed fingers refused to obey him.

Suddenly the girl whimpered, and the knowledge that
she was still alive galvanized him. He watched the rattler's
flat head move, tongue darting in and out, small eyes fixed
on its target, and calculated his own striking distance. The
snake lifted more of its length from the deadly coil. Quicker
than the eye could see, Logan twisted his booted foot from
beneath the talus, and the rattler shot out in a swift blur
of strength. Death struck, and was struck down in its turn,
as Logan's arm came down and the knife-sharp edge of rock
severed the snake's spine. Again and again the rock came
down until the thick, ropy body ceased its twitching and
went still.

Dripping with the cold sweat of reaction, Logan eased

off his boot, the fanged head and six inches of snake still hanging from the thick sides. He was glad he'd worn them, with their double walls of heavy leather and the thick moss insulation in between. He owed Hank Montgomery and his Paiute wife a great debt for adding the boots as a bonus with their last transaction. The next time their paths crossed he'd find some way to repay them.

He crawled over to the girl, every inch of the little journey painful beyond belief. Logan saw that his arm was black and blue along most of its exposed length and covered with long scratches. Although his entire body ached and throbbed, it seemed to be intact. He was fortunate to be alive and with full use of his limbs. His hand went to his medicine bag, tied to his belt. Perhaps old Buffalo Heart was right in declaring that he'd been born under a lucky star. At least where physical protection was concerned.

Hannah seemed to have been granted the same benefits. Except for the layers of dirt and a bruise near her right temple, she was unharmed. That in itself was a miracle, for Logan's horse had fallen beside her but not upon her, and the lingering warmth in its cooling carcass had protected her through the cold mountain night. He reached out and brushed the hair from her face.

"Hannah?"

She opened her eyes. They were wide and blue and innocent—and as blank as the morning sky. She shrank from his touch, but Logan pulled her up into his arms. "It's all right. You're safe. We're both safe."

He spoke softly and patted her back. After a few minutes the stiff little body relaxed against his chest and one hand clutched the front of his buckskin jacket. Hannah began toying with the fringe, and he felt a pang. Anna had done the same. Forcing away the pain, he smiled down at her.

"Well, little lady, we're safe and sound. Are you hungry? I'll bet you are." The sound of his voice soothed her even more. "I'll just skin this ugly customer, and in a short while we'll have us some rattlesnake steak. Then we'll be on our way."

She didn't respond. Hannah had found a shiny stone and was examining it closely, like a merchant inspecting a fabulous diamond. Logan jiggled her elbow. "I'll take you to your mother. You want to see her, don't you? Want to see your ma?"

Hannah nodded and gave him a dazzling smile. Logan grinned and leaned back against his dead horse. He was battered and bruised and hungry, with a thirty-mile walk ahead of him, carrying a small girl and a large saddle. It was enough to daunt any man, but he was incredibly, absurdly happy. He hadn't been able to help Anna, but at least this little one would be all right.

Hannah fell asleep in his arms, and he held her for a while, just for the bliss of it, then put her down and made a small fire. Once it was going good he began to skin the snake. There was more meat on the horse, but Logan never even entertained the thought as others might have. There was food and there were friends, and the two didn't cross categories in his mind. Friendship had been one of the cornerstones of his existence, and his estrangement with Small Eagle and self-imposed exile from the Cheyenne had been a trial by fire. He hadn't realized until now just how much it had cost him.

Suddenly Logan felt more at peace inside than he had for some time. Every man needed a home, a place or people to return to, a place that tethered a corner of his soul and kept it from floating away to become just one more lonely star, adrift in the blackness of the night sky.

He smiled. The past was put into its proper perspective. He and his foster brother would set the hurts and jealousies of the past aside as if they had never been. All that stood in the way was a quick trip to Fort Laramie, where he could unite Hannah with her mother.

Then he was going home.

Two men came riding side by side through the pink dawn, heading up the Laramie River toward its confluence with the North Platte. They rode well and carried quantities of fine pelts behind their saddles, but they had the well-fed appearance of men who lived in ease and comfort, not the knife-edged look of mountain men. Leaving the river, they angled northwest and began to scan the land ahead as if searching for something particular.

"Up there," the taller of the two said. "Straight past the shoulder of the hill. Should be right on the other side."

It wasn't long before they came upon the trail laid down by Angus McGrew's ill-fated wagon party: buff-colored earth churned to dust by hooves of horses and oxen and worn-out boots, and the grooves worn deep by the iron wheels where the wagons had gone single file. The tall man gave a soft bark of laughter. "The first of the overlanders— and most likely the last."

His companion pulled the ends of his mustache. "You think you're so damned smart, Eugene, but you talk too goddamned much. Gonna dig yourself a hole you can't crawl outta one day."

"Shut up, Shorty." He gave a scornful look at his companion's gray hat and the bullet hole that marred its brim. "The next time you collect your wages and go to Santa Fe, buy yourself a new hat. Makes you look like a fool."

"Me and this hat's been together four years. It's my good-luck piece. If I hadn't 've been wearing it, the bullet mighta gone right through my head."

Eugene shot him a withering look. "Sometimes I'm not so sure it didn't."

The sharp rowels of his spurs bit deep into the horse's sides and sent the gray bounding forward in long, nervous strides. By the time Shorty caught up with him, Eugene was at the edge of a meadow where sharply tilted rocks rose up to form a sheer-sided canyon. "Will you goddamn look at that. Looks like we got us a massacre, here."

Shorty reined in and pulled his bandanna up hastily to cover his mouth and nose. The stench of death was everywhere. "Shit! I never reckoned on this. You never told me you was gonna do this."

Eugene shrugged. "The boss said he didn't just want to

discourage any more settlers from coming through here—
he wanted to stop them. This ought to do it."

He rode out into the meadow, past the scorched wood
and the scattered bodies, both human and animal. The
Vandergroot wagon was still upright, although it had partially burned, and two of Small Eagle's arrows protruded
from the wooden frame. Shorty followed reluctantly as Eugene leaned down from his saddle and broke them off.

"Look here, Shorty. See these turkey feathers? Cheyenne
arrows. Seems like the mystery is already solved. Seems like
the Cheyenne are going to have to answer for this."

Shorty was in no mood for his partner's queer humor.
"Let's get outta here. This place gives me the creeps. Not
even a goddamn bird singing."

"It wasn't so quiet here yestidy. Not by a long chalk."

Eugene jumped down from his horse and moved among
the dead, searching their possessions. He found a few coins,
two lockets, and Letitia Renfrew's silver teaspoons. "Not
much pickings left. I wanted to get me a souvenir."

Something caught his eye on the Vandergroot wagon. It
was the shiny medallion Nils had found half-buried on the
banks of the Missouri, which he'd hung on the wagon for
good luck. Eugene scrutinized it, front and back.

"I reckon this is one of those medals that the Corps of
Discovery gave out when Lewis and Clark came up the
Missouri in 1804." He tucked it inside his pocket. "Make
a nice keepsake, don't you think? I got me a notion to have
it set into something. Maybe a belt buckle, or the front of
my saddle."

Shorty turned away in disgust. "I don't reckon any man
in his right mind would want a reminder of this. C'mon.
Let's light out for Fort Laramie and tell them what we
found."

"Hell, you're really spooked, aren't you? Well, let's just
make a circuit of the place first. Collect our evidence."

They went in opposite directions, circling around the
perimeter of the meadow. Shorty felt a shiver run up his
spine, as if he were no longer alone. He tensed for attack,

then let the strain ease away just as rapidly. A moan, disembodied and directionless, whispered around him. Whoever
hid among the rocks was no threat to him; but among the
sage and tufts of wildflowers, there were a hundred crevices
and folds where a body could be hidden. Eyes narrowed,
he searched for the slightest movement that might give a
clue.

"Where are you?" he called out. "I can't help you if I
don't know where you're at."

There was no answer. Whoever lay among the shadows
of the canyon walls was terrified that he was one of the
attackers, coming back to finish his evil work. Shorty tossed
a pebble off to his right and listened hard. With its rebound
came another sound from behind him as the injured person
instinctively recoiled.

"I won't hurt you," he said firmly. "I'm a white man.
I've got food and water. Just let me know where you are."

Something moved among the rocks, a deeper brown
against the umber walls, and he started toward it. A piece
of metal gleamed dully. A rifle barrel, he thought, and
ducked aside. There was no need. Even if it was loaded
and ready, the poor creature holding it had no strength to
cock it or pull the trigger.

Pity struck him as he crept up beside the victim. Jezus!
They'd really done a job on her!

Kneeling, he held his canteen for her to take a drink.
A young girl, brown-haired with terrified dark eyes. Her
lips were cracked and bleeding, her body bruised and
abraded so that the visible flesh was more purple than any
other color. She tried to drink but couldn't swallow, her
mouth was so parched. Wetting his bandanna, he held it
to her lips and moistened them. She rolled her eyes away
in a flash of white, frantic with fear and something more.
He realized she was trying to signal that she was not alone.

Shorty looked in the direction indicated and spied a
woman of middle years with long auburn tresses huddled
on her side beyond a line of sagebrush. She was so streaked
with dirt and mud that she'd seemed a part of the land

itself. Her hair was black with dried blood around the crown where a piece of scalp had been cut away, but the flap was still partially attached. Something had scared her attackers away. Despite the trauma of the scalping and the loss of blood, she clung to life by a desperate thread. One that would break before long. "Indians," she whispered.

Shorty brushed the flies away and wiped her lips with the dampened bandanna and thought furiously. He couldn't just leave them here to die, but what the hell would Eugene do? He rose and got back in the saddle and rode to the other man.

"We gotta put together some kinda wagon and hitch it up to our horses. Got us a couple of survivors to take to Fort Laramie. Can't leave 'em here to die."

Eugene's face twitched. "Survivors! There can't be any survivors. You know that as well as I do."

Licking his dry lips, Shorty tried not to look in the direction where the two women were hidden. He hooked his thumbs over his belt and frowned. "Witnesses," he corrected himself. "Witnesses to an Injun attack."

He watched the wheels and cogs turning inside Eugene's head and kept his right hand loosely over the butt of his gun. Eugene rubbed his jaw thoughtfully, then broke out in a sly grin. "You're right. The boss wouldn't like us to leave them here to die. Not witnesses to an *Indian* attack."

Looking around, he pointed at the remains of the Ebbersoll wagon. "We can make a cart of sorts from that to carry them." An idea seemed to strike him as humorous. "Why, all the newspapers back east will get ahold of the story. They'll call it the Laramie Massacre."

He poked Shorty in the ribs. "And they'll call us heroes."

Logan had expected to make it back to Fort Laramie in less than two days, but black clouds swept through the region, sending down a fusillade of hailstones so big they left bruises. For three days the sky cracked open, and rains like he'd never seen before poured down, accompanied by howling winds. They took shelter beneath a huge ledge of stone.

Past noon on the fifth day he arrived at the outskirts of the trading post with Hannah wrapped in his long shirt. A party of Sioux warriors was traveling up the flat plain behind the outpost, and a group of Arapaho squaws were setting up their tipis near the river. All in all some sixty people went about their business or idled in the afternoon sun.

Logan was thankful for his coloring, a legacy from his unknown parents. No one challenged him as he strolled through in buckskins, his dark hair caught over his shoulder with a thong. To the white men lounging by the gates he looked like just another half-breed Indian. Inbred caution made him reconnoiter the area before marching boldly inside the fort. He was passing a wagon loaded with trade goods when a grizzled Scots trapper stepped around the side. Logan thanked his luck that Hannah was still sleeping and pulled the blanket up to ensure she was well hidden as the man stopped in midstride. Keen blue eyes narrowed in doubt until they were almost swallowed up by the wrinkles.

Logan's insides tensed. The moment of truth had come, the first test. He took matters in his own hands, closing the gap between them. "It is a good day that we meet again, Malcolm Robertson," he said in the Cheyenne tongue.

The trader's frown vanished. "Wolf Star, by all that's holy! Thought I was seeing a ghost. Heard you'd disappeared somewhere up along the Yellowstone, years ago."

Logan smiled and settled back into his Indian identity. It was more natural than the one he'd worn as "Logan" in the white man's world. The lines of his body shifted subtly, as did the rhythms of his speech. "A man might hear many stories, none of them true."

"Aye, that's the right of it. Come and sit by my fire and fill up your belly. My woman's roasted an antelope haunch." Starting toward a tipi set off by itself, he let Logan follow and threw out a casual-seeming comment. "You fill me in on what Small Eagle is up to these days. Haven't seen him since the Rendezvous in thirty seven."

Every sense in Logan went on the alert. His foster brother should have arrived days ago with the woman. Logan tread carefully. "A man camping by Falling Star Rocks, he told me I would find Small Eagle here."

The Scot slowed his pace. "He hasn't been anywhere near the place since early spring, and if he wants to keep a whole hide, he'll stay away a lot longer. If he's to blame, they'll skin him alive and hang him from the flagpole."

"What are you saying? For what deed is he blamed?"

"A party of emigrants bound for California was massacred two days from here along the river. Cheyenne arrows found in one of the wagons. Had those special marks on them like Small Eagle always uses."

"Arrows found in a wagon, you say. But were arrows found in the bodies of the slain?"

Robertson scratched his whiskers. "That's a mighty good point, Wolf Star. You were always a canny one. The emigrants were shot or hacked to death. But the two females who were rescued afterward say it was Indians that did it all right. The young one is mending well, but the other one died soon after. Folks are up in arms about it."

The very air vibrated with danger. The smell of roasting antelope wafted on the crisp air, but there would be no convivial meal for Logan tonight. If Hannah awakened now, if one person saw him, a Cheyenne brave as far as the world could tell, carrying a white child—worse, if one of the survivors identified Hannah—there'd be no time for explanations: he'd be shot dead on the spot.

He looked grave. "That is evil news, indeed. I do not think I will stay here as I planned. May the Great Mystery bring you prosperity and health, Robertson. I cannot tarry."

"I think you're wise to move on, under the circumstances."

The trader watched as Logan mingled with a group of Arapaho and vanished in their midst. Robertson stared. The Cheyenne believed Wolf Star had magical powers—and he was beginning to believe it himself.

While the Scot was still pondering the matter, Logan

made a few swift purchases: a horse that was fast and strong, a warm buffalo robe, a packet of jerky, and he was on his way, just another "redskin" blending in with his fellows until the fort was far behind.

From the top of the ramparts, Josie Carter, healed from exposure and shock, if not from the emotional devastation, walked beside the wife of the chief company man. Mrs. Fleming guided her to a sunny spot on the ramparts. "Fresh air and sunshine is what you need, child. You've got to get out and face the world."

Josie turned her head away. She didn't want to face the world beyond the sheltering walls. It was a terrible place, offering only pain, misery, and shame. It had stripped her of everything she valued—even her identity. She had no memory of anything except the past before she and her husband had joined the wagon party. It had been a terrible shock to find herself in the middle of nowhere, and it was worse to be the battered victim of rape in everyone's eyes.

Mrs. Fleming understood Josie's feelings. There had been a day outside Edinborough when she had fallen victim to a stranger's unprovoked violation. She knew too well the overwhelming fear that followed and wouldn't allow Josie to sink into a despair from which she might never arise.

"I know it's painful, my dear, but you can't hide here forever. Perhaps tomorrow you'll accompany me for a short walk outside the gates. Just to the river and back."

Josie's stomach twisted into knots. Out there where everyone could see her? With a hundred wild Indians running loose? After what they told her had happened? After living with the pain and the scars and the scalding shame? She was sick of being pointed at and whispered about.

She glanced involuntarily at the open plain below them and then out across the western wall. Unfortunately it was just as Logan rode away. She was very long sighted. It was Logan's ill fortune that she had looked out at the exact moment Hannah awoke and poked her blond head out of his blanket.

"Oh, no! Stop him!" She clutched at Mrs. Fleming's

arms. "Someone must stop him. He's got a child. He's taking a white child."

It was more bad luck that Mrs. Fleming saw it, too, saw Logan push Hannah's head back down and pull the robe up over her. It was even worse that an ex–military man called Colonel Armstrong happened to be in Fort Laramie at the time. Armstrong's eyes glittered and he smiled coldly: Even if the girl's claim was unfounded, he could work the episode to his employer's advantage.

Don Miguel would be pleased.

Eleven

IN THE GHOST LIGHT OF APPROACHING DAWN, Small Eagle bathed in the stream near his solitary overnight camp. He had ridden out to hunt alone, to be away with his thoughts and away from the woman who dominated them. A light fog hovered a few feet off the ground so that his piebald pony appeared to be a creature of mists and shadows, gathering form and substance as he watched. Later, when the sun rose higher, it would be a fine day.

He carried his bow and a quiver full of new arrows, fletched with striped turkey feathers and painted with the alternating bands of yellow and brown and the single red dot. Since he and Wolf Star had gone on their first hunt so long ago, he had marked his arrows with his own personal sign. On that summer morning the two foster brothers had shot at the same antelope: one arrow had pierced the animal to the heart, while the other had barely nicked its rump. Despite his protests his father, Notched Arrow, and the other men had awarded the honor of the kill to Wolf Star. Even now, when the incident had been forgotten by everyone else, Small Eagle remembered. His wide hand clenched around the bow. That arrow had been his. His!

As he approached, the pinto whickered softly and offered its muzzle to him. Small Eagle stroked it absently, his mind going to the woman who slept in his lodge in Deer Creek Meadow. She was like no creature he'd ever seen or imagined: her strange, milky skin, her white woman's scent, and her eyes . . . her eyes! They were filled with shifting

145

lights, like the rippled reflections at the bottom of stream, and they had haunted his troubled dreams.

Small Eagle no longer thought of her as the Silver Woman his brother had spoken of. She was Warrior Woman, and he wanted her with a hunger that exceeded anything he had ever known. Wanted her and meant to have her, not by force or fear, but of her own need. And the sooner the better, for any day now Wolf Star might arrive.

His feelings were a confused amalgam of many things: admiration, desire, and the male need to possess mixed with a burning curiosity. Underlying all these was an urgency that had nothing to do with the woman herself, but everything to do with the jealousies and defeats of the past and his need to triumph over Wolf Star.

A chill wind sprang up out of nowhere, and a winged insect crawled along his forearm. He crushed it between his thumb and finger without even being aware of it. Recently, after many years' absence, he'd heard a voice as familiar as his own, one that had had no physical presence. That was when he'd known that Wolf Star had turned his back on the white-eyes world and his face toward the Cheyenne. At first Small Eagle had rejoiced, eager for the companion of his childhood, the friend who had been beside him all his days, like another self.

From their earliest days this power to call out to one another, silently but profoundly, had existed. Buffalo Heart had explained it was because they'd slept in the same cradleboard and been nourished by milk from the same breasts; but Small Eagle knew as well as the old seer that the source of the power resided in Wolf Star, the brother he loved and admired and envied and sometimes hated.

And now, complicating everything, there was the woman. She would be his, must be his. Not only in body, but in heart and mind and loyalty. She would be the one thing that his foster brother would covet and envy; and never obtain. But in order for it to work out as he planned, Small Eagle knew there was no time to lose. He must bind the woman to him before Wolf Star returned. Whatever it took to win her, he would do it.

It did not seem like an insurmountable task: he was a favored warrior, strong and handsome, a man who owned many horses, one any woman would be proud to take for her husband. But he must go carefully, for the woman had unknown and powerful medicine—eyes that could steal a man's soul from him. But first there was the hunt. He found a spot that had served him well before, a place where the upthrust of rock on two sides formed a funnel of land leading down to the river, and picketed his mount. Choosing a screened vantage point downwind, he settled in to wait. Just after dawn the antelope would come down to drink. Small Eagle chanted the prayer that would bring one to him and send his arrow deep and true.

"Come to me, antelope brother, give up your life to me, let your blood flow out into the earth that I might live." He felt at peace now that he'd made his decision and was instantly rewarded by a glimpse of pale hide gleaming through the trees. The arrow was nocked and ready. The bow bent as he pulled back the string of twisted sinew. Small Eagle felt the tension rise within himself as well. The chant continued in his head:

"Come, antelope brother, that you might nourish me, and live again. Come to me!"

The thong of twisted rawhide tautened, the arrow poised on the brink of flight. *"Come, my brother,"* Small Eagle sang softly. *"Let my arrow fly straight and true. Let it pierce your strong heart, your brave heart."*

And then the pale form moved out into the clearing, neither antelope nor deer, but a form even more familiar: Wolf Star!

From his aerie, Small Eagle watched his human brother riding down to the water, and for longer than necessary the arrow remained pointing down at Logan, aimed toward his heart.

Even when he'd awaited Wolf Star's coming near Spirit Mountain, Small Eagle had been divided. Part of him longed for the deep friendship they had shared, yet another, darker part of him felt resentment that was based on fear. Once again it would be Wolf Star who outshone all the rest at riding and hunting and raiding. Once again it would be Wolf Star to whom the men turned for leadership and at whom the young maidens smiled and sent shy, sidelong glances.

The words of the prayer echoed in his mind. *Come, my brother. Come to me. Let your blood flow out into the earth that I might live.* A film of sweat covered Small Eagle's upper lip. He drew the bowstring back the final increment and let the arrow fly.

Down below the bluff, Logan rode unsuspecting toward the river. Over the past days he'd thought mainly of Hannah's safety and comfort. Now he thought only of the woman whose child he had rescued from the renegades.

The woman. The Silver Woman. She had no other name, but every time her image came into his mind it was burned away by the visions of the blazing cabin and the skyward rush of sparks. She had taken possession of his thoughts, entrenched herself so deeply in his existence, waking and sleeping, that he hadn't realized the extent of it until now. Logan wished that he knew her name. Then he could label her and put her away in one of the locked compartments of his mind. Then she would have no power over him.

He angled down toward the river. There was no use dwelling on the woman. She was his responsibility for only a few more days. By then she'd back be back at Fort Laramie with Hannah, to await the next group of travelers heading east. To part with the child would be a wrenching experience, for Hannah's gentle, loving ways had won his heart; but life itself was always a matter of meeting and parting, of leaving or being left and of going forward alone. He would forget about them and pick up the scattered pieces of his life. Settled in among the people who had raised him, he would become again a Cheyenne brave and find the peace that he had sought so long and which had always eluded him.

Logan's lips twisted wryly. He certainly hadn't found it during his life among the white-eyed ones. So much for the bond of blood.

Suddenly the hairs rose along the nape of his neck. Danger. Somewhere above, on the bluff. He had the horse turned and his rifle ready in the blink of an eye.

As Small Eagle released the bowstring, he made a minute adjustment that altered the arrow's path. It sped through the air with a rush of sound and pierced the ground less than a yard in front of Logan.

Logan's horse tried to rear, but he controlled it and managed to keep Hannah from falling at the same time; but if she hadn't been secured by his soft leather belt, she would have tumbled off amid the flailing hooves.

Logan frowned up at the bluff. He had recognized the markings, of course, but the man who stepped out into the sunlight confirmed it: Small Eagle, up to his old tricks again.

Logan reined in his anger. This time he was determined not to let the old rivalry flare up. If jealousy still smoldered in Small Eagle's heart, he must be the last to fan the flames, no matter what the provocation; for once he reached the circle of Cheyenne lodges the man called Logan would vanish forever and only Wolf Star would remain.

The struggle had been long and hard. After years of wandering he had finally made peace with the demons that had driven him forth in the first place. But that had been in the past he was putting behind him now. Let Small Eagle enjoy the pranks he should have long outgrown. Logan's heart was full. His exile was ending. He was coming home.

He stopped to examine his horse's foreleg, and a moment later Small Eagle jumped from the ledge and landed lightly beside him. "I did not mean to frighten your mount, Wolf Star. Is the injury severe?"

"I'll have to walk him home. He won't be able to take my weight, but he can still carry Hannah."

Small Eagle turned his attention to the girl, who stared

at him placidly from the animal's back. "Hannah," he said cautiously. Her hair was fair and golden as summer sunshine, but otherwise she bore little resemblance to the woman he thought was her mother. The bones of her face were square and less refined, and her eyes lacked the quick intelligence that sparkled in the depths of Warrior Woman's.

She pointed to Logan and then the way ahead. "Go," she said softly. "Go!"

Logan looked up from his examination. "Don't worry, Hannah. You'll be back in your mother's arms before the sun is overhead."

"Not," Small Eagle pointed out, "if you walk all the way. We have moved from the Place of Plenty. Our lodges are above the bluffs, in Deer Creek Meadow."

Logan was greatly annoyed. He'd be lucky if he made it by nightfall. "I should take your pinto—but I'm not fool enough to go riding into the camp on your horse, without you by my side. I might get an arrow or a bullet through my heart before I got close enough for anyone to recognize me."

He wasn't exaggerating the danger. When raids or wars were frequent, men shot before waiting for positive identification. More than once in many bands, returning warriors had been mistaken for attacking foes. Logan had no wish to test the matter.

"Then," Small Eagle said, "I will take the girl to the camp and alert them to your coming. We will have a feast waiting for you."

Logan hesitated. The strain of the past few days had been more than physical. He was dog-tired. Hannah's safety had occupied him initially, and after Fort Laramie his own had concerned him as well. Added to that had been worry that Small Eagle and the woman had run into unforeseen hazards. His irritation showed. "Why didn't you go to Fort Laramie as we had planned?"

"As you rode off, Wolf Star, you shouted to me to take the woman to Fort Laramie. But you did not wait to hear my reply." Small Eagle eyed him squarely. "I did not think it was a wise plan, my brother. The men of Fort Laramie might have blamed our people, the Tsistsista, for the slayings—for who knew what the woman would tell them in her grief and terror? But if you brought the little warrior to her, she would have understood that we were not the same men who had destroyed her people. I expected you to overtake us along the way."

There was not a single argument that Logan could dispute, and his vague and unworthy suspicions shamed him. There could be no other reasons than those Small Eagle stated for taking the woman to the Cheyenne camp, for his dislike and mistrust of the *ve-ho-e* were real. After a moment's deliberation Logan decided that it would be best to let Small Eagle take Hannah to her mother in Deer Creek Meadow.

Over the time they'd been together he'd developed an affection for the gentle, dreamy-eyed girl. With every foot of the way he'd imagined—and eagerly anticipated—the moment of restoring her to her mother. And after all his fine plans, it would be Small Eagle who rode triumphantly into camp with Hannah in his arms.

He lifted Hannah down from the horse and handed her to his foster brother. "Don't be afraid. This is Small Eagle. He'll take you to your mother."

She let Small Eagle take her without objection, toying with the necklace of beads and bear claws that hung around his neck. Logan felt a pang of disappointment when Hannah didn't protest. Small Eagle shifted her against his shoulder, surprised at how easy it had been. He was anxious to be on his way. "Blue Morning Flower and Buffalo Heart will rejoice to see you."

"And I to see them."

When they were gone Logan checked his horse again. Better to let it rest an hour or so before going on. He made a poultice of moss, water plants, and mud and applied it to the strained foreleg. Then he stretched out beneath a tree on the grassy bank. He had all the rest of the day before him, and there was no real reason to hurry.

Bettany put down the doeskin shirt she was making for Blue Morning Flower when she heard the shouting. At first she couldn't believe her eyes when she saw the blond child riding before Small Eagle as he came along the row of lodges. Then she was on her feet and running. Face shining, she ran up to him and took the child he held down to her. "Oh, Hannah! Hannah!"

The girl's arms wound around her neck, and Bettany held her stepdaughter against her breast. In her heart she'd thought that she would never see Hannah again, but it seemed that at least some of her prayers had been heard and answered.

While Bettany kissed and caressed and filled Hannah's ears with sweet endearments, Small Eagle stood apart, observing. If he had thought Warrior Woman beautiful before, it was nothing to her beauty now. Her face was as blindingly radiant as the sun, and he longed for her warmth as the Earth, caught in the grip of Old Man Winter, yearned for the long, sunny days of the Time When the Cherries Are Ripe.

He let Bettany take Hannah into the lodge, followed by Blue Morning Flower and two of the older girls. A child was a child after all, a creature to be coddled and played with and loved, whether light-skinned or one of their own; and with so few among their band they made much of Hannah, giving her choice tidbits to eat and a string of smooth, shiny shells which she promptly put in her mouth. Her comical look of dismay brought a ripple of laughter from the onlookers. Hannah glanced from Bettany to the others, then broke into an answering smile of delight. In that moment she captured Blue Morning Flower's heart as surely as she'd captured Logan's. It would be good to have a child within her son's lodge. Perhaps, in time, there would be more.

Later, when Hannah looked sleepy, Bettany was about

to put her down for a nap, but Small Eagle gave the customary cough and entered. Without a word being exchanged, Blue Morning Flower picked Hannah up in her arms and went out. The two girls followed, the older one after a single speculative glance from over her shoulder.

Bettany cringed inwardly and tried not to show it. The moment had come. When Small Eagle had promised to find out about her children, she had known what payment he would exact. Now he had kept his word to her, and now she must make good her own promise. Schooling her features, she rose to her feet. Her palms were sweaty.

Even across the twenty feet of space separating them, Small Eagle sensed her emotions. He closed the gap slowly, thinking that he would gentle her until she showed no fear, touch her until she sighed with pleasure. For so many nights he had dreamed of this moment: she would be soft and warm, her body as wonderfully luminous as her face. Her breasts would fill his hands, softer than doeskin, with their pink, pebbled centers to tempt a man's mouth. A bolt of desire jolted through him, igniting the smoldering desire, burning away the last of his restraint.

Small Eagle quickened his step, suddenly aflame with a roaring, unquenchable need. He could not wait until nightfall. Not when Wolf Star was already on his way here. History must not repeat itself. She was his woman. His and not Wolf Star's. Until today he had pretended that she was only an object of curiosity and arousal, but most of all a playing piece in a game. The truth revealed itself to him. He wanted her, and he would have her. The game was ended, here and now—and he was the victor.

He reached out and placed his hand over her breast. Beneath his palm her heart beat wildly. Bettany stood quietly, awaiting his next move, afraid the wrong action on her part would catapult her into something she couldn't handle, hoping against all her instincts that he had not come to extract the payment she had promised.

Immediately she was ashamed of her ingratitude. Hadn't her marriage to Axel been similar? Her services as wife and

mother and cook in return for passage west? A few words
spoken before a preacher, a plain gold ring, and she had
been prepared to share the most intimate secrets of her body
with a man who had been a stranger.

This man of another race had saved her life and effected
Hannah's rescue. If he had no marriage lines or gold ring
to offer, what he had given her was priceless, and she must
never forget that.

He was so close now that his breath stirred her hair.
Bettany looked down at her hands. They were shaking.
Small Eagle followed her glance. His fingers closed firmly
over her wrist, and he placed her hand over his own heart.
Bettany felt the heat of his body and the accelerating
rhythm of his heart. He tried to unbutton her bodice, but
his fingers were unfamiliar with the task. He yanked impatiently at them, and she put out a restraining hand. "I'll
. . . I'll do it."

Turning to hide her embarrassment, she slipped the glass
buttons from their loops, one by one. When the garment
was undone she didn't know what to do next. Small Eagle
took charge. He stepped close to her back and pulled the
dress down over her shoulders, catching the wide straps of
her chemise at the same time. When she was naked to the
waist he reached around and cupped her breasts in his
palms, kneading them gently. Her nipples tingled and
swelled to his touch. Bettany was glad he couldn't see her
face and read the fear—or see the first faint stirrings of
something she didn't understand.

He pushed the clothing down past the flare of her hips.
Her skin was like the smooth shiny cloth that Smoke Along
the Ground's two wives had purchased at Bent's Fort the
previous summer, and she had a soft fragrance of her own.
He inhaled, pressing his cheek against her shoulder, watching his hands as they kneaded her breasts and moved down
over the womanly roundness of her abdomen. She shivered
but did not pull away. Elation sang in his blood. *Ah, she
desires me, this white-eyes woman, as I do her.*

He stripped the rest of her clothes away and pulled her

back against his loins, then lowered her to his sleeping pallet. He brought her to a kneeling position and held her when she tried to turn onto her back. He had heard the white people made their love in such an unnatural manner, but it was not his way or that of his people; and as his wife, she must learn his ways.

Gently, firmly, he indicated that she was to remain on her knees with her back to him. He caressed her buttocks and thighs and then leaned forward to touch his cheek to the contours of her spine. Her breasts were like ripe fruits against his seeking palms, and her woman scent overwhelmed him. He parted her legs and touched her intimately, feeling the spasms that ran through her body and thinking they were caused by pleasure. She quivered like a wild mare beneath his seeking fingers, and he made soft sounds that were meant to soothe, but had an opposite effect.

Bettany tried to close her mind against the shock of his touch and against the tendrils of sensation that were curling outward from the center of her body. Waves of cold ran over her skin, followed by waves of heat. She was unprepared for the piercing, and when he mounted her and thrust deeply she cried out once, sharply. But he held her tightly as he plunged himself into her, and his own hoarse cry was filled with triumph and passion. Bettany squeezed her eyelids shut against her tears.

Afterward he drowsed with his arm possessively over her while the sounds of camp life went on around them. Bettany, who had never even undressed before another woman, found herself lying naked with an equally naked man. She was sore and thoughtful. He had seemed to find enjoyment in the act, and she was relieved to have pleased him. He would have no reason to regret their bargain.

Even when she'd been afraid and wanted him to stop, she'd suspected that she might be sorry if he did; and if she hadn't wanted or enjoyed the experience—although there was a time when she had felt something pleasant happening, something building inside her that never reached fruition—

she was glad at least that it had been Small Eagle who took her over the threshold of womanhood and not her late husband. Axel had made her feel . . . soiled. Yes, that was the word. But this uncivilized Cheyenne warrior had made her feel desired.

She became drowsy herself but was unable to sleep. So this strange act she had shared with him was the dark, mysterious secret of what happened between man and woman. It certainly wasn't the stuff of poetry. Unless something was wrong with her. Some essential lack of womanliness or the capacity for passion.

Suddenly Letty Renfrew's bizarre advice came back to haunt her; but Bettany didn't think of curtains to take her mind off what had happened. Instead she thought of Hannah and all she owed this man who slept beside her.

It was dusk when Logan approached the Cheyenne encampment in Deer Creek Meadow. His old friends and their families gathered to greet him, and Buffalo Heart welcomed him as the son of his heart. Blue Morning Flower put Hannah down and hurried to embrace the foster son she loved so dearly, the son who had ridden away many years ago and had not returned until now.

"Ah, Wolf Star. I prayed that I might see your face again before I died."

Logan's heart overflowed. "My own prayer was similar." No matter who the woman was who had borne him, Blue Morning Flower was his true mother. She would not have abandoned him in the blizzard.

A feast had been prepared as Small Eagle had promised, and there was much joy and merriment. Logan searched the milling throng. Only his foster brother and Hannah's mother were missing.

"Where is my brother, Small Eagle? And where is the mother of this little *ve-ho-e* child?"

An outburst of laughter followed his questions. Smoke Along the Ground laughed loudest but was first to explain. "Blue Morning Flower has had to give up her lodge for a few days to her son and his new wife. *He-ha!* At this rate we shall not see them for weeks, for they have been making love all day. That one, he never tires."

Amid more jests Logan stood like a man paralyzed. "His wife?"

"Yes, and she is a brave woman, although not skilled in our ways. But she learns quickly. I am glad my son chose her. It is good for a man to have a wife and children in his lodge."

Logan was stunned and furious. "Has he taken leave of his senses? She must go back to her own people or they will make war upon us."

Blue Morning Flower sensed trouble and tried to head it off. "They do not even know that she is alive. Warrior Woman does not want to go back. She has taken my son of her own choice. He is a fine warrior, one any woman would desire for her husband."

Logan's face was terrible to see. He turned and walked away, into the night. No one dared follow.

The plaintive hooting of an owl sounded from one of the trees, and Logan stirred restlessly. Most of the Cheyenne had retired to their lodges for the night, but from his vantage point he could see a few men still talking and couples moving away toward their lodges. This was the Time When Horses Grow Fat, the season when the creatures of the woods and meadows set up their lodges with their chosen mates. All around he'd heard their rustlings as he walked the far boundaries of Deer Creek Meadow, making no more sound himself than the sighing of the night wind. Men followed the same cycles of nature, and in the circle of tipis the ancient patterns were being repeated.

He leaned his head back against a tree trunk. Over the mountains' dark bulk, light rippled across the sky in sheets of red and orange. Wildfire, leaping through the heavens. Loneliness swept through him in answer. There was no going back. Time had changed things among the Cheyenne, just as it had changed him. Just as it had changed the world. His thoughts took a dolefully poetic turn. More white men would come with their wagons, sweeping across the plains like wildfire, destroying the old ways. The boys he had known were men now with their own sons, but their children would never know the freedom or the peace that he and Small Eagle had known, growing up together.

His restlessness grew worse. Logan tried to fight it, but step by step he was drawn back toward the lodges. The thin-scraped hide walls glowed like embers from the firelight within.

Inside, the occupants were preparing to retire. They wouldn't sleep, not for a while. Small Eagle had made that clear to him—and to the woman. They had joined the feast belatedly, and Small Eagle had avoided any confrontations. Logan hadn't wanted to look at them, but time after time his eyes were drawn to his brother—and his brother's wife. Silver Woman.

Logan had watched the woman closely. She had stayed beside Small Eagle, glancing at him shyly from beneath her lashes; and when the time came to retire she had seemed willing enough, he thought. Certainly there had been no fear or signs of coercion. And that was that.

So much for the foolish dreams he'd harbored. Tonight, while he made his bed beneath the stars, his foster brother would lie upon a soft pallet with his new wife in his arms. He found Small Eagle's lodge among the others, the walls translucent from the light of the lodge fire.

A shadow moved, a small womanly shadow that added fuel to the fire in his loins and coldness to the chill spreading outward through his chest. He had been alone so long, but he'd been sure it would end with his return to this band of Tsistsistas. Instead he felt more isolated than ever.

Abruptly Logan turned away from the tipi and wrapped his blanket about him. One by one or two by two, the remaining men and women drifted away from the firelight into their own lodges, leaving him alone in the darkness.

Logan emptied his mind and concentrated on the glowing firelight. He had gotten through the time in prison by focusing all his powers upon one object, as Buffalo Heart had taught him, studying it in infinite depth until he merged with it. Until everything else was blotted out, even the pain.

Especially the pain.

But tonight Buffalo Heart's magic failed. Logan left the fire and wandered off into the darkness. He found the smooth saddle of rock where he had sat so many times before in years past, and leaned back against it. The stone was still warm with retained heat from the day's sunshine, but cooling rapidly. He longed for coolness to ease his heated body and quench the fire rising in his blood. A hopeless anger filled him. No woman should be able to create such turmoil in a man's heart.

Logan brought out his medicine bag, finding by touch the oval piece of silver and gold that was his special talisman. The religious medal fit in the hollow of his palm, light yet so cold that it stole some of the warmth from his hand. Where had it come from? Who had sewn it carefully inside his infant's swaddling? A woman, no doubt. But who had she been—and why had she even bothered?

Twelve

Mexico: 1811

"My daughter is unpunctual," Don Miguel said in irritation.

It was his custom to spend a half hour with his family and any guests before the household met for evening prayer, discussing matters of religion and philosophy. Ysabella had made it abundantly clear that she saw no reason to be included. The role of the women was to sit in the background, occupied by embroidery or some such work and listen quietly to the words of wisdom, as was proper.

Luis leaned back in the high leather chair. "Unpunctuality is a common womanly vice. Even my wife—a paragon of womanly virtues, is she not, Estrellita?—has no more sense of timeliness than a stone."

Estrella, sitting in a corner with her needlework, stiffened but didn't respond. The attempt to mollify his brother-in-law didn't succeed. Miguel frowned and addressed the third man. "Such womanly vices lead in time to other laxness. It offends my pride, Don Enrique, that you should witness my daughter's failings."

Don Enrique, that portly man to whom Miguel hoped to affiance his daughter, turned an unbecoming shade of red. He had neither the inclination nor the training to debate wisely with a man of Don Miguel's faculties. Words were sometimes like snakes, twisting around first this way and then that, changing their meanings to trap the unwary. He cleared his throat.

"Tardiness is a small peccadillo compared to true sins: a mere offense against one's fellow man rather than offense against God."

The spark in Don Miguel's eyes made the suitor think he had erred, but his regret was fleeting. His answer had been honest and in accordance with his conscience and the rules of heaven. It was the only way he knew to live with himself and his God.

Don Miguel was far from displeased. He took the blunt response as a good sign, for he had feared that Enrique had a dull disposition. Meekness in a husband caused discord within the family. A man must rule his hacienda as a king ruled his kingdom, lest there be anarchy. He poured his guest another glass of brandy and passed the decanter to Luis. Perhaps they could indulge in one of the philosophical discussions that were so dear to his heart. He sipped his brandy.

"And what is 'true' sin, my friends?"

Luis stretched out his long legs. "The greater sins are those which are a direct affront to God Himself. Sacrilege, worship of false gods, persecution and martyrdom of the clergy and the faithful. But these are not as frequent, I think, as the lesser sins."

It was not the custom for the women to engage in these debates, only to be present. Estrella had been engrossed in her embroidery in the far corner of the parlor, but her attention was focused on her brother-in-law's response.

Don Miguel nodded. "These sins affront God but are directed toward our fellow man—theft, lying, coveting another's goods or wife. The sin of lust."

Their frank discussion astounded Don Enrique. Such matters were not for the ears of modest women. It was no wonder that Dona Estrella had tried three times to thread her needle and three times missed the eye.

Luis had noticed it, too. He savored his brandy, rolling it around on his tongue. "And what of the sins that are an outrage to both God and man? Should the punishment of these belong to man or to God? I refer to murder, rape, and incest."

Estrella gasped as the needle stabbed her finger and a drop of blood welled up. Like a woman in a trance, she watched it grow until it spilled over and dripped on the white linen caught in her wooden frame.

Ysabella's erstwhile suitor was now on the verge of apoplexy. He did not wish to be rude to his host, yet it was more than time to change the subject. "I think," he said at last with an apologetic smile, "that nothing you or I might say over a glass of brandy could touch on all the ramifications of sins so grave as these. I will leave them to the courts of law and the judgment of God; for if they are not punished in one, they will be surely be tried and sentenced by the other."

Ysabella hurried into the *sala*, her face set in sullen lines. Luis rose with the others, then came to stand beside Estrella and admire her handiwork. "Why, you have pierced your finger. I have known you to be many things, Estrellita, but never clumsy."

She sat silent while he bound up her hand with his own handkerchief. When it was done, Luis smiled down at her tenderly. "How fortunate that I am here to rescue you from yourself."

It was late when Estrella checked on her niece. Ysabella sat at her desk by the light of a branch of candles, barefoot and in her white nightgown. "What, still awake? You should be asleep, *querida*."

The girl finished the line she was writing and set down her quill. "I have started a journal like yours. Tío Luis brought me this one from Mexico City. Is it not elegant?" Ysabella was thoughtful. "I wish Father would let me read my mother's diary. I am old enough, and I should like to know more about her."

A bolt of fear shot through Estrella. There was some knowledge it was best to leave alone. If Julianna's diary had not already been destroyed, it was high time that it was. "I will speak to your father."

Estrella kissed her niece and went out, pulling the door carefully shut behind her. Her own room was around the corner at the far end of the passage. In the morning she would move her things to one of the empty chambers closer to Ysabella's. The morning sun, she would explain, wakens me too early. Yes, that would do nicely.

The door to her own room stood ajar, and very little light came through the open windows, but it was enough so there was no need for a candle. She entered and shut the door. As she slid the bolt across, a piece fell to the floor with a jangle. Juan would have to repair it in the morning. He could make one for Ysabella's chamber at the same time.

After a brief hesitation, Estrella lifted a small chest and put it in front of the door. Then she stripped off her garments and hung them on pegs in the carved and painted cupboard. There was nothing to fear. She was a woman grown and not a naive girl, unable to protect herself.

She undid the laces that held the bodice of her shift together, then poured water in the washbasin and dipped a cloth in it. The cool water was refreshing after the day's heat, and she wiped it over her face and throat and down between her breasts. If only she could wash away the turmoil within her so easily. It had been five years since Luis had left the hacienda, and she had never expected to see him again. Should she speak privately to him—or to Miguel? Or should she continue her burden of silence? Estrella dipped the cloth into the water again and wrung it out.

She hadn't heard a sound, but a hand clamped over her mouth and an arm snaked around her, pulling her back against a hard chest. "Allow me to do that for you, *querida.*"

She recognized his scent, his voice. Luis! She could envision the dark flush across his handsome features and the small smile of triumph that must be flickering over his lips. "Luis, let me go or I shall scream." Her words were muffled behind his strong hand.

"You should have lit the candle and checked the room before you bolted the door. Anyone could be lurking in the corners of your chamber, *querida*. A murderer, for instance. Or a rapist overpowering you."

His arm moved up to press against her neck, compressing her windpipe. "I could throttle you before you made a sound. But I have other plans for you tonight. It has been too long."

He took the cold, wet cloth and stroked it over her breasts until her nipples were hard and erect. Then he pushed it down below the waist of her open shift to caress her abdomen. She reached out for the pitcher and tried to swing it backward at his head, but Luis caught it easily.

He turned her around in his arms. "Why do you pretend to fight with me, Estrella? You know that you have longed for this moment."

He was right, and she felt sick with the knowledge. After all this time she had thought herself immune. She had convinced herself that she found him loathsome. But one touch of his hands on her naked skin and all the old feelings came pulsing back to life.

Tears sparkled in her eyes. "Why do you humiliate me like this?"

"We are two of a kind, you and I, although you would never face up to it." Luis drew her closer, his face half-hidden in shadows, and ran the ball of his thumb over her bottom lip. "We should have married, Estrella."

She wrenched herself away, tears of rage and humiliation filling her eyes. "Knowing what you are!"

Even in the moonlight she could see his face darken. His fingers dug into her shoulders. "You would throw my mother's shame in my face?"

She wasn't listening. "Go away, I beg of you. Leave this place at once and never come back. What we . . . what I once felt for you is dead. Dead as I am. Every night I thanked God that you were gone, and every night I prayed that you would stay away from me."

"Yet you have never married, you live the lonely life of

a virgin." He voice was low and husky against her throat. "Be truthful, Estrellita. I have ruined you for every other man."

"What man would want me, once he knew? You have ruined me in many ways. I am unmarried because I have no desire for any man."

"Do you not?"

She stepped back, but he came closer in the dark. So close their bodies were touching.

His long fingers captured her wrist and held it, while his thumb caressed the sensitive underside. A spasm jerked through her body, but she was unable to pull away. "Feel how your skin quivers beneath my touch. Just as it did that first time. Do you remember, *mi amada*? You did not push me away then. You took me as your lover."

She turned her head, overwhelmed by memories: the grove beside the stream, the scented grasses of the meadow—the need, the heat, the irrevocable moment of his piercing. The wild joy and the dark shame that came after it. "Once you were my hero, Luis. I loved you innocently. But I was young and sheltered, too inexperienced to withstand your practiced seductions. I trusted in my love, trusted that you would never hurt me."

His anger flared. "I never forced you. I gave you what you wanted, but up to that final moment, I would have stopped if you'd ever once said the word. You wanted me, Estrellita. Just as you want me now."

As if against her will she faced him again, surveying the aristocratic line of cheek and jaw that haunted her dreams. "You have the face of an archangel, Luis. But I think you are the Devil himself."

"You blame only me. But I think, Estrellita, that we are cut from the same cloth. Like your late sister-in-law, Julianna, you are a whore at heart."

"No!"

His teeth gleamed whitely as he smiled, lowering his mouth to hers. She endured his kiss without participating, but he put his hand upon her breast and felt the accelerating rhythm of her heart. He cupped the fullness of her breast in his palm and heard the hiss of breath between her lips.

"I have missed you, *querida*. I have thought of you and of what I am going to do to you now a hundred times—a thousand times."

His knee thrust between her legs and she lost her balance, tangled in the long skirt of her shift. Luis caught her as she fell and lowered her to the small runner that lay beside the bed. Her face and breasts were exposed, pale as alabaster in the shaft of moonlight, and she knew that he had planned even this. Already her gown was bunched up over her hips and his hands were exploring the insides of her thighs, tenderly, urgently.

Estrella could not quell the great surge of longing that washed over her. Her soft cries were part protest, part acknowledgment of her terrible need. Five years. *Five years!* Luis lowered himself over her, and she reached up to him, weeping. "We will both burn in hell for this."

"Ah, my sweet life, but first I will show you heaven on earth." He touched and teased and toyed with her until she was wild with desire, hating him and hating herself for it. Yet when he entered her she cried out in welcome, arching up to meet his thrusts. Five years! Five years of loneliness and denial, of physical longing to be held, caressed. Consumed.

Luis took her roughly, as he knew she wanted to be taken; but afterward he held her in his arms and covered her face with possessive kisses. "When I lie with Pilar, in the hope that she will give me heirs of my loins, it is your face I see behind my closed eyes, your body I feel beneath my hands." He touched her cheeks. "You are mine, Estrellita. Say it. Say it!"

Although her body was still flushed and damp with sweat, her face burned with shame in the silvery light. "You are another woman's husband, Luis. This cannot—must not—happen again. I will not allow it."

"You say that now, but you don't mean it. Your own body betrays you, *mi amada*." His voice was fierce with triumph. "You are mine for the snap of my fingers."

"I hate you." Her palm connected hard with the side of his face. "From this night on, my door and windows will be barred. Stay away from me or I will kill you. And stay away from Ysabella until the day you leave."

Luis took her hand, the one that had struck the blow, and kissed her fingertips. "Ah, jealous little cat. Who would expect that such passion lies below so cool and pristine a surface? But that is what draws me to you. Ice beneath the fire, and fire beneath the ice."

He wove his fingers in her hair and yanked her head back, exposing her throat, and ran the tip of his tongue down it to the V of her breasts. She went weak and pliant in his arms. Luis's mouth moved lower.

"But didn't I tell you, Estrellita?" he murmured. "My dear wife is consumed with her imagined illnesses and the care of her house. I am not eager to return to that, I assure you. And your brother seeks my assistance here.

"I am to help him build up his empire so that someday Ysabella's son might inherit it."

The corners of Luis's lips twisted. "He will give me gold for my assistance, but not land. Never the land. How could someone as proud as the aristocratic Don Miguel share his estates with a man he knows to be 'tainted' with mestizo blood!"

Estrella tried to break his spell. "If you hate him so, then leave. Go back to California and your wife. Let me spend out my days in peace."

Her efforts crumbled away at the intimate touch of his hand, and a shudder ran through her whole body. Luis exulted in his control over her. She must never know that she was really the one who controlled, that his passion for her was the real reason he'd come back despite Miguel's unsuccessfully hidden disdain. What had begun as vengeance had ended in obsession. The seducer had become the seduced.

His mouth skimmed hotly over the crest of her hip, the

satiny skin of her belly, then lower until she was helpless
to protest. "My beautiful Estrella," he whispered hoarsely,
"you are under a misapprehension. I have no plans to leave,
ever. I have come back to stay."

Thirteen

Deer Creek Meadow: 1840

Bettany watched Elk Horn, one of the Contraries, back out of his lodge. The warrior societies, like the Red Shields and the Dog Soldiers, made sense, but she couldn't understand why some of the men did everything backward or opposite. Small Eagle had explained that Elk Horn was afraid of thunder, as if that would make everything clear. It had only confused her further. Then there were the *Hee man eh*, the "half men/half women," who dressed like old men but otherwise adopted the ways of women. The *Hee man eh* were camp favorites and noted matchmakers, and Hannah was fond of Elk Horn and his comrades.

Slowly Bettany had grown accustomed to life in the Cheyenne camp. At first all the Indians had looked alike to her, but as the days went by she realized she had been blinded by ignorance and fear. She had discovered that they were men and women who felt the same emotions she did, who laughed and loved and sometimes wept the same as she. But at other times they seemed as alien to her as people from the moon.

Their humor sometimes struck her as cruel, but she admired their stoicism and their ability to survive in such hostile circumstances. Their delight in family life and joy of living warmed her heart, but it was their acceptance of Hannah that mattered most.

She had been accepted into the community of the band far more readily than Bettany had imagined possible—far more readily than a Cheyenne child would have been in any white community. Bettany understood that her own acceptance was provisional, and walked carefully between her world and theirs. Any serious misstep could result in disaster—for herself, for Hannah, and for Nils. She hadn't given up hope that Small Eagle would effect her stepson's rescue, just as he had managed to bring Hannah safely back to her arms. And then—what?

The choices were few and unsatisfactory. Could she stay among the Cheyenne, forfeiting forever her chance of being among her own kind and surrendering Hannah's and Nils's futures as well? Or could she turn her back upon the man who had saved her life, by leaving him at the first opportunity? Small Eagle considered her his wife, but she did not think of herself that way. Of one thing she was certain. Small Eagle would not let her go willingly.

Any attempts to reach a white settlement would have to be made clandestinely, and with no assurance of being taken in if she ever reached it. If the talk among the wagon party had been correct, the only form of life considered lower than Indians was a woman who had consorted with them. Even for the children, could she face the scorn and revilement that would be her lot?

Torn in so many directions, Bettany lived in an agony of indecision and divided loyalties. She tried to lose herself in her daily tasks, emptying her mind of all but the work at hand. The attempt was unsuccessful. As she stretched a hide, the nape of her neck prickled. All morning she'd had the feeling she was being watched. Looking up, she saw Small Eagle and two Arapaho braves lounging beneath a tree a dozen yards away, discussing yesterday's hunt, from the looks of their gestures. It was the fourth man, a little apart from the others, whose eyes turned her way.

Thorson rode up and dropped a brace of sage hen at her feet. "Here's your supper. And you'd better stop staring at a man who's not your husband like that or there'll be trouble. The Cheyenne don't cotton to carryings-on."

"Don't be ridiculous. That is Wolf Star, Small Eagle's brother."

She'd noticed him before, even though he always kept his distance. There was a separateness about him that had caught her curiosity. The others seemed to hold him in respect, even affection; yet wherever he went he was surrounded by a circle of isolation as if he were a spirit moving through the ranks of men. A shiver ran up her spine. "There is something different about him."

Thorson chuckled. "Aye, that there is. He's a white man, raised since he was a squalling pup by Small Eagle's folks. Found him in the snow, protected by a she-wolf and her mate."

"Protected by wolves? A highly unlikely occurrence, I should think."

"According to these folks, Wolf Star's special, said to have powerful medicine. Long ago Buffalo Heart prophesied that Wolf Star would save the Cheyenne from great evil one day. They set great store by omens and such."

Bettany sent him a wry look. The big Swede had his own superstitions: around his thick neck hung a fob with a Masonic emblem, a crucifix of Spanish silver, a Chinese coin with a square hole in the center, and badge of doeskin beaded with the Cheyenne symbol of the Morning Star.

He grinned back. "Every little bit helps."

Hannah came skipping up to Bettany and thrust out a scrap of carved wood for her to admire. "Pretty."

Bettany examined the article. It was a clever piece of work. She could see where the natural contours of the root had been followed with only a deft cut here and there to find the shape of a young foal with its lanky legs tucked beneath its body. "Yes, it is very pretty. Where did you get it?"

Hannah started to point, then frowned. The man who'd given it to her was gone. As soon as Bettany took the carving in her own hand, she guessed its maker. She rubbed the ball of her thumb over the smooth wood, taking pleasure in the satiny feel of it. Her interest was piqued. Wolf Star.

A white man living among the Cheyenne. She might be able to use him to her advantage.

The wind sighed through the cedars high above Deer Creek Meadow as Bettany strolled beneath. She had taken Hannah up along another branch of Deer Creek. Hannah ran ahead, then stopped, enchanted by sapphire wings fluttering among the wild roses.

"Look!"

Hannah was learning to speak at last. To speak Cheyenne: her delighted cry at noticing the colorfully winged insects had been in the Indian tongue. Bettany sighed.

"Yes," she answered in careful English. "Butterflies. Beautiful blue butterflies."

Hannah looked up at her in such a puzzled way that it was clear she was already forgetting her own language. How simple life had been back at the Susquehanna orphanage and even on the rigorous Oregon Trail. Bettany's present life, while simple in style, was incredibly complicated. There were so many other things to consider—and so many riddles without answers.

While Bettany was caught up in her musings, Hannah had settled down on her side to watch some ants at work. If left alone, she would stay that way for hours, lost in some private world of her own. The heat of the sun and the nearness of water were too much for Bettany. She stepped to the edge of the creek. It flowed deep and silent here, a place of mysterious shadows and moss-lined pools.

Quickly slipping out of the moccasins she had received in trade for her boots, Bettany dangled her feet in the water. It was too tempting. In a flash she was out of her garments and into the creek. Her soles touched deposits of stones polished by years of wear, and the water rippled past her like flows of silk. Without soap she could do little more than soak, and she stayed near the bank where she was close to Hannah.

A loud splash upstream startled her, and she saw the sparkling droplets crash back into the creek. What kind of animal had made so much noise? Curious, and more than a bit apprehensive, she scrambled to her feet as a dark shape cleaved the water. It arced toward the shallows and curved up, erupting into a patch of brilliant sun. For a few seconds her vision was obscured by the glory of the splashing water as it caught the sun and threw it back. When it settled down she saw the cause.

It was no woodland creature but a man, his bronzed body spangled with droplets of light. His back was to her, and she stared openmouthed, not at his sinewy strength and solid muscle, but at the pale skin below his waist. Skin very like her own. He turned at her soft gasp. Wolf Star. Bettany gaped at him.

He splashed through the shallows. "What the hell are you doing here?"

"I was just . . . but . . ." Bettany was thoroughly confused. "But you speak English."

That made it worse somehow. She averted her eyes, but not until after she'd seen a good deal more of him than she'd intended. And he had evidently seen as much of her. Bettany crouched down beneath the water, vainly hoping that the shifting patterns of light upon its surface would offer some cover.

Belatedly Logan grew aware that her embarrassment was greater than his own. Still, he couldn't look away. A dozen seductive images taunted him: the sheen of her skin, like precious pearl beneath the water, the supple shapes and curves of her body, her long hair floating out about her shoulders like strands of silver in the dappled light. Moments passed and he could neither move not speak. She took his breath away.

Bettany was under a similar spell, but one cast by fear. Until now she hadn't realized his height and apparent strength. Although the Cheyenne were a tall race, this man was much larger than Small Eagle, and his angular face was so dark and grim that it filled her with alarm.

He took a step toward her, and the water streamed down his ribs and beaded along the corded muscles of his arm.

Bettany groped in the stream bed for a suitable rock but
had to dig her fingers in to grasp it. It came loose suddenly,
and she overbalanced and catapulted backward into the
creek. She banged her head against the bank and took in
a gulp of cold water. Logan acted reflexively and grabbed
a handful of her long hair, yanking her up violently. She
came up sputtering and coughing, with her scalp on fire.
The struggle that ensued left him with a bruised rib and
toothmarks on his arm and ended with Bettany pinned
against his chest.

"Damn it. I was just trying to help you," he said furiously.

"Is that what you call it? I can do without your help. Let
me go."

"Very well. But the next time you go bathing, make sure
your 'tub' isn't already occupied."

He released her and turned away while she scrambled up
the bank and snatched up her clothes. Taking Hannah by
the hand, she hurried away from the meadow; but long after
she was gone he could still feel the warm imprint of her
body where it had touched his. The ache inside him grew.
He swore softly beneath his breath. She was his brother's
wife.

For the first time he doubted the wisdom of returning to
live among the people who had raised him. Unless he
learned to control it, his envy of Small Eagle would corrode
his soul and eat its way into his very heart.

Bettany went down to the creek for fresh water, passing
a group of men along the way. One shifted his position ever
so slightly to watch her progress. She didn't have to look
to know it was Wolf Star. Since that day at the river they
had avoided each other, but she was increasingly aware of
him. When she handed him a portion of food and their
fingers touched, however briefly, it was like touching a hot
coal. They seemed to be connected by a thin silver thread
that vibrated to the slightest change in mood or position.

It was unnerving. Bettany was glad that it was not Small
Eagle who made her feel so giddy and aware and off-balance.

Then it would be harder to put her careful plans into ex-
ecution when the moment arrived. Soon, she hoped, Nils
would be with her and she could begin. When Nils came
to camp she would go on as she had the past weeks, making
no outward changes but continuing to cache supplies. Then
some fine morning when Small Eagle and his comrades were
out hunting, she would steal a horse and ride away with
Hannah and Nils to Fort Laramie.

After their meeting in the river, Logan pretended she
didn't exist. The weather was mild and he made his bed
outside, away from the others. It was a habit he'd acquired
trapping alone along the Yellowstone. His stays in St. Louis
and Santa Barbara, living behind walls and beneath roofs,
had made him appreciate a night beneath the open sky all
the more. The time he'd spent in jail with Halsey and his
men had given him a greater abhorrence of confinement.
And the aftermath of his sojourn with Cassie and Anna
had taught him not to let anyone get too close again. He'd
been in danger of forgetting that lesson.

Night after night he slept alone, listening to the sounds
of nocturnal creatures and the whispering of his own heart.
He had come back to the Cheyenne, knowing that it was
where he belonged, sensing his destiny lay with them; yet
night after night he watched Small Eagle and his new wife
retire to their tipi and fought his jealous desire.

On the night of the new moon the rains came, and he
sat inside Small Eagle's lodge with Runs Far and Limping
Elk, telling tales of long-ago days. Blue Morning Flower
had curled up earlier on her pallet and was fast asleep. How
many inclement evenings had they passed in just this way
before?

Logan leaned back against the painted backrest, listening
to his friends and pretending the intervening years had
never existed: he and Small Eagle had never quarreled, he
had never left the Cheyenne, and the old harmony had
never been disrupted. Then the woman leaned forward into
his line of view, destroying all his peace.

The woman. He tried to think of her that way. Not as

Counting Coup Woman or Warrior Woman. Certainly not
as Bettany Howard or Bettany Vandergroot, although he'd
learned her white woman names. The wind howled, blowing smoke back into the room, and she rose to adjust the
"ears" of the lodge by altering the position of the long poles
affixed to them. Her breasts strained against her garment,
and he had to look away. The lodge cleared, but the boom
of thunder and the rattle of hail seemed to shake the ground.
Runs Far laughed as the thunder crashed again.

"I must return to my own lodge. Can you not hear my
old woman shouting for me? How loudly she calls!"

The others laughed at his joke. The wife of Runs Far was
a gentle woman with a voice so soft, it was difficult to hear
across the width of a cook fire. "Go quickly," Small Eagle
told him, "for a good wife is as important to a warrior as
his horse."

Everyone laughed except Bettany. She understood suf-
ficient Cheyenne now to follow their conversation, but she
hadn't lived among them long enough to recognize her
husband's words for the compliment they were. To compare
a woman to a horse!

Logan read her thought as if she'd said it aloud. She
didn't understand. How could she? But either her annoy-
ance or the heat of the fire had brought a bloom of color
to her cheeks. He thought if he touched her face, it would
be warm against his palm and soft as the downy feathers of
a newly fledged bird. And he thought that he had no business thinking such things about his brother's wife.

Drawing his buffalo robe about him, he prepared to follow
Runs Far from the lodge. Small Eagle stopped him. "Only
a foolish man would attempt to sleep outdoors in the face
of such a storm. You will stay here tonight, within my
lodge."

Logan felt the air thicken about him, stifling his lungs.
He tried to make light of it. "I have been wet before."

For once Small Eagle refused to agree. "Already there is
talk. They say that you would rather live like a wild creature
than accept the hospitality of my lodge."

There was challenge in every line of his face and a kind of hurt pride that Logan recognized. "Very well." He took a place on the opposite side of the fire from the one customarily reserved for members of the family and rolled up in his robe.

Small Eagle noticed but didn't comment. He also meant to roll up in his robe and go to sleep; but the banked fire dimmed beneath its coat of ash, and the scent of Warrior Woman's hair was like the fragrance of wildflowers on the wind. Desire bloomed within Small Eagle's loins. He reached out and covered her mouth gently with his hand against her murmured protests. Her flesh, so soft beneath his seeking hands, inflamed him more. She was a modest woman, he knew, but with the robe thrown over them she had no reason to protest.

And as for Wolf Star, what of it? This was the way of a man and wife.

Bettany had become used to her husband's customs, but Blue Morning Flower was a sound sleeper. This was different. Beyond the dim glow of the fire a man lay awake. A white man. She remembered how he had looked, rising in splendor from the waters of the creek like a primeval god. She remembered every line of his body, outlined in fire as the sunlight caught the film of water covering him. She remembered the flash of hunger she'd seen in his eyes, before they'd shuttered against her. She closed her own.

Logan heard the rustling and the murmur of voices and recognized them for what they were—not merely the sounds of a man and woman sharing the most intimate of acts, but a declaration of ownership, a tally of possessions. The old animosities had been buried, but they hadn't died. He could see into Small Eagle's thoughts with as little effort as it took to understand his own: *Know what I have that you do not, my brother, for I have seen the longing in your face and read your heart.* He wondered, if the circumstances were reversed, if he would feel the same way.

Logan slowed his breathing and tried to slow his pulse the way Buffalo Heart had shown him after his Vision

Quest. He had often passed the terrible nights in St. Louis by leaving his body behind while his soul soared free. Tonight the power he sought was gone and he was tethered hopelessly, helplessly, to earth.

Fourteen

SMOKE ALONG THE GROUND WAITED UNTIL THE
pipe passed back to him again. "Then it is agreed," he
announced. "The Comanche and their allies seek peace.
We will send a delegation to the southern Cheyenne to
arrange a meeting at Bent's Fort."

He began calling off the men in the circle by name,
skipping over Logan, Small Eagle, and most of the younger
ones. Small Eagle protested heatedly. "Have I not taken
part in many meetings before? Is my tongue not persuasive
enough, or is it my prowess as a warrior that you doubt?"

Logan put a restraining hand on his arm. "After the false
story I heard at Fort Laramie, it is better that you do not
display yourself so publicly yet."

"Malcolm Robertson is a fool, and so is anyone who
thinks I am afraid to face any white man who may speak
against me."

It was time for Buffalo Heart to intervene. "Your honor
and valor have never been in doubt, Small Eagle, but what
Wolf Star says is true. It is best if you remain behind." He
nodded his head. "I have spoken."

Logan went out, and Small Eagle followed his foster
brother. It was a warm day with a light wind, the kind that
stirred a man's blood with possibilities of adventure. He
was ill pleased with the decision of the council.

"I will not stay here by the fireside like an old woman.
There are many fine horses among that band of Utes at the
Place Where the Bear Died. Horses too fine for Utes, but

good for the Tsistsistas. Come, Wolf Star, let us go raiding."

Logan shook his head. "Take Horse Nose and Knows His Brother and their nephews. I'll stay behind with Spotted Bull and Five Calves." He kept walking, aware that his companion had stopped in surprise. Logan was halfway to the river before Small Eagle caught up with him.

"Always you were the boldest of warriors, the first to count coup, the last to fall back before the enemy. The white-eyes have done something to change you."

"If I am different, the cause is within myself. My eyes have seen too many things. . . ."

Logan stared off across the bluff toward the river, and for a moment his vision was dazzled—not by the bright sun, but by the soaring sparks and the burning cabin reflected from his soul. "I have grown weary with death and killing. Life is too short to squander it at foolish, deadly games."

Small Eagle went away, dissatisfied and baffled. Raiding kept a warrior quick and strong. It was not a game.

On a cool, clear morning when the sky was as blue as a robin's egg, Small Eagle prepared to ride out with his hand-picked group of braves. First they would proceed to the lodges of the Arapaho, their allies, and add one or two of their most daring warriors to the raiding party. The whole camp was out to see the raiders off, shouting encouragement or teasing comments. Not quite masked beneath the commotion was unspoken concern, at least among the women. All except the youngest children understood the hazards involved: when the raiding party returned their numbers might be fewer, and somewhere in Ute territory a husband, brother, son, or friend anticipating victory might meet with death instead.

Even Blue Morning Flower was not exempt from a touch of anxiety, but her only remark gave no clue of it. "Your husband," she said to Bettany proudly, "is first among all the warriors."

On White Thunder, his favorite pony, Small Eagle was

indeed the embodiment of his people's legendary heroes. More than one woman felt the impact of it, and at least three thought, with pangs of deep regret, of what might have been. To Bettany he looked strong, confident, and full of savage beauty; but her admiration for that beauty held the detachment of someone admiring the grandeur of a mountain or the simple grace of a hawk on the wing. Her eyes were not those of a lover.

Small Eagle was very aware of it. The only time she showed any real animation was when she played with her daughter or watched the girl from afar. Then the lines of strain eased from her face and her strange clear eyes—eyes whose silvery depths hid her every thought from him—kindled with a special light. Frustration filled his chest until he felt as if it might explode. If only she would look that way for him.

Only for him.

He wanted from her more than the mild acquiescence she gave; he wanted passion. He wanted to know that she hungered for him the way he did for her. Moderation and chastity were the rule among the Sand Hill People, but the qualities he'd deemed as deeply ingrained had evaporated like fog to reveal the landscape of his inner self. It was a brooding place with sharp edges and shadowed corners, where dark emotions bubbled up dangerously close to the surface. The previous afternoon, when she'd seen Wolf Star with her daughter, she had smiled warmly at them, and Small Eagle had been overcome with jealousy. For a terrible, rage-maddened moment he'd thought the smile was for Wolf Star. The sentiments that had seared his soul then shamed him now. There had been black murder in his heart.

Bettany had her own misgivings. What would the future hold for herself and Hannah if her "husband" died on the raid?

Small Eagle made a sweeping movement with his arm. "When I return," he vowed to her, "I will bring with me many fine horses. I will give them to you."

She tried to show enthusiasm, but the puzzled expression

on Small Eagle's face told her she hadn't totally succeeded.

Small Eagle's pride rankled. What could he say or do to make her await his return? The answer came to him like a gift. A crafty light shone in the depths of his dark irises.

"I shall seek news of your small warrior who was taken from you. There is word of a white child among the north-western tribes. I will seek him out. If he is yours, I will bring him to you."

Nils. He hadn't forgotten!

Bettany's excitement and gratitude were profound, and Small Eagle knew that he had spoken wisely. He had offered her wealth and she had been indifferent, but the mention of the little warrior had made her face shine like the sun.

He signaled with his lance and started forward with the others in his wake. When I return, he vowed, I will win her heart to me forever.

The group led by Small Eagle reached the Arapaho camp on the third afternoon, having stopped to hunt along the way. As a gift they brought with them two antelope and three plump sage hens, which were well received. Whistling Bear spoke to his young widowed niece, Red Paint Woman:

"Since no man of the other bands pleases you, perhaps you will be taken with Small Eagle. He is a noted warrior and rich in horses and hides, with only a pale-eyes woman to tend his hearth. Furthermore, he is handsome in the way that women like, with a strong, straight body. You could do worse than to select a man like Small Eagle to share your lodge."

Red Paint Woman needed no convincing. She had known Small Eagle in her youth and admired him, but their paths had gone separate ways; but the moment he had ridden into camp all her early feelings came back, magnified by her predicament. At her husband's death all his be-longings had been given away, in accordance with the cus-tom. Red Paint Woman had come back to her uncle's lodge to start anew. Now the opportunity was at hand, in the person of her childhood hero.

She rose immediately and began directing the butchering of the kill and the preparation of the food. The other women looked at one another, communicating by a certain gleam in their eyes or an almost imperceptible lift at the corners of their mouths: Red Paint Woman had chosen her next husband.

In the morning Small Eagle set out with the other raiders from the Arapaho village, filled with good spirits. On the second day they came across a group of Comanche camped between Two Rabbit Rock and Split Stream. The smell of roasting meat tempted them closer, and Small Eagle recognized Antelope Chaser from a distance.

"The Comanche is far from his own territory. I do not know what has sent him here."

"Perhaps the mystery is not so great," Whistling Bear joked. "Perhaps he has come here to provide us with a tasty meal." They laughed as they rode into camp.

Antelope Chaser was glad to offer them hospitality, reflecting only to himself that a year before they would have been at war with one another.

As they sat around the fire, Whistling Bear sank his teeth into a tender strip of meat and bit off a juicy morsel. "Elk Horn says that you have taken a small warrior into your lodge," he said after swallowing the morsel. "A white-eyes child."

"It is true." Antelope Chaser wiped the grease from his chin. "When the grass first grew tall and the trees were freshly budded, two men brought him to me. He is quick and bold, and will make a fine war chief one day."

Small Eagle remained silent, pretending he hadn't heard and wishing viciously that the Arapaho had kept his mouth shut. He hoped the subject would pass, but Whistling Bear kept at it.

"Small Eagle has, in his lodge, a white-eyes woman. She says her son was taken away when her wagon was attacked before the new moon. He has vowed to find this boy and take him to her."

Both Antelope Chaser and Small Eagle tensed. Their gazes met across the fire, revealing nothing. For reasons of their own, neither wanted there to be a connection. Antelope Chaser looked grim. The boy belonged to him now, as surely as if he'd been born a Comanche.

Small Eagle's thoughts were in turmoil. He had not expected this. Not so soon. His promise to find Bettany's son had been an empty one, meant to assure she would not run away in his absence. He had been sure the boy was either dead or far north among the Blackfeet or Snakes.

His dilemma was compounded by his uncertainties over his white-eyes wife. She tolerated his advances, but there was no eagerness in her eyes or in her body. As long as he held out hope of restoring her son to her, she would stay with him. Once she had both her children, who knew what she would do?

The Comanche responded first. He deemed it wiser not to mention the exchange of gold. "This boy cannot be the one you seek, my friend. He has no parents. He was given to me by his male relative, who could not keep him."

"Ah, then it is another child entirely." Small Eagle's voice was neutral, his body stiff as his lance.

The same rigor seemed to affect Antelope Chaser's muscles. There must be no doubt in anyone's mind that his new son belonged with him. He thought of a way to quell any doubts. Kearns and Ludo had both ridden bay geldings.

"The men who brought the white-eyes boy to me," he said at last, "had hair like fire. They rode a small gray and a chestnut with a lightning blaze on his forehead."

"Ah," Small Eagle said again. "The men who took my woman's boy away from her had hair like the tassels of ripened corn. Their mounts were a black mare and a brown spotted pony. They were not the same men."

Antelope Chaser held out another strip of meat to Small Eagle. The juices sizzled and dripped, as palatable to each as the falsehoods they had just uttered. When they parted in the morning, each warrior was glad to be on his way;

and each was equally determined to avoid contact with the other for many years to come.

With the man of their lodge away, Bettany and Small Eagle's mother came to depend upon one another. Young and strong, Bettany was able to perform tasks the older woman found arduous because of her arthritis, and Blue Morning Flower was happy to oversee Hannah while Bettany tended to the heavier chores. Mutual need grew to mutual respect. It was rare for the two of them to leave the encampment together, but one glorious morning they set out with several other women to gather firewood. Blue Morning Flower knew all the best places to search.

The air had an unusual brilliance and clarity. Even the colors seemed exceptionally vivid to Bettany. The trees and grasses burned with emerald and topaz lights and the sky overhead was so blue above that she fancied it had been hollowed from a sapphire. Sadness came in the midst of the uplifting mood, as it did so often. She paused for a moment in silent prayer for those who hadn't lived to see the glory of this morning, those whose bones lay scattered about the meadow amid the wreckage of their dreams.

"Hurry," Mouse called out to her, "or your fire will go out and you will be left to eat your meat uncooked."

Bettany wandered away in search of some dry wood she'd seen among the rocks the previous day. The landscape screened her from the others, so she was startled by the sound of hoofbeats and the shrill cries of alarm. She peered over a rock to see a line of horsemen strung out across the meadow, facing the drop-off. Her first thought was that the raiding party had returned; but there were no horses herded before them, and the shouts of the Cheyenne women were not cries of welcome but shrieks of fear. In the split second that she hesitated, the line hooked at one end, closing her off from the others. The women were trapped between the attackers and the sheer drop.

She saw a squaw go down before the flying hooves, and another tried to break between two horsemen to the trees.

Bettany recognized Mouse. The young squaw stumbled and almost fell but suddenly jerked erect, arms flung wide. Bettany thought her eyes had tricked her, until she saw the gout of blood. A wooden lance protruded through Mouse's body, holding her eerily upright. Then the impaler dropped his lance and she fell to the ground, dead before she hit the grassy surface.

The horsemen were between her and the other women. There was no way Bettany could help her companions, except to run as hard as she could for the village and alert the men. She ran like a madwoman. Her legs burned with the effort, and her lungs were on fire. They were much farther from the village than she'd realized. The screams from the meadow spurred her on, summoning reserves she'd never tapped before. At the top of the slope she gasped for air, unable to shout loudly enough to sound the alarm. All that came out was a hoarse, desperate croak. Bettany's legs could barely support her.

Logan on his way up from the river, raced to meet her. She was almost too spent to speak and grabbed at him with bruising fingers. Only the strength of his strong arms kept her from falling.

"What is it?"

She struggled for breath and gestured desperately. "In the meadow . . . killing them . . ."

He didn't wait for more. The fear and horror in her voice said enough. "Get the women and children up to the ridge. Now!"

Logan raced for his weapons and the nearest horse. "Attackers!" he shouted to the other braves. He was thundering toward the ravine with the others as Bettany reached the edge of camp.

He reached the meadow as a marauder began to scalp a body, and dispatched him with a deadly arrow. His horse was shot out from under him, but Logan rolled free. Using the dead horse's carcass as a bulwark, he sent another of the besiegers face downward with a shaft through his heart.

Other horsemen arrived from the camp, and in the ensuing melee so much dust was kicked up that it was difficult to see at times. Bettany ran down the line of lodges.

"Enemies! They're killing the women," she cried to the others. Since she had reverted to English they didn't understand, but all knew that something terrible was happening.

The members of the soldier societies grabbed up their weapons and the war shields that hung before their lodges. He Laughs, one of the Contraries, who did everything by opposites, almost forgot to enter his backward. A moment later he backed out, carrying a curious two-stringed bow topped with a lance head, and joined the other braves. Bettany had thought of the Contraries as clowns, not warriors, and saw that once again her perceptions had led her astray.

There was no time for other observations as the camp mobilized. Children were whisked away and weapons readied by those who had them. Summoning her last burst of energy, Bettany ran to her lodge.

Hannah sat in the sunlight just outside the door, oblivious of the uproar around her. She was playing with colored beads strung on a piece of dried sinew, sliding them up and down singly and in groups. It was her favorite game, one that could keep her occupied for hours. Her entire attention was focused on the beads, on their brightness, and on the cool feel of them between her small fingers.

Round, round, round. Red, red, red. Round, red, round, red.

The words were simple and represented concepts she could grasp because they were immediately before her. She could see and touch them. But when they were put away she forgot about them and focused on other things until they were brought out again. Each time it was a new discovery.

Round, red, blue. Round blue.

Bettany had taught her the names of the colors. At first Hannah had thought they were the names of the beads. It had confused her. How could this one be white when that one was white? And if this bead was blue, why was that one blue, too? But after a while it began to come to her more easily—not as a conscious, rational thought, but as if Bettany were saying the word softly inside her head.

Hannah could almost tell the colors by the way they felt to her sensitive fingertips. Closing her eyes, she touched her tongue to one. Red. It tasted red. She opened her eyes and crowed with delight. Red, red, red.

When Bettany swooped her up, Hannah was suddenly jolted out of her secret, narrow world and into the larger one filled with sharp voices and sudden movements. The string of beads dropped in the dust, and she began to wail.

Bettany didn't want to waste time, but she couldn't chance it. The Cheyenne children were trained to be silent when necessary, but Hannah hadn't learned that survival trait. A crying child could give away a hiding place and bring destruction down upon them. Stooping quickly, she retrieved the beads and slipped them over Hannah's head for safety. Hannah wrapped her fingers around them, and her crying ceased. Bettany grabbed the Kentucky Rifle and ammunition she'd salvaged from her wagon and hurried out.

The other squaws and older children were already dragging and carrying the younger boys and girls toward the relative safety of the ridge. They knew that if the attackers were a large party, they might be hunted down as they raced across the scrub and stone that stretched between them and the high ground, but in the village they would have no chance at all.

Out in the meadow, where the bodies of three attackers lay sprawled in death, and the blood of the slain women still glistened among the supple grasses, not even a birdcall broke the stillness. Logan looked down at Mouse's corpse and then away, sick at heart. Visions of a massacre he'd witnessed as a young boy were overlain by one of Cassie sprawled on her bed inside the cabin. Finally it seemed it was Bettany impaled by a splintered lance, the crown of her head a bloody mass surrounded by strands of her long silver hair.

The image shimmered and vanished, but the reality was just as terrible. He found Blue Morning Flower crumpled behind a rock, so bloody at first that he couldn't tell the severity of her wounds or even where they were. As he lifted her in his arms she gave a short sigh and her head dropped back. He held her a few precious seconds, this woman who had been his mother, who had taken in a foundling and raised him as if he were a son born of her womb.

Gently he laid her down again, placing her arms at her sides. Her flesh was still warm. How fleeting the spirit was, that it could leave the body so quickly. How tenuous the ties that held it in place, so that one moment a person was alive, the next dead and yet still warm. His mother.

He touched her hand. "They will pay for this. And it will not be easy. I promise you that."

There was such bleakness in his eyes when he rose that those who saw it stepped back. Mere minutes had passed since the attack. Logan scanned the area. The five surviving foe had vanished among the uplifted shelves of ground, but their tracks clearly marked their direction. They had gone west alongside the irregular wall of rock that snaked from the meadow into the distance. It ended at the sheer cliffs of a U-shaped valley of sand and stone, from which there was no outlet. The only other entrance was a small section where the rock face had been sheared from the greater bulk by some ancient cataclysm. It ran parallel to the main entrance but some five hundred yards beyond.

Logan squinted toward it, shielding his eyes against the glare of sun off the bone white rocks. It could form a deadly trap—but for the hunted or the hunter? A premonitory warning crawled like a centipede between his shoulder blades. "Something is not right."

He bent and picked up a rifle. "These thunder-sticks are the newest and best that the white men have. How did these men get possession of such weapons? Look at the bodies of the fallen enemy and their clothing. They are not members of any one tribe."

With a sharp stick he sketched the layout of the valley, indicating where the attackers might lie in ambush. "They could wait here until our party is past, then attack from the rear. I smell a trap."

Spotted Bull agreed. "Wolf Star speaks wisely."

Breaks His Bow, Spirit Woman's elder brother, muttered beneath his breath. "And I smell a coward. Wolf Star has changed since his earlier days among us. He wishes to sit by the fire, like an old woman, and warm his bones. I will follow them and kill them. Nothing less will satisfy me."

Mouse's husband, Five Calves, was angry and bitter. "I will warm my bones along the vengeance trail. Let those with no fear ride with me."

He kicked his pony and galloped off, flanked by his brothers, and the majority of the others joined him in a blood frenzy.

Logan turned to his friends. "Who among you will stand with me?"

Twenty warriors joined him, among them Spotted Bull. The two conferred, then divided the others into two uneven groups. The smaller one he left to guard the village, the larger to ride with him around the grove and down the far side of the ravine. Speed was essential, but the terrain forced them into single file.

It was chancy. The grade was precipitous, strewn with rocks, and badly eroded. A horse could stumble and fall, taking down not only his own rider, but those coming along behind. Logan led the way to break the path, with Spotted Bull in the rear. He slanted down the incline, picking his way with as much caution as he could afford without sacrificing the crucial element of time. He reached a succession of stony terraces and paused beside the long wall of rock. It was wider than he thought, as much as eight feet in some places. He directed his horse out along it for several yards. From his eagle's aerie he had an excellent view in all directions.

Below, Five Calves, Breaks His Bow, and their company rode hard after their quarry. Unknown to them, a war party waited in the cut at the valley entrance. They would enter in frenzied pursuit of the marauders and be caught between two hostile parties. Surrounded and surprised, they'd have no chance at all.

Logan signaled to Spotted Bull, pointing first toward the valley, next to the horsemen hidden along the river below the village. He would continue on alone, along the wall of rock and Spotted Bull would ride after Five Calves and Breaks His Bow. Whoever the attackers were, one thing was sure: they meant to eradicate every man, woman, and child in the Cheyenne camp.

Logan urged his pony out onto the smooth rock parapet, patting its neck soothingly. The bond of trust between man and horse calmed the beast, and it proceeded without incident, feeling its way at the narrowest sections. Logan knew that as long as his pony kept its concentration on the ground ahead, they could make it to the other side, but if the animal realized the danger on either side, it would panic and send them both hurtling down to their deaths.

Breaks His Bow was first to reach the narrow mouth of the valley. The tracks of those they followed went straight before them, and ahead was a cloud of dust stirred up by the hooves of several horses. He was relieved because his outburst earlier had shamed him. "Wolf Star was wrong. This is no trap for us, but for them."

The words were hardly out when a shower of stone rained down upon him. Not an assault, but a warning. Wolf Star was poised high above them on the wing of rock at the valley's summit. He held out his hand and wheeled his pony around. They followed his example, when suddenly the air was rent by war whoops. A horde of war-painted horsemen poured through the side cut behind them, and the battle was joined.

Making his way gingerly toward the rim of the valley, Logan heard the sounds of battle. His visage grew grimmer. His instincts had been right, but that brought him no sat-

isfaction. Grief had clouded the usually keen judgment of
Breaks His Bow and Five Calves. As he tried to find a route
down into the valley itself, Logan saw three riders slip
through the rocky cut. Gifted with long sight, he identified
them easily as the ones who had escaped from the meadow.

Three to one. He'd faced worse odds before. Logan turned
his pony and skittered down the perilous slope.

Their raid against the Utes was successful, and Whistling
Bear and Small Eagle arrived back among the Arapaho
lodges exhilarated with their victory. Behind them the
cloud of approaching dust heralded the first sight of their
spoils—sixty fine ponies. Red Paint Woman hurried out
with her congratulations and promises of a fine feast. Later
that night, when the cook fires were dark red embers, she
managed to meet Small Eagle outside her uncle's lodge. He
knew the meeting wasn't accidental and was curiously
pleased. Red Paint Woman was very beautiful, and her
attentions soothed his bruised spirits.

Her eyes were dark with mystery, her arms graceful as
she held out a belt of fine quillwork which she had started
as a gift for her late husband. While the raiders were away
she had cleverly picked out the design that represented his
emblem and added in the Cheyenne symbol of the Morning
Star. Small Eagle would never know, and if he guessed, he
wouldn't care. She would make sure of that.

"I have no use for this poor work of my hands," she told
him slyly, "and my uncle has many of his own. I would be
pleased to think it graced so bold a warrior."

As she handed it to him, their hands brushed. It was
deliberate on her part, but Small Eagle didn't move away.
He was enthralled with his white-eyes wife and could not
get his fill of her; but a man wanted a woman to desire him
as he desired her. While Warrior Woman had never refused
him, she seemed indifferent. In the half-light the expression
on Red Paint Woman's face told him that it would be
otherwise with her.

Small Eagle struggled with his Cheyenne upbringing.

Chastity and moderation had been instilled in him since birth, but now he wondered why. The Arapaho celebrated life lustily and seemed no worse for it than the Tsistsistas. They were tested by the same famine and floods that his own people suffered and blessed by the same abundance and beauty. Why should he deny himself the comfort of this willing woman?

Red Paint Woman leaned forward to hand him a delectable morsel, and her fragrance was all around him like a cloud. He inhaled deeply and made his choice in that instant. His fingers wrapped lightly around her wrist, arresting her movement. She looked into his eyes and smiled, a slight upturning of the corners of her mouth that set his blood singing. When he released her she rose quietly and walked away. The lowering sun outlined her graceful body and dazzled his eyes. She turned sharply left past the last lodge and eventually vanished among the trees.

He wanted to run after her but controlled himself, even having another helping of food. Then he left, as casually as he could manage, and also disappeared among the trees as twilight settled around him.

"It is clear that your niece will soon leave the protection of your lodge," Old Claw Keeper said. "When Small Eagle returns to his people he will have a new wife with him."

Whistling Bear was pleased. The Cheyenne was a warrior of courage and wealth, a good ally and a fitting mate for his relative. "His blood is overhot, that one. Another day and night of withholding himself and his bones would melt from the heat of it."

If Small Eagle could have heard the comments of Whistling Bear and the others, he would have flushed to know his thoughts were so transparent. But nothing would have altered him from his course. He found Red Paint Woman lying on a blanket she had laid out earlier for just this purpose. Some men might have been chagrined to think she had been so certain of him; Small Eagle was pleased to know that she wanted him so eagerly.

He pulled her skirt up, too impatient to wait until she

stripped, and felt the growing pressure in his loins. Her
buttocks were round and smooth beneath his palms, and
the scent of her readiness competed with the aroma of pine
and earth. He thrust into her quickly, and she met his every
movement with an avidity of her own. The explosive force
of his coming brought him great pleasure and release.

But afterward, when they lay naked together beneath the
cedars and his mouth sought the soft brown tip of her breast,
he brought it to hardness with his tongue, imagining it was
pink against pearly flesh. Imagining it was Bettany's breast
he tasted in his mouth. He didn't remember crying out Bettany's Cheyenne name in his moment of greatest ecstasy.

But Red Paint Woman did.

She lay awake after Small Eagle fell asleep, realizing her
task was not as easy as she had thought. She heard the rider
come into camp just before darkness settled and raised herself up on one elbow. It was her young cousin, Porcupine,
who had been staying with Breaks His Bow among the
Cheyenne. It was late for him to arrive. Something was
amiss.

Curiosity won out. Making sure that Small Eagle was in
sound slumber, she dressed quickly and stole away. She
would be back before he awakened. She moved through
the shadows of the lodges until she reached her uncle's fire.
Porcupine had come straight from the Cheyenne camp to
Whistling Bear with news of the attack.

Red Paint Woman was alarmed for more reasons than
one. On the grander scale it seemed that strange and destructive forces had been let loose like a dire plague; in a
more intimate way it affected her plan to win the Cheyenne
warrior to her. When Small Eagle learned of the attack and
his mother's death, the Arapaho woman knew that all
thoughts of love would flee his mind. The timing was disastrous for her.

Fortunately, most of the others had gone to their lodges
and were wrapped in their robes for the night. Hunkering
down beside her uncle, she whispered her idea. "Let nothing
be said of this tonight, for it is too late for any action to

be taken now. Porcupine must leave now and return when the sun has risen over the top of Owl Rock."

"What good will this do?" asked Whistling Bear.

Her hand clutched at his arm. "I will rouse Small Eagle at first light and lead him up to the Place of Many Flowers. We will not come down until the sun is setting—and I tell you this, when we come down I shall have his vow to take me with him as his wife."

Whistling Bear grinned suddenly. Among the family his niece's secret name was One Who Will Have Her Way. How accurate the naming had been.

"Go back to your lover," he said. "It shall be as you say."

By late morning the Cheyenne council had already been in session long. Under the leadership of Wolf Star and Spotted Bull the enemy had been caught between two attacking wings. The bottleneck near the mouth of the enclosed valley was strewn with bodies of the enemy; but the three who had escaped after the slaughter in the meadow were not among them—and neither was Wolf Star. Great storm clouds had come with a sound like the flapping of massive scavenger wings. The destructive rain that followed had obliterated any tracks.

Now they must agree on future plans. "I say that this is not a good place," Turtle said for the second time. "Let us move camp before evil visits us again."

It was nearing the end of the Time When Horses Grow Fat, when they had arranged to join the scattered bands of Tsistsistas and take part in a great buffalo hunt. But to do so they would have to travel in the opposite direction from which Smoke Along the Ground and his delegation would come. After each man had stated his opinion the decision was made, and the heralds went out to announce it.

"The enemy has been killed or routed. We will remain here until the new moon. If Smoke Along the Ground and the others of our band have not returned by then, we shall go ahead to the agreed meeting place."

Bettany was relieved. She wouldn't have had the slightest

idea of how to take down the lodge or pack their possessions efficiently for another move; but most of all it would have been heartless to leave the newly dead behind upon their lonely scaffolds. Blue Morning Flower had been kind to her, and Bettany's grief was sincere. She mourned Spirit Woman and Mouse as well, but violent death had become such a part of her life that it was beginning to seem like a natural pattern.

"Come, Hannah. Your dinner is ready." She was handing the bowl of food to her stepdaughter when a hush fell over the camp. Bettany turned quickly, expecting some new danger. It took her ears a few seconds longer to pick up the sound of hooves in the distance.

Logan cantered up the broad meadow before slowing to a trot. He rode through the camp until he came to her lodge. He dismounted and strode to where she sat, holding out a grizzly trophy: a circle of scalp the size of a silver dollar on the end of a hank of hair.

Every eye in the camp was focused upon them. Bettany knew what was expected of her. Small Eagle was gone, and outside of himself there was no other man of Blue Morning Flower's line to acknowledge that the blood debt had been paid. Belatedly she had fathomed why the men were exempt from ordinary chores. At all times, and with an instant's notice, they had to be ready to defend the village and the lives of their families from attack.

Holding out her hand steadily, she took the lock of long, straight hair attached to the bit of dried, puckered scalp. It smelled like a rind of cooked ham.

He must have smoked it over the fire, she thought with cool detachment. The events around her were unreal and dreamlike. She suddenly realized that the thing in her hand had once been part of another human being. I am holding the scalp of a murdered man in my hand as casually as if it were a skein of knitting wool.

Almost immediately a fierce sense of satisfaction filled her chest, and she corrected herself. No! Not a murdered man, but one who had been justly executed. She suddenly understood the cleansing power of vengeance. The keen, primitive joy of taking an eye for an eye.

She realized she had become as savage as her companions.

Dismay and disgust routed out the fleeting pleasure of victory. If a few short weeks among the Cheyenne could wear away her thin shell of civilization, only God knew what black passions months, or even years, among them might reveal hidden deep within her soul. Bettany put the scalp on the ground before her and rose. She scrubbed her palms against her skirts, not knowing if anyone saw and not caring if they did.

"You're hurt," she said quietly, noting the dried blood along his bare arm that she had at first mistaken for crusted red ocher. It was deep and crudely bound. "Come inside and I will cleanse it for you and apply a healing poultice."

"I have not finished my business."

He pivoted around. Breaks His Bow stood a few feet away. Logan held out another scalp to the brother of Spirit Woman, and to Five Calves, husband of Mouse, he presented another. As he distributed the last proof of his revenge, not a single word broke the silence.

Beyond his shoulder Bettany had a clear view through a gap in the hills to a remote stand of trees. Their gnarled and leafy branches bore strange fruit: the bodies of the dead women, wrapped and placed on platforms erected among the limbs, in accordance with their custom. Blue Morning Flower and the others had been avenged.

Logan turned a steady eye on Five Calves and Breaks His Bow, the men who had called him coward. They were the first to avert their gazes. In the silence that followed, Logan walked away toward the place where the dead had been left.

No one dared to follow.

Logan's task was finished, but he felt no peace. He avoided the company of the other braves and made his bed beneath a cottonwood by the river. When he finally slept, nightmares rode his dreams. He was lost in drifting snow, blinded by the glare. Bettany appeared, reaching her hands out to him, but as he touched her she grew cold as ice and turned to silver. He was left alone in growing darkness, the medallion that was his talisman inside his clenched fist.

Awakening, he felt the medallion in his medicine pouch digging into his hipbone. He shifted and saw Bettany lying on the other side of the lodge, her hair gleaming like polished silver in the moonlight streaming through the smokehole. Logan was groggily aware that his past and future were inextricably twined. But he would not know the future unless he first unraveled the shadowed secrets of his past.

Fifteen

Mexico: 1811

The Hacienda de Medina was aswirl with sound and color. It was the third day of Don Miguel's fiesta in honor of his daughter's saint's day, and Quinn Logan was glad he'd accepted the invitation to attend. A *niña* in a white blouse and red skirt clung to her mother's brown hand, rubbing her eyes. Quinn grinned at her, and the girl smiled shyly before burying her face in her mother's skirts. He passed two men throwing dice against a stable wall and a blind old man plucking rich, intricate notes from the heart of his guitar for a group of listeners.

He ducked between two outbuildings, grinning again when he spied the young vaquero who had both his hands inside the blouse of a buxom mestizo girl. Not twenty minutes past he had seen the same couple in the midst of a heated lover's quarrel, the young man alternately castigating and imploring and the girl filled with cold disdain. But interesting things happened during fiesta; and that was why Quinn was here.

His destination was the wide space at the far end of the pasture, where a spectator stand had been built next to the special corral. It was there that the wealthy Creole families sat beneath a gay yellow awning in readiness for the coming bullfights. Señorita Ysabella Maria Constanza was cutting quite a swath through the ranks of guests and servants alike. Instead of the full, sashed skirts and graceful blouses of the other women, worn with shawls and elegant mantillas, Don

Miguel's pride and joy was decked out in an ensemble that would have looked right at home in New Orleans—at one of the better fancy houses.

Quinn shook his head at the green silk gown, elaborately draped and tasseled beneath a shocking décolletage, and so heavily trimmed in gold floss and embroidery that it might have better adorned the walls of an Arabian harem. Where she had ever gotten such an outfit was more than he could imagine; and thus was Don Miguel's reaction, when he came from the stables and saw his daughter in all her glory. From halfway across the meadow Quinn saw the pride and fury as she flung her head high and stamped her little foot. She was no match for her father.

With face aflame, Dona Ysabella flounced away in the direction of the hacienda, refusing her aunt's company in no uncertain terms. Quinn chuckled. Then he watched as Don Miguel leaned down and spoke privately to Dona Estrella. Her cheeks grew crimson, but she held her ground. Another *hacendado* came to speak with her brother, interrupting the tête-è-tête. Estrella took advantage of the distraction. Snapping her fan open, she summoned a servant with a tray of cool drinks and addressed a comment to the woman seated beside her as if nothing had happened. Only her eyes betrayed the hurt and anger she felt.

It was a gallant performance, and Quinn's admiration rose. A few weeks earlier he would have bypassed the casually offered invitation to the fiesta and thought nothing of it. But that had been before he'd gone to San Felipe and witnessed the drama in the hotel ballroom.

It was none of his business at all. From everything he'd seen, Dona Estrella was a very private woman. She'd be mortified to know he'd seen and overheard—much less guessed—so much. Nor would Don Miguel thank him for meddling in his affairs. Yet there was something about the woman he couldn't shake off. She wasn't a real beauty like her niece, and she seemed to have learned none of the little feminine tricks that could captivate and snare a man. And he'd always preferred blue eyes to brown.

So, he asked himself wryly, why am I here at this god-damned celebration when I should be halfway to Albuquerque by now? Jennings is going to want my hide for dawdling like this when there's business to do.

Estrella rose from her seat and began making her way through the throng in his direction. She moved, he thought, as effortlessly as a petal wafted on the breeze. Quinn threw down his slender cigarro, combed his thick hair with his fingers, and changed his route to intercept her.

Jennings could go to hell and take Albuquerque with him.

She looked up, startled, as he stepped into her path. Quinn doffed his wide-brimmed hat. "*Buenas tardes*, Dona Estrella."

"Good afternoon, Señor . . . Señor Logan, is it not?"

Quinn reddened like a choirboy caught stealing from the poor box. "It is . . . and it isn't." Great work, he fumed, for a man known for his silver tongue.

"Are you enjoying the fiesta, señor?"

Quinn took her hand in his. "I'd enjoy it much more if you'd take a turn around the garden with me. It's devilish hot today."

Estrella was about to refuse when, from the corner of her eye, she saw Luis heading toward them. "That is an excellent suggestion. The sun is merciless."

She slipped her hand through his arm, and together they ducked beneath an archway and into the walled court beyond.

It was a charming place of contrasts, not attached to the house, but leading off the front *portal*, with its own double arcade on either side. Roses glowed like drops of blood against the dark green vines that climbed the posts and trellises. Fallen petals of a glossy white flower littered the ground like snow. Shrubs and flowers from Spain and China were juxtaposed with thorny succulents and spiky blooms native to the surroundings. Quinn knew somehow it was her hand that had shaped this place, her heart that was

buried here. That reflection shocked him. She was very
much alive and warm at his side; why had such an odd
thought struck him? This was a place for things to burgeon
and grow, not for them to end.

They crossed to a vine-shaded corner where a bench
waited invitingly. The air was immediately cooler. Instantly
the tension seemed to drain from her, and Quinn felt a sort
of peace seep into his bones as well. The sounds of the
crowd were muted here, no more intrusive than the whisper
of the wind through the great sprawling sycamore that an-
chored the central garden. Estrella's hand was still tucked
in his arm, yet she seemed unaware of it. In fact, he decided
ruefully, she seemed equally oblivious of him.

A bejeweled hummingbird hovered near her head to sip
nectar from a delicate lavender blossom, and neither of
them moved. It went from flower to flower, light catching
its rainbow colors and the impossible blur of its wings.
When it darted away at last, Estrella smiled warmly at her
companion. "You are a restful man, Señor Logan. Thank
you."

He was surprised. "For what? For staying still a moment
or two to enjoy one of God's gifts of beauty?"

Estrella smoothed her skirt with the palm of her hand.
"Some men would have tried to catch it," she said flatly.

"That would most likely kill the poor, fragile creature."

"Yes." She withdrew her hand. "But some men wouldn't
care. It is only important to own, to possess. And if they
cannot, they would rather kill than see it fly away to someone else."

Quinn suspected she'd been recalling an actual event.
Her lips trembled just a moment before she could hide it.
He felt as if he'd been kicked in the stomach, hard. If
anyone hurt this woman, if any man dared . . . Sweet Christ
on the cross! What in God's name had come over him?

But he knew. He knew.

He should have pulled her into his arms then and there.
The hesitation was too long. Estrella rose fluidly as Luis
called her name from just beyond the archway. The ner-

vousness was back. Suddenly she was like quicksilver, shimmery and insubstantial in the sunlight. "We should get back to the others. The rooster pulls will be starting soon, and perhaps you will want to participate."

Quinn shrugged. He liked a good cockfight as much as any man, but the idea of men racing by on horseback and trying to pull out roosters, buried to their heads in sand struck him as too outlandish. "It doesn't tempt me in the least."

She glanced up at him. "Perhaps you do not know that my niece, Dona Ysabella, will give out prizes to the winners, and the grand winner will get to lead her out on the dance floor at the fandango tonight."

He grinned down at her. "No, I hadn't heard that. But what that has to do with me is more than I can figure."

A tiny frown line formed between Estrella's brows. "Forgive me if my conclusions were too hasty. I thought perhaps you had come courting, Señor Logan."

He stared at her so long, and with such a peculiar expression in his eyes, it held her paralyzed. Then he raised her hand to his mouth and pressed his lips against her fingers.

"I have indeed, Dona Estrella. I have indeed."

She was too taken aback to speak or snatch her hand away. His mouth was warm and strangely intimate against her skin. It made her feel cherished. Precious.

The sound of Luis's boots on the walkway broke the spell. "Estrella! What is the meaning of this!"

But Estrella didn't know what the meaning of it was, only that all her command had deserted her and that she was in a state of utter confusion. She darted away, as quickly as a hummingbird, through the other arch to the *portal*. A trace of her light, spicy cologne lingered behind.

Quinn turned to face the intruder. Luis stood with his feet planted apart, hands at his waist in a challenging pose. "Señor?"

The message was unmistakable and the provocation great. For several seconds the men bristled at each other like two dogs with one bone; but Quinn was in no mood to participate in a brawl on Don Miguel's property and get himself barred from the hacienda. These Creoles were mighty protective of their women's reputations. He made an exaggerated bow to his host's brother-in-law.

"I was paying my respects"—he stressed the word—"to Dona Estrella. She is as gracious and virtuous as she is beautiful."

Luis drew in a hissing breath. His skin was pale with suppressed emotion. Quinn recognized the blaze of anger in the man's eyes. He didn't recognize the pain.

After the American strolled past him and out of the garden, Luis fought to control his rage. Another hummingbird zipped among the vines nearby, unnoticed. Even the gardens had faded away into a red mist. That first night of his return, Estrella had melted into his arms as he had dreamed and planned she would. Since then she ran from him as if he carried the plague. But she had let that rawboned American kiss her hand so familiarly. Let him try anything more and he would pay for it, dearly. Estrella would be his. She *was* his. And he must show the world that she belonged to him.

His temper cooled and he lost himself in daydreams. Pilar did not exist. Estrella would create a garden at his hacienda. There would be hummingbirds and roses as they walked in it together. She would bear his name and his children. He would no longer let her flutter free and aimless as that hummingbird.

A tiny bundle of iridescent feathers flashed by, and Luis's hand shot out to the seize it; but when he opened his fingers there was only a handful of crushed blossoms.

Hanging lanterns of red and yellow swayed overhead in the breeze, as gay as the music filling the air. A dance floor had been made of hard-packed dirt, watered and stamped and left to dry again and again until it was as solid as stone but with the resiliency of wood. Estrella, whirling around in Quinn's strong grip, was giddy with the dancing and the excitement. She felt like a girl again, still innocent, still looking forward to each new day instead of looking back. She could even forget Luis, sending cold looks at them from the sidelines. She could even forget that she was supposed to be keeping an eye on her niece and relinquish chaperonage to Manuela.

"Will you be in San Felipe long, Señor Logan?"

He looked down into her eyes with a slow smile. "As long as it takes, *alanna.*"

A slight frown appeared between her eyes. "I do not know that word, señor."

"Don't worry." He relinquished her hand as the dance ended. "I'll explain it to you someday."

He bowed and left her with her new partner, and Estrella looked after his retreating back. Ah, if only she could turn back time. If only Luis had never returned so that she might pretend, at least for a few happy hours, that she was still young and innocent and courted by Señor Logan. If only . . .

But the music started and she was swept into the steps of the dance. Luis, lounging against a wall, was surprised when one of the serving women handed him a note with his glass. Eyebrows raised, he slipped a coin into her hand and went off to the library where he could be private. The lamps had not yet been lit, and with the door shut behind him the room was in deep shadow.

He ambled over to one of the long windows facing the court to avail himself of the light and unfolded the square of paper. There was no signature, but that didn't matter: the writing was as familiar to him as his own.

The ruin of the old *indio* quarters. When the lanterns are lit for the dancing.

He was jubilant in victory. Estrellita could not resist him. He had won!

A voice startled him. "Who is the lucky woman, Luis?"

"Miguel! I did not see you sitting there all alone in the dimness." Luis quickly tucked the note into the pocket of his *chaqueta.* "Why are you not outside enjoying the afternoon with your guests?"

"Time enough for that. I came in here to think." He took the decanter and poured out some fine Madeira in two crystal glasses. "Do you know the American called Quinn?"

"By name and reputation."

"What do you hear of him?"

"That he is an honest man, ready with his fists and his wallet. A successful trader and a formidable enemy." Luis took the glass Don Miguel handed him and sprawled on one of the leather chairs. "What is your interest in Quinn?"

The older man sipped his Madeira ruminatively. "It is not so much my interest in him, as his interest in the house of de Medina. I believe he has come here a-courting."

"The gringo looks too high for a bride. And Ysabella is almost contracted to Enrique de la Vega. That is well-known throughout the district."

Don Miguel turned a sardonic look upon his brother-in-law. "I do not think it is Ysabella he has in his eye. Of course, she would never stoop so low—but it is Estrella that he wants."

Luis moved so quickly that he knocked the Madeira to the floor. The heavy crystal decanter landed near the edge of the rug and was unbroken, but the stopper cracked and the Madeira spilled out in a sweet puddle over the fringe and along the tiles. He stooped with an apology and one of his lithe movements to retrieve it. Don Miguel waved him back toward his chair and rang for a servant. Luis hesitated, then bowed.

"Excuse me, but I have forgotten to give the groom instructions about my chestnut mare. She must be pampered like a princess, you know."

But once outside he avoided the stables and headed to the site of the original small house the first de Medina had built on the hacienda. The place was now the home of the sick old man who had been Don Miguel's overseer in younger days. It was deserted, for even the invalid had gone to the fiesta, carried there in a chair by two strong men.

Beyond the casa lay the ruins of the old *indio* quarters where the Indian laborers had been housed before the uprisings a decade earlier.

Only the end section stood intact, its scorched walls silhouetted against the dusky blue of the sky. It had been used for storage a few years and then abandoned altogether to the insects and field mice and clandestine lovers. Luis opened the outer door and stepped over shards of broken pottery and empty sacks. The door to the inner room was locked, but he felt along a space between the low vigas until his fingers touched metal. The key turned easily in the freshly oiled lock, and he went in.

It was blacker than midnight, and at first he couldn't make out any shapes. But he knew Estrella was there by her soft breathing and the light, spicy scent she always wore. Luis closed the door and locked it by touch alone; but then he had done so many times before. "Estrella, light the candle."

A scratch, a flare, and then a growing circle of light blossomed in the far corner. He tugged the heavy rug into place to keep the light from showing beneath the door in the outer room. But when he straightened he saw that his companion was someone else. "Ysabella!"

She threw off her shawl. "How did you know me? I kept my face hidden."

"If I held my hat before my face, would you not recognize me? Little fool, everyone here knows you, and if they were unsure, they would remember you from the same gown. I doubt there is the like in all of Monterrey."

Ysabella preened. "Is it not beautiful? I saw it in a dressmaker's book that came from London and had it made up in Mexico City. Papa did not like it much." Her face clouded. "He told me to go to my room and change—as if I were a *niña* still!"

"*Madre de Dios*, why did you not do so instead of coming to meet me!"

She was offended. "I couldn't change my gown. Then everyone would know that I had been ordered to do it, and

I could never hold my head up for the rest of the fiesta. And if you didn't want to meet me, then why are you here?"

"Because I thought that . . . Never mind what I thought." He unlocked the door. "Blow out the candle. I will leave first and pray that no one saw us both here together. What would they think? . . ."

Ysabella flounced over and put her hand on his arm. "But you used to meet Tía Estrellita here when you were younger. Juana said so." She shrank back at the look on his face. "What is wrong? Why do you stare at me so?"

"You are tiresome and silly. That was when we were children playing at games. It is different between a grown man and woman. And though you act like a child, you are no longer one, Ysabella."

Tears fell, but so easily that it was obvious they were a talent rather than a sign of distress. "You are being unkind to me, Luis. I thought you would understand and help me with my problem. I need your advice."

"About what, that you cannot seek it beneath your father's roof?"

"*He* is my problem." Her face was wild and sulky in the flickering light. "He has arranged a betrothal for me—with Don Enrique, with the marriage to take place in three months' time. Oh, Luis! I would rather die! He is an old man!"

Sparks shone in the depths of Luis's irises. De la Vega was his own age. "You are foolish beyond permission. He is a man of wealth and position, still in his prime."

He pinched Ysabella's chin between his fingers, none too gently, examining her delicate features and rosebud mouth that had never known more than a boy's unpracticed kisses.

"It takes a man of experience to tame a passionate young woman such as yourself."

For a moment the air was charged with something dark and forbidden. "Oh, you are as bad as my father." Ysabella flung herself between him and the open door, her fingers clenched around the opening of his *chaqueta*. "You must persuade him to forgo this betrothal. He will surely listen to you."

"Not when it concerns the marriage and breeding of his heirs." His laugh was low and bitter. "Who should know better than I?" Luis leaned down until his face was close to hers. "Go back, Ysabella, and take the marriage your father has arranged. Go before it is too late."

Not understanding, yet frightened, she did as she was bid; but after she was gone he blew out the light and walked back alone toward the gay lanterns and music. He had warned Estrella that he would find a way to punish her if she kept encouraging the pretensions of the Irishman.

And now he knew how.

The old covered arbor was rickety with age, and the vines that swarmed over it were no longer fruitful. In Estrella's childhood it had been a favorite playhouse. The long benches had been beds for her dolls; the wooden cover securely bolted over the old stone well, a table for her miniature dishes. Later it had been her place to dream. Now it was her refuge. Her confessional. She removed a loose stone from the outer course of the well and took out the slim journal, the ink and sharpened quill. Into the pages she poured out her secrets and her prayers. She dipped the quill into the ink and filled the page in her elegant script.

> He is still here. Every day becomes more difficult. Each time I swear it will be the last, each time I fall into sin again. I do not know what to do.
>
> I would ask to be admitted to the convent as a novice, but even if Miguel would agree to it, how could I pray among those holy women when I am filled with sin? When my body burns and lusts for him? And there is Ysabella, as innocent, as passionate, as I was at her age. How could I go away and leave her unprotected?
>
> Ah, Mother of God, intercede for me in heaven.

Estrella heard the scrape of a boot on the stone flags and hastily hid the journal and her writing things in their accustomed place. She came out of the arbor as if lost in idle contemplation but stopped abruptly in alarm. Luis stood before her, blocking the path. She saw his horse tethered down in the wildflower meadow. "Why did you not ride up here instead of sneaking about like a thief?"

"And give you the chance to slip away when you heard the hoofbeats? You have been avoiding me since the fiesta—so I have come to seek you out instead." He reached for her hand. "You see what power you have over me, *mi alma.*"

She pulled away and tried to brush past him, but he caught her by the arms and forced her to step back beneath the arbor. His face was flushed, his eyes filled with the lazy heat that in the past had melted her bones and left all her fine resolutions in ashes. Estrella fought it. "Why do you torment me! Go away. Go back to your wife in California and leave me in peace!"

He pressed her against the massed leaves and tangled his hands in her hair, shaking the pins from it with his fingers until it tumbled over her shoulders. "The only peace either of us knows is when we are in each other's arms."

His mouth hovered over hers, the firm lips that had crushed her own a hundred times, that had made her breasts tingle and ache, that had set her skin ablaze with sensual fire. They skimmed her cheek, the line of her jaw, whispering, urging. "Ah, *querida,* I think of you night and day. I want you waking and sleeping. And I will have you."

Estrella groaned as she slipped under his spell. It was happening again. The familiar hungers grew. Even as warnings screamed inside her head, she was dizzy with excitement, with need. Her traitorous body curved against his hardness. Her breathing changed and quickened. Luis's hand slid into her bodice, seeking her breast. As her breath hissed between her teeth, he lowered her to the bench that ran the length of the arbor, pressing her against the wood. Suddenly she felt the hard bite of metal against her skin and gasped out a protest. Luis rolled onto one elbow. "What is this?" he asked.

He brought out the gold chain and the oval religious metal hanging from it. A madonna on one side, the obverse featuring a heart pierced by seven swords. Light shining through the central, heart-shaped ruby cast a glow upon Estrella's skin, a single drop of blood against her white breast. She tried to snatch it away from him, but he was too quick for her. Luis laughed when he saw her expression.

"Ah, I think I understand. It is a talisman—to ward off the devil himself. Did you really think it would keep me away? Or make you impervious to my . . . charms, shall we say?" With a quick movement he had her bodice completely open. "Let us test its powers."

He let the golden links fall over one of her breasts, so the medal fell below its rosy tip, then lowered his mouth over it, hot and damp and seeking.

"No, Luis! Don't . . . ," Estrella cringed as he sucked her nipple into the warmth of his mouth, but the deep tug of desire that followed almost overcame her shame at his blasphemy. At her own weak body that was moist and yearning for more. After so many nights of tearful prayer, all the novenas and rosaries to beg for courage and the strength to resist.

She saw herself reflected in his pupils, recognized the light of unholy joy in them. She realized that this was part of his pleasure—forcing her to forget the teachings that had been drummed into her from childhood, to turn her back on everything she valued most. And every time he taught her something new about the ways of making love. About herself.

Things she didn't want to know.

The heat faded, leaving her blood thick and cold. For the first time in her life she saw Luis clearly, without the sheen of glamour that had made him the idol of her childhood and the focus of her first, girlishly romantic dreams. Time and again he had vowed that he loved her; but he was destroying her. No man destroyed the thing he loved.

She ceased her struggles. He had pinned her beneath his weight, gloating over his inevitable dominance of her, anticipating the sweetness of victory. There was cruelty in his smile. Why had she never seen it before? "Let me go, Luis."

It was a command, not a request. He laughed at her. "How foolish you are to pretend anew each time, Estrellita. You are mine willingly. I have made you love me, as I vowed I would."

"I loved you once, foolishly and blindly. It was like a disease, but now I am cured. I see what you are, and it chills me. There is no love in my heart for you, Luis. I hate you . . . and I pity you."

Her cool, dispassionate tones took him aback. There was a change in her body, from liquid and yielding to a rigid block of wood. The look on her face was neither desire nor fear, but disgust. He had lost her. Completely. Irrevocably. His grip slackened, and she wriggled free. Shock held him paralyzed for a few, stunned seconds, and she almost escaped. Luis hadn't realized the depth, the violence, of his feelings for her. The rage and jealousy and despair came over him in a crimson-black wave that swept away reason.

He caught her as she tried to flee and swung her around. "You are like your brother. You think I am not good enough for you because my blood is not pure."

There was no gentleness in his hands, none of the lover's touch. His handsome face had become an ugly mask, reflecting his twisted emotions. Estrella was terrified as he ripped at her clothes, bruising her flesh. He tried to throw her down upon the bench once more, but she caught hold of the trellis and held on with all her might. The old wood parted, and they fell to the flags.

The wind was knocked from Luis as Estrella landed atop him. In her fear she struck out at him again and again, until she saw the blood. The piece of broken lattice in her hand had slashed through the top of his shirt to the skin beneath. Another red streak cut across his collarbone. Appalled, Estrella dropped the weapon. He had made her a whore, and now almost a murderer. She rose, reeling with reaction while he tried to stem the flow with his hand.

She stood over him, her eyes blank and lusterless. "I swear to God, Luis—if you ever touch me again, I will kill you. Or myself."

He stumbled to his feet, cursing, but she was already running through the meadow, running from Luis and from herself as well.

Sixteen

Mexico: 1840

Father Ignazio was faithful to the spirit of the dead woman who'd entrusted the secrets of her past to him. He must see that Dona Ysabella's soul found rest by discharging the duty she had laid upon him, but he was not finding it an easy task. There were a dozen obstacles at every turn—the current one, the Very Reverend Father Emmanuel Siguente, aide to a prelate of the archdiocese.

"As you know, Father Ignazio, Bishop Delgado is a very busy man. His time is severely limited." The secretary rolled his eyes and heaved a heavy sigh of sympathy for his superior's workload. "I will review the matter first."

Father Ignazio had a great deal of awe for the bishop's place in the hierarchy of the Church, but he also had his duties to perform. And in his eyes, God far outranked the bishop. He held the wooden box more securely in his strong brown hands. "I must speak with Bishop Delgado myself. Privately."

Father Siguente stiffened ever so slightly. "I regret that this is not possible. . . ."

"It is," Father Ignazio said distinctly, "a matter that concerns the honor of his family. To be specific, the family of his most esteemed cousin Don Miguel Alvarez de Medina."

"His cousin Don Miguel. . . ."

Those four words were the magic phrase that Father Ignazio needed. Although the *hacendado* had moved his headquarters to Santa Fe, Don Miguel still had friends among the lords both spiritual and temporal. Father Siguente was not blind to the opportunity that lay within his grasp. Rapid advancement could come to the man who aided, not only Bishop Delgado, but his influential cousin Don Miguel Alvarez de Medina.

There was a softening in the lines of Father Siguente's face, a hardening of the ambitious light in his eyes. "I am sure an audience can be arranged on a matter concerning the bishop's cousin. Wait here, if you please. I will inquire whether he is free to see you."

He left quickly and was back within a few minutes. "The bishop will see you in his private study. Follow me."

The knot in Father Ignazio's stomach tightened as he was led down a grand corridor, past the long dining room with its highbacked chairs and dark paintings, past the large reception room furnished in the style of imperial Spain, and beyond it into a smaller passage. Father Ignazio had never been in this section before, which obviously led to private quarters. In fact, he had never been farther inside these hallowed walls than the reception room and the secretary's sanctum.

As they hurried along, his companion didn't balk at the opportunity to ingratiate himself further with questions regarding Don Miguel's health and welfare. He was surprised and disappointed that Father Ignazio had never met the wealthy *patrón*. "But I thought that you had come as Don Miguel's emissary?"

Father Ignazio smiled his sad smile. "I have not come on his behalf. To speak the truth, I am sure that Don Miguel would wish me at the bottom of the sea if he knew of my purpose in seeking this audience."

While the other man digested this strange turn of events, they went through an ancient door and out into the sun's splendor. The sharpness of light off the stone blinded Father Ignazio, and he caught his toe in a pavement crack. A hand caught his elbow to keep him from stumbling.

"You must watch your step most carefully, as you are

unfamiliar here," Father Siguente said with every evidence of sincerity.

There was something in his tone that made Father Ignazio wonder if another, deeper meaning was implied. He shook away such thoughts. I am only out of my element here, and this matter weighs upon me so heavily that I see dragons wherever I turn, he thought. I shall be relieved to place it in the care of one far holier and wiser than myself.

They crossed the courtyard to a long arcade, and the secretary knocked twice at a simple door, opened it, and announced the visitor. He stepped back and waved Father Ignazio inside. "I will be nearby, should I be needed."

The door closed behind him. He expected more grandeur, but once his eyes adjusted to the change in light he found himself in a sparsely furnished room. A wooden table, blackened by age and decades of polish, was set across one corner, so the lone occupant might look out to the court on one hand or to the plain crucifix upon the adjacent wall.

The bishop was a lean man, sunken-cheeked and hollow-eyed. Father Ignazio's heart plummeted. Although the room was comfortably warm, he was sure the blanket and pile of shawls neatly stacked on a wooden chest had just been removed from the bishop. It was clear that this frail shepherd of Christ, the spiritual leader of an immense territory, was only a man. A man who was obviously dying.

Then their gazes met, and Father Ignazio saw the intensity of the spirit that blazed out through those dark-rimmed eyes. They held intelligence, power, and the faith to move mountains. Perhaps he had not made this trip in vain. The bishop held out his hand, and Father Ignazio knelt to kiss the amethyst ring that was the seal of temporal and spiritual authority. "Pray be seated, Father Ignazio."

There was only one other chair in the room, a grand affair of carved wood and burnished leather held in place with brass nail heads that were the size of acorns. Bishop Delgado sat back in his own chair. "I understand that you have come to me on a matter of some urgency."

Father Ignazio cleared his throat. "And of great delicacy.

I regret to say that it impinges upon the honor of your cousin Don Miguel Alvarez de Medina. It is a dark tale, Excellency, and I do not know what should be done with it."

With economy, he related the story of Dona Ysabella and her dying wish. When he had finished he put the box upon the table and brought out the letters. "These, Excellency, will tell the rest more clearly—more piteously—than any words of mine could do."

The bishop eyed him steadily, then took the letters and began to read. Father Ignazio waited anxiously. It seemed to take a long time. He would have liked to pace, but it wouldn't have been seemly. Not within these peaceful walls or in the presence of such holiness. Not with matters of such grave importance. He contented himself by running his long fingers over the line of brass nail heads along the arms of his chair.

A fly buzzed. The clock ticked endlessly. Through the windows he watched the shadows lengthen on the far side of the arcade. A bird perched on the head of the stone St. Francis, then flew away. The pattern of the nail heads was becoming imprinted upon Father Ignazio's fingertips.

At last Bishop Delgado put the letters aside and lifted his head. His eyes looked very old and very tired. "You have done right to bring these to me. I will decide what the next step must be—and if there is to be one. These are very serious charges, my son."

"'Serious charges'?" Father Ignazio blinked. Mild words indeed for the accusations made in the letters: unnatural lusts, incest, and murder.

Before morning mass, Father Ignazio took a stroll through the grounds. The sun was warm, but the air was clear and cool in the shade. In the distance the mountains raised their heads beyond the adobe walls, aloof and mysterious. He felt the tranquillity of the place seep through his skin and soak deep into his soul. For the first time since Dona

Ysabella had shared her secrets with him, he was almost at peace.

When the priest returned to his room, Dona Ysabella's small coffer waited on the tiny side table in a patch of sunlight. The polished wood shone with golden splendor, but he knew the darkness it held inside. At least inside these walls he had felt secure enough to leave it behind. For the past weeks it had been his personal millstone, weighing his spirit down. Even now the bishop must be evaluating the same questions: Must the corpse of past evil be dug from its grave and displayed in the naked light of the present? To whom was more owed, the living or the dead? Should temporal justice be invoked, or was it far better to leave the judgment in the hands of God?

Father Ignazio had already reached his conclusions, and now it was only for the bishop to validate them. Soon the matter would be out of his hands completely. Bishop Delgado was a man both wise and holy. Whatever decision he made, Father Ignazio was sure it would be just. There was a rap on his unlocked door, and Father Siguente entered. He looked like a man who had been up all night.

"I regret that Bishop Delgado cannot grant you an audience today. Or indeed for many days, if ever. He has suffered an attack of some sort during the night. Presently he is in a deep slumber from which he has not yet roused. The infirmarian is not hopeful of a happy outcome. . . ."

"This is terrible news. I shall pray for him." Father Ignazio was in a quandary. "I do not know what to do without instruction. I am only a humble man." He glanced at the wooden coffer and back. "Forgive me for bothering you with my own cares when you have so much responsibility now, but who will conduct the bishop's business in the interim?"

The skin of Father Siguente's face drew tight as a mask. "It is to me that both the burden and the honor falls in the interim. But I regret I cannot meet with you to consider your matter at the present. You are needed in Santa Fe, I understand." He indicated the box with a wave of his hand. "If you wish to leave your documents with me, I will of course read them and offer you what counsel I can, but it may be weeks before I am free to do so."

"Perhaps that would be the best course to follow. I will pray for guidance." He made no attempt to give the box to Father Siguente. After a short, hostile pause the other cleric went out.

Alone again, Father Ignazio sat on the hard bed and sighed. It seemed the burden was still his to carry, at least for a few more days. Such a small thing to weigh so heavily upon his conscience. Idly he picked up the box and lifted the lid. Inside, instead of the folded papers, was a heap of torn and crumpled scraps.

"Mother of God!" In his dismay he dropped the box. The joints parted, and it split into several pieces. Father Ignazio ignored the broken wood as he knelt down on the floor. Doubting the evidence of his eyes, he picked up a handful of the papers. He recognized the style of the writing, but only parts of words could be made out. It would be impossible to reconstruct the letters.

He released the scraps, and they floated to the floor like bits of ash. The griefs and sins of the past were now nothing but unsubstantiated memories existing solely in his mind. To Father Ignazio's knowledge, he was the only living person aware of all the facts. Unless, that is, the unknown who had destroyed the letters had read them first. But who? And why?

He would have to rethink the situation.

As the priest stooped to retrieve the broken casket, he noticed something unusual about it. A piece of finely tooled leather might have been used to line a coffer, but why would it be hidden by another rectangle of polished wood? As he examined it the priest realized that there had been a false bottom built into the box. It was not a lining, but a thin leather-bound volume wedged inside the enclosed space.

He withdrew it carefully. His indrawn breath was a hiss

of surprise. The dark blue cover was embossed with an intricate border and centered front and back with a familiar crest. That of Don Miguel Alvarez de Medina.

The priest's hands shook. Scraps of old rumors floated through his head, but he had promised to see this through. Opening it, the priest plunged himself even deeper into the heart of the mystery.

It was a journal, filled with script in a feminine hand and designated "Volume II." A slip of pale blue ribbon was sewn in for a bookmark, and a faded blossom, lovingly dried and pressed, fell out when he opened it. Although the petals were crackly, they retained their original rose color and the faintest hint of perfume. He wondered who had put it there and what occasion it had marked.

The same delicate hand had scribbled something on the end paper behind it, as if in great haste. He had to squint to read the faded writing. It seemed he had opened it backward:

> Thus ends Volume II of my confession of
> sins, which I cannot tell to my poor priest—
> and may God have mercy upon me.

With trembling hands he turned it over and read the first sentences. After a few pages he stopped, overcome. These writings had never been meant for his eyes or any others. He felt like a voyeur leafing through a litany of private pain. This diary was the secret confessional of a young woman denied the solace of the official sacrament of penance. It held the outpourings of a bruised and troubled heart.

He rubbed his hands over his eyes. Did his promise to Dona Ysabella cover this journal also? He supposed it did. Steeling his nerves, he forced himself to flick through the next few pages, pausing to scan when certain names leapt out at him.

At last he closed the diary, unable to force himself to read further. The simple words, the raw emotions in it, were far more incriminating than the letters had been. He looked for a place to hide it. There was none.

Mother of God, what am I to do now? he asked himself. The priest tucked the slim volume securely inside his garments, but the despair and anguish of decades past still filled the room.

Whoever had destroyed the letters might feel safe now, because they hadn't known about the diaries and their further testimony. But perhaps that same mind would realize all the evidence had not been destroyed: there was still the knowledge of what had happened in his own, very accurate memory. Father Ignazio crossed himself, asking for the guidance of the Holy Spirit; for he suddenly felt very cold and very, very much afraid.

It was after the noon meal that Father Ignazio sought out a harried cleric with the look of one too busy to delve into matters that didn't concern him. "I do not wish to bother Father Siguente when he has so much to deal with during the bishop's illness," he said. "Please convey my best wishes to him and tell him that the matter has, in a most peculiar way, resolved itself."

The secretary to Father Siguente was relieved that at least this task would be simple. He smiled with the banked eagerness of a host learning that unwanted guests were leaving before their scheduled departure date. "You are returning to Monterrey?" he asked, mistaking Father Ignazio for a priest who'd come seeking an audience with the bishop.

Father Ignazio realized the secretary's mistake and answered with subtlety worthy of a Jesuit. "Monterrey! A place that is dear to my heart. How anxious I am to see it once more."

Before setting out, the priest spent an hour on his knees in meditation. After all his prayers, his decision was unchanged: evil must be torn out, root and branch. The saying had been a favorite of his grandfather's.

But when he left the compound and reached the road, he didn't take the way that would have eventually led him to his birthplace. Grimly, knowing his journey would be both dangerous and difficult, Father Ignazio headed north on the Camino Real. He had business with two men in Santa Fe. One was the formidable Don Miguel. The other, if he lived, was a man named Quinn Logan. Between the two of them he would surely find the answer to the puzzle.

He suddenly shivered in the warm sunshine. He remembered another saying of his grandfather's: "When the past casts long shadows, no man can escape them."

Seventeen

Santa Fe: 1840

Don Miguel rose before sunrise while his manservant was still asleep in the adjoining alcove. His joints were stiff as he climbed out of the huge bed that had traveled from Madrid to Mexico City, then to the Hacienda de Medina, and, at last, here to Santa Fe. It was said to be the only real bed except for the one owned by His Excellency, Governor Manuel Armijo. Don Miguel had been born in it, and he intended to die in it.

His thoughts turned to death more and more these days. His nightly dreams were restless, haunted by faces of the dead. He passed the niche that held the beautifully worked statue of his patron saint without really noticing it. It had been many a year since he had prayed.

A cock crowed, a dog barked, and the sun rose in a pearly sky. Gradually the light flooded the hills and glinted on the snowy peaks of the Sangre de Cristo Mountains. The household awakened and set about the morning chores. The old don went up the steps to the rooftop to survey his kingdom. It had shrunk greatly in the past years and was not nearly so wealthy and grand as the estate he'd left behind in Mexico almost three decades earlier. He lived like a rich man now, but once he had lived like a king— with all the prerogatives.

The Hacienda de Medina, which he had planned to hand down to his son—and failing that to a grandson—was no more than the ashes of his dreams. He was an old man, sliding into the shadows. At times, when he grew weary, he wondered why he bothered to go on. But he was a de Medina, the descendant of royalty, the last of a proud and ancient line. And when youth and strength fled, pride was all that was left to a man.

Don Miguel had always had more than his share. Perhaps, he thought, that was why the women in his life had had so little. Julianna! Estrellita! Ysabella! The old man's fists doubled in, and he felt the icy fingers clamp around his heart, squeezing. Squeezing . . .

His hands fisted with the effort to hold back the memories. Pain came back, pressing down upon his chest like the hand of God. Don Miguel waited some time before it eased, and his skin was damp and gray; but after it passed he was himself once more.

He forced his mind away from his infirmity and tried to clear his thoughts, but other problems intruded. This troublesome Father Ignazio, for instance. A man with a conscience is either a saint or a fool, he mused. Of the two, Don Miguel would much rather deal with a fool: a saint with a conscience could be a dangerous foe.

A rider came across the valley, kicking up feathers of dust, and the old man stiffened. Then the figure drew nearer, and he recognized one of his men from Santa Fe. A few minutes later a servant tiptoed up to the old eagle's aerie. "Colonel Armstrong has arrived, Don Miguel."

"I will see him in the *sala*."

The servant bustled off, but Don Miguel sat a while longer, surveying his kingdom. He had sold the Hacienda de Medina in Mexico—lush acres, fine cattle, superb horses—for this: twenty thousand acres of dry New Mexico scrub that would support sheep but not the steers and cows he had formerly raised. The house was old, parts of it built by the first Spaniards in the area, but it had none of the luxuries he had been accustomed to in Mexico, either. It had been a gamble, one that had not yet paid off thus far. But it would.

Somewhere near his twenty thousand acres, masked by

rock and sand and juniper, was a gold vein so rich it would make the bounty of the Ortiz mine seem like a mere handful of coins. He had a bag of the nuggets to prove it, grape-size pieces so pure they could be molded by the pressure of his fingers. He wanted that gold more than he'd wanted anything except a true heir to inherit his kingdom. He'd had no heir, but he would find the gold. It was the thought of it that kept him alive. That and his pride.

He rose and joined the colonel, a lean man with piercing blue eyes. The military bearing and extreme neatness of dress made most people accept the man's story that he'd recently resigned a commission in the U.S. Army to pursue private enterprise. His version was slightly skewed. The whole affair still rankled the bogus colonel. He'd lost his commission five years back because of a certain raid on a Pawnee village.

"I hope you have brought me the news I have been waiting for," Don Miguel said by way of greeting.

Armstrong smiled. "I haven't located the vein yet, but we're close. Damn close!" He reached into his pocket. The nugget he pulled out was larger than a walnut. "This assayed as pure as they get. And I found another site up along that wash called Old Woman Creek."

"Then why are you here, wasting your time and mine, when you could be investigating further?"

Armstrong's face purpled, but he held his temper outwardly. He needed Don Miguel on his side for a few more months. "Indians," he explained. "The whole goddamned place is crawling with Cheyenne."

A singularly unpleasant light shone in his host's eyes. "Ah, you don't like the *indios*? But I am certain I had heard that you were particularly fond of them—or at least of their women and children."

It was touch and go for a minute. Armstrong took a deep breath. "Why the hell anyone cared that a few Indian women were raped and killed was more than I'll ever understand. As for the children, why, they'd just have grown up into a passel of thieving, raiding murderers. If the Indian

problem isn't solved soon, the land will be soaked with
blood. If it comes to that, it's far better that it not be white
blood."

The old don was tired of baiting his hired man. "Get
the Indians off that land before they discover the gold and
begin trading it for bullets and whiskey. Until I can afford
to buy those five thousand acres from the government of
New Mexico, we must keep word of the gold from leaking
out. If Governor Armijo gets wind of it, he'll take the land
for himself and we'll be shut out in the cold."

"Don't worry. I'll clear those Cheyenne out." Armstrong
rubbed his chin in satisfaction. It would be just like the old
days. Later he could get the whites involved with Josie
Carter's story of a Cheyenne riding away from Fort Laramie
with a white child. It didn't matter that no such child was
found to be missing—people believed what they wanted to
believe. He left shortly, chagrined that he hadn't been
invited to stay for supper.

Don Miguel was glad when the colonel was gone. A man
might own a vicious dog for hunting the wild boar, but he
did not sit down to eat with it.

The servant was back. "A letter for you, Don Miguel.
It was brought up with the caravan from Ciudad Juarez."

Don Miguel waited until he was alone and broke the
seal. The writer was one Fray Domingo, a monk of a nursing
order near Ciudad Juarez. It seemed, the good brother
wrote, that Father Ignazio would have to postpone his visit
to Don Miguel in Santa Fe, as he was seriously ill with the
influenza. The disease was particularly malignant this season
and had already caused many deaths. It was very likely,
Fray Domingo implied, that Father Ignazio would never rise
from his sickbed at all.

Folding the letter, Don Miguel placed it in his pocket.
A pleased smile played over his saturnine features, and he
thought of an old proverb: "Man plans—and God laughs."

So much for Father Ignazio.

Eighteen

BETTANY ROLLED OVER FOR THE TENTH TIME.
Hannah slumbered by her side. The night was cool and
crisp. Good sleeping weather, they had called it back in
Pennsylvania, but she wakened from troubled dreams and
was unable to fall back to sleep. Although the dreams were
now only tattered remnants, fading rapidly, she knew they
were about her father. He'd been close, so close she could
reach out to touch him, but had vanished before her eyes.
Then the dream had altered to the meadow by the ravine,
and she'd been running to warn Mouse and Blue Morning
Flower. Running in vain. . . .

Since the attack Bettany hadn't had one uninterrupted
night's sleep. She got up and checked on Hannah. The
child had been fretful all day. She was curled up on her
side with one arm around the small leather doll Feather
had given her, heartbreakingly vulnerable in her slumber.
What kinds of thoughts went through her mind, what did
she think of the people who came and went in her life so
rapidly? How much loss could a child endure and remain
unscathed?

How much could she?

The lodge was too empty with only the two of them.
Blue Morning Flower's place was only a cleared space nearby
in the darkness, and Small Eagle's pile of robes lay waiting.
Once he returned she might be able to close her eyes with
some confidence, but Bettany was not anxious for her husband's return.

The families of Mouse and Spirit Woman and the two
men slain fighting the enemy had slashed their arms and
legs in mourning until the blood flowed from their limbs.
Others had wailed like banshees or cut their hair to show
their grief. They had given away the belongings of their
slain kin within hours of their deaths. When Small Eagle
returned and learned of his mother's death, he would do
the same. Bettany wondered if he would expect her to follow
suit; but that was not the reason she dreaded his home-
coming. She wrapped up in her robe and tried to court
sleep, again without success.

A rustle from outside the lodge brought her upright in a
flash, reaching for the rifle that was never far from her side.
She rose as silently as a shadow and drifted toward the
entrance. As she untied the flap to peer out, she realized
that someone was lying on the ground in front of it. She
widened the space for a better look and recognized him
even before she saw his face: Wolf Star. If dreams of her
father haunted her sleep, this was the man whose presence
or absence haunted her waking hours.

Bettany gazed upon him for several seconds, unmoving.
After the first initial gasp of surprise, she held her breath.
The urge to reach out and touch his cheek almost overwhelmed her. She leaned down, aching to smooth his thick
dark hair with her fingertips, wanting to feel the strength
of his arm beneath her palm. Knowing that if he was her
husband, she would have welcomed him to her.

She quickly fastened the entrance flap and stretched out
in her robe. Her fears were eased. She and Hannah were
alone, but not unprotected. Within minutes she was
soundly, blessedly asleep.

Logan was awake. He'd known when she peered out the
flap, heard her soft intake of breath, smelled the soft
woman-scent of her body. He had only pretended to be
asleep, but he'd sensed the moment when her hand had
hovered near his temple, dreaded and longed for her touch.

Inside the lodge, Bettany wandered in happier dreams.
Outside, Logan lay awake till dawn. As soon as it was light

he got his horse and rode out into the hills, away from temptation.

Despite the breeze the day was hot and sticky. The children played quiet games with sticks and stones, and even the dogs felt the heat. They lay in the dust with their tongues hanging out, occasionally lifting their heads to sniff at some interesting smell before dozing off again. Bettany and Hannah seemed to feel the heat the most. When Singing Wolf, one of the Contraries, tried his antics to make her laugh, Hannah was fretful instead. On the excuse of needing fresh water, Bettany took her down to the stream, where the trees offered some shelter from the sun, and lingered there for the luxury of being alone. There was little privacy in the Indian village.

It seemed cooler by the water, but whether that was real or only her imagination, she didn't know. Settling her back against a mossy trunk, she rested amid the green-and-gold shadows with Hannah's head in her lap. Suddenly she was startled by a quick succession of splashes in the stream. She went completely still. It was reflex now to freeze and become part of the scenery at any unexplained sound. Even Hannah had the same reaction, but hers was born of terror rather than caution. Another splash, louder than the first, gave Bettany a sense of the direction they were coming from. Without moving her head, she slid her gaze sideways and saw a streak of dark brown pass by.

She patted Hannah's hand and spoke softly. "It's all right. Come see."

They crawled through a gap in the ground cover, where there was a better view. Hannah put her hands over her mouth in delight. A group of otters was at play beside the stream. One slid down the sloping bank into the water, all sleek grace and sinuous beauty, and dove beneath the surface. She surfaced, rolled on her back, and floated serenely by. The others followed in sequence, every movement seemingly filled with glee and the exuberance of being alive on such a wonderful day.

Bettany had never seen otters before. They were much larger than she'd imagined, over four feet from dark button noses to the tips of their tails, and they moved with agile elegance. Hannah was as fascinated as Bettany, watching the lithe creatures scramble up the bank by another path, tumble and roll around merrily, and streak down their mud slide once more.

Time passed with only the sounds of their play and the occasional hum of insect wings. Bettany could have stayed stretched out on the bank all day with Hannah beside her, watching the otters frolic. It was the first time she'd been completely light-hearted since she'd left the orphanage and her girlhood behind her.

An otter paddled lazily by on its back, preening its whiskers. It spotted her along the bank, twisted with incredible nimbleness, and vanished, to pop up almost within arm's reach. The clever eyes looked into hers, and Hannah laughed aloud. The otter did a quick revolution and surfaced again, inviting them to join in the game.

Suddenly the otters streaked away, as if at an inaudible signal. Only their noses and the tips of their heads were exposed, and they left wakes of inverted V's streaming behind them along the dappled surface. Before Bettany could turn to see what had startled them, a shadow fell across her and another reflection joined hers.

Wolf Star.

Her heart thudded against her ribs, and she was afraid to turn around. A dried blossom floated past, whirled away by the force of the water. Bettany understood how it felt. She was caught up in something that made her feel that she was also being swept along as helplessly.

Logan wished he hadn't alarmed the otters. The delighted expression on Bettany's face and its smaller image in Hannah had pulled the blinders from his eyes. He loved his brother's wife. The knowledge, swift and devastating, robbed him of speech.

His silence unnerved Bettany. She had thought of him all day, trying to analyze exactly why his nearness should

fill her with a wonderful awareness of security and a terrible
sense of unease. Her own behavior was a paradox to her,
because she drew such comfort from his presence. He slept
each night outside her lodge and was always gone before
dawn, and she had gone to great pains to avoid him during
the day, but one fact could not be denied: they were bound
together by some extra sense, a web of invisible silver
strands, that grew stronger and more sensitive every day.

Confused, not knowing what to say or do, she rose as if
he weren't there and scooped up water in her container.
Hannah was looking around for the otters, bewildered by
their lightning disappearance. Bettany held out her hand.
"Come along, Hannah, they're gone."

For a moment she thought he would just stand there
without saying a word. As she tried to pass him he stepped
directly in her path. Bettany's head tipped back. How much
larger he seemed now that they were so close. She could
smell the sweat and his deep, male scent and hear his
indrawn breath. She could almost hear the beating of his
heart. Her pupils widened.

Logan felt his pulse speed up. She wasn't as indifferent
as she seemed. Although her shoulders were squared and
her jaw firm, there were subtle feminine shiftings in her
body—small, instinctive alterations of carriage and expression that a woman made when she was attracted to a man.

It took all his will to keep from pulling her into his arms.
He was shaking inside with the need for her. He'd faced
Halsey and his men with far less trepidation. But Halsey
hadn't had strange silver eyes that pierced to the center of
his soul. He wondered if every time that she looked at him
she remembered the scalps and saw a man with bloodstained
hands.

He was never one to hang back when directness was
required. "You're angry with me. I want to know why."

Bettany had become so accustomed to replying in Cheyenne that at first the English words sounded like a foreign
tongue. "Angry? That's ridiculous. Why should I be angry?"

He didn't touch her, but his eyes held hers while they

said all the things he could not put into words:

Because I was blinded by my grief for Anna and left you with my brother while I went after Hannah.

Because you are a white woman and you think that, as a man of the same blood, I should aid you in returning to your own kind.

But you are a white woman living as a Cheyenne wife, and even though you do not know it now, you can never return to your former life. You will never be accepted. You are forever tainted by your association with us. You don't understand yet. But I do. . . .

Bettany couldn't read Logan's face. She pushed past him hurriedly and went up the slope. She could feel him watching her all the way back and returned to her lodge in turmoil. At the edge of the river, when Wolf Star had looked at her so darkly, she had been gripped by such strong feelings that her knees had almost given out. For just a moment she had thought he was going to sweep her into his arms. And for just a moment—one wild, breath-stopping moment, she had wanted him to.

She was ashamed of her fierce response. If not for Hannah at her side, who knew what might have happened? Dear God but she had to get away before it was too late, before she violated every principle she had been brought up to honor. But not before Small Eagle came back with Nils. Only then could she begin making plans.

For the rest of the day she went about her chores without glancing up once to seek him. There was no need: the thin silver threads that bound them had thinned into a single, tenuous filament as the sun rose high in the sky. When it snapped she knew that he'd left the camp.

Logan wrapped up in his robe and stretched out beside Bettany's lodge. Another night of restless sleep and uneasy longings. If Small Eagle didn't return in the next two days, he'd . . . what? Abandon a white woman and child among the Sand Hill People without a man to protect or hunt for them? No, he was tied to the place like a warrior staked to the ground to face the enemy charge. He must show equal valor, although he'd much prefer to run: battle, pain, and death he understood, but not this woman or the bonds that held him to her side.

Hell and damnation! He couldn't remember where in his wanderings he'd picked up that phrase. It certainly suited the situation. The flames that burned within were consuming him, licking away at his cautions and loyalties. Eating away his will. Perhaps this was what the parson had meant by hellfire, but his notion of Christian religion was hazy. White by birth, he was Cheyenne by every other means of reckoning. A god who allowed himself to be hung upon a cross was no god to his mind; yet something in the parson's stories had compelled his interest. Miracles of loaves and fishes, the dead raised to live again. He would have liked the parson to tell him more, but there had been no time. Not after they had begun to build the gallows.

They had laid the parson's god in the grave and rolled a stone before it, but Logan had not been as willing to go meekly to his own death. The morning of the hanging he had made his break. A life had been lost in the process, but it hadn't been his. He had followed Halsey and his men along a blood-soaked trail and had finally come back to the place where he belonged. Ten years of life in the white man's world. Ten years he could have sloughed off like a lizard shucked its skin. If they hadn't taken the shortcut and come upon the wagons. If he hadn't looked into a pair of clear gray eyes and lost his soul in them.

Logan folded his arms behind his head and stared up at the sky. He'd never known the stars to be so bright and full. Or himself so empty. Smoke Along the Ground was somewhere on his way back from Bent's Fort after settling matters for the great meeting with the other tribes, and Small Eagle was no doubt returning from a successful raid. And here he lay, playing watchdog outside the lodge of a woman who ignored his very existence. A woman who belonged to his brother.

Bettany was just as confused. She had come to rely on

Logan without even being aware of it. The following morning as she rose from her sleeping pallet he coughed and entered. In the half-light his face was thinner and interestingly shadowed, his profile like a hawk's for fierceness and for grace. Who was he, this bronze-skinned white man who thought of himself as Cheyenne? What hopes and thoughts, what dream and memories, lived behind his strange golden eyes?

He turned those eyes her way, and she was caught in them like a doe caught in the light of a hunter's lantern. She couldn't look away, and neither could he. Slowly, like a man reaching for something so precious, so fragile, the mere touch of his fingertips could shatter it, he put his hand against her cheek. She forgot how to move or breathe. Whatever might have come next was banished by the thudding of hoofbeats outside.

Small Eagle had returned.

She pulled back sharply. Logan emerged from the lodge into the sunlight as Small Eagle dismounted and gave his pony to one of the younger men. Dried blood crusted his arms and legs where he had cut them in mourning, and the youthful look was gone forever from his face. His eyes narrowed when he saw Logan exit the lodge.

"How is this that you lie abed until the sun is high, while our mother's killers go free?"

"Blue Morning Flower is avenged. Their scalps decorate your lodge pole."

Double guilt washed over Small Eagle, for not being there to defend against the attack and for not being there to avenge the death. Always, *always*, it was Wolf Star who took his own rightful place. Who knew what other responsibilities he had usurped?

Small Eagle pushed past him into the tipi, just as Bettany was slipping on her outer garments. With her sleep-heavy eyes and nervous manner she looked like a woman arising from a bed of love.

Small Eagle's vision was dimmed by jealousy and the long shadows of the past. All he saw was his woman, who had always covered herself before him, half-naked in the lodge, which his brother had just left. He shouted at her—harsh, ugly words he didn't even know he said.

"Small Eagle!" Her gasp of fright he interpreted as one of guilty dismay.

Always quick to anger, held in check only by the importance of self-control and public opinion among his people, he felt no need to curb himself inside his own place. He grabbed Bettany by the hair and yanked her to her feet. His face was dark with fury, only inches from hers as she struggled to escape. She was terrified that he meant to kill her on the spot. There would be no time even to wonder why.

The force of his reaction was almost beyond Small Eagle's control. Rage and pain threatened to burst out in violence. He could have snapped her neck with one blow. For an instant, a lifetime, her fate hung in the balance. A shudder ran through him, and he flung her away. Bettany cried out as she was thrown off-balance and landed with a crash among her cooking utensils. Her scalp prickled and burned as if it had been ripped away from her skull.

Hannah awakened and rubbed her eyes, and Bettany froze. Small Eagle stood over her, breathing heavily, and she was afraid to move and set him off again. When he stepped toward her she instinctively prepared to ward off the blows she was sure would fall. "No!"

As her arm brushed the side of her face, she felt wetness there. The stinging in her arm seeped into her awareness and once there became a throbbing pain. The edges of a broken pot had cut into her forearm, and warm blood flowed down her hand and dripped between her fingers. She didn't know her face was streaked with transferred blood.

Frightened by things she didn't understand, Hannah began to wail. Outside, Logan heard the commotion and ran back toward the lodge. He found Hannah shrinking away from Small Eagle and Bettany covered with blood, scrabbling toward the girl. He caught Small Eagle's arm. "Have you gone mad?"

Small Eagle shoved him away, but Logan clung to him, trying to drag him outside. As Bettany watched they grappled with each other and ended up on the ground, grunting and rolling through the cold ashes of the fire. They fought in earnest, exchanging blow for vicious blow. She was frightened out of her wits.

Grabbing Hannah up, she ran outside and thrust her into the arms of the first woman she saw. By now it seemed that half the camp was aware of something wrong, and knots of people clumped about the lodge. The whisper went through them. "It is Wolf Star and Small Eagle who contend with one another."

With Bettany standing outside, pale and smeared with blood, the object of the clash was obvious to all. She felt them withdraw from her, the outsider who had brought discord between the brothers. Bear Claw, one of the official peacekeepers of the camp, came to the front of the growing crowd but refused to enter. What a man did outside his lodge was one thing and what he did within it another; but if the participants came out, he was quite prepared to take action.

"Do something," Bettany demanded. When he folded his arms over his chest, she wheeled away from him and grabbed a pole from the meat-drying rack. She charged into the lodge without any clear idea of what she could do but knowing she must try to stop them.

The lodge shuddered as the men inside wrestled. Except for the sickening thuds it was a silent struggle. Then, as Bettany watched helplessly, it ended. The two men were getting to their feet, their sweat-slicked sides heaving. Small Eagle had taken the worst of it, and the skin along his jaw was bruised from where his face had been forced down into the ground.

The white heat of anger had gone out of him; but there had been a time when Small Eagle might have gone for his knife, had Wolf Star not prevented it. The knowledge of it lay thick in the lodge. Small Eagle was ashamed. He had forgotten for the moment about Bettany and the jealousy that had inflamed him. He remembered only that in a moment of rage he had wanted to kill his brother.

Logan's face was stern. "The woman committed no evil. And neither did I."

The chagrin Small Eagle suffered made him abrupt. "You did not wrong me. I know this." He couldn't meet the other man's eyes.

Logan turned to Bettany. "Are you all right?"

Her fear evaporated. Now it was her turn to be angry. "I'm fine, thank you! What else could I be, stranded in the wilderness surrounded by squabbling savages who go for each other's throats like animals with no prior warning! Well, I've survived two massacres in the past months, and I can certainly survive a few more cuts and bruises."

She stormed out of the lodge, followed by Logan and Small Eagle. As she reached to take Hannah a woman named Many Quills reached out. "Come with me. I will bind your wound."

The crowd parted to let them through. Head high, Bettany let Many Quills assist her toward her lodge. The low chuckles that came in her wake infuriated her. She was sure they were laughing at her expense. It was left to Logan and Small Eagle to deal with their actual comments: "Warrior Woman is indeed brave."

"Yes, for she has vanquished both Wolf Star and Small Eagle. See how they hang their heads like chastised children."

Shoulder to shoulder, the two men who'd fought so unmercifully earlier glared at the onlookers. For those few minutes they were united. But when the throng dispersed they each went in separate directions.

As the day wore on Small Eagle's shame grew. In the madness of his jealousy he had turned upon his wife and brother with false accusations of adultery. And it had been he who had lain with a woman who was not his own. Red Paint Woman, like others of her tribe, was generous with her favors, but among the Tsistsistas chastity and constraint were the rules. There was no reason he couldn't take a second wife, or indeed a third or fourth, as long as he could provide for them. It was the custom of his people—but it was not the custom of the *ve-ho-e*.

Thorson had explained this to him once. In the white-eyes culture a man could only take another if his first wife died or if he put her away from him. To have more than one at the same time was a grievous sin and an insult of great proportions to the first wife. Even among the Tribes such matters did not always run smoothly. Thorson had learned this at first hand. When his Arapaho woman had learned that he'd taken another wife among the Pawnee, she had tried to kill him. Thorson was very proud of the long scar that marked his chest and told the story often when he was drunk.

Small Eagle's mind was full of how close he'd come to disaster. When Wolf Star had first come into the lodge in response to Bettany's cries, for a moment—a terrible moment—he had almost gone for his knife. Wolf Star would have been completely unprepared for such an attack. One swift, lethal move and it would have been done. Sweat stood out on Small Eagle's brow as he imagined the sickening feel of the blade plunging home between his brother's ribs, as he envisioned the sudden ashy pallor and Wolf Star staring up at him with eyes that asked "Why?" before going blank with death.

It had been that close. And he was certain that Wolf Star knew it.

Their previous rift had sent Wolf Star out into the white man's world, and only tragedy had sent him back. If he left again, he would never return. Small Eagle would lose his brother, his friend, his rival, who always was and always would be a part of himself. It would be like chopping off his own leg or cutting out his heart. They had been carried within the same cradleboard, nourished at the same breasts. And a Cheyenne who killed one of his own people was banished forever from the Tsistsistas.

He was about to ride after his brother when he realized

that Wolf Star had left all his belongings behind, and he
would not go this time without taking leave of old Buffalo
Heart and Smoke Along the Ground. There was still a
chance to undo the damage.

He sought out Buffalo Heart and found him resting beneath a tree. The old man's eyes were failing, but his ears
were sharp and his instinct keener. He didn't say anything
when Small Eagle joined him. There was wisdom in silence.
Buffalo Heart waited until he felt the last of the poison
drain out of Small Eagle's soul. It took a long time, for it
had been there a great while. The evil crawled away. He
saw it from the corners of his eyes, moving like a muddy
cloud into a patch of sun, where it vanished in a shimmer
of light.

"The sun is warm, and I drowsed as old men do. I had
a dream," Buffalo Heart said in the way he began many of
his stories. "I thought this dream was meant for you, but I
was not sure. If it is yours, you will know it."

Small Eagle shifted slightly and waited until the old warrior continued. "I dreamed that a man took and ate an
antelope haunch which did not belong to him. He became
ill with it, and the illness spread throughout the camp."

The younger brave sat patiently, but it seemed there was
no more. "What happened then? What is the meaning of
this dream?"

Buffalo Heart put his wrinkled hand along Small Eagle's
sinewy forearm. "You are the only one who can answer
those questions. If it is your dream."

He rose and went to his lodge, but Small Eagle stayed
beneath the tree, lost in thought. The old sage's words
stayed with him while the sun melted into a puddle of gold
on the horizon. The sky was tinged with violet hues when
he started slowly back to his lodge. A breeze had sprung
up, blowing wild and free. It swept down from the north,
edged with loneliness that whistled through his soul. Small
Eagle wrestled with himself, with the past, and with the
future he envisioned. It was only when he saw his brother
approaching the camp that he made his resolve. A shooting

star blazed high above the earth and was extinguished. He took it for an omen.

Logan came across the river and saw the shooting star's fiery streak. Dusk was rising from the ground to meet the fading glow of the sky. The row of trees, the line of tipis, and the high ground beyond all blurred and blended together in the twilight, shapes and images from a dream. And that was what it had been, all his fine expectations of picking up the pieces of his former life and making them whole again. Making himself whole again.

He witnessed the falling star and also saw it as an omen, a troubling one. The other stars were fixed in the heavens, sure of their places in the natural harmony of things. But some, like this one, like himself, were only transients lost among the orderly workings of the universe. He thought of the medal in his amulet pouch. Perhaps it would provide him with the vital clue to who and what he was, and to where he really belonged. Perhaps no such place existed. Some men carried their own shadows with them no matter how far or how long they rode.

Ahead he saw the painted designs on Small Eagle's lodge through the veil of dusk. He slowed his horse to a walk as he entered the camp, memorizing every sight and sound and smell. They would have to last him a lifetime. There was no way he could stay on.

Inside the tipi Hannah was sleeping restfully after a fretful night. Bettany had spent most of the day inside with her, away from prying eyes. When she heard the hoofsteps and the voices just outside, she tensed and then busied herself with her normal tasks.

She was quiet when Logan entered and began gathering up his things, but she watched him closely. He took his extra ammunition, canteen, and the hide robe Blue Morning Flower had given him. Before her death she'd begun a shirt of fine buckskin, but it was only half-done. Folding it gently, he put the shirt back in the reed basket where she'd left it and smoothed it with his hands.

Bettany turned her face away, fighting down her panic.

He was leaving. Logan had somehow become the center of her universe. If he left she would be alone as she had never been before. She couldn't bear it. And she was suddenly so angry, she couldn't speak even if she had wanted to. He finished his task and started for the door but paused when Hannah woke up and smiled at him. She made one of her unintelligible happy sounds and reached her hand out to him. He hunkered down beside her and ran a finger down the curve of her cheek.

There was such tenderness in his gesture and such profound sorrow that Bettany felt as if her heart would break watching it. She came toward him, impelled by forces too strong to resist. "Don't . . . don't go."

Logan looked over his shoulder and stared, not sure he'd heard correctly. His eyes met Bettany's for a long moment before he wrenched his gaze away and stood. They were so close he could almost feel her warmth. As he tried to move back she clutched his sleeve. "Then take us with you."

Before he could reply Small Eagle entered, so intent on what he wanted to say that he failed to sense the tension in the lodge between the other two. He strode over to them and started right in.

"Wolf Star, you are my brother in every way but in blood. As children we slept in the same cradle. We suckled at the same mother's breasts and called the same man father. We took our first steps together. We played and hunted and grew to manhood side by side. Even in the years we lived apart there remained a bond between us that was never broken. I felt your pain as you felt mine. I speak the truth."

Logan bowed his head in acknowledgment. "You speak the truth, my brother."

"From infancy we have shared everything, and there is no reason for it to be otherwise now. Whatever I have is yours as well."

Logan looked up, and his eyes caught the light, glowing like yellow lamps as he hefted his belongings. "I am content. This is all I need."

"No. You are restless and filled with unease. It is time you took a woman."

Bettany had been following their exchange, but her Cheyenne was faulty and she wasn't quite sure what she'd heard. Then Logan looked at her, and she felt the blood drain from her face. Small Eagle pressed his point. In atonement for his jealousy and near murderous rage earlier, he would make the ultimate sacrifice, one that was an outrage to his Cheyenne upbringing, yet the only medicine that would salve his soul.

"There is no other man to whom I would say this. Until you take a woman of your own, until you set up your own lodge, we will share everything within mine." He squared his jaw. "Everything, including the woman."

Bettany had no doubts this time. If she had, the stunned expression on Logan's face would have vanquished them. She felt as if she'd been hit in the stomach, dizzy and nauseated and filled with fear; but there was another part of her that was quickened and breathless with yearning.

Logan took a deep, shuddering breath. His eyes caught Bettany's for a terrible, burning moment. She clasped her hands together until her nails scored her flesh and didn't know it. All her being was concentrated upon him: the fate of her entire world hung upon his reply.

No matter what it was, it would destroy her. Perhaps destroy them all.

Her thoughts were written plain upon her face. Logan felt the bottomless pit yawning open before him. The slightest misstep would send them all hurtling over the edge. His face twisted into an anguished mask.

Bettany held her breath, waiting. Then, with a smothered oath, Logan pushed past her and went out.

Nineteen

HIGH SUMMER RETURNED TO THE PLAINS, AND THE
old patterns of life were repeated. Bettany moved with the
Cheyenne band to the branch of the Republican River that
Small Eagle called Where the Willows Were Broken. It
was farther south then their usual warm weather camp, but
there was much coming and going between them and their
new allies, the Comanche and Apache. Every time a rider
came into camp she looked up, hoping yet dreading that
it would be Logan. Each time she was forced to realize that
her sense of disappointment was far keener than her relief.
Otherwise life went on, running in the same narrow channels.

Six weeks to the day that Small Eagle had returned from
the raid with his fine string of ponies, Whistling Bear rode
into the Cheyenne camp accompanied by several of his kin.
The buzz of excited gossip ran through the spectators. The
horses and travois were loaded down with a quantity of
things, including a fine assortment of hides and pelts, the
property of Red Paint Woman.

The women set about unloading the goods, and soon the
skeleton of another lodge was erected from the travois poles
and covered. Rumors abounded. The women whispered to
one another: Red Paint Woman had come to stay. Whistling Bear paid his respects to Smoke Along the Ground,
Buffalo Heart, and the chiefs of the soldier bands. "I do
not see Small Eagle among you," he said when the courtesies
had been observed.

243

Everyone in camp knew why the Arapaho had come. Smoke Along the Ground kept his countenance neutral. "My cousin is with the band but not in the camp. He has followed the water down toward Crooked Fork."

Whistling Bear continued to exchange news with his companions, but no one was surprised when he got up shortly—or that his way led him down the stream toward Crooked Fork. The Cheyenne braves exchanged glances and a few sly smiles.

Bettany was already at the fork where two branches made gentle zigzag bends, following the cracks laid down by some ancient cataclysm in the far Northwest. She was hot and sticky and wanted to cool off in the water away from chattering voices and prying eyes. Since Logan's departure every day seemed exactly like the one before it. And each day took her deeper into savage territory.

She was barefoot and bareheaded most of the time, lean and brown as an Indian. It had been weeks since she'd spoken her own tongue, months since she'd seen a white face. Even Thorson would be welcome, if only to hear English spoken and learn any news. Not that he would be any help to her. The more she became like the Cheyenne squaws around her, the more desperate she was to get away. Yet how was she ever going to find her way back to civilization alone? They were now deep in the heart of Indian lands, and she had no clue as to where she was.

Suddenly she was very homesick for the sound of her own language and the faces of her own kind. What she wouldn't give to see Mamie Ebbersoll come walking over that sandy ridge or to hear Sean O'Connell's lilting brogue! Even Letitia Renfrew's endless complaints would be music to her ears. And it would be a bit of heaven to be back on the trail through the wild roses of Ash Hollow or sitting around the cook fire with Nils and Hannah. The fourth face she envisioned wasn't Axel's. It belonged to a man with hair as black as night and eyes as gold as the morning sun.

The man who left the band when Small Eagle had offered

to let him share her favors. She would never forget that night. Logan's face just before he turned away was graven deeply in her memory, tortured and torn by his conflicting emotions.

Her own feelings had been in turmoil, too: fear, anger, pride, shock—and greater than them all, the soul-deep longing that Logan would agree and take the burden of guilt from her own conscience.

Instead he had gone away.

Voices drifted from the camp. She looked up and saw Small Eagle coming toward her. She wished she could avoid a private meeting with him. Since Logan had left, the tension in their lodge ran high and his physical demands upon her grew.

Small Eagle was restless and troubled. He did not know why Wolf Star had left the Tsistsitas but knew that this time it had been for good. And he was glad of it.

Wolf Star's leaving should have brought him closer with his wife, yet each time Small Eagle touched her she withdrew more, retreating inside herself where he could never follow. His frustration was keen. The more he asked of her, the less she gave; the more he desired her, the more she turned from him.

Halfway across the meadow he spied Whistling Bear's approach. Like the rest of the encampment he knew why the Arapaho had come and could only be glad that Red Paint Woman had not followed her uncle to the creek. Although he was a great warrior, Small Eagle felt at a disadvantage with women. Who could tell what any woman would do—especially one of the *ve-ho-e?*

He shouted across to Bettany. "Hurry, woman! Whistling Bear has come with his relatives to honor my lodge. Prepare a feast for our guests."

Bettany went across the meadow to the place where she'd found unripened berries a few days earlier. If the other women or the birds hadn't gotten them first, she might be able to collect enough for the guests.

Crickets whirred and chirped in the brush as she picked

the brambly berries and piled them on the shawl she'd placed upon a convenient rock. There were many bushes, but only a few berries to each. By the time she'd gathered enough, the sun was appreciably lower in the sky. There was no supper cooking at her fire, and she supposed that Small Eagle would be angry.

Bettany started back at a brisk pace and was surprised to find a savory mixture of roots and sage hen bubbling and ready to be eaten. In addition, small cakes had been made of elk-heart berries and the gluey residue of boiled rawhide shavings. There was even some kind of dried meat wrapped in thin leaves to dip into a bowl of hot drippings. She'd never seen so great a feast among the Cheyenne before.

Small Eagle sat cross-legged beside Whistling Bear and his younger brother, Two Wolves, tucking into the food with gusto. She expected Small Eagle to scold her or show his displeasure in some concrete way. There was a hard set to his face and a glint of anger in his eyes at Bettany's approach, but his calm greeting surprised her.

"This is a good thing you have done, wife, to set so fine a feast for my lodge."

Bettany suddenly realized he was not speaking to her, but to someone standing behind her in the shadows. She turned around to find an Arapaho woman behind her.

Red Paint Woman met her questioning look with a satisfied smile that grew from a small flicker of pleasure to a great victorious blaze.

The Cheyenne camp boiled with rumor. A war chief named Seven Bulls returned from the Arapaho camp with good news: their longtime foes—Comanche, Kiowa, and Apache—wished to make peace. They had asked for a meeting to be arranged at a mutually agreeable site.

The Cheyenne chiefs met in conference and later had a huge lodge, made from the coverings of two lodges, set up in the center of the encampment. There was much to discuss.

"How can we trust these men?" Breaks His Bow said,

refusing to smoke when the pipe came to him. "I think it is a trap."

Smoke Along the Ground had seen his brothers fall in the past spring to Comanche arrows. He puffed on the pipe. "Many of our warriors die each year in wars and raids against the enemy. Peace would be a good thing for all."

The pipe came next to Buffalo Heart, and the others waited expectantly to see what he would do. The old man was wise in the ways of this world and the next, and his words would carry great weight. Buffalo Heart held the long stem and communed with his spirits.

"Long ago three brothers shared a lodge with their families, but they quarreled and fell out. In the Moon When Plums Ripen each set out to bring down a buffalo, that he might feed his family. The first man was gored by the great bull's horn, the second was trampled beneath the great bull's hooves, and the third could not catch the beast and perished of hunger.

"From another lodge, three brothers set out together. Together they brought the great bull down, and they lived in peace and harmony for many years."

Smoke Along the Ground saw the questions in eyes of some of his fellows: Why does the old one speak of brothers and hunting, when it is of enemies and peace that we must talk? He addressed his elder. "What is this matter that you speak of?"

Slowly Buffalo Heart looked around the circle of chiefs and at the young men sitting behind near the door. "All the Tsistsistas, all the Comanche, Apache, Kiowa, and Arapaho, are few compared to the great numbers of *ve-ho-e* who will soon come across the wide river and fill the plains. As in the story of the brothers, only those who work together will survive."

They digested his meaning and decided to leave the decision to the Dog Soldiers, the warrior society known for its bravery and ferocity. The Dog Soldiers voted to accept the peace and arranged a preliminary meeting at the mouth of Two Butte Creek, where a past flood had piled great

heaps of driftwood, even whole trees. Small Eagle returned
from this second meeting, where fine gifts and horses were
exchanged, to announce that the peace council would be
held along the Arkansas River just below Bent's Fort.

There was great excitement in the camp, and Bettany
and Hannah were the only ones untouched by the news.
Bettany felt isolated since Blue Morning Flower's death and
the arrival of Red Paint Woman. There was nothing Bettany did that the Arapaho did not do ten, twenty, a hundred
times better. Red Paint Woman took every opportunity to
make her look foolish and worse.

Bettany suspected that the Arapaho woman acted out of
fear and jealousy but knew a good deal of the behavior
directed toward her was justified—at least from Red Paint
Woman's point of view. What good was a wife who didn't
know the proper way to scrape and tan a hide and who
couldn't tell a healing plant from a poisonous one? Bettany's
last foray to glean edible berries and medicinal herbs had
ended up with a violent stomachache, and even days later
she still felt queasy from it.

Only Small Eagle seemed immune to the tension within
his lodge, and as he divided his attentions equally between
the two women, he saw no reason for it to exist. It was
better for a warrior not to meddle in women's things, at
least as long as there was no state of war between them.

Bettany could hold her own, but she feared for Hannah.
Red Paint Woman was unkind to the girl in many subtle
ways. There was no physical punishment of children among
the Cheyenne band, and Red Paint Woman seemed good-
hearted with children, yet she had no patience with Hannah's slowness. One day when she had the cook fire going,
she repeatedly had to warn the girl away from the fire. At
last, tired of futile lectures, Red Paint Woman simply jerked
her away by the arm.

No real force had been used, and Hannah was more
frightened than hurt. She began screaming for all she was
worth—high, piercing wails that assaulted the ears. Bettany
had witnessed the entire incident from a distance as she

was returning from digging some roots. In her fury she dropped them and came charging into the camp. She pushed by Red Paint Woman and swept her foster daughter up in her arms.

"Don't you dare touch her!" She'd reverted to English, but Red Paint Woman understood her tone.

"If you wish the child to be safe, you must teach her properly. You are not doing what is expected of you as her mother."

Bettany saw that every woman in earshot was watching and agreeing with the Arapaho. Didn't they understand that there was something . . . different about Hannah? Or— and the thought was frightening—if they did realize it eventually, what would they do about it? On the wagon train Angus McGrew had told stories of Indians abandoning children with defects. Was that true or just another of his senseless lies?

The chill of apprehension faded. No, children were too loved and longed for among the Cheyenne. But Bettany was still upset. "She is my child. You have no business chastising her."

"Only one of the *ve-ho-e* would have such a ridiculous idea. The peace and safety of the entire camp can be destroyed by the foolish actions of one undisciplined person." Anger made a deadly weapon of Red Paint Woman's tongue.

"The girl is not right in her head. It would have been far better for you, and for us all, if Wolf Star had not gone to rescue her. Small Eagle warned him against it. He should have listened to Small Eagle and left you both to die among your own kind. Then there would be peace within this lodge."

Bettany was caught totally off guard. *Logan* had saved her. Saved Hannah. And Small Eagle had argued against it. The knowledge stunned her to immobility. Her former gratitude to the Cheyenne changed to caustic, burning anger. She was unable to sort out how much of the deception was Small Eagle's, how much the product of her own mis-understanding.

"Come, Hannah." Bettany turned and fled to the dry wash that was Hannah's favorite place to play, but she could not outrun her anguish. She hardly noticed when Smoke Along the Ground's little daughter joined them. The old dry wash was cracked and scoured from past torrents, and sometimes pretty stones could be found there, washed down from the mountains. Leaping Girl darted up and down the broken slope like one of the small brown lizards she had disturbed. Suddenly she straightened up. "See what I have found."

A piece of metal glinted in her palm, yellow as a marigold. Bettany examined it. It was a mass of small grooved cubes, and she'd seen its like before. Fool's gold.

"Very pretty," she told the girl, but the words were automatic. *She'd* been a fool, exchanging the real for the false. But she was fooled no longer. All ties of gratitude to Small Eagle had been severed by Red Paint Woman's revelation. In hindsight now it seemed so obvious, having learned the two men's characters so well: Small Eagle would not have felt any obligation to a white woman and child—and indeed, why should he? But Logan had not been able to ride away and leave them. *Logan,* not Small Eagle. Her sacrifice had been in vain. More than that, it had kept her from Logan, the man she loved.

Bettany was startled. The words that formed in her mind rang with the knell of truth: *the man she loved.* The knowledge released a flood of pain and loss. Oh, Logan.

A happy shriek roused her from her ruminations. Hannah was exclaiming eagerly over her discovery of one of the "shiny rocks." Bettany watched them searching among the dried, crusty soil. Leaping Girl took a stone and threw it down into the wash. Bettany picked one up idly and pitched it down the slope. The physical action released some of her tension. She tossed another and another. The fourth one her fingers encountered had a different feel, much too light for its mass.

Her fingers uncurled, and she blinked at the rounded chunk of metal in her hand. It was pale as butter and the size of a walnut. Gold. *True* gold.

Now that she knew what to look for, she saw several other pieces scattered at the bottom of the wash. She picked them up and searched for more as an idea jumped into her mind. The gold was the answer to her prayers. By the time she'd scoured the wash she had enough nuggets to fill her cupped hands. Enough to bribe her way back to civilization with some passing trapper. Even Thorson might be tempted.

Bettany could hardly wait to implement her plans, but within a few minutes of arriving back at the lodge they were driven from her mind by a more immediate worry. The smell of grease dripping into the cook fire filled her with nausea. She moved a distance upwind from it and leaned back against a tree, while Hannah played happily with her string of colored beads.

The sick feeling didn't pass. Instead Bettany's queasiness grew. She hadn't really felt well since the episode of the poisonous berries—but Hannah had eaten some and not become ill.

A chill passed over her. How long had it been since the wagon attack? The facts she'd repressed surfaced, and the unwanted knowledge hit her like a blow to the stomach.

The irritability and nausea that plagued her were suddenly, irrevocably explained. She was more than two months pregnant.

Twenty

LOGAN HAD LEFT BETTANY AND SMALL EAGLE BE-
hind him, yet they remained with him over the passing
weeks, the ghosts of what was and of what might have
been, haunting his thoughts. He was in no mood to be
sociable and avoided Bent's Fort and the company of his
fellow man.

Texas called him. He'd spent a few years there before in
his wanderings. A man could always find some kind of work
to lose himself in, and no one asked awkward questions. It
was out the Llana Estacado that his path crossed those of
two riders. He dismounted to check. The sign scattered
over the ground was recent, and no effort had been made
to hide the tracks of their unshod ponies. Comanche, he
thought, secure on their own lands. One of the riders was
considerably lighter than the other. Not troublemakers,
then. No war party traveled with women and children.

Logan considered a moment. He'd been alone with his
thoughts and memories, finding them bleak company. Suddenly he felt a longing to hear another voice, unusual in
a man who could travel alone for weeks in perfect contentment. He had often gone his way alone, but he had
never been lonely. Bettany had changed all that. He needed
companionship and conversation, even the edge of danger,
to clear his mind. To make him forget.

He bagged a brace of rabbits, more than enough for his
own needs, and followed the hoofprints. He found a Comanche warrior and a small boy sharing a meal of berries

and flat pieces of tough bread made from cornmeal. The man's face was known to him. Logan and Antelope Chaser had met by accident at Bent's Fort a year ago. And the boy . . .

Logan looked from him to Antelope Chaser. As far as he knew, the Comanche had neither sons nor nephews— yet the boy addressed him as "Father." The small warrior was dark-skinned from the sun and dressed Comanche fashion, but he bore no resemblance to the older man. He also spoke Comanche with a faint, almost indistinguishable accent. That made Logan curious. Something about the way the boy moved and sat and held his head was different, too.

This would bear investigation. Standing on the edge of their temporary camp, he held up the rabbits as a visible peace offering and cleared his throat to announce his presence. "Greetings, Antelope Chaser. I bring good meat to fill your stomach."

The boy reached for his bow, but the older man stopped him with a gesture. "Let him come to us. I have no quarrel with him."

The boy obeyed but kept his hand upon his bow, eyes wary as Logan approached. The Comanche brave offered a portion of their food. "Welcome, Wolf Star, brother to Small Eagle. My son and I have been on a journey to find the wood to make him a warrior's bow."

He held out a piece of wood that Logan recognized: bois d'arc, it was called, and osage orange. The Cheyenne also favored the wood, which came from the Medicine Bow Mountains far to the north. "It will be strong and true."

The boy seemed pleased. "I will smooth it myself and glue a strong buffalo sinew to it. When it is finished I will paint the inside red and"—there was hesitation over the word—"and yellow," he finished. He lapsed back into silence as suddenly as he'd spoken and shifted uneasily.

Logan addressed the older man. "I did not know you had a son, Antelope Chaser."

The Comanche's eyes clouded briefly and then cleared.

"My son was born into another tribe. He lived with his mother among the Apache until it was time for him to become a warrior. It is often our way."

Logan didn't think so. Intuition was stirring, making gooseflesh along the backs of his arms; but this was no time to voice his thoughts. "I'll prepare the rabbits, then, while you start the fire. Your son can help me."

The boy looked sharply at Logan, but when Antelope Chaser raised no objection he obeyed. Antelope Chaser murmured something low that Logan couldn't overhear.

Pretending not to notice, Logan led him a little away. "The grass is soft and makes a good place to work." As they gutted and skinned the carcasses, he noticed that the boy was eager but inexperienced. That didn't necessarily mean anything. Skinning rabbits was usually women's work.

He waited until Antelope Chaser had gone in search of dry firewood and mumbled a few words beneath his breath. The boy sent a mild, questioning glance his way, but seeing that his companion was occupied, he went back to his task.

Logan mumbled a few more words, then made his speech perfectly clear. "My name is Logan. If you are Nils Vandergroot, I can help you. I will take you to your mother and sister," he said—quietly and in English.

The boy kept on working, his concentration focused on his task. Logan went back to skinning the hares, satisfied. It had only been a foolish hunch. His mind was so full of Bettany, he felt her influence everywhere and had jumped to a wrong conclusion. When they were done Logan went to wash his hands in the sand while the boy took the meat over to the cook fire his father had prepared. Antelope Chaser spoke in low tones.

"What did he say to you?"

"I do not know, Father. I did not understand his words."

The Comanche was pleased. So was the boy.

As he arranged the rabbits for cooking, Nils had to fight to hide his glow of satisfaction. If his pa and new ma had loved him, they would have come searching for him a long time ago, before Ludo and Kearns had traded him away for the gold. It didn't matter now: he was happy with Antelope Chaser and the life of the Comanche camp, where he was much favored and doted upon by all. His old father had quarreled with everyone, but Antelope Chaser was a mighty warrior and counselor, respected and admired. It was good to be the son of so great a chief.

Nils frowned. He had willingly turned his back completely on his old way of life, and he would never go back to it. Never! Now he was Comanche. One day he would be a great warrior among them. And anyone who tried to take him away from Antelope Chaser would suffer for it.

This white man with golden eyes and a Cheyenne name was a danger, for he had spoken aloud his old, hated name: Nils. He was not Nils. Nils was dead.

He was Setanta.

Nils thought of waiting until Logan was asleep. It would be easy enough to plunge his knife into the soft parts of the man's throat while he slept or to push it in between his ribs. Yes, it would be easy. Or he could throw it at him from behind, a silent and deadly missile cleaving the air— like so! He hurled his knife forward in a clean, straight line.

The blade was buried in the cedar's trunk, right up to the hilt.

The weather changed, and Logan's travels brought him down along the Pecos. Avoiding settlements and the more raucous company of his fellow man, he eventually came upon a small ranch. It had once been well managed but now had an untended look, as if the tasks to be done far outstripped the number of persons available to do them. Logan rode up to the small wooden house, forlorn among its unkempt fields. He was twenty yards from it when the door opened and a length of shotgun barrel poked out.

"State your name and business, stranger."

The voice was female, high and thin with strain. Logan reined in. "The name is Logan. I'm looking for work, ma'am. Honest labor for an honest day's wage."

A woman in a figured calico dress edged out into the shade of the overhang, cradling the gun at the ready. "Ain't no money here to pay a body's wage. Ain't hardly enough to feed us. You'd best be on your way."

"If you don't have money to pay me, ma'am, I'll work for a room in the barn and my meals." He looked out over the fields. "As for food, this place could support itself quite well, with a little manpower put into it."

She stepped into the light, a stringy young woman burned brown by the sun, with a wistful face. She eyed Logan in silence. He looked strong and healthy, and she liked the looks of him. "Why'd you pick this place?"

"It was the first one I came to. I'm looking for a place to winter. In the spring I'll be on my way."

For a few more seconds she weighed the situation. "I'll have to ask my ma and pa. Sit yourself down and rest your bones."

Logan got down carefully, as she still held the gun. She glanced over her shoulder. "Yancy, Beau! Come here and introduce yourselves."

Twin boys came out, freckled and rangy as the woman, although only a year or two younger. It was plain, Logan thought, who wore the pants in this clan. As he approached, she wiped her hand off on her apron and stuck it out awkwardly for a handshake.

"I'm Nell Byrd. This here's my brothers, Yancy and Beau."

The boys bobbed their head and shook hands with the same lack of grace as their sister, but for all that their faces were friendly—almost eager. Logan recognized the look: it had been a long time since they'd spoken with anyone outside the family, longer still since they'd had news of the outside world. It was a lonely life.

He smelled something wonderful baking in the oven. Bread or fluffy biscuits, light and melting to the tongue. His mouth watered. "Would your parents be about?"

Nell indicated the rise beyond the house. "I'll go talk to 'em about you staying on."

She walked away, the hem of her dress whipping about sturdy brown ankles and feet coated with Texas dust. Nell seemed almost a part of the landscape, as elemental as the low hills and the scattered trees. If these were the kind of people who settled this land, they would endure and prosper, Logan thought. He perched on a log awaiting the ax. Yancy brought him a tin cup of water so cold it almost numbed his mouth and then scooted away with his twin to the safety of the house. He'd kept his arm so close to his side and used it so adroitly that Logan hadn't noticed at first that it was withered.

He glanced up at the rise and saw Nell standing there all alone, as if deep in conversation. He rose, slowly, and moved to where he had a better view. Two wooden crosses were side by side in the bright Texas sunshine, guarding the house and fields.

Nell returned, completely unself-conscious. "Pa says you can stay if you're clean and sober. God knows we need a man's help around here." She smiled shyly, looking almost pretty for a few seconds. "Ma says it's all right to trust you. She said you have a nice face."

Without losing a beat she turned and hollered over her shoulder. "Beau! Take his horse and rub it down. Yancy, show our new hand where to stow his things."

Logan followed the boy with the withered arm to the barn, where there was clean soft straw. The tack hanging from the pegs was oiled, the metal parts polished, and two horses in the stalls were sleek and curried—better fed than their owners. It was well that he'd come. The place needed a man's labor until the three kids could get on their feet. He'd hang around till spring, doing what he could. Then it would be time to move on. Otherwise it would be too easy to get attached, to learn to care.

He didn't ever want to care again. It hurt too much. You had to leave or they left you.

No matter which way it happened, it wasn't worth the pain.

Twenty-one

Mexico: 1811

Quinn cantered up the road leading through the de Medina lands. His business led him in the vague vicinity of San Felipe, and he found himself drawn like a magnet to the sprawling hacienda of Don Miguel. His excuse was thin, but it garnered him a gracious invitation to break his travel overnight. It was exactly what he'd been hoping for. He wanted to see Dona Estrella again.

The lady had taken hold of his imagination. Quinn didn't understand it. She had neither the healthy animal sexuality of a portside whore nor the conscious seductiveness of a high-class prostitute. It was an appeal he couldn't identify— or resist. He didn't have the same affinity for the company of Luis Allende. The mere mention of the man made his hackles rise, and when he heard Allende had suffered a freak accident when thrown from his horse, it was hard to muster enough sympathy to sound convincing.

When Estrella greeted him in the *sala*, she looked so cool and beautiful in sapphire silk and lace that his heart skipped a beat. Her reaction was more mundane; in fact, she seemed so distracted that it piqued his male vanity. Conceit wasn't among Quinn's vices. He didn't feel he was the certain answer to a maiden's prayers, but he hadn't expected such an aloof response, either.

"Perhaps you don't recall our previous meeting," he said in a serious breach of etiquette.

"I beg your pardon, Señor Logan." Her color heightened.

"Of course I remember your visit. And I am . . . delighted
. . . that you are to be our guest this evening to celebrate
my brother's saint's day. I . . . I was out too long this afternoon . . . so hot! A touch of the sun, you understand. . . ."

She was rambling, and they both knew it. When Quinn
took her hand in his, he felt the fine tremors that shook
her. Don Miguel was speaking to a servant, and Quinn
grabbed his chance. "You are in distress from more than
the heat, I think. If you are in trouble—if I can be of
assistance to you in any way, Dona Estrella—you have only
to say the word."

She stiffened. "That is kind of you, but completely un-
necessary, señor."

The rebuff was so abrupt, his face reddened. "Perhaps
you are already regretting your brother's hospitality. I'll take
my leave in that case."

He was still holding her hand, and for just a moment
she returned its pressure. "Please . . . please stay. It is not
often that we entertain guests these days. I . . . I would be
glad of your company."

The look she gave him held gratitude and a dawning
trust that caught them both by surprise. Quinn had the
strangest urge to sweep her up in his arms and carry her off
to his horse, to ride away into the sunset and never look
back. Their hands dropped, the moment passed, and Don
Miguel rejoined them. Quinn had the odd feeling that for
the rest of his life he might regret not doing it.

The evening meal was served outside in a pleasant court.
Both Don Miguel and his brother-in-law wore silk velvet
over fine white linen, as fine as kings, and Luis Allende's
gilt buttons were studded with topaz the color of his shadowed eyes. Quinn was decidedly underdressed for the company; it wasn't the first time, but it was the first time he'd
given a damn about it. He hadn't cared when Ysabella had
come into the *sala*. Her fresh beauty and engagingly innocent attempts at flirtation might have amused him on
another occasion, but the edgy atmosphere of the place had

gotten beneath his skin. It was like the stir in the air preceding a rainsquall. The crosscurrents made the hairs rise at his nape.

When Estrella joined them, pale and still agitated beneath her surface calm, Quinn had sucked in his breath. He wanted to get up and go to her, enfold her in his arms, protect her—from what? Her life was fairly isolated but luxurious, as evidenced by her rich gown of azure silk and the fortune in pearls around her ivory throat. "I see that I have kept you waiting for your meal," she said breathlessly.

Luis smiled tightly. "A man who would not wait for you, my dear Estrellita, is no man at all."

She shivered, a small involuntary movement that only Quinn seemed to notice. He held out his arm to her. "Allow me." As they promenaded out to the courtyard, she chattered with a brittle, forced gaiety. A sense of foreboding came over Quinn. He'd seen it before: the quality his grandmother had called "fey"—the frenetic ebullience that came before disaster. It carried through the evening.

The courses of the meal were served in formal elegance with branched candelabra on the long trestle table. A moth, white with lavender veining, flew too near the flame. It tried to dart away. There was a faint hiss, and it fell to the cloth with blackened, smoldering wings. Quinn brushed the moth's remains from the table. The others had all seen it. Don Miguel and Ysabella paid scant heed: it was only an insect. But when he glanced across at Estrella, she had a stricken look.

"You will think me foolish, señor. But it was alive only a moment ago, alive and beautiful."

Luis set down his goblet. "It went too close to the fire— and paid the price. That is one of life's most important lessons. That is an old saying among our people, Señor Logan: 'Take what you want, the Devil says—and pay for it.'"

Estrella's spoon clanked against the edge of her gold-and-silver dessert dish. Ysabella chided her saucily. "Those are to be part of my trousseau. They are very old," she told

Quinn, "and once belonged to a queen of Spain. My father is very proud of his lineage," she added ingenuously.

Luis laughed. "With good reason. Through the generations the de Medina line has been kept . . . *pure*. And we see in you, my beloved Ysabella, the fairest flowering on the ancient vine."

He smiled at her over the gold rim of his glass, then turned his limpid gaze to her aunt. "Don't you agree with me, Estrella? The man who claims her will be fortunate indeed."

Estrella looked away hastily. Quinn sensed the panic in her, like the futile fluttering of the moth just before the heat withered its delicate wings. A chill ran down his back. A ghost walked over my grave, he thought uneasily, and took another swallow of his wine.

That night, despite his travel weariness and some excellent brandy, he found himself unable to fall asleep in the comfortable bed. How his old friends would laugh if they knew that the defenses of his hardened bachelor's heart had been breached at last—that the man who had averred that women were put on earth for only two purposes, that romantic love was a female fantasy, and that he would never be caught in a parson's mousetrap was lying awake in a positive sweat, eating his words, one by one.

Quinn tarried at the hacienda for several days, enjoying his talks with Don Miguel and the innocently flirtatious ways of his daughter. Dona Ysabella, he told himself, was a rare handful indeed. It was rather like watching a fledgling hawk fluff its feathers and hop about the nest, pretending to fly. But when the stunning little heartbreaker grew into womanhood, she would soar on her youth and beauty— and pounce on the man she selected for her prey. It was fortunate that her disposition was as sunny as it was willful. He only hoped she wouldn't fly too high.

Estrella had been noticing his interest in Ysabella. As she walked with Quinn through the rose garden, she brought the subject deftly around to the girl. "Ysabella is both beautiful and accomplished, Señor Logan."

"So I would expect in your niece, Dona Estrella."

"Her lineage is impeccable, also."

Quinn hid his grin. "So I have heard."

"And," Estrella added, "she is, of course, my brother's only heir." She sent him a glance from the corner of her eyes. "One day she will be a woman of great wealth."

Quinn stopped and faced Estrella. "I don't know why, but you remind me of a man trying to sell off a horse—and a spavined one, at that."

"Oh, no. Ysabella enjoys excellent health."

He tipped her chin up with his finger. "If I wanted to hear about your niece, I would have invited *her* to go for a walk with me."

His eyes captured hers for a long moment. Estrella was the first to look away. Pulling back, she started once more down the walkway, her cheeks becomingly flushed. The air was so charged between them that he began to hope she was not as indifferent as she always seemed. Whether to press the point or go easy was the problem. Interruptions could come at any minute, and he took a chance.

Quinn led her toward the archway. "I feel like a monk pacing back and forth inside these walls. Let's get away toward the river. There's an interesting old arbor. . . ."

He never had the chance to finish. She was gone with a gasp and a flurry of skirts, leaving him to curse and wonder where he'd gone wrong.

Estrella managed to avoid Quinn Logan until he left on the appointed day, discouraged. She watched him ride away with great sadness. *Mother of God, what was I thinking of to encourage him for even a moment? I, with the stain of black sins upon my soul!*

If her life had been different, she could have been happy with a man like Quinn Logan. There was strength and goodness in him. But Miguel would never have let her marry the American. His pride ran too deep, and he would have scorned an offer from a man he considered a common merchant. A son of peasants. Hadn't he refused an alliance with Luis in no uncertain terms?

Of course, that wouldn't have stopped a man like Quinn Logan. If he truly wanted her, Estrella knew, he would have thrown her over his saddle and carried her off, dowerless. And she would have gone gladly. It was too late now, and had been too late since that first time Luis had found her alone in the arbor. She had been a young girl, flushed with her first beauty and the unnamed yearnings of her ripening body. Flattered by the attentions of the dashing Luis, seduced by his honeyed words and her own desires.

Estrella blinked away her tears and went back into the house.

By noon the following week the *hacienda* swarmed with carriages and men and women on horseback. There was to be a bullfight and all sorts of amusements at Don Enrique's home to honor his new wife. Don Miguel had had to swallow his anger and disappointment at his daughter's refusal to entertain Enrique's suit. Resigned, he had graciously opened his house to guests for his neighbor's wedding feast; Ysabella, however, remained in his disgrace.

Estrella went into the *sala* where Ysabella was holding court. Miguel stood to one side, listening to Luis. "I have never seen her more lovely. Your daughter will add more hearts to her chain before this day is out."

Miguel watched his daughter, frowning. "I fear she goes beyond what is pleasing. Ysabella is young, headstrong, and passionate, a combination I know all too well."

"She is her mother's daughter."

Estrella looked as if she'd been struck, but Miguel nodded broodingly. *Her mother's daughter.* "It is true. Every expression, every gesture, is the image of her mother at the same age."

The enchanting Julianna Allende had married Miguel in accordance with the wishes of her father, Don Alfonso Allende. Her new husband, considerably older and wiser in ways of the world, had planned to mold her into an ideal mate, the perfect complement to himself. For the first two

years she had been a docile, if subdued, wife. After Ysabella's birth she had changed. Subtly at first, so that he
blamed it upon a hundred different reasons; later Luis said
he had noticed it immediately upon returning from his first
journey to Santa Barbara.

Miguel's hands clenched into claws as he remembered
the pain and humiliation of those days. His dreams of fur-
thering his dynasty with a worthy consort had soured
quickly. The secret glow new to Julianna's eyes had
quenched itself when she turned them upon her husband.
She was restless and aloof by day, resigned by night. Several
times he had awakened to the sound of her weeping.

He had set traps for her, but she had been clever. He
had found her out, forced a confession from those beautiful,
lying lips. In the end, however, he had never been able to
shake from her the name of her lover. If he had, there
would have been no duel of honor. He would have shot
the man down like a dog and left him to die. That would
have helped to salve his pride and heal the wound; instead
it had festered like a chancre, burrowing deep. Even Julianna's death had not cured him of it.

He would rather see his daughter sealed up within the
convent, or dead, than have her take the same path her
mother had chosen. Anger ebbed as his carriage was brought
around.

It was time to depart for Don Enrique's hacienda, which
adjoined his own estates. Miguel was to escort Dona Margarita, an old family friend, and her two haughty daughters.
Ysabella and Estrella had decided to go on horseback, with
a small party, which scandalized their elders but was quite
accepted among the younger set; after all, it was not as if
they were riding off the de Medina property. The carriages
left first, taking the old trade road. Within a short time
the riders left, going across country. As some lingered to
admire the various views or fell behind for other reasons,
they split into straggling groups. One, composed of the
youngest, raced across the wide meadows in bursts of speed
and laughter.

They were halfway to the neighboring hacienda before Estrella realized her niece was not among them. She didn't want to raise a fuss but turned back to the following clusters of riders. "Have you seen Ysabella?"

No one had. She saw young Esteban Vaca stopping with two young women in the shade of a wooded grove and rode out to them. Ysabella was not with them. "She forgot something and turned back shortly after we left the stable yard," said Esteban.

Estrella glanced back toward the hacienda. There was not a soul to be seen. "What can she be thinking of? She cannot ride alone all the way to Don Enrique's."

Esteban hastened to reassure her. "She is not alone. Don Luis accompanied her. He said, if you should ask, to say that he would extend to her the same loving care as he would to yourself."

The air seemed to buzz with a thousand bees. Estrella fought the vertigo that came as the blood drained from her face. "Thank you. I will ride back to meet them."

She wheeled her horse about and trotted away. Once beyond the crest of the low hill, she kicked it into a gallop and headed back to the house, too afraid to even pray. Luis had not approached her once since that afternoon in the arbor, but a dozen times a day he fingered the scar beneath his collar and watched her thoughtfully, Estrella had been sure he was only biding his time. She had dismissed the remarks he'd directed toward Ysabella, thinking it was her he really meant to bait. No, no, she was only being foolish. Surely not even Luis . . .

Pounding over the earth, she tried to calculate how much time had passed since the two had returned to the hacienda. Her heart sank. More than an hour. Alarm changed to terror when she reached the stable yard without meeting them and discovered their horses were not within their stalls. She ran into the house and through the rooms like a madwoman. The scrap of paper was lying on the floor near Ysabella's bed.

I must see you alone. Turn back at the old
oak tree. You will know where to meet me.

Where? Where! Estrella ran from the room and out into
the courtyard. Suddenly she knew where she would find
them. Gathering her skirts, she hurried out past the stables
and outbuildings and down beyond the old house, stumbling
over roots and ruts and anthills. She arrived at the adobe
ruins gasping for breath.

Inside, it was dark, the inner door closed. Thank God,
thank God! She was sick with relief and had to lean against
the wall for support. Then she heard a soft cry, like an
animal in pain. Her heart lurched against her ribs. Estrella
moved cautiously across the earthen floor toward the inner
door. A faint glow showed beneath it, but whether daylight
or candlelight she couldn't tell. Like a sleepwalker she
reached for the iron handle. The door was unlocked and
swung open on freshly oiled hinges.

The sight that met her eyes burned itself into her soul:
a candle guttering in a porcelain saucer, a heap of hastily
discarded garments . . . and Ysabella sleeping naked in Luis's
arms.

He rolled up on one elbow and smiled at Estrella. "I
warned you, *querida*, that I would have my revenge."

The look he gave her was shot full of deep, corrosive
anger and overflowing triumph, mingled with a terrible,
twisted love.

Twenty-two

Cheyenne Territory: 1840

Red Paint Woman took the bone scraper from Bettany's hand. "No." She brought the honed edge down along the stretched mule-deer hide. "Like so."

Bettany watched, then took the scraper and tried to imitate the gesture. Red Paint Woman sighed and put her hand on Bettany's, guiding it with the proper motion. The pressure of the blade increased slightly, and the alteration in angle was only a fraction of an inch, yet it made all the difference in the world.

Now that she had the feel of it, Bettany was able to make a decent job of it on her own. Her companion took up a spot on the other side, and they worked together until the hide was thin and clean. Red Paint Woman had been very patient, and Bettany was grateful for that, even though she didn't understand the other woman's motive.

Red Paint Woman nodded her approval. "You learn quickly. It is good."

"I would not have learned if you had not been so patient with me. Why do you help me?"

The Arapaho looked at her as if the answer were plain to anyone but a complete idiot. Then she lowered her eyes. "You are Small Eagle's woman. You must be a credit to him."

There was more than irritation in the reply. There was grief, anger, puzzlement.

Their band had joined up to travel with the Suhtai band

of Cheyenne for the agreed-upon gathering at Bent's Fort. There was much feasting, and the men danced before the big campfire and told stories of their war exploits. Bettany had no patience with it. It had taken her a while to understand that the bravest act for warriors was to touch the enemy by hand or lance. The killing appeared almost an afterthought and only made the Cheyenne seem more alien to her, their raids and battles nothing but a lethal, barbarous game.

Red Paint Woman, however, seemed fascinated. When it was Small Eagle's turn to boast of some feat, her dark eyes were fixed on him and her face shone with the light of his reflected glory. Bettany stared at the Arapaho. Why, she loves him! And she suffers for it! she realized.

It was a revelation. She had been afraid to acknowledge that Red Paint Woman and the others were every bit as human as she, that they were merely of another culture and not another species. Afraid because, as the days became weeks and months, she felt herself slipping away, losing her separateness and identity. Becoming like them.

Already she ate with her fingers as if it were the only way she'd ever learned. How long before she forgot how to eat with a fork and spoon altogether? How long would it take before she sat like Red Paint Woman, nodding in admiration at Small Eagle's tales of running another human being through with a lance or splitting a skull with his ax?

Her deliberations were interrupted by the sounds of a woman arguing loudly from within a nearby lodge. It was so strange that Small Eagle stopped in midsentence and turned to watch with the others. Elk Shield came out of his lodge, his face like granite. Snail had a sharp tongue and a temper to match, unusual among the band who reverenced moderation, and there had been trouble between the brave and his woman for some time.

A stir ran through the circle of men before the fire, like a breeze rustling through a stand of cottonwoods. Bettany was about to say something to Red Paint Woman, but the Arapaho shushed her. "Watch."

Small Eagle finished his story, and Smoke Along the Ground began another. Then Buffalo Heart chanted while a young brave danced out his own story to the beat of the drum. Everyone seemed to be waiting for something, and Bettany felt like a child excluded from the secrets of the elders. Elk Shield rose next and began to stamp his feet and whirl around, accompanying himself by hitting a drum with a stick. He went around and around, and the air of expectancy grew.

Suddenly he waved the stick in the air. "This is my wife. I toss her away." He flung the stick toward a group of men, and they ducked and dodged. Elk Shield faced them. "Let him who wants her take the stick and her with it."

There were no takers. Red Paint Woman was satisfied. "Snail is rash and unwise. Now she has no husband and Elk Shield has no wife."

"Just like that?" Bettany was appalled by the ease and quickness of dissolving the marriage. "What will happen to her now?"

"It is a disgrace for a woman to be thrown out by the drum. Perhaps some other man will want Snail, but I do not think so. Her tongue is like a scorpion's stinger. She will take her lodge and belongings and go back to her clan in the Suhtai band. She will live among them until she finds another husband."

Red Paint Woman looked across at Small Eagle, handsome in the fire's glow, and her face softened. Then she sent Bettany a mocking glance. "A woman who is wife to a brave warrior and does not appreciate him is nothing but a fool."

Later that night, when Bettany was half-asleep, Small Eagle reached for her. She cringed from his touch, but his hands were strong and possessive, and she knew he wouldn't desist until his need was fulfilled. Why can't it be Red Paint Woman he wants? she thought bitterly as he pulled her robe away and fastened his hungry mouth to her breast. Or, a wild, agonized part of her cried out, why can't he be his brother! A shudder of sensation shot through her, potent and unexpected; but the knowledge that she lay with one man and desired another was too startling, too painful, to contemplate.

Bettany stiffened as Small Eagle's hands stroked the inside of her thighs. She endured his fondling with gritted teeth. His entering was painful to her, unsatisfying to him. When he finished she could feel his bafflement and growing frustration at her lack of response. Her eyes filled with tears in the darkness. Time and again their bodies were joined in the most intimate of physical acts, yet they were both condemned to loneliness, each needing, each wanting, what they could never have.

Small Eagle rolled away with a smothered sound, then rose and went out into the night. As Bettany pulled the robe over her, she thought she heard Hannah awaken and snuffle softly. She got up and went to the girl, only to find her sound asleep. The weeping was so faint she would have decided she'd imagined it, if not for the thwarted love she'd glimpsed earlier on Red Paint Woman's face.

Bettany wiped her eyes and buried her face in her arms. She and Small Eagle were not alone in their misery. The sooner she reached Bent's Fort and put her plan into effect, the better it would be for all of them.

Bettany stepped around the other sleeping forms in her lodge. She was still wrapped in her buffalo robe against the morning chill and hadn't taken the time to dress in her eagerness. Untying the entrance flap, she peeked outside. New light washed the sky. Behind her Red Paint Woman stirred on her sleeping pallet and raised up on one elbow.

"Are the lances still there?" she asked sleepily.

"No." A thrill of excitement raced through Bettany. "We are moving camp today."

The day she had waited for was finally here. This morning the camp at High Rocks would be dismantled for the journey to Bent's Fort and the great rendezvous between the tribes. After the first numbing realization that she was pregnant, Bettany's determination had grown. Her baby would not be born and raised among the Cheyenne, raised as a naked heathen. That was how she thought of it: *her* child.

But she would have to get away before anyone guessed her secret. Her hand went protectively to her abdomen as she turned from the entrance. Red Paint Woman saw the gesture and took in a swift, sibilant breath. As Bettany passed her she reached out and grabbed the end of the buffalo robe, yanking it free. At that moment Small Eagle roused and opened his eyes. He blinked in surprise and leapt up from his bed.

"Why did you not tell me that you are with child, wife? Did you mean to keep such good news to yourself? I do not think you could hold such a secret long."

"I am not with child," she stammered. "I am growing fat with the horses and buffalo." Hannah was still asleep. Bettany snatched up her garments and slipped them on, dashing out of the lodge before he could stop her.

She went up the hill to the stand of young spruce and aspen and wept with frustration. She must get away soon. She must! If Thorson had came back, she might have tried to bribe him with the gold she'd found, but he'd gone north to visit one of his wives and children up along the Yellowstone.

After Bettany was cried out, she felt better. There were things to be done—for the sooner the band set out for Bent's Fort, the sooner she would be free. By the time she went down to pack for traveling, she'd formed the outline of her plan.

The great meeting of the tribes at Bent's Fort went well for the Cheyenne and Comanche and their allies. For Bettany it was much less successful. Hundreds of tipis, painted with mementos of their owners' exploits, already lined both sides of the Arkansas. The Comanche were across the southern side, the Cheyenne and their allies on the north bank a distance from Bent's Fort, and the entire plain was a shifting, moving mass of people and animals.

Bettany selected a site for the lodge and set it up quickly

with the able assistance of Red Paint Woman. There was nothing she could do that the Arapaho could not do three times faster and better; but it was to her that Small Eagle reached out in the night more often than not. Knowing the other woman lay awake, angry at times, weeping silently at others, only added to the strain within their lodge.

She glanced down the river in the direction of the trading post operated by the Bent family. Through the intervening trees she could make out the glimpses of the thick adobe walls and an occasional horseman. Once the meetings were well in progress, she could slip away with Hannah on some pretext and seek shelter with them, but there were hundreds of Indians here, all sworn allies now. If she asked the Bents for sanctuary, there would be nothing to stop them from attacking the fort and taking her back against her will. It was difficult for her to bide her time, but it would be far better to wait until the rendezvous broke up and then slip away in the commotion of breaking camp.

Her plan was seriously jeopardized when she and several others ate some meat that had been poorly preserved at the Arapaho camp. Between the food poisoning and the nausea of early pregnancy, Bettany was ill for three days. The episode left her weak and in a frenzy of anxiety that she would lose her opportunity to escape. Only the afternoon before they were to break camp did she feel strong enough to venture away from the lodge.

While the other women were clustered in groups or visiting with friends or relatives from other bands, she set out toward the fort. Her heart pounded with joy when she saw a white man resting against a tree, a hundred yards away. His back was to her, but she could see his trousers and coat of brown superfine and crowned hat. He withdrew something from his pocket, and she saw a glint of gold chain connected to the case of his timepiece. It must be one of the Bents, she thought excitedly.

Suddenly he moved away, and she was afraid she'd lose him among the trees before he reached the wide plain surrounding the fort. The place would be filled with Cheyenne braves. It was urgent that she talk to him in private. "Sir? Sir! Please wait. . . ."

She hurried over the uneven ground and caught her dress on a branch. As she stooped to free it he looked over his shoulder. The man's face was darker than Small Eagle's and every bit as Cheyenne. A necklace of bear claws was draped over the crisp white shirt, and he'd stuck a feather through the topmost buttonhole. She recognized him: Stone Ax, a war leader from one of the other bands, known for his love of finery. Evidently he'd traded some furs for the incongruous clothing of a town banker.

He hadn't seen her, and he was close enough to the river that its roar had blotted out her soft calls. Bettany kept her head low and hoped he wouldn't notice her. After a moment Stone Ax went on toward the fort. Bettany shook with relief. She stumbled over exposed roots and around a clump of bushes until she came through a shady grove and into a wide clearing.

A group of Apache women were digging for roots with sharpened sticks. She was about to retreat and go around them when one of the squaws straightened up. Bettany stared in disbelief. "Letitia?"

It was impossible that this was Letty Renfrew: the scarecrow with wild eyes and dirty hair bore little resemblance to the meticulous woman from the wagon party who had once collected buffalo chips with white gloves. For a moment Bettany thought she was in error. There was madness in the woman's eyes, and a furtive, animal cunning.

At closer range Bettany wasn't sure if her first impression was correct. She hurried toward her, and the woman threw up her arms as if to ward off blows. Then the woman howled like a beast and ran away, a feral thing guided by primitive instinct instead of intelligence. The other squaws made angry comments among themselves, but Bettany didn't understand their language. They left their digging and went off in pursuit of the poor demented creature who, Bettany feared, had once been Porter Renfrew's wife.

Horrified, Bettany tried to run after the woman and got

tangled in a thorny ravine. By the time she extricated herself, they had vanished. She remembered the prophecy the half-breed woman had given Letty Renfrew at Fort Laramie: "You will live so long you will be weary of life."

She was still in shock from the encounter when she came upon the trade wagon in the grove beyond. Bettany racked her brain for some way to help the woman. If she could find out which band the woman was with she could ask the Bents for assistance in helping her; but she knew that there was no real help for the wild, mad thing with matted hair, who resembled Letty Renfrew.

She wondered if Small Eagle would be able to do anything to help her locate the woman. She felt the small pouch of gold nuggets beneath her skirt. The yellow metal was of limited use to the Indians except for trade—but if she was able to buy goods with her gold, she might be able to make a trade with the Apaches herself. This trader might strike a deal, and that would serve very well. Then she could take Letty back to Fort Laramie when she went. Meanwhile it was essential to act as normal as possible.

A rangy trader in buckskin trousers and a leather vest had put some wares on display for a group of Arapaho squaws. The large wagon behind him looked like something from a gypsy caravan and had Cole's Trading Company painted on it in big green letters. His wares were on display in front.

He had several of the iron kettles that were so highly prized among the tribes, packets of needles and glass beads for quillwork, tin cups and bowls, an assortment of penny whistles, a bugle stamped with the insignia of the United States Army Corps, and yards of gaily colored calico. The women were pawing through some of it, thumping the kettles and conferring over the packets of beads. One took a length of fabric and draped it around her like a cape, chattering and posing for her companions.

The trader grinned at them and pulled at his thick mustache. "You like those? Well, I got plenty more. And you ain't seen nothing yet, ladies. Wait'll you get a load of this."

He whisked a woman's outfit from within his wagon, a long-sleeved blue dress printed with forget-me-nots, complete with petticoat, tight-laced corset, and matching ribbon-trimmed drawers. There was even a pair of ankle-high kid boots with rows of shiny black buttons. To Bettany's luxury-starved eyes, it was like a glimpse of an alien, half-remembered world. They were so beautiful! She couldn't take her eyes from them: they would be perfect for implementing her plan.

She waited nervously while the others bargained, afraid the novelty of the white-woman's garb would tempt them. Her fears were groundless. Although the squaws didn't understand the trader's words, they could figure out the gist of his comments. They had only amused contempt for such useless items.

"Who would wear such a cage about their ribs?" one said, "You speak truth, Little Frog Hops," another agreed. She pointed to the dainty drawers: "And of what good are such flimsy breeches, so short they do not reach one's knees? Ah, I would not be seen in such a garment."

When the trading was done and he saw the women had finished buying, the man began putting items back inside his wagon. The squaws drifted away, happy with their purchases. Bettany lingered. When he reached for the clothing, she ran up to him.

"Wait! How much . . . what will you take in trade for the dress and all the rest?"

He looked at her, hard. The windblown dust and sun-browned skin could not conceal the bone structure of her face or the clear gray of her eyes. "Well, I'll be damned! A white woman. Where'd you come from, sweetheart? Outta that whiskey bottle I drank?"

"From . . . from the Cheyenne band. Down by the willows."

He reached out and caught her by the arm. "You're real enough all right." His eyes took on a crafty light. "Cheyenne, huh? A squaw woman. A woman like you could do better. I'm lighting out for Santa Fe now. Why don't you come along with me, dolly? I'd show you a good time."

Bettany's knees shook. "Oh, yes! Please take me with you. I've been trying to find some means to get away. Sir, you are the answer to my prayers."

The trader grinned widely. "Sweetheart, you're the answer to mine. Name's Cole. Wilfred Cole. Step inside and we'll get acquainted better."

"My daughter . . . she's sleeping in the lodge. I'll go get her."

"Plenty of time for that later. Come on in and set yourself down while we get to know each other."

Bettany felt she couldn't blame him for wanting to hear her story first—after all, he was surrounded by Indians who might turn hostile at any moment. He climbed up the step and held out his hand to her. Hesitating just a moment, she accepted it and let him help her up. She was able to stand up beneath the high cover, but there wasn't really anyplace to go. The back was loaded down with trade goods, and a few crates were stacked behind the driver's bench with a mattress rolled out beyond. He waved a hand at the forward crates.

"Makes a good barricade in case of attack. A man can't be too cautious when he travels alone. My partner was took by the Pawnee when we went through their territory. Skinned alive, so I heard."

He said it as casually as if discussing the weather. Bettany was appalled, but Wilfred Cole was her one best hope at the moment. "I'm very sorry to hear that."

"Me too, little lady. It gets mighty lonely along the trail, and a man wants someone to talk to. Someone who can watch his back for him."

Bettany folded her hands and perched upon the crate. "I can load and fire a rifle, Mr. Cole, and have become quite handy with a knife as well."

"How'd you get hooked up with the Cheyenne? You ain't no squaw woman like I surmised at first."

"The Cheyenne war chief called Small Eagle rescued me when my wagon party was massacred. I have lived among them for several months and they have treated me kindly, but I wish to return to my own kind."

He sat on the mattress near her feet. "Just what is it you want me to do for you?"

"I wish to obtain passage to the nearest white settlement, or back to Fort Laramie if necessary. Originally I had planned to go to the fort and ask the owners to give me sanctuary, but I think it would be far better if you would just take me with you."

Cole looked her over appraisingly. "You're right about that. You see, Bent's wife is an Injun. He'd have to side with her kin or they'd be overrun, don't you see."

Her eyes grew wide at how close she'd come to disaster. The merchant scratched his armpit. "Well, that's what you want from me, but what've you got to offer in trade?"

She didn't want to squander the gold nuggets. She'd need them to start anew somewhere. "I could cook for you, Mr. Cole, and do your washing. And 'watch your back,' as you said earlier."

"Ain't enough for the danger you'd be putting me in, sweetheart. You gotta do better than that."

This was just the kind of situation she'd anticipated. Fortunately she'd put most of the nuggets in a small pouch sewn inside her skirt and the rest in a twist of cloth tucked inside her bosom. "Will this be enough?"

Cole wasn't staring at the glittering gravel but at her bodice, where, for just an instant, he'd seen a flash of milky skin beneath her tanned throat. He put his hand on her knee. "You know what I want, honey, and I mean to sample it right now. Yessiree."

Before she knew what he intended, Bettany found herself flat on the lumpy mattress with the trader atop her and her skirts hiked up to her thighs. His hands were rough and bruising in his eagerness, and he didn't seem to believe that she was unwilling. "Come on, loosen up, sweetheart. Show me whatcha got. . . ."

"Get off me! Let me go!" She kicked and struck at his shoulder wildly, trying to wriggle free, but he pinned her down with his weight. Bettany raked her nails along his face, drawing blood.

"Damn it now, girlie. You've made me bite my tongue." The taste of his own blood angered him. The trader's hand covered her mouth and nose so tightly, she could hardly breathe. Her teeth caught the web of skin between his thumb and right index finger and she bit down, hard. Her reward was a sharp yelp from her attacker and a stunning blow to the left side of her head that made everything go temporarily numb.

"Don't play games with me, sweetheart," he whispered harshly in her ear. "There's only two things Injuns do with white women, fuck 'em or kill 'em. You're still alive, and that means you're nothing but an Injun whore. And if you're good enough for an Injun, honey, you're plenty good enough for me."

Bettany knew the struggle was in deadly earnest now. Marshaling her reserves, she battered at him with her fists. One flailing hand caught him hard on the side of his jaw. He slammed his forearm across her throat, cutting off her wind. "Don't mess with me, girlie. You'll enjoy yourself if you just relax. . . ."

"Please . . . no!"

Her skirt was up to her waist, her pregnancy evident. Cole cursed when he felt the swelling mound of her abdomen. "Won't have nothing to do with an honest man looking for a bit of fun, but you let one of them Injun bucks poke you. Well, this is what I think of Injun half-breeds. . . ."

He pulled back, then struck her in the abdomen with his knee. They were hard, vicious shoves. The pain was sickening, the fright worse. He would have his way with her and kill her. She was suffocating from lack of air, no match for his strength. For the briefest fraction of a second it seemed easier to die than to endure. For that one flicker of thought Bettany almost gave up; but she was a fighter.

She hadn't come this far only to perish at the hands of a rapist. And there was the baby, too. *Her* baby.

She got one arm loose and fumbled desperately for her knife. It was on the other side, impossible to reach. She flung her arm out and back, hoping her fingers would touch something she could use as a weapon. Then her groping hand touched the outline of a leather sheath attached to her assailant's belt.

Bettany knew she was on the verge of blacking out. With a supreme effort of will she yanked his knife free and struck out blindly at him. The blade connected, its honed edges biting deep into living flesh. Blood gushed over her fingers and ran up her arm. There was a horrible choking, gurgling sound. The body weighing her down jerked stiffly once, as if from a heavy blow, then went limp.

She lay gasping beneath him, eyes closed, spent with fear and effort. When she tried to push him off, she was unable to budge him. Suddenly he rolled off and she was free. Small Eagle squatted beside her in the wagon, his face grim. "You have fought well and bravely, Warrior Woman. But you have brought danger to yourself and to all by your actions."

He gave her one of the colorful blankets from the wagon's stores. "Go down to the river where we saw the turtles this morning and bathe. I will send Red Paint Woman to you with clean garments. Then you must return to camp. Say nothing to anyone about this. Not to Red Paint Woman or to me. Now, go!"

Trembling and unable to take in everything, Bettany pulled the blanket over her blood-soaked dress. A blood-stained Bowie knife lay on beside the trader. She was glad his head was turned and she couldn't see his eyes. They would be open and staring and . . .

Her mouth filled with bile, and she clambered awkwardly toward the front of the wagon. When she reached the driver's bench she glanced back, just once. Small Eagle was already rolling Cole's corpse in another blanket. She jumped down, dodging through the growth along the river until she was well away, then retched until her stomach was empty. When she was able, she went along a small side stream created when part of the bank had crumbled in the spring rains. There was no one in sight.

She splashed in, clothes and all. The water was breast high and slow-moving, the site protected by scrub and young cottonwoods. She dragged in shuddering, agonized breaths, watching the blood flow away into thin brown tendrils that spread and vanished among the ripples. Her mind wheeled about in dull, self-accusing circles. She had saved herself, but at a horrible cost.

She immersed herself in the river and tried to calm down as she removed her clothes. She felt too sullied to pray for forgiveness. Was what Cole had wanted in exchange for helping her any different from what she had given Small Eagle? Yes! part of her cried. That had been for Hannah and Nils, and Small Eagle had treated her honorably by his own reckoning. In his eyes she was his wife, even if it was not so in hers. No! another part judged: you cannot defend your honor if there is no honor to defend.

Sick at heart, Bettany moved deeper among the reeds and ducked her head below the surface, a baptism of the flesh that left her feeling no better than before. She waited a long time for Red Paint Woman to come, and when she did Bettany recoiled. The garments she had brought with her were the petticoats and ribbon-trimmed drawers and the calico dress with the blue forget-me-nots. She realized Small Eagle had sent them, thinking they would please her. Drying off on the blanket, she stepped into the garments. She vowed to wear them as long as she could, a punishment like the scarlet brand of an adulteress. Forget-me-nots to mark a murderess.

When she passed the clearing the wagon was gone, and she followed Red Paint Woman back to the lodge, her wet clothes over her arm. Although they would still be serviceable, the stains would remain.

Small Eagle returned near sunset. He ducked beneath the lodge flap and sent Bettany one brief glance that both warned and reassured. Some of her tension drained away. Whatever Small Eagle had done, the death of Wilfred Cole would not be traced back to her.

Later she noticed that Smoke Along the Ground's wife wore a pair of kid boots with twin rows of shiny black buttons and that Spotted Bull had a blanket of red-and-black plaid. When Red Paint Woman brought the evening meal in a new iron kettle, Bettany found she had no appetite. She moved away until she sat at the edge of the firelight. Even here the red glow flickered across her hands, giving the illusion that they were freshly stained with blood. For an instant she relived that terrible moment before pushing it out of her mind with a silent scream.

Abruptly she left the fireside and walked to the banks of the Arkansas. It flowed black as the river Styx beneath the pale quarter moon. She held her hands out before her. In the muted silver light the illusion had vanished. They looked as they always had, if browner and more callused. But they had killed a man.

They were the same, but she would never be.

Twenty-three

Texas, March 1841

"That's a nice table you made, Mr. Logan." Yancy ran his good hand over the smooth plank top.

"One of the many things I learned in my travels."

"Nell will be right pleased with it. Is it a birthday present for her?"

Logan shook his head. "I'm afraid not. It's more of a goodbye present." He heard the hiss of breath the boy took in and went on. "I always said I'd stay till spring and then be on my way. It's time I was gone."

He couldn't meet Yancy's gaze. He knew what he'd find there. Don't care, he had told himself a hundred times. Don't love. But he already cared about the three youngsters who had struggled so valiantly to save their parents' dream.

Yancy shuffled to his feet. "Nell's been crochety these past weeks, but I was hoping you wouldn't hold it agin her. She really likes you."

"I know." That was just the problem, Logan thought. Although the twins had grown taller than their sister, they were merely large boys. Nell was a young woman, feeling the first stirrings of a woman's needs and with no other object to focus them on than himself. He'd stayed too long.

"She's a fine girl," he said. "And I think Lem Jenkins agrees with me on that."

"Lem! She won't have nothing to do with him. Why, she used to fuss at him as much as she fusses at you."

Logan smiled. "She will again."

An hour later Nell came squelching across the muddy ground to the barn. He'd put a lean-to on the end for his private room. Usually she barged right in, speaking whatever was on her mind at a clipping gallop. This time she knocked before opening the door. She was wearing her "good" dress, with her hair neatly parted and brushed. He saw with a pang of tenderness that she had pinned it up to make herself look older—or to make him think of her as less of a girl.

From the threshold she could see his few possessions folded and ready to pack in his saddlebag. "You're really going! I . . . I didn't believe Yancy."

But she had. Her anger was just a veil over the dread that she had felt on hearing Yancy's words.

He pulled his wool shirt from a peg. "The ranch is on solid footing now with the buildings and tools in good repair and a smokehouse full of venison and pork. With what you can raise and grow and trade, the three of you will do all right. And Lem will help you any way he can. I think you know how much he cares about you."

"Lem! I don't care about Lem! I care about—"

She broke off and bit her lip as Beau pushed past her with Yancy on his heels. Logan felt his resolve wavering. Maybe if he stayed on a bit until she switched her idealized affections to young Jenkins, it would make his leaving easier.

Beau gestured to the rough track that served for a road. "There's Comanches a-coming!"

Logan looked past Nell's shoulder. One brave and a young boy. "Stay calm. If it was a raid, they wouldn't have brought a boy along."

Nevertheless he reached for his rifle as he spoke. A moment later he recognized the visitors: Antelope Chaser and his son. They halted their ponies just out of range. Lowering the rifle, Logan went out to meet them. "Greetings, Antelope Chaser. I did not think to see you here."

The Comanche returned his greeting. "I heard that you were lodged in this place and have ridden long to find you.

I have also heard of trouble coming to the Tsistsistas. A
leader of the white horse soldiers is gathering his men to
ride against your people. He will use any means to destroy
them."

"Where did you hear this information?"

Antelope Chaser's face took on a look of grim humor.
"There was a man who violated and killed the daughter of
an Apache war chief. We apprehended him and gave him
to the women. Before they were through with him he told
us many things."

Logan didn't doubt it. "What has set them off this time?"

The Comanche turned to the boy, who had been silent
up till now. Antelope Chaser's son met Logan's gaze stead-
fastly.

"They say a woman of the Tsistsistas killed a white trader
for his goods at Bent's Fort. They say the woman is Small
Eagle's wife. They say her hair is silver."

"I will have Singing Leaf help me fold the lodge cover,"
Red Paint Woman said, waving Bettany aside. "You will
only be in the way."

Gratefully Bettany rubbed the aching small of her back.
Taking down the tipi was a major chore for a woman in
her advanced state of pregnancy, and she was glad to have
Small Eagle's wife take charge. That was how she thought
of the Arapaho—Small Eagle's wife—while she, of course,
was something other. Bettany tried not to dwell upon it.

Her gravid body was heavy and clumsy, and there seemed
to be no more room for the baby to grow inside her. Back
in the green hills of the Susquehanna she would have been
expected to stay out of the public eye in the last months
before her baby was born; here among the bleached-bone
rocks and juniper scrub she was expected to fulfill all her
normal duties. In fact, she would be on horseback before
the yellow sun rose much higher.

The interior packing was done, everything bundled
neatly inside pots and baskets or tied up in robes. Moving
awkwardly, Bettany went to the lodge of Yellow Cake to

see if she needed help in wrapping up her belongings, but everything was already done. Bettany remembered the water vessels hadn't been filled yet and took them down to the river. The Cheyenne refused to drink water that had been standing through the night—if it was not fresh, it was not "living water" and was therefore unacceptable for drinking.

She was unable to bend to dip the containers from the bank and had to stand in the river to fill them. It was much higher already than in previous years, the other women had commented, and Bettany found it difficult to keep her balance in the swift current. The gurgling of the flow at first covered the sound of an approaching horseman. She looked up and froze as a man in buckskins came into camp at a gallop. It was a dangerous thing to do. In the heat of excitement he might have been mistaken for an enemy bent on counting coup. Small Eagle had his rifle at the ready but lowered the barrel. His voice carried clearly. "It is Wolf Star."

The men crowded around him, and Bettany walked slowly up from the river in time to hear part of the exchange. "But why?" Smoke Along the Ground was asking. "Have we not lived in peace and left them unmolested?"

The Cheyenne anger and disbelief was apparent to Bettany even from the space of several yards. The land, they said, had room enough for all. Now that they had smoked the pipe with their former enemies, the warring would cease and their young men could live to become old men. Buffalo Heart joined them, ignoring the pain of his arthritic joints.

"You say he is bringing more blue coats with him to attack the Tsistsistas. This puzzles me. The horse soldiers have their own warrior society rules and must have a reason to ride against us."

Logan dismounted. "They say a woman of the Cheyenne killed a trader near Bent's Fort."

A murmuring of dissent rippled through the assembled men. "We know of no such occurrence."

Bettany turned to stone a few feet away. My God, what had she done!

Small Eagle was strangely silent. Logan's glance went to him like iron filings to a magnet. He knew his brother too well.

"Such a thing happened," Small Eagle acknowledged in low, angry tones. "He tried to dishonor the woman, and he might have meant to kill her. In the struggle she vanquished him instead."

There was an utter absence of sound, like the airlessness that came before a storm. Logan's hands clenched and a muscle worked in his jaw. "You must get fast horses and take her away so she is not recognized."

Smoke Along the Ground frowned. "We must leave this place immediately and head up into the hills where they cannot follow." He indicated Bettany, standing to the side, paralyzed. "The woman cannot travel fast. She is near her term."

Logan spun about and stopped, staring at her. There was a sudden pallor beneath the bronzed skin stretched across his cheekbones. His eyes went dull, like tarnished brass. Then it passed, and he was the man she knew as Wolf Star once more, so masculine and beautiful that her heart ached for it. He turned away without speaking. There was no need. The bleak despair in his face had said it all.

Small Eagle rode up to the front of the traveling party and found Bettany. "Once we reach the Place Where Many Antelope Died you will be able to rest."

She nodded, grateful for his concern not only for his unborn son, but for herself as well. Once through the gap the main party could travel on to one of the high, rugged valleys while a party of warriors stayed behind to ambush the attackers and drive them off.

This wasn't the first instance of Small Eagle's thoughtfulness. He saw to it that she had choice bits of meat to eat and that she was shielded from the cold with his best buffalo robe and jacket. Even Red Paint Woman, who had no reason to love her, was showing surprising solicitude. It was good, Bettany had come to realize, to have another woman in the lodge. The more clumsy she'd become, the more she'd appreciated the aid of the Arapaho woman and her forced companionship. In fact, in the last few months their relationship had changed considerably. They'd developed a curious, shared sisterhood; although it was never effortless, it was often comforting. Small Eagle's other wife had become her friend. They would never be close, but they could rely on each other, and it had all come about that terrible day Bettany had defended herself against the trader's attack.

Red Paint Woman wanted a child of her own desperately, but there was no sign of one as yet. Initially Bettany would have gladly changed places with her; but for many months now the little creature kicking and growing in her womb had taken on its own personality in her mind. She hardly remembered that Small Eagle had fathered it and never thought of the baby as being a half-breed. Son or daughter, the baby was hers in a way that no one else had ever been.

The sun rose higher, and the air warmed pleasantly. Already the low hills were visible in the distance, buff and brown dappled with evergreen scrub and tender new shoots. Bettany even thought she could make out the gap as a narrow notch in a rising curve of terrain. She stiffened her resolve; she could hold on that much longer.

The long hours in the saddle were exhausting. In a minor truce, Red Paint Woman had agreed to let Bettany use her padded, high-backed Spanish saddle. Even with its support her back ached terribly. Her abdomen was so tight and distended, she could scarcely draw a decent breath. She couldn't imagine six more weeks of it until the baby came.

By the time they reached the river's main fork she could hardly stay on her pony. At least the day was mild with little wind and a warm sun. She gritted her teeth and hung on.

The front of the long cavalcade was almost at the place where they planned to ford the river. After reconnoitering

the banks, Small Eagle and Spotted Bull turned their
mounts away from it and traveled halfway to the rear to
confer with the others.

"The water is running high this year." He indicated an
amount that was more than the length of a man's arm.
"The current is swifter than any time in my memory."

Smoke Along the Ground was concerned. The warm
spring weather of *Mahk e o me' shi,* the April Fat Moon,
had caused melting in the highlands, and the runoff was
already apparent. It was early for the flash floods, but their
past history could be read in the piles of brush and driftwood
that lay up the slope on either side of the river. The trunks
of whole trees, some with shredded branches and roots,
were heaped on the hill beyond the bend. When the floods
came here, they came full and they came hard.

"Can we cross it safely, or should we seek another site?"

Spotted Bull looked up at the cloudless blue sky and
shrugged. "There is no rain here, but who knows what is
happening in the great mountains? But if we do not cross
and the river floods, we shall be delayed here for many days,
perhaps weeks."

Small Eagle knew what Smokes Along the Ground was
thinking: If they turned aside, they would endanger the
lives of all the camp, for the enemy was large in number
and well armed, while they were only a few; furthermore,
if they crossed quickly, it might be their enemies who were
forced to turn away instead.

He squinted into the distance, where a thin haze of dust
shimmered in the clear air. It might be the rest of the band
coming to join them—or it might be the enemy. Six men
could hold off a war party for several hours, and the range
of their bows exceeded that of the *ve-ho-e* rifles; but once
the Cheyenne arrows were spent, the attackers would close
in and finish off the women and children quickly. Small
Eagle didn't think it was worth the risk.

"I cannot say what the afternoon might bring, but if it
is decided that we should cross, then it would be best if we
do so in haste, before the river rises further."

The debate lasted only a few minutes. The leaders had decided that they must cross. When Logan rode up from his place in the rear guard, the first riders were starting across and the women were dismantling their travois and binding them on their ponies.

To Bettany the water seemed like a living thing, rushing high and swift between its deep banks. She was unused to riding horseback in the first place, and crossing a river in the saddle was something she had little desire to experience. Spotted Bull gave the command: "We cross. Go quickly so as not to delay the others."

Bright Cloud, a young brave, went first. His sister, Pearl Finder, went down the steep incline on her spirited mount and plunged into the water without hesitation. Her pony found its footing on the river bottom without difficulty, and several others picked their way down the narrow gully toward the water. Bettany was terrified. Instead of urging her horse forward, she let it sidle back until it bumped into another.

In the ensuing confusion Red Paint Woman looked to her husband, but Small Eagle was far to the rear. She didn't want to risk the saddle, of which she was so proud, by having Bettany wait to cross. Why, even a child could see that the water level had risen again. This stupid *ve-ho-e* will never cross unless something is done. She picked up a switch and cracked it over the rump of Bettany's horse and sent it lunging down the bank.

Logan, far to the rear, had learned of the high water and came trotting up to reconnoiter. He reached the fording place as a cry went up from those waiting to cross. He had just enough time to see the high ripple of water surging downstream toward them like a second layer over the top of the river, pushing a load of twigs, branches, and other debris before it. It was a warning swell, like a bow wave, and the wall of water that sent it tumbling past the banks would come crashing along behind it at any moment.

He saw Bettany's pony panic and slip, before righting itself, as the wave approached. Without hesitation he urged his big bay into the churning river. The horse was frightened but trusted its master completely. It paused a fraction of a second before plunging into the swirl of froth and foam and soon was breast deep in the torrent. Logan was halfway across and almost at Bettany's side when Bright Cloud's pony discovered it could no longer feel the river bottom beneath its hooves.

Instead of trying to swim the last few feet, it tossed its head from side to side and fell sideways with a splash. Pearl Finder cried out and leaned down, holding her hand out to her brother, but man and mount went tumbling downstream, sweeping her away as well. Bright Cloud's dark head vanished beneath the roiling current, to bob up a hundred feet down the river before being lost from sight once more. Of Pearl Finder there was no sign at all.

Although it was putting up a valiant struggle, Bettany's pony was rapidly losing ground to the river's forces and would soon follow suit. As she turned helplessly toward him, Logan threw a loop of rawhide rope over her head and shoulders. Once her arms cleared the loop, she grasped the rope instinctively and hung on with all her strength. They'd almost made the far bank when her horse was swept hard against it, bruising her leg to the bone.

The doomed beast shrieked in terror, but its cries were muted by the noise of the approaching flood. It rose above the normal flow of the river by eight feet or more, almost to the top of the embankment. The sandy soil seemed to explode as the banks were undercut, showering dirt and grit everywhere. Churning, foaming, the dark mass of water swept inexorably down upon Bettany as she struggled to escape, her throat so paralyzed she couldn't even scream.

The floodwaters bore down upon her with a horrible, throaty roar that drowned out every other sound, including her scream of terror.

Twenty-Four

THE GIANT WAVE'S ROAR OVERRODE THE SHRILL screams of the onlookers and the bone-scraping shriek of Bettany's terrified horse. The animal's head was raised, throat strained and mouth gaping open, but nothing could override the furious bellow of the river as it caved in banks and ripped trees from their ancient moorings.

With steady hands Logan guided his own mount through the swirling water. He had plunged in downstream of her, and having a few more seconds before the floodtide reached him made all the difference. The bay scrambled up on the bank in a supreme effort of equine strength and courage. Man and horse moved like a single creature with one heart and mind.

His rope tightened around Bettany, and she was snatched from the water mere seconds before the flood's main onslaught. Logan saw that his horse was too spent to carry them both. He dragged her from the bank, threw her joltingly upon his bay, and sent them plunging up the high ground to safety.

Racing behind them on foot, he managed to reach Bettany's side before the water roared over its former boundaries, snapping some trees and uprooting others with its raw, primitive power. The spray from it flew through the air in droplets that shone like rust-stained pearls.

The rawhide rope bit into Bettany's flesh under her arms and across her swollen breasts, but she didn't try to pull it free. It took all her strength to hang on to the bay's mane to keep from falling. She was shaking so badly, she didn't realize the horse was trembling, too. Logan came up beside her. "The water's still rising. We'll have to go higher before we can rest."

She nodded, too tired to speak, and he led them up into the hills. When they were out of danger he lifted her gently down. Her legs wouldn't hold her. Cold, soaking wet, and shaking with fear and reaction, she clung to Logan like a lifeline. Her hands clutched at his shirt, and she buried her face against his wide chest.

Logan held her as tightly as her gravid belly allowed, his face buried against the curve of her neck. Her skin felt cold, and wave after wave of shudders shook her frame. He released her abruptly.

"You're chilled to the marrow. We've got to get you warm or you'll come down with lung fever."

He went to his bay and patted its foam-flecked neck. "Easy, Shadow, old friend. It's all right now, but we'd have been lost in the torrent without your strength and spirit." The gallant creature's sides heaved as it gulped in great raspy breaths, but it lifted its head and nudged his shoulder affectionately. Logan smoothed its long Spanish nose. "I'll have you set to rights shortly."

He removed the oilskin packet he'd secured to the horse's back. Inside with other items were a rolled buffalo robe and a heavy wool shirt. He tucked the robe around Bettany and rubbed his pony down with the shirt.

He thought that Bettany might sleep in the aftermath of their ordeal. When he was finished he discovered that she had managed to gather fuel and start a good fire with the tinderbox she carried in the pouch attached to her waist. Sun-browned, hair darkened by its wetness, and wrapped in the buffalo robe and hunkering awkwardly near the fire, she looked like a bedraggled squaw. Her hair had come loose from its braids, and there were scratches and bruises on the left side of her face and all along her left arm. There was little resemblance now to the white woman they had rescued from the wagon party massacre. What had he done to her, and to himself, by sending Small Eagle to her rescue?

He took some jerky from his blanket roll and handed her a piece, watching while she chewed and finally swallowed. Even with her face filled with strain and fatigue she had the power to rip his heart from his chest. The burning wood gave a loud pop and sizzle as the flames encountered a bit of moisture within. The only other sound was the distant rushing of the river in flood. He realized they hadn't spoken a single word to each other, at the same time she began to speak.

Bettany's voice was as taut and high-pitched as a twanged wire as she allowed herself to vocalize her fears. "The others . . . what happened to them?"

He met her gray gaze levelly. "Most escaped. A few were swept away when the bank caved in—Stone Elk Woman and Weeping Rock, Black Leg's youngest daughter. I couldn't tell about the others. It all happened too fast."

"And . . . and Hannah?"

"I didn't see Hannah anywhere."

Bettany stared into the heart of the flames. "She was with Red Paint Woman, near the bank, when I started across with Bright Cloud."

After that there was nothing to say at all. She leaned her back against a tree while tears spilled down her cheeks. When night came they rolled up together from opposite sides of the buffalo robe for warmth. The sky was overcast without even the stars for comfort. Logan listened to Bettany's breathing as it changed to a deep and regular rhythm. Her abdomen made a small mound of its own beneath the robe.

Logan's mouth twisted into a wry smile. He had spent so many nights imagining what it would be like to share his blanket with her.

Somehow, this wasn't exactly what he'd had in mind.

When the dull light of dawn came seeping through the trees, Logan stirred. Bettany was already awake. Her eyes were vacant and staring, and he thought she had succumbed to the listless, empty state that sometimes followed terrible events; but slowly the color came back into her cheeks and her rigid posture eased. He rolled on his back, searching the maps of his mind for the best routes back to their band. There were none. There were dozens of creeks and tributaries. Until the flood ebbed and the waters were safe to ford, there was nothing to be done. They were marooned on a vast island of high ground.

He sat up and realized she'd gone still once more. Suddenly she gasped and clutched her abdomen. It was much too early for her to have the baby, but he knew this was no false start. Already beads of sweat had formed along her brow. From the way the whites of her eyes were showing around their smoky irises, Logan had the sinking feeling that she knew as little about the mysteries of childbirth as he did.

He did know one thing: the dark clouds gathering overhead promised more rain and flooding. If there was time, he'd have to get her to shelter before the sky opened. From past journeys he knew there was an old shack a few miles ahead off the timeworn trail. It was little more than a shed with a roof, but if the place still stood, it would at least keep them fairly dry. Logan stooped down beside Bettany. "We can't stay here. Do you think you can ride a little more?"

Instead of answering she doubled over as another contraction overwhelmed her. It felt as if her back were about to break. The ache began at the base of her spine and grew until it encompassed her sides and distended belly. A rushing, buzzing sound blotted out Logan's questions and even their relevance. For an eternity of seconds the world narrowed to only herself and the deep, gnawing pain. When it passed she was white and shaken.

Logan knew there was no time to waste if he meant to get her to the shack. He lifted her in his arms before the next assault and placed her on his patient bay. If that didn't work and she couldn't hold on, he'd tie her to the horse. And if *that* didn't work, he'd carry her in his arms.

Fortunately he didn't have to do either.

They wound their way higher into the hills, where the vegetation of the plateau began to give way to aspen and beech. The slopes of the distant hills were steep, their upper reaches cloaked in forests of green fir and pine. An irregular line of blue to the west marked the high, rocky spine of the continent where the floodwaters had been born from the early snowmelt. Bettany's labor slackened, and she had only a few more pains over the miles.

She was exhausted when he finally led the bay up toward the ruined shack. It was nestled in a bowl of green hills, just as he'd remembered it—but the place had been considerably improved in the intervening years. A crooked lean-to of recent vintage had been added at one end to house animals, and the roof had been repaired. Flat stones had been placed before the door, and a few early wildflowers had sprung up near the sheltered south wall. The shutters hung open at the single unglazed window, and bits of colorful fabric fluttered and danced in the breeze. He felt decided relief. If there were curtains at the windows, there had to be a woman inside.

Logan put his hand on Bettany's arm. "The situation might be hard to explain. I think it would be best if we say that we're married."

He spoke in English. She answered quietly in Cheyenne. The irony struck her belatedly.

Leaving Bettany with the rifle, he advanced toward the dwelling, calling out: "Hello the cabin!"

The door remained closed, but there was no sign of a gun barrel in a window opening. Logan called again to announce his intentions and went up to rap at the weathered plank door. It swung open without a creak on oiled leather hinges. The room was bare of furniture except for a table fashioned from a piece of metal and a wooden wheel from a *carreta,* and a rude bed frame formed from the other parts. Their manufacture showed a very high level of creativity and a very low level of skill. The place was tidy and clean, with a thin layer of inevitable dust, and to Logan it looked like heaven.

After a quick check around the outside, he helped Bettany into the cabin. "No one's been here in some time. I don't think they'll mind if we make ourselves at home."

There was no place for her to sit but the bed, which was only a thin sheet thrown over a pile of sweet-smelling dried grasses. Bettany looked around. The rough boards had been newly chinked, and a parched wisp of vegetation that had once been a columbine was stuck in a chipped bottle. Someone had taken good care of the cabin. "Wolf Star? . . ."

"Speak English. We don't know whose place this is or what their feelings are toward the Cheyenne. And don't call me Wolf Star."

"What shall I call you, then?"

"Logan."

"Is that your first name . . . or is it your surname?"

"Just Logan."

"It seems a strange choice—an Irish name for a man who could pass for an Indian."

"It was my father's name."

With those words he closed himself off to her. His defenses were impenetrable, and she didn't even try to pierce them; but there were so many questions she wanted to ask, so many things she wanted to know. How had the son of an Irishman come to live among Small Eagle's people? Perhaps his father had been a trapper who'd taken an Indian wife, as was common practice. That would explain his dark coloring and sparse beard. She had seen him pull the whiskers out with shell tweezers just as Small Eagle did.

Thorson had related to her the story of how Wolf Star had been found in the snow, alone and surrounded by wolves. Why had he gone out into the white man's world, and why had he returned instead to the Cheyenne? Where did he learn to speak English? The more she knew him, the more curious she was about his background and history. But his curt words had held the sound of a door slamming shut, and she was too tired to pry.

Logan had rummaged beneath the bed and brought out a wooden box. He pulled out a length of rope, two more candles, a bar of soap that smelled like lilacs, and a camisole of soft bleached cotton with two dozen hooks and eyes down the front. There was something else in the bottom, wedged beneath a thin piece of unfinished board. He pried it loose with his strong fingers and pulled out a pair of dusty satin slippers. A rosette of frilly fabric adorned their tops, and the soles were paper thin. Long ribbons trailed from either side of the insteps.

Bettany laughed at Logan's expression as he turned them over in his hands. He was clearly puzzled; the slippers were useless for all practical purposes. "Who would waste good money on something as worthless as these? You couldn't walk a hundred yards in them before they fell apart."

Bettany laughed. "Why, they're dancing shoes. They were never intended to go beyond a ballroom floor, or a moonlit terrace."

Now Bettany noted odd details that hadn't registered before: an abandoned bird's nest in one corner, a bit of mildewed ribbon tied to the bedpost, a rusted straight razor with a broken blade set carefully on a window ledge, and a small pamphlet of psalms in a thin board cover. Two stubby candles were stuck in place with their own wax, one on a broken piece of pottery, the other in a small square of metal whose use she didn't know. She wondered whose bed she was sitting on and hoped its owners wouldn't mind if she rested there awhile.

"Where do you think they have gone, Wolf . . . er, Logan? What do you think has happened to them?"

He had picked up a piece of torn paper and was frowning at it. He put it back on the table. "I don't know." His glance was penetrating. "I should forage for food. Will you be all right for a short while if I leave you?"

Bettany nodded. Her water hadn't broken, and the dreadful pain in her back had ebbed to a faint ache. "The pains have stopped. Red Paint Woman said it often comes and goes with a first child."

Logan took her word for it. Birthing was women's business and not included in the traditional education of a Cheyenne brave. He stopped just short of the doorway. "I'll leave the rifle with you."

She raised her eyebrows. "I have my knife."

"I have my bow." He went out and returned with the rifle. "If there's trouble—of any kind—a shot from that will have me back."

Bettany stood at the door and watched him ride away, feeling very alone. A breeze ruffled the curtains and stirred the hair at her temples. Something rustled behind her, and she turned as quickly as her cumbersome body allowed. The paper had blown off the table and was skittering across the hard-packed dirt floor. She retrieved it clumsily. The writing on it had been done with a piece of charred wood, and though the spelling was poor and the letters ill formed, their message was as clear as the day it had been written:

> Joe, Im sik of bein left alon in this plas
> wint to las cruzis wif Brigs yu kin folo me
> or yu kin go to hell

The signature was an ornate scrawl that could have been "Ruth" or "Roth" or—with a stretch of the imagination— even "Rachel." Bettany didn't know whether to laugh or sigh. This valley would be like the ends of the earth to a woman left alone by her man, but she could picture all the dismay of the hapless Joe when he returned and found the note. She hoped he had followed her to Las Cruces. There had to be some happy endings.

Well, at least she knew now why the cabin was untenanted. But why hadn't Logan? He'd said he didn't know where the owners had gone. Belatedly she understood. Logan couldn't read.

Before she had time to ponder this, the pains returned with terrible force. There was hardly time between the end of one and the beginning of the next. This time she knew her labor had begun in earnest.

The contractions that came in an almost continuous assault left her gasping for relief. From the base of her spine to just beneath her ribs her body felt as if it were being torn asunder. Her water broke with a small, warm gush, and she was frightened. Even Red Paint Woman's often grudging assistance would have been welcome.

She had no idea how long it would take for the baby to be born, but she knew that the first one usually took many hours. When pain clawed through her again, stronger than before, she was sick with fear. How could she survive ten or twelve or twenty hours of this? She wanted Logan. She needed his help, but more, she needed his strength. Everything would be all right once he returned, but they needed fresh game. It would be wiser to wait as long as possible before she summoned him.

And then her contractions came hard and fast, and she was no longer able to stay on her feet. She groped her way to the bed and lay down upon it on her side, biting her lip to stifle a cry. She felt as if she were being rent apart. The successive waves merged into one long agony. Despair alternated with terror; she had waited too long.

Her hand edged out for the rifle, but the effort seemed beyond her remaining strength. Something was very wrong. She felt another gush of warmth and lunged desperately. The momentum carried her off the bed and onto the floor. Something ripped free inside her. The pain was excruciating, blinding Bettany with its fury. She felt consciousness slip away and went eagerly to meet it until she remembered the baby inside her womb. *Her* baby. She struggled against the encroaching blackness. At last her fingers curled around the gun.

Logan was on his way back after a successful hunt when he heard the shot. At first he thought it was a rumble of the approaching rainsquall, but lightning split the sky almost immediately, and when the thunder came it was a giant's roar, so loud that the ground shook and the air trembled. The voice of the storm was nothing like the high-pitched echo that had preceded it.

He goaded his horse into a gallop and streaked across the
meadow and through a gap in the hills that led to the
sheltered valley. The closer he got to the cabin, the greater
his sense of urgency grew. Once he imagined he'd heard
her cry out his name, but he knew it could not possibly
have carried over the noise of the wind and the pounding
hooves.

He arrived at the cabin in a state of controlled panic.
The clouds had gone from gray to black, and rain came
down like the outpouring of a broken dam. In the false
twilight the cabin looked eerie and void of life. The pony
took shelter beneath the crooked lean-to, and Logan burst
into the dwelling. Inside it was dark, but he could tell the
bed was empty. Then another flare of light rippled jaggedly
across the sky, and shadows and images jumped out at him.

Logan's breath hissed between his teeth. She was lying
in a pool of dark water, between the table and the bed.
But there had been no water in the cabin before. He rushed
to her side and knelt to lift her. His hands were warm with
her blood. Bettany roused enough to cry out. "The baby
. . . it's coming."

A jolt pierced his body, bringing a rush of urgency. Once,
as a young boy, he'd fallen through thin ice into a freezing
pool of water. He felt the same way now, desperate for
action yet almost paralyzed. This was woman's work. He
fought down the panic. Her life was in his hands—but what
the hell was he supposed to do now?

Her skirts were soaked. He pushed them up and saw that
birth was imminent. There was no time even to put her
on the bed. The head crowned, and the baby was born in
a gush of fluid. Logan swore. He had an unconscious woman
and a limp, purple-mottled baby on his hands. He lifted
the infant gently in his outstretched palms. A boy.

Stillborn.

Bettany moaned, and as Logan shifted his weight he lost
his grip on the slippery little form. Instinctively he grabbed
the baby's leg around the calf, and the boy hung upside
down, a darker shape in the increasing grayness of the cabin.

Suddenly the baby coughed, choked, mewled like a kitten, and coughed again. Logan was startled into action. He thumped the baby on the back, and it coughed again, more clearly. The newborn drew its first, lusty breath and sent it back out immediately in a great wail of angry protest.

Logan pulled off his shirt and wrapped up the bawling infant, his ears assailed by furious, high-pitched cries. He was so surprised that the baby lived, he almost forgot that the cord had to be tied. Removing a thong from the top of his jacket, he tied it firmly in a knot at what he hoped was the right spot and then rolled the boy up in his shirt once more.

He was afraid to look at Bettany. The delivery was finished, and there was so much blood everywhere! He put the baby to her breast, knowing a child's suckling was said to ease the bleeding. He turned his attention to Bettany. The deadly flow had stemmed, and her arm was still warm beneath his hand. He leaned over her and felt her breath tickle his skin as light, as insubstantial, as a bit of dandelion fluff. The fear that held him loosened its cold grip but didn't let go. She still lived, and for the moment that was enough. He tried not to think of what might happen later.

The baby was still suckling, and Logan took the time to light the candles. He carried Bettany to the bed. She moaned and tried to speak, and he was encouraged. "Don't talk. Save your energy."

His words soothed her, and she closed her eyes. Once she was settled he got water from the half empty rain barrel, and bathed her sweaty face and body. He used the rest of the water to clean up the wailing, squirming infant; neither of them enjoyed the process very much. Wrapping the boy up tightly once more, in the way Cheyenne mothers swaddled their infants, he placed him between Bettany and the wall. The fussing and cries stopped now that the child felt warm and secure.

Logan whiled away the interminable hours sitting at the bedside. Now and then he was able to get some water down Bettany's throat. He had nothing to accompany his thoughts but the clamor of thunder overhead and the dull ping of hail against the roof and walls. Even the hours in his jail cell had passed more quickly, he thought.

The storm blew over in a wild gusting of winds that sent a draft down the chimney, showering hot sparks over the dirt floor.

Bettany stirred. Logan put his hand over hers. "It's all right. You're going to be all right."

"The baby . . . ?" she whispered.

"A fine, sturdy little one. You have a son."

"A son." Bettany opened her eyes and smiled at him. To Logan the interior of the cabin seemed a hundred times brighter.

Twenty-five

BETTANY'S RECOVERY WAS QUICKER THAN LOGAN
had expected. She hadn't lost as much blood as he'd feared
from the complications, and he forced her to eat as much
meat as he could—"for your son's sake." It always worked.
He roasted game and fowl and made broth from the scraps
and bones and stood by her side until she finished her
portion.

Bettany was half-asleep when the baby began to fuss.
Logan saw that she was awake and brought her a cup of
broth. She wrinkled up her nose at it. For the past few
minutes she had been dreaming of an old-fashioned Thanks-
giving dinner, her plate heaped with chestnut dressing,
boiled cranberries, and potatoes and gravy. Waking up to
a bowl of plain broth was a severe disappointment. What
she wouldn't give for a glass of buttermilk or cool lemonade.

She pushed it away, but Logan was insistent. "You must
keep your strength up."

It was lukewarm, and she drank it down quickly. The
broth was keeping her milk flowing, she admitted grudgingly
as the baby began rooting at her breast. Absorbed in her
infant's needs, she began to unfasten her bodice. Logan
turned away.

As the infant suckled she looked down at him, smiling.
So this was the little stranger she had carried so many
months, the boy who would grow to manhood and have
sons of his own one day. Her eyes shimmered with joyous
tears. "How beautiful you are, little one! How perfect!"

His eyes opened wide at the sound of her voice, and he paused to look up at his mother. "Ah, see how intelligent you are! What shall I call you, my darling?"

The baby went back to his nursing with renewed vigor. Logan laughed. "He is *Mok' so is.*"

Bettany sent him a darkling look. "'Potbelly' might be the nickname for small boys among the Cheyenne, but it is not what my son will be called. He'll have a proper name."

The whims of pregnant women and nursing mothers were meant to be humored—to a point. "What name would you give your small warrior, then?"

"Samuel. Samuel Emmett Howard, after his grandfather."

Bettany frowned. That didn't sound right. "No, there can only be one Sam Howard. I'll give him my mother's maiden name." She ran her hand over the baby's downy head. "Grayson Howard. That is your official name. And not *Mok' so is.*"

Logan balked. "What kind of name is that? It is *ve-ho-e* words that are only sounds, meaning nothing. My brother's son must have a Cheyenne name."

Bettany was getting tired. "Then let him have both. You can choose it for him, if you like."

Logan was pleased. He gazed down at the baby, hardly able to believe that this wizened little creature was his brother's son. As Small Eagle's nearest male relative, it was his responsibility to see that things were done properly. He tucked his index finger in Grayson's hand and grinned when the tiny digits wound around it firmly. "He is strong."

To choose a name was an important task. The boy's spirit would derive strength and protection from the right one. Logan went to the window and threw open the shutter, searching the sky for inspiration or a sign. The storm had passed over them and was venting its might on the low hills beyond. Thunder grumbled, and the cabin walls shook. It reminded him of the anxious hours after the delivery, when he had feared that both Bettany and her son might die. The name came to him suddenly, and he knew it was right.

Logan took the baby from Bettany and carried him to the open window. He lifted the boy-child high so that he might see the roiling black clouds and the great flares of light in the distance. Unlike most infants, the noise of the thunder didn't seem to frighten him. Instead the boy howled his wonder and delight.

"See the great power of earth and sky and know that it is yours, *Woh'k pe nu num'a*. From this day until you grow to manhood you will be called this." And he also decided that, as the nearest male relative present, he must give the boy his secret name that few would ever know: Wolf Born of Thunder. It was a name his father would be proud of—a warrior's name.

Logan carried the baby over to Bettany and placed him in her arms. At that moment he was more the Cheyenne warrior of his youth than at any time in the past ten years. Bettany sensed it, but only dimly. She had never felt closer to Logan—or more aware of the gulf between them.

He placed his hand on the baby's head. "Here is your son. His name is Gray Thunder."

She nestled the baby against her breast. "Gray Thunder. Grayson Howard, Gray Thunder."

The compromise was accepted in silence. The baby yawned and closed his eyes. Bettany followed suit. Logan watched them drift into sleep together. Through the window he saw the sun trying to peek out, gilding the edges of the clouds. A rare peace settled over Logan. He had never known its like before.

Ipewa. It was good.

The days warmed and lengthened, the grasses grew tall, and deer came to drink at the nearby creek. Bettany had recovered enough to travel, and her baby thrived. The river flowed swiftly, but the waters were no longer high, yet Logan didn't mention leaving to seek out the Cheyenne band. Neither did Bettany.

They spoke only of things that had happened since the baby's birth, and the world had narrowed to this valley,

this cabin. The pain of Hannah's loss was real to both, but
this existence was something apart, a segment of their lives
removed from the real world. Time did not exist. There
was only the present. Then the ease between them seemed
to slip away, eroded by the tension between them. A glance,
the unintended brush of his arm against hers, and they
jumped apart; yet Bettany's eyes sought his face more and
more, only to find him watching her. She pretended to
ignore him as much as possible. It was increasingly difficult
when he absorbed every waking thought that was not de-
voted to her child and her chores.

Days melted into weeks. Logan was absent more than
usual and spoke less and less. He was restless and abrupt at
times and spent the evenings staring into the fire while she
worked or played with her son. He never spoke of leaving,
and she wanted to know what was in his mind. Afraid that
speaking of it would make it happen, she approached the
problem obliquely one afternoon.

She was making soap from ashes and animal fat, boiling
it in a battered kettle he'd unearthed from a pile of odds
and ends in the lean-to. Logan was stripped to the waist,
magnificent in the golden sunlight, his long hair held back
with a thong. He stretched, lithe and tawny as the mountain cat she'd spotted the day before. He loved the heat.

"It's good to bake in the sunshine after the winter bitterness has passed. Good for the body and good for the
soul."

Bettany seized her opening. "The days grow hot, but the
nights are still chilly."

"They are always cool here, and in winter the snow will
be halfway to the roof."

"Then I will make some robes to keep us warm before
the season turns." She paused, hoping his reply would give
her some clue to his plans. Logan didn't answer. He got
up and walked away.

While the soap boiled down Bettany set to work on her
special project. She took a hide she'd scraped and tanned
until it was soft and thin and cut it into squares. She

roughened one side with a scraper and then prepared a mixture of berry juice and ground charcoal from the fire. When Logan returned he found her dipping the end of a stick, chewed to a brushlike consistency, into the dark fluid. He stood behind her as she made painstaking marks with her improvised ink on her makeshift sheets.

"What are you making?"

"A book for my son. A record of his birth." She was pleased with her handiwork. Although not beautiful, it was legible, and that was what mattered.

> Grayson Howard, son of Bettany Anne Howard of
> Pennsylvania and the Susquehanna orphanage.
> Grandson of Cecily Grayson and Samuel Howard,
> Born early spring, 1841

She'd stopped there, without the knowledge to finish it appropriately. "Where are we?" He looked at her strangely. "I mean," she explained, "what would this place be named on a map? It's very important that Grayson should know it."

Logan grinned. It seemed a silly thing to him, but he made one up, knowing she would never be content otherwise. "Mountain Cat Valley on Bettany Creek, south of the Arkansas River and east of Santa Fe."

Bettany set down her brush, and he saw that he'd offended her. "Your people set much store by records and books."

"They are your people, also."

"No. The white man is as alien to me as the Tsistsistas are to you. I want nothing of their world."

He was so vehement that she didn't press the point. On an impulse he couldn't explain, Logan took out his medicine pouch and spilled the contents into his palm. "Can you read this?"

She picked up the medallion and examined it, then shook her head. "It's another language. Latin, I think. See here—

Mater—that means mother, I believe. The rest I can't decipher."

He was disappointed. As he was about to replace the items, she noticed the scrap of vellum with English words in fading letters. The ink was the color of dried blood, and the name *Logan* was written in ornate script. She picked it up, careful to prevent cracking along the folds. It was difficult to make the words out at all. ". . . it is better that he be left in the snow for the wolves . . ."

She felt as if she'd been kicked in the stomach. Perhaps it was just as well he couldn't read. At first she had intended to teach him, so that he could write more than his name. After all, Logan could reckon with numbers easily. But then he would know the terrible words, the damning words, on the scrap of paper. It was easier to coast, to let the days slide past in a safe routine. Bettany sang to Grayson and told him stories, although he was far too young to understand them. It was a way of tying her son to Nils and Hannah, the children who were lost to her now, and perhaps forever. Logan liked to listen. It was another bond between them, a moment each day when their thoughts ran together—on safe, neutral subjects.

As Grayson grew, Bettany shortened his name to "Gray." It suited him, with his smoky brown eyes. He was an alert baby and sturdy in frame and constitution. She imagined she saw her father's strong features in the chubby planes of Gray's sleeping face and was pleased to see how much the shape of his hands resembled her own. There was, she was sure, no resemblance at all to the Cheyenne brave who had fathered him. He would be totally her child.

Bettany imagined him growing to boyhood in the cabin where he'd been born, playing with sticks and shiny stones while she attended to her chores. She would sing him all the songs she knew, as she'd done for Hannah, and someday tell him the stories that Nils had loved. She would pass the long winters teaching him his numbers and how to read. Logan was always there in the background of her fancies, yet she tried not to think of him or cast him in any special role.

It was only in her dreams that he came to her and cupped her face between his hands or drew her down beside him upon some mossy bank. Each time she dreamed of him she would awaken, heart pounding and sick with longing, only to have it all fade away with the dawn.

Logan was aware of her pleasant fantasies concerning Gray, but he knew they couldn't stay at the cabin forever. He could provide for their physical needs even through the cold winter to come. For the present they were both fully content with no other company than their own; but eventually the word would get about of a man and his woman with strange silver hair. To recognize that moment would be to force a choice he didn't want to make.

One morning Logan went off hunting on foot, and Bettany had nothing to do but look after herself and the baby. Seven weeks old now, he was alert and vigorous. The only argument she and Logan had had was over him. Logan thought she should swaddle her son like an Indian child. It gave babies a sense of comfort and security. Bettany would have none of it. It was unclean and the weather was too hot, she'd told him, and the heavy wrappings would give the infant a fever. At the present moment Samuel Gray Thunder had nothing on at all.

She envied him. She'd put on the camisole that Logan had found in the box to support the weight of her breasts, heavy with milk, but it was too uncomfortable in the heat today. Bettany removed it. The baby began to fuss, and she slipped open the bodice of her dress to feed him. He rooted for her breast and suckled contentedly. Happiness flowed over her in warm, contented waves.

She switched him to the other breast and smiled. So this perfect little manikin was the baby she'd carried so long. His eyes had been blue gray to start but were darkening to the color of peat. She had wanted them to stay gray or blue. She had put his Cheyenne heritage from her mind, but it lurked in the background, unacknowledged. Bettany couldn't admit he would grow up to resemble his father. He was *her* baby. Hers alone.

The afternoon grew warm and lazy, and so did she. When the baby finished nursing, she fell into a light, dreamlike state, aware of her surroundings yet not really awake, merely floating along in a contented haze, looking forward to the cool night to come. She drifted deeper until she was far away in Pennsylvania, lying in a summer meadow beneath a serene blue sky, surrounded by wildflowers and the drone of pollen-laden bees. Hannah and Nils were chasing butterflies together and . . .

The door opened suddenly, jerking her mind fully awake, yet her body lagged behind in responding. It was only the sight of Logan frozen in the open doorway that made her aware of how she must look, with her hair damp and tangled and her bodice open wide to the waist. "Oh! I . . . I didn't expect you so soon."

Her voice partially awakened the baby, and he made soft, hungry sounds that made her breasts ache and tingle with their fullness of milk. Bettany was disconcerted. In the Cheyenne camp mothers nursed their children openly, and she had expected to do the same; but this was different. The dark flush on Logan's cheekbones and the response it evoked in her removed it from a natural occurrence between mother and child. It became an incident of profound sexual intimacy between a man and a woman. Her face flamed. She struggled to pull her dress closed over her swollen breasts, but the fabric was caught beneath her elbow. She sat up, leaning forward to button her dress.

Logan hadn't moved. The flush of heat had spread over his face, and there was a fierce pulling in his loins. Her breasts would fill his palms with their weight and warmth, her skin as soft as rose petals against the roughness of his hands. A pearl of milk trembled and spilled. Logan was filled with a fierce, terrible hunger.

The raw desire in his eyes awakened her own slumbering sensuality. Heat spread out from the center of her body, firing her veins with longing. She struggled against it, lips parted and eyes wide and dark with emotion. She was afraid, and Logan knew it. Both sensed but neither could acknowledge that they had been moving toward a critical point, a dangerous line that once crossed would alter their lives forever. Her breathing quickened, and she licked her dry lips. Logan took a half step toward her.

Then the baby awakened fully and started to cry, as if sensing something disturbing. Bettany bent to pick him up, and as she looked back Logan was just vanishing out the door, slamming it closed behind him. The sound was incredibly loud in the afternoon stillness. She felt suddenly forlorn, as if a vital organ had been cut out of her living body or an artery severed.

She put her son at her breast, lay down with her back to the room, and wept long, silent tears. When night fell she took everything out of the wooden crate and made a bed for the baby from Logan's wool shirt. Grayson was already sleeping through the night and would not waken until well into morning. Assured that he was content, she stripped and bathed herself with lilac soap and water from the dented bucket and shampooed her hair.

She had hoarded the soap before to make it last, but now she was prodigal with it. As she dressed again Bettany sniffed the back of her hand and the inner bend of her elbow. Her skin had picked up the light, elusive fragrance. It was odd, she realized, how a little thing like perfumed soap could make a woman feel feminine, almost pampered, after being away from civilization so long. She didn't feel very civilized.

After she had dressed again she was aching with restlessness. She paced the hard-packed floor, listening for the sound of hoofbeats that didn't come. She took a loose ribbon from one of the dancing shoes the unknown Ruth had left behind and tied it in her hair. Then she sat on the edge of the bed for a long time, pulling the other ribbon through her fingers, and waited for Logan's return.

•   •   •

The light had gone out of the sky, and the day's warmth with it. Bettany carried in several of the seasoned logs stacked inside the lean-to and fed them to her small cook fire until the cabin was filled with a mellow golden glow. For some time the evening meal had simmered in its juices, but it was after dusk when she heard Logan's horse coming across the meadow. Her heart sped up to match its rhythm. She glanced over at the baby, sleeping peacefully in his snug little crate, and wondered that the tumultuous drumming of her pulse hadn't wakened him: it sounded like thunder in her own ears.

Tiny bits of moss and dried mud fell from the chinking of the opposite wall, accompanied by various thumps and bumps. She pictured Logan in the lean-to on the other side, the muscles of his arms and back corded as he rubbed down the bay and settled it for the night. She pictured his hand smoothing the horse's coat, his long fingers firm but gentle, and imagined them touching her skin. The shiver that ran through her was half pleasure and half fear. By the time he pushed the cabin door open, her breathing had quickened and her palms were damp with sweat.

She busied herself dishing up tin bowls of stewed meat, more to avoid meeting his eyes than anything. He took a seat on the stool in a dark corner where he was completely in shadow, yet she knew he watched her every movement. Bettany was aware of his gaze lingering on the back of her neck, the curve of her waist, the swell of her breast. What was he thinking? What did he want?

What would he do if she suddenly faced him and asked?

The strain grew in the silence of the thick walls until she wished the baby would awaken and she could immerse herself in tending to him. At the thought her breasts tingled and ached with the let-down of milk, and the front of her bodice was damp with it. It reminded her even more forcibly of the episode earlier and the embarrassment that had followed it.

Bettany put Logan's bowl on the table quickly and turned away with her own dish of food. Her hands trembled with the effects of her inner turmoil. Earlier she'd eagerly awaited his return. Now she wished he'd go away again.

Logan's thoughts ran along the same track. If he hadn't ridden across the river, he wouldn't be trapped now in the tangle of disordered emotions. But neither would the woman. Neither would Bettany. He forced himself to say her name in his mind. Bettany. Bettany of the silver eyes and silver hair, who haunted his dreams and imaginings. His spoon scraped against the metal bowl. *Bettany*.

He put the bowl down and stood abruptly. There was an awkwardness about it, unusual in a man of such physical grace. Bettany took a step toward him, afraid he would leave. "Don't go . . ."

She had said the same thing to him before, under other circumstances. It was in both their minds. He came another step closer, impelled to her. This was the moment they had been traveling toward since the day he'd first set eyes on her. He had known it, somehow, from the start. Logan saw the pulse fluttering at her throat. His eyes shone gold with reflected candlelight, the planes and angles of his face hardened, sharpened by the hunger he could no longer deny.

Bettany was caught up in the same spell. Her fingers twisted together with the effort to hold on to sanity, because once she let go . . .

Logan touched her cheek with his fingertips. His hand dropped to his side as if burned, but the intensity of his gaze held hers. Her words tumbled out without conscious thought: "That night . . . when Small Eagle offered . . . offered to . . ." She couldn't say the words aloud. She looked up at Logan. "Why . . . why did you refuse?"

His answer was torn from the depths of his soul. "What is one mouthful of food to a starving man? Or a single drop of water to a man who is dying of thirst?"

Bettany's lids flickered once over her eyes, and she let out her breath slowly. Her head arched back in the age-old gesture that was both invitation and surrender. With an anguished moan, Logan closed the gap between them and pulled her into the hard circle of his arms. The strength and warmth of his body, the hunger of his mouth on hers, were far greater than she could ever have imagined. No man had ever kissed her before. She was totally unprepared for the powerful sensations, the whirling giddiness, the agitated longings of a passion so long denied. She was starved, ravenous, for him. For a moment she was totally out of control. She tried to break away, frightened by the power of her own emotions.

Logan's embrace lightened, but he didn't let her go. He couldn't. All his world was bounded by the span of his arms. "Bettany . . ."

His voice was low and ragged, like her breathing. He lifted her chin and looked down into her eyes. There was naked desire in his, mixed with great tenderness and more than a hint of sorrow. His look ignited a flame in her blood. The heat spread through her body, carrying with it a curious state of exaltation that was halfway between joy and tears.

She reached up to hold his face between her hands. Inexperience made her shy, yearning made her bold. Her face shone with it. Bettany let her fingers slide over his sculpted cheekbones and along the curve of his mouth. He lowered his head and kissed her again, lightly. Lingeringly.

She rested her head against the solid muscle of his wide chest, hearing the strong drumming of his heart in tune with her own. There was such strength in him—of body, of purpose. She drew upon it, absorbing it into her soul. Nothing else existed.

He kissed her hair, her forehead, her closed eyes. When his mouth came down on hers again, the kiss began gently, almost reverently. Before they were aware, it exploded into a wild, singing force that swept them up in its glory. Locked together, their hands and mouths touched, memorized, explored.

They had to pause, at last, just to catch their breaths. Logan's head was flung back, his face illuminated, his long fingers tangled in her hair. Bettany thought her heart would stop with the pure joy of it. She wanted no barriers between them, even of the flesh. Slowly she undid her bodice, button by button, and slipped the deerskin dress from her rounded white shoulders. She heard his sharp intake of breath. There was no going back now. The hooks of her camisole were next, but her fingers trembled.

He tried to help, but his hands shook too much for the tiny bits of metal. His fingers caught the top of her camisole and ripped it open. Hooks and eyes went flying, and her breasts were exposed, full and heavy to his seeking hands. How he had waited and longed for this! Her skin was silk and velvet beneath his callused fingers, her mouth milk and honey. The months of denial inflamed their urgency. She tilted back her head as his lips sought her throat with a dozen burning kisses. Every one of them left a tingle of fire along her skin until she was aglow with passion.

Logan swooped her up into his arms and carried her to the bed. He stripped his clothes off in quick, clean movements that stirred her blood. She had never known arousal before or the sharp pull of desire that tugged at her loins. She was in an agony of need that only the touch of his mouth, his hands, his body, could quench.

He straddled her, the sculpted contours of his thighs and arms standing out in high relief. She reached up to run her fingertips over them, feeling the steely muscles and sinews beneath his bronzed skin. He was beautiful, overwhelming in his masculinity, calling up every primitive feminine urge within her.

She was pliant as a young willow in his arms, bending to the force of their passion. Her skin was soft and dewy as a peach, and his lips memorized its taste and texture and the way little wisps of hair curled along her forehead and at her temples. His mouth roved lower, seeking the scented valley between her breasts, the arch of her ribs, the soft curves of her abdomen. She knotted her fingers in his hair and pulled him up, needing the reassurance of his embrace.

Logan looked down at her. "I want you. I want you, Bettany."

A shiver of need ran through her. She ached for him. "I want you, too."

She turned away from him, in the only way she knew, and suddenly they were no longer alone in their bed. The knowledge that another man had known her was like acid in his veins, eating at him. He blocked the images that tumbled into his mind and rolled her back, pressing her shoulders down into the bed. His desire for her overcame the corroding jealously and banished the uneasy guilt.

He slid his hand between her thighs, and they parted willingly. She was as ready as he. With a cry that echoed from her lips, he plunged inside her. Bettany gasped in pleasure and surprise. He cupped her smooth buttocks in his palms and rocked against her, watching her face. His slow thrusts brought her arching off the bed, grasping for him in her fervor. Her fingers dug into him, and she was warm and liquid with rapture.

His chest skimmed her breasts, the nipples hard and straining up to meet him. Every touch was like a fiery lash, burning into his skin. He'd meant to take his time, prolonging the moment for them both; but he was only human. He drove into her with mounting fury until he felt her stiffen suddenly. The spasms that shook her engulfed him, propelling him over the edge of ecstasy and into the void. They clung to one another, lost in a wild, exhilarating frenzy of passion.

When it was over he brushed the tears from her eyes with the backs of his fingers and kissed her lids. The communion between them was so deep, there was no need for words. Bettany curled up against him. Safe, loved.

Complete.

Twenty-six

THE SUMMER DAYS PASSED SLOWLY, BUT IN TIME
the aspens changed to yellow, masses of them covering the
lower slopes of the foothills with a shimmer of living gold.
The nights grew chill while Bettany and Logan lived snug
in their cocoon of happiness. It was enough for the moment
to be together. They spoke neither of the past nor of the
future, and any plans spanned no more than a handful of
days; they could not stop time, however, and the ticks of
the invisible clock were measured by the growth of her son.
A hundred times a day Bettany thought of Hannah and
Nils, and hugged Grayson tightly to her breast.

One bright afternoon, after he'd been gone overnight,
Logan came back and gave her a bundle wrapped in faded
cloth and tied up with heavy twine. "I met a trader heading
for Santa Fe."

He looked eager and just a little apprehensive. Bettany
untied the cloth, as excited as a child on Christmas morning. Inside were all sorts of treasures: a pack of shiny needles
and colored thread, a length of yellow-and-white calico, a
tortoiseshell comb, and three slim books with cloth covers.
Her hands reached for the books first.

Although the covers were cheap and the bindings poor,
they were nonetheless precious. The thickest one was a
collection of poetry, with the title in peeling gold leaf, the
second a book of best-loved psalms, and the third was a
child's school primer. Her face was shining as she threw
her arms around him, the primer in her hand.

"Thank you. I could ask for no greater gifts. But how did you guess that I love poetry?"

A sudden flush stained his high cheekbones. "I didn't. I had no idea what they were." He shrugged. "But the trader said a woman would like them."

It was her turn to color. She didn't know quite how to respond. "Would you . . . would you like me to teach you to read?"

Logan opened a book at random, frowning at the strange black symbols. "These marks. They are just lines on paper. What is it that makes your people treasure them so? Why do you read?"

She'd never had to think of it before. "Why, for knowledge or for pleasure. To learn what people think or how they live. To find out their histories."

"Among the Tsistsistas knowledge is handed down from person to person, and pleasure is taken in the telling and listening to stories. Old Buffalo Heart knows the history of his people back to when they lived near the lakes they call the Big Waters. His stories are shared by all who wish to hear at one time, instead of one person reading alone."

Bettany searched for the proper words to explain. Buffalo Heart knew more legends and stories than anyone of his band. "One book can be read by many—even a hundred years later. If only a few people know the tales and if they die or go away, those tales may be lost forever. With books, that knowledge is safe as long as the book endures."

She touched the volume of poems with her fingertips. "Some, like this, are for pure joy. To make us think and feel and know what someone else has experienced. To marvel at how alike—or how different—we are." Flipping open a page at random, she found an old favorite.

> All that we see or seem
> Is but a dream within a dream.

Logan didn't say much, but later when he was out beneath the stars he thought of those words. There was magic in them. Magic in the rhythm and the sound. Magic in the meaning. The lines seemed to speak directly to his soul. He understood them without understanding how—or why—he did so. Perhaps there was something to these books after all.

After that, Bettany read to him a while every day. Several weeks went by before she noticed the primer was missing. She went about her chores, smiling.

The days grew shorter, and the air turned brisk. Autumn touched the valley, and the breath of Winter Man blew down from the hills. Logan rode out one morning under a hard blue sky. A skitter of yellow leaves danced across the ground before him. It was the crisp kind of weather he loved, when something in the wind set the birds wheeling in formation from the cottonwood groves, the same something that called to old longings buried deep within the human soul.

He passed beside a grove of aspens, and ravens burst from the branches like a gleaming black cloud, in a cackle of sound. They were used to his comings and goings. Something else had set them off, but he found no sign anywhere. Perhaps it was only the lure of adventure calling on the breeze.

Usually he hunted south or west of the cabin, but he changed his habits and went north to the river instead. The spring flood had left its mark in the caved-in banks and masses of debris strewn everywhere. Uprooted trees lay snarled together at the bend, forming a low, natural dam and setting up the probability of another disaster in the near future.

The current was slow and only a few inches deep below the logjam. As Logan crossed his mood was somber. The river had taken the lives of Pearl Finder and the others, and it had given him Bettany. He had taken her joyfully and never counted the cost. Until he watched Grayson growing day by day and saw Small Eagle's features and expressions in the baby's face. It was unsettling.

Logan had always regarded infants as rather indistinguishable lumps of humanity until they attained a certain age. Resemblances to family members, he'd been quite sure, were nothing but wishful thinking on the parts of doting relatives. He knew how false his preconception had been. There was not a single day when he didn't look at Bettany's son and find there a reflection of his own guilt and torn loyalties.

The horse splashed through the shallows and up the mossy bank. The hills rose in sandy waves to the horizon, dotted with juniper and twisted piñon. Beyond lay the fir- and spruce-clad slopes he knew so intimately. The sun hadn't reached its pinnacle yet when he picketed his mount and climbed to a stony ridge. He made himself comfortable and waited. He had a wide view of the valley below and the gap in the next line of hills.

By midafternoon his patience was rewarded. Two scouts reached the rim of the valley, then turned to signal to their unseen followers. Logan recognized Split Tail's pony by the crescent-shaped blotch on its right forequarter. Small Eagle's band, moving south to their winter camp. Logan was jerked awake from the contented dream of the past months. He could no longer pretend that his actions had hurt no one. Suddenly he was filled with impressions: loss, anger, numbing sorrow. They seemed to belong to him but gradually focused and diminished as he located their source. Somewhere, just beyond the valley's crest, his brother rode grieving for his first wife and the child he thought he'd lost.

The phenomenon shook Logan deeply. It had never been so powerful before. Although miles separated them, he had heard the "call" of Small Eagle's emotions winging toward his aerie. Had heard it and experienced the pain as if it were his own. Logan cursed the bond that connected them so strangely, so inescapably, to one another. By tomorrow evening Small Eagle would be camped with the rest a few miles from the cabin.

He moved slowly, like a man caught in quicksand, and made his way back down the ridge. The moment of decision had come. Logan rode back to the cabin. Bettany opened the door when she heard his mount's hoofbeats echo in the gathering dusk. He stared at her, his face so strained and pale beneath his tan that she put a hand to her breast to still her racing heart. "What is it? Are you hurt?"

Logan swung down from his horse and came to face her. He took her face between his hands, and his eyes took on their haunted, golden sheen. "I've never known such joy as we've shared here these past few months. I can hardly bear to see it end, even though I always knew it could never last."

Bettany's breath caught in her throat. The pain in her chest was so sharp and sudden that she felt she'd been stabbed. "What . . . what are you saying?"

"The Cheyenne are making for the winter grounds. They'll be camped at the river tomorrow. We'll be up by first light and set out as soon as possible."

The words she'd been dreading had been spoken. She was totally undone. Didn't he know they belonged together? "No! You can't take me back! I won't go. I won't!"

He pulled her into his arms and kissed her mouth with sudden fierceness. "Take you back? I could no more do that than I could cut out my heart." His eyes searched her face. "Don't you know that?" he asked softly.

She reached her fingers up to trace the shape of his mouth. "I was so afraid. . . . Oh, Logan! I love you so. I couldn't bear to be parted from you."

Bettany hoped he would say he loved her, too, but he only looked at her with a deep, terrible sorrow. "We can't undo what's done. There's no turning back for me. For us. . . ."

It was a bittersweet acknowledgment of what she had hoped to hear him say aloud. It was, it would have to be enough.

His hand cupped the fullness of her breast, his lips caressed the curve of her throat, as she melted against him. His mouth sought hers, and the passion of his kiss said more than his words had done. Desire and need mingled with the male instincts to possess and protect. They made love with an urgency that astonished them both and left them shaken in its aftermath. Much later Bettany lay beside him with her head upon his breast, feeling the rise and fall of his chest and his breath tickling against her hair. She thought he'd fallen asleep until his hand stroked along her naked back, his fingertips tracing the gentle curves of spine. He sighed. "I'd better get up and get things together for our journey."

Other, more immediate things, had pushed their traveling plans from her mind. "Where are we going?"

"To look up Juan Abrue, an old friend of mine. He has a small ranch just north of Santa Fe."

The eastern sky was aglow as they set out at dawn. Bettany was sad to leave the cabin behind. Within its rude walls she had found the only true happiness she had ever known. To leave it seemed to be tempting fate. The only comfort was being with Logan night and day on the way to Santa Fe and learning to really know the man she loved so passionately. Her view had narrowed to the grace of his profile, the proud angle of his cheekbones, the firm curve of his lips.

They maintained a brisk pace over the days that followed, as if fleeing from whatever might pull them asunder. Bettany didn't care where they went or how long it took them to get there. Her world began in the circle of his arms and ended there, morning and night. She knew the texture of his skin, the silky feel of the thin scar along his jaw, the scent of his hair. The sound of his footsteps was as familiar as the deep timbre of his voice—but there was so much about him that he kept locked away.

There was a fire in him, and light that shone out at odd times; but there was also darkness, covering an immeasurable pain. She ached to ease it but didn't know how. Time and again she came up against the barriers that let her only so close and no closer. At times a brooding came over him that left him silent and aloof for hours. Bettany suspected he was thinking of Small Eagle.

She tried not to think of him at all. She'd sensed the bond between the two men who called themselves brothers. Even during their rift, when Logan had left the camp for those many months, the connection had still been there. And now she had come between them, irrevocably.

Her feelings about their breach were mixed. She knew the rift caused him pain, and she struggled with her own emotions. Small Eagle had been kind to her. No, he'd been much more than that. He had cherished her in a strange way, as if she had been some kind of unique possession to show to his friends. And he'd let her think that he had brought Hannah to her. Her anger still smoldered.

Bettany felt she owed him nothing. She had made no promises, broken no vows. Although she had submitted to him, she had done so for Hannah and for Nils. There had been no desire on her part, none of the fierce glory that she found in Logan's arms. Grayson was *her* son. Her one real regret was that because of her there was permanent estrangement between Logan and the man he considered his true brother. The memory of Small Eagle was like a ghost, riding up into the hills with them, and when Logan fell silent for long periods she knew which lonely paths his thoughts wandered.

The closer they got to their destination, the more anxious Bettany felt. The landscape changed, becoming drier and less hospitable to her eyes. Sage, juniper, and saltbush sprinkled the ground with stands of prickly pear. She had always thought of mountains as green and wooded, like those she'd known in Pennsylvania; but although the higher slopes of the distant mountain range were furred with evergreens and their highest reaches white with snow, their lower flanks were sparse and bare. But she was with Logan.

Fish were dreaming idly in the stream, and Logan had decided to catch some for their midday dinner. He was used to going all day on little more than water and jerky or a bit of meal, but a nursing mother required more frequent feeding. While Bettany brushed her hair with her quill brush, he hunkered down on the bank and observed the fish awhile. The sheltered pool near the opposite side looked like the best bet. With his uncanny grace of movement he slipped into the icy water, unaware that Bettany was watching him.

The contrast between them made her smile. Logan could lose himself in whatever he was doing, while she was always conscious of the outside world encroaching upon them. Even now, while she admired the symmetry of his body, the play of muscles across his back and shoulders, part of her was always aware of Grayson sleeping near at hand, of what they would eat for their meal. Of Small Eagle among his band, thinking that they had both been washed away by the torrent or buried beneath tons of debris.

Logan had no such difficulties. At the moment all his concentration was upon the fish hovering near the stony bottom in a gentle wave of fins. She envied him his single-mindedness, that intense focus that made him—and all the Cheyenne—live in the present moment. Perhaps it was because their way of life was so precarious, balanced on a thin tightrope between abundance and disaster. Because they never knew from one hour to the next whether or not they would be alive to enjoy it.

"Hah!" At the splash from the river and Logan's triumphant cry, she looked up, startled.

A glittering arc of droplets rained down nearby, accompanied by a soft thud. He'd caught a fat fish between his cupped hands and flung it up on the bank, where it flapped about in a shimmer of silver scales. Bettany smiled and put a few more sticks on the fire she'd built earlier. Scant minutes later he flipped another from the brook, as fine as the first.

"How did you do that?" Bettany asked when he sat down beside her.

Logan grinned, teeth white and strong against his dark skin. "It is a boy's trick. I could have caught them more easily with my net. But it would not have been as satisfying."

"Oh! You did it for fun."

Now he was puzzled. Some of her concepts were alien to him. A thing was done because it was necessary, and if it could be done in an enjoyable manner, that was merely an added benefit. "I did it so we might eat."

Bettany laughed and shook her head. "There are times when we seem to speak a separate language."

He took her hands in his, his features suddenly serious. "You must understand this, Bettany. I'm not what or who you think I am. Because I look like a white man—because I bear a white man's name and blood, you expect me to act like one. To *be* one. But you must never forget that I am of the Tsistsistas."

His jaw tightened. "In my heart, in my soul, I am Cheyenne."

She met him gaze for gaze but was the first to look away. He let her go and began cleaning one of the fish. Bettany took out her knife and started on the second. He was right. She knew it deep down, and it frightened her. The man he really was and the man she wanted him to be were two different persons entirely. He might never be able to reconcile those differences. And he could never go back. Not now.

The previous winter, when a young wife had run off with an Arapaho, her husband had accepted a string of horses in payment and the debt was considered over. To Bettany's puzzlement, there had seemed to be no rancor between the two men once the matter was settled. Red Paint Woman was more practical about the situation and thought the outcome a good one: Bear Speaks had increased his considerable wealth and status by several fine ponies, and Lost His Finger had the woman he'd coveted for his wife.

But Red Paint Woman had told her of another couple who were hunted down and killed by the aggrieved husband. If Small Eagle found out that she was with Logan, which would be his choice—the payment or the knife? He might suffer anger and loss of pride and the bitterness of betrayal, but in the end it would be Logan who would pay the greater price, alienated forever from the man he called brother and the people he considered his own.

Perhaps someday he would hate her for it.

Wrapping the fish in green leaves, she prayed their love would never be put to the test. Hers was deep and boundless; but she was daily more aware of how little she knew of Logan, of how often she misread his thoughts or tried to fit them within the framework of her own education and experience.

She dug a hole in the hot sand and put the wrapped fish in it, then poked them beneath the level of the fire to bake. At least Santa Fe was far enough away from the usual Cheyenne lands that they might never have to face that particular trial.

While she was worrying about the past and future, Logan's mind had turned again down a more immediate channel. "The sun is warm and the boy sleeps."

His mouth touched her temple lightly in a way that sent shivers down her arms. He began to work her dress up over her legs, brushing the back of his hand along the insides of her thighs. Bettany felt her blood heat with the call of his. She helped him strip away her clothing.

When she opened her arms to embrace him, Logan sat back upon his heels instead. Her skin was white as snowdrops, her hair like a net of gold. Bettany was equally enthralled.

He was beautiful with the sun outlining his physique and shining through his hair like a halo. She loved his lean face, the sharp cheekbones beneath the bronzed skin, the firm nose and mouth, and the jagged white scar beneath his jaw that felt satin smooth beneath her fingertips. She smiled up at him, eager for his embrace, her mouth soft and full with desire.

He held back a moment, his eyes filled with the deep emotions he found so difficult to put into ordinary words. He lowered his body onto hers and began kissing her face, her throat, her breasts, until she was wild for him. She traced her hands over the muscles of his back and arms, reveling in their strength. Her need for him was like a wildfire in her blood, matched by her desire to shower him with all the love it was in her power to grant. She gave herself to him willingly, fully, and afterward they lay in each other's arms while Grayson slept and watched the cloud castles form and dissolve in the sky.

It was much later, when Gray awakened and she sat nursing him beneath a tree, that Logan wandered over to the packs and removed an item. Bettany, playing pat-a-cake with her son, to his utter delight, didn't notice until Logan began to speak from just behind her.

> But true love is a durable fire,
> In the mind ever burning,
> Never sick, never old, never dead,
> From itself never turning.

She twisted around in surprise. He was perched on his saddlepack, reading from the volume of poetry he'd given her—reading Ralegh's poem, which she had never read aloud to him at all. Tears of pride stung her eyes. All those hours when she'd thought he was off alone hunting or brooding, he'd been teaching himself to read.

Rising, she went to him, holding the baby against her shoulder. "How did you do it?"

He flushed. "I memorized as much as I could of what you read to me. Once I'd heard it a time or two, it was easy. Then I took the book and the primer. A hundred times I was ready to admit defeat. Then one afternoon, while you were napping, it all changed." He still seemed amazed by his achievement. "The little squiggles became words."

Bettany beamed up at him. "You are a very remarkable man."

"What, to learn a thing that you mastered as a child? That, to me, is more remarkable."

"I grew up with words and letters. You did not." She ran

her hand up to his shoulder in admiration. "New worlds will open for you now."

A shadow fell across them as a dark bird winged low across the sky, hunting for prey. An unfortunate creature in the ravine below had attracted its fatal attention. Suddenly the bird plunged down in a feathered blur, then rose again to the accompaniment of terrified squeaking. Bettany looked away, hoping it was not an omen. She would be very glad once they reached the safety that Santa Fe offered.

Santa Fe

Colonel Armstrong rode into Santa Fe ahead of the pack train. This trip would show a big profit for himself and the other shareholders. While the wagons were unloaded he crossed the plaza and went down the maze of streets to his favorite hangout. The cantina was crowded. Rosalia's place was the best of its kind in town, the girls clean and comely with the fast-fading prettiness of youth.

The room was filled with smoke and laughter. The vigas that roofed the room were sooty from the cigars and *cigaretas* that had burned away to ash beneath it, and the dirt floor was packed as hard as cement. Armstrong ignored a feminine squeal from a dark corner but turned sharply when he heard a chair turn over and fall. A man had Rosalia forced back across the table with her blouse yanked down to reveal her breasts to an interested crowd.

"You think you're too good for me? Me and my friends will see just how goddamned good you are."

The colonel was across the room in a bound. "Unhand her, Eugene!" He pulled the man away roughly. Rosalia slid off the table and arranged her clothing to cover herself. The colonel leaned forward, eyes like cold pebbles. "You will apologize to the lady, Eugene."

"Lady! She's a goddamned whore!"

"You will apologize."

Eugene swallowed. "Sorry, ma'am."

Rosalia looked uncertainly from one to the other. She had never heard of anyone quelling a mad dog with a soft voice and a look. Armstrong smiled grimly and waved her away. "Go on. It'll be all right. He won't bother you again."

The stare he gave Eugene sent a chill down the man's back. He quickly doffed his battered hat and changed the subject. "Well, Colonel. Didn't expect to see you for another day or so. I took care of that little matter up along Old Woman Creek. There's a few less 'Paches running loose out there these days."

"Good work. Did you find out anything about this big gathering that's rumored?"

"It's fact, now. Gonna be a big powwow—Cheyenne, Comanche, Arapaho, 'Pache. A whole passel of Injuns." He tipped back his hat and watched Armstrong closely. "About one short day's ride east of Crooked Neck Creek."

The colonel's reaction was everything Eugene had expected and more. Armstrong's face was purple with rage. "By God, they're banding together now! There'll be no stopping them. Those vermin will overrun us and kill every man, woman, and child. It will make the Pueblo revolt look like a Sunday school picnic!"

Eugene hooked his hands in his belt. "You got another little job for Shorty and me, boss?"

"Not yet. I'll send you word when Ludo and Kearns get in. We'll go from there." Armstrong didn't invite his companion to sit down.

Eugene's mouth twisted in a sly, mocking smile. The colonel thought he was better than the men he hired to do his dirty work for him, but his hired gun disagreed. He knew there was as much blood on Armstrong's hands as there was upon his own—how it got there was the only difference. But he was too canny to let his boss know how he felt. He'd seen the colonel in action before. Armstrong could strike like a snake, swift and deadly.

As he was about to walk away he remembered something and turned back. "There's talk that an hombre I've been looking for is with one of the Cheyenne bands. I want to take care of him myself." Eugene's hands clenched into hard fists. "The son of a bitch killed my brother."

"If you can give me a good description, I'll pass it on to the others."

"I can do that all right. He's tall. Taller even than most Cheyenne. Got a thin scar along his jaw and the queerest eyes you've ever seen. Yellow as a wolf's."

Twenty-seven

SMALL EAGLE AND SMOKE ALONG THE GROUND
were cautious as they neared the arroyo. They were deep
in the heart of Comanche-Kiowa territory. Except on raids,
they had never ventured so deep into the lands of their
former enemies. This particular part of the countryside was
unknown to either one of them, although Antęlope Chaser's descriptions had proved accurate until now. Where they
had expected to find a narrow pass carved by a river long
dead and forgotten, there was now an enormous slide of
fallen rubble stretching up to the sky.

Only that morning as they prepared to mount, their
horses had shivered and balked. Almost immediately Small
Eagle and Smoke Along the Ground had felt the ground
shrug and tremble beneath their feet. As they skirted the
massive landslide the same thought was in both their minds:
Had they started out a day earlier, they would be lost beneath that crushing weight of earth.

"We will have to scout in either direction for a crossing,"
Smoke Along the Ground said. "Otherwise a man must
pick his way up and down the high ridges and around the
places were the land folds in upon itself."

Small Eagle scanned the landscape. "I will go up beyond
the river."

As he splashed across to the far side, he wished for the
tenth time that they had arranged this meeting in their
own territory. It was Antelope Chaser, speaking on behalf
of his uncle and the other chiefs, who'd insisted otherwise.

"Since the coming of the horse soldiers," he had warned, "many things are changing. You must see this danger and report it to your people, that they may understand our urgency."

It was midday before Small Eagle found an indication of a way around the impassable walls of stone. The way was steep, and he couldn't tell what might await beyond the sharp slope. He picketed his horse and made his way up and over. Difficult on horseback, but not impossible. It was as he clambered down the other side of the rocky shelf that he spotted the hoofprints. He squatted down to discover what the sign could tell him: recent. They had come this way before the sun was overhead. Two horses, two riders—one much lighter than the other. A leisurely pace, with no heavy loads. They seemed to know the country.

He brought his pony up the incline and followed the sign, hoping it would lead him to a good crossing place. He found the remnants of their camp an hour later. Fresh horse droppings, the place where fire had been smothered and covered, readily identified by the warmth of the sandy soil. Small Eagle dug up a bit of fish discard. The meat was still moist upon the bones. They had made a long stop here. The grass was bent enough to show the imprint of their bodies, where they had lain in an embrace for quite a while.

The corners of his wide mouth lifted. It was a fine day for a man and woman to lie beneath the sky together. If he were back at Deer Creek Meadow now, he would take Red Paint Woman away from the lodge where they could could do the same. Her belly was just beginning to swell with the early stages of pregnancy. The child would be born while the snows were still upon the ground, well before the flood season. He was glad of that.

The sadness came over him, as it did so often. To lose a wife and child was a terrible thing, but one that had happened to many before him and would happen to many long after he was gone. It might be that he had broken some unknown rule of the white man's god, and that Warrior Woman had been taken from him because of it. Small

Eagle did not understand this *ve-ho-e* god, who ordered his followers to turn the other cheek to one's enemies. What foolhardiness! Fortunately for them, the white men did not obey their god in this matter and fought their enemies with rifles instead.

As he came over a rise of land, Small Eagle halted his pony. Two mounted figures descended the trail at the entrance to a wide valley scattered with juniper and piñon and fleshy-leaved prickly pear. For a moment they were lost behind a stand of rock, and the landscape seemed forlorn and untenanted. The sun reflected from the heated rocks until the scene shimmered with it, and Small Eagle had to blink his eyes.

Ghosts! He blinked again, but nothing changed. And, he realized, ghosts did not walk—or ride—by day; nor did they leave tracks upon the ground.

Logan gestured to the rocky shelves rising up just ahead. "We'll stop here for the night. It's as good a place as any."

While he took care of the horses Bettany hung Grayson's cradleboard from the low branch of a spruce and looked for a comfortable place to lay their robes. There was an easy peace to their traveling days, and she would almost be sorry to see them end. Except for an occasional settlement of a few scattered adobe huts with half a dozen inhabitants, they hadn't seen another soul since leaving the cabin. She wondered idly if Logan had been purposefully avoiding known trails. Even across the vast distances of the western lands, news and gossip traveled fast. The whereabouts of a dark man and his silver-haired woman might eventually reach Small Eagle.

She was thinking of the Cheyenne and what his reaction might be when he suddenly appeared on the ledge above her. His gaze was fixed on Logan coming up from the river, and there was hatred in his eyes. Bettany pointed. "Logan! Up there!"

His head jerked up. Logan had only a split second to identify his attacker. The knife that would have buried itself

in Small Eagle's chest or belly went intentionally wide.
They grappled and fell, rolling down the bank toward the
river. The two were equally matched in size and strength,
but Small Eagle's attack was fueled by his fury. Logan, trying
only to constrain him, took the worst of it.

His forehead was gashed above the eye, and the flow of
blood blinded him. He had to end it now, before it was
too late. Holding the wide edge of his knife against Small
Eagle's throat, he pressed down, cutting off his air. Small
Eagle's face grew red as he fought to pry it away. Another
push, another inch, and it would be over. Instead Logan
released the pressure. The years of love and brotherhood
went too deep. This could be settled in some less deadly
way.

His challenger seized the opportunity. Small Eagle threw
Logan off. His knife flashed out and was deflected, but not
before it had slashed through Logan's buckskin shirt to graze
the skin beneath.

Bettany couldn't bear to watch the combat, knowing that
she was the cause and fearing what the outcome would be.
Logan twisted free and jumped to his feet, blood pouring
down his face from the cut. Small Eagle's breathing was
labored, but his face was triumphant as he closed in for the
kill, his lips drawn back from his teeth in a deadly grimace.
Logan's face mirrored it.

Bettany knew she had to stop them somehow. "No! What
are you doing?" she cried in Cheyenne, throwing herself
between them. "You, who have been as brothers!"

Logan came to his senses first. Bettany was not in danger.
If Small Eagle had meant to kill her, he would have done
it already. There was only one thing to do to put a stop to
this.

"I will not fight my brother." He stepped back, threw
his knife into the ground beyond his reach, and waited for
Small Eagle's response.

Bettany was afraid to blink. The Cheyenne crouched for
the spring, his knife blade poised. For the span of a single

heartbeat Logan's life hung in the balance. Then Small Eagle straightened and sheathed his knife.

"From this day forward I have no brother," he announced. "My face is forevermore turned against you. Your name will not be spoken within my lodge. I will not rejoice at your happiness. I will not mourn at your death. From this moment you are my enemy and I am yours. When we meet again it will be as foes, and only one of us will walk away."

He pivoted on his heel and started for his pony, then he saw the cradleboard. While Logan and Bettany watched from opposite sides of the clearing, Small Eagle strode over to where Grayson hung from the branches in his cradleboard. A fine boy, with lighter eyes, but the shape so like his own that he would have recognized him anywhere. Grayson looked back at him, interested and unafraid.

A great sorrow came over Small Eagle such as he had never known before, a smothering blanket of it that pressed so heavily upon him he couldn't move. Slowly Small Eagle fought it and won. Removing his choker of bone and bead, he slipped it over Grayson's neck. It hung down to the baby's waist, but his little fingers grasped the choker and clung to it.

Small Eagle touched the boy's face. "What is the name he is called?"

Bettany's throat was so constricted, she could hardly answer. "Gray Thunder. *Woh'k pe nu num'a,*" she said at last.

He was startled and pleased that his son had been given a Cheyenne name. A strong name. A warrior's name. "*Woh'k pe nu num'a,*" he repeated. "*Ipewa.* It is good."

His gratification and surprise were touching. Bettany's heart broke for him, for Logan, for herself. For Grayson, who would grow up apart from his Cheyenne heritage, caught forever between two worlds, as Logan was.

Leaning forward, Small Eagle whispered something into Grayson's ear. The baby waved his hands, entangling them in his father's hair and cooing happy sounds. Small Eagle released the boy's grasp, then turned and leaped upon his pony, his face carved from stone. He rode proudly past Logan—his cradlemate, companion, rival, and brother—without a single glance of acknowledgment.

As he left them, Logan felt a burning, tearing sensation in his chest, as if a part of his heart had been ripped out. The loneliness that followed proved more forcefully than Small Eagle's words that their bond was irreparably severed, the rupture complete.

Bettany wanted to run to Logan, to put her arms around him and offer silent comfort; but she sensed it would be the wrong thing to do. He needed to be alone now to deal with his grief. The grief for which she had been the unwitting cause. If not for her, Logan would have settled down among the people who had fostered him and, in time, taken a Cheyenne woman to wife. His days and his fate would have been ordered; instead it was chaos and exile.

For Logan the road to Santa Fe would be a long and lonely one. So would every other road he traveled, for the rest of his days.

Twenty-eight

"THERE IT IS. SANTA FE." LOGAN WAITED FOR BET-
tany to rein in beside him.

Her first sight of the town in the flat valley below was a
surprise. She had heard that, just as in ancient times all
roads led to Rome or Babylon, west of the Missouri all roads
led to Santa Fe. This great meeting place of the Southwest
was the destination of El Camino Real, leading up from
the sunny heart of Mexico, as well as the Santa Fe, Cimar-
ron, Old Spanish, and many-branched Comanchero trails.

Because it was the major trade center in the vast area,
with hundreds of thousands of dollars in goods sold and
exchanged each year, she had envisioned a city like those
she'd known back east. Santa Fe was nothing but a mud
village built in the valley alongside the Río del Norte. It
was a lesson in how far she had come from her own civilization. There was not a bit of clapboard or red brick or a
single gable to be seen anywhere. Instead of high-peaked
roofs and dormers, there were flat one-and two-story adobe
structures, roofed with grassy sod.

The few windows she saw were blind, with shutters closed
to the streets or sheets of translucent mica in place of glass
in the square panes. But there were men and women and
children and goods and food aplenty. After well over a year
in the wilderness, Bettany thought she had never seen such
a beautiful sight.

Logan grinned at her beaming face. He'd intended to
pick up a few supplies and press on but changed his mind.

"Would you like to stay the night in town? There's a *fonda*—a hotel—down on the corner of the Plaza. We could enjoy a few comforts there." His grin widened. "It would be a shame to let one of their comfortable beds go to waste."

"Real beds? With real mattresses?" It sounded too good to be true, and she feared he was teasing her.

"Real beds—and real bathing tubs. We'll have one sent up with buckets of hot water, first thing."

As they descended toward the town, Bettany's delight gave him pleasure. It had been well over a year since she'd known any of the civilized comforts she had once taken for granted. The streets were rutted, dust-clogged and filled with mules, horses, oxen-drawn *carretas*, dogs, and people. A party of soldiers rode north in a double column, light flashing from their saber hilts. The Plaza, which was Santa Fe's commercial heart, was lined with vendors displaying their wares, from strings of peppers and bins of vegetables to spicy frijoles, freshly prepared.

Logan pointed out the Palace of the Governor, a long, low building on the north side of the Plaza that didn't—in her eyes—quite live up to its name, at least from the exterior; but after living so long in a hide tipi, it came close.

Bettany was fascinated by the people around the Plaza: old men with donkeys, small boys with hats wider than they were tall, and young women in Spanish-style flounced skirts and wide-necked blouses, their faces painted with a caked, white substance. "To keep their complexions safe from the sun," Logan explained. "They'll wash it off at sundown."

Two of them, smoking the little black cigaretos, whispered and pointed her way, then laughed behind their hands. Bettany was conscious of her browned face and arms but decided she'd rather be as she was than make such a spectacle of herself. They rode up to the inn. Bettany was still gawking.

"I can't believe we're finally here. Fireplaces and windows, carpets and real chairs and tables, bowls and plates and forks, bathtubs and real soap and clean clothes and clean-washed sheets."

He grinned at her delight. "I can't be sure about the sheets, but everything else is available. For a price."

It had been many months since she'd thought about having to pay for things. Among the Cheyenne everything was made or bartered. It occurred to her that Logan might not have the money to pay for a room. When they dismounted she took the bag of gold nuggets tied into her clothing and placed it in his hand. His fingers closed over it. "What's this?"

"Look inside," she said mischievously.

He did. "Where in hell did you get this?"

"I found the nuggets along a little wash northwest of the summer camp. The place they call Where the Boy Was Found. There's another bag at the bottom of Grayson's cradleboard."

"Leave them there for now." Logan quickly slipped the bag inside his shirt and scanned the Plaza. No one was watching. "It's a good thing no one saw what you had. Men's throats are slit for less than this."

Bettany was chastened by her carelessness. In growing to know and avoid the dangers of the plains, she had forgotten that civilization had its own: less fierce, perhaps, yet more numerous, because instead of nature's occasional tantrums, it was the more indirect treachery of man preying upon man.

They entered beneath the *portal*, going through a door in the thick adobe walls. Bettany had the sensation of passing from warm golden sunlight into a cool netherworld. She found herself strangely uncomfortable within the four massive walls, imprisoned in a dark and airless cage. Panic fluttered briefly in her chest. She had to remind herself, forcibly, that such enclosed rooms were once her daily habitat.

Logan spoke in Spanish to the woman in charge. "We want a room for the night. One with a real bed."

Bettany was sure she looked totally disreputable and

feared they'd be refused a room; but the woman nodded as
if men accompanied by blond women in Cheyenne dress
with a child in a cradleboard were guests every day. Perhaps,
Bettany thought, they were. This was Santa Fe, the northern end of El Camino Real, the Royal Road, terminus of
the Santa Fe Trail. Mountain men and traders, aristocratic
señors and señoritas, Indians and missionaries, soldiers and
adventurers, all passed this way. The old *fonda* had probably
seen many more unlikely visitors than herself. Someone
entered the inn, and sounds from outside accompanied—
"Los carros! Los carros!"

As she examined her surroundings more thoroughly, Logan paid for their lodging. The woman asked him a question
about their arrangements, and he shrugged. He bent his
head to Bettany as if conferring over some point, but there
was a sudden air of tension that communicated to Bettany.
Logan's eyes held hers, dark as Spanish gold, as he pressed
a few coins into her hand.

"Go to the entrance. Walk normally. When you're almost outside shout out something. Anything! Then run as
fast as you can and lose yourself in the crowd. Disguise
yourself and get across the river to the Church of San Miguel
in the Barrio de Analco. I'll find you there."

She didn't wait to ask why. Months of living among the
Cheyenne had attuned her senses. Out of the corner of her
vision she spied a man observing them from the shadows.
There was danger here, and arguing would imperil them
all. She put her hand on his arm, a quick light touch, and
then strolled over to the entrance.

Glancing outside, she pretended that something had attracted her attention and paused on the threshold. Then
she filled her lungs with air and screamed. Outside in the
Plaza few heard over the noise of the incoming trade car-
avans. Inside the quiet *fonda* it caused astonishment. Every
gaze was fixed on the doorway, and three or four onlookers
ran out to see what had caused Bettany's cries.

The man who'd been watching Logan was distracted.
When he looked back his quarry was gone. Eugene stared

at the place where Logan had stood mere seconds before and cursed viciously.

Bettany wove her way rapidly in and out of the throng. Two loud sounds came clearly over the normal uproar accompanying the entrance of a wagon train, but whether they were shots or the crack of a carrier's whip was impossible to tell. She was too terrified for Logan's safety to wonder what was wrong and why.

Plunging between two *carretas*, she ignored the shouts and oaths of the drivers, running, not for her life, but for Logan's.

It was doubtful that her own safety was in jeopardy, unless someone had seen her leave and followed her. Bettany pushed past two stout women and stepped into the shadow of a half-open doorway. It was a shop with goods for sale or barter. Resourcefulness was second nature by now. She was able to parlay some of her silver into a full red skirt, white blouse, striped rebozo, and a big basket with handles.

Arranging the shawl to cover her hair and the cradle-board, she placed Grayson in the basket and carried him along on her arm. He smiled, amused by this new method of conveyance and the novelty of seeing his mother's face while they traveled. The street was still as crowded as before, and Bettany mingled with the passersby.

Ducking in the angle of two walls, she pulled the voluminous skirt over her buckskin dress and slipped the blouse over her head. The blouse looked a little lumpy, but the shawl hid it. Along the way she'd seen two or three women wearing the wide hats favored by the men or carrying them on their back. One of the straw sombreros might come in handy to disguise Logan if need be. She added that to her purchases and wound her way to the bridge.

The towers of a church were visible, and she headed toward them, hoping it was indeed San Miguel. This section of town was poorer, the population primarily Indian. She pulled the rebozo down over her face more to hide her fair hair. With her disguise and skin tanned by the sun, she

blended with the inhabitants without notice. Her stomach
was growling with hunger, and she used gestures and her
remaining coins to buy a mixture of beans and spices
wrapped in thin, flat bread.

The vendor, an Indian woman, didn't seem to notice
anything amiss. Bettany was pleased with her disguise. To
the casual observer she was now a woman of Santa Fe,
heading home to her family. Now the hard part came, and
she settled down along the wall where a few vendors and
idlers squatted and waited for Logan.

It was a long wait.

The sun set in a lake of crimson and purple, the bells
tolled the closing of the day, and the wooden mission gates,
set in thick adobe walls, were closed against the night. One
by one the others left, except for an old man who'd fallen
asleep beneath his sombrero. Eventually his son came looking for him and escorted him home, scolding gently. Bettany was alone with Grayson in the rapidly cooling night
air. Holding him against her breast, she wrapped the rebozo
more tightly around them both and prayed.

The search of the livery stable had been fruitless. Eugene
kicked a bale of hay with his boot, sending out a cloud of
dust. "Goddamn it, he must be hiding somewhere. I saw
him go in here with my own two eyes."

The smaller of Eugene's two companions scratched his
head with a grimy nail. "Maybe you got the wrong place.
Those two eyes of yours ain't getting any younger."

"Shut your mouth, Shorty. I know I winged him, and I
know he ducked inside this place. Check the stalls from
that end again."

Eugene and the other men inspected the stables with
guns drawn, jumping when they got too close to one another. "Watch where you point that revolver, you idiot."

After another twenty minutes they gave up. Eugene was
filled with deadly persistence. "Shorty, go over to the *fonda*
and see if he's come back. Find out which horse and gear

is his while you're at it—and if it's gone, God help us when the Colonel finds out."

Eugene holstered his Colt. As they headed out toward the street a single drop of blood fell from the ceiling to splatter on the packed dirt floor below. Logan lay on the wide reinforcing beam that ran twelve inches below the vigas supporting the roof. From beneath, the space between them seemed only an inch or two, but Logan knew this place like the proverbial back of his hand.

After evading Eugene he'd made the mistake of trying to get back to the inn to retrieve his things. The shot had caught him unexpectedly, and only his knowledge of the town had saved him. The streets were narrow, the houses clustered here and there, and Eugene had spotted him again as he'd circled back toward Juan's house. There was only time enough to get to the stables and hide. He had managed to get up to the beam and squash between the crudely dressed tree trunk and the smaller vigas. It had been damned difficult to do, and he scarcely had room to breathe. The only fortunate thing was that the pressure upon his wounded shoulder had kept it from bleeding freely and giving him away, but he feared he done some damage to it wriggling into place. Getting down was going to be a lot harder.

After waiting to ensure they had really gone, Logan managed to extricate himself. On the way up he'd launched himself from the wall of the nearest stall, but he couldn't reach it for the return journey. He landed with stunning force, rolling away to absorb the impact and protect his injury. The effort left him dazed and clammy. Dragging himself up, he remembered to scuff over the bloody trail on the dirt. An old jacket hung from a peg, and he put it on gingerly. It was a struggle that left him dripping wet with reaction.

He managed to get down the street without undue notice and slipped inside an ancient cantina. Ignoring the bartender, he went directly to the wooden stairs leading to the second story. Blood was running down his arm and soaking through his sleeve. He hoped he hadn't left a trail behind him; a quick glance showed nothing but dust on the scuffed boards.

The hallway was fairly dark and quiet with all the doors closed, but he picked up occasional sounds of low laughter and the scraping of a chair on the wooden floor at the end of the hall. The cool dimness was refreshing after the heat of the day. He felt curiously feverish, and his vision was blurred. Logan's steps faltered as he neared the last door.

His wound hadn't seemed that serious at first, and the period of numbness had prevented him from feeling the initial pain. Now his arm ached dreadfully one moment and burned like a white-hot brand the next. The slightest motion made it feel as if jagged blades were ripping along its length and down to the bone. Logan braced it with his other hand but had to release it to knock. He twisted a fraction too far. Pain assaulted him in sickening waves. Sweat covered his face, and his palms were slick. He had to get out to the hacienda while he was still able to do it under his own power.

Leaning against the door frame, he blotted his brow with his kerchief and waited for the nausea to pass. Only a while longer to keep up the pretense. His meeting was with Rosalia, the dark-eyed owner in charge of the unadvertised activities that took place in the upper rooms. Rosalia was as famous for her discretion as her amorous talents. She would bring Juan to meet him without asking questions he didn't want to answer.

He scratched at the thick door, and it opened instantly. Logan pitched forward into the room. He saw the floor come up to meet him but never felt the impact. He was rushing through a dark void toward the cold light of a small and distant star.

The evening star appeared, a stubborn glow against the fading sky, growing brighter moment by moment. At first Bettany was glad to see her old friend; then she realized that she had watched it for years, waiting for a man who had never returned.

She shivered with the sudden invasion of cold that spread through her body and finally coalesced in her chest. The tears that streaked her face were like shards of ice. The sky darkened to soft purple velvet, embroidered with enormous diamond clusters. Bettany had never seen stars so huge and bright, so seemingly close she could touch them if she dared. The immensity of the heavens dwarfed her until she felt small and insignificant. She had prayed for hours, for all the good it had done.

The temperature had dropped, and she wished she had her warm buffalo robe but was thankful for her doeskin garments beneath the skirt and blouse. If it got much colder, she would have to find shelter. Although he was hardy, Grayson was too young to withstand the cold unprotected much longer. Her coins were gone, but she still had the two pouches of gold nuggets gleaned from the dry arroyo. If worse came to worst, she would barter for a night somewhere and be back at first light.

She hunched closer to the wall, which radiated back the heat soaked up throughout the day, marveling that Gray could sleep so peacefully while she was in so much turmoil. The cold was seeping into her limbs, making her sluggish. Very shortly she would have to come to a decision. Dry rustling near a building down the street took her mind from her immediate problems. Her hand went to the hilt of her knife. The whisper of movement repeated but didn't seem ominous. Dogs or rats nosing through the refuse.

Or, she realized belatedly, Logan trying to attract her attention. She rose cautiously and edged through the shadows and around the end of the low building. It came again, a sort of dry whistling, the way she and Maud had used to call to one another from across the stairway at the orphanage after Miss Olmstead was asleep. Those signals had led to nothing more ominous than made-up ghost stories or girlish fantasies about what their lives would be like once they were grown. She hoped these odd whistles were just as innocuous.

Rounding a corner, Bettany passed beneath a gnarled tree and between two small houses. She was halfway down their length when a hand shot out of a dark doorway, grabbed her arm, and yanked her inside.

"I am a friend. Señor Logan sent me."

Bettany stopped struggling. The hand was taken from her mouth and her arm released. "Come with me. I will lead you to him."

She had no choice but to follow. They went along the deeper shadows close by the walls, then two left turns and past a longer row of buildings and across the bridge, leaving the barrio behind. Her serape-covered guide was a woman, but other than that Bettany had no clues. They skirted the Plaza and hurried down a side street. At last a door gaped inward, a black rectangle set in the adobe walls, and her guide pushed Bettany through it. Music and laughter filtered through a closed door.

"This way," the woman said, and went up the steps. It was dark as a cave, but at the end of the hall the light from the single candle beckoned. The room held a tall chest, a wooden chair, and a mattress covered with a colorful blanket. Logan was stretched out upon it, his chest and shoulder wrapped in bloody bandages, his skin tinged with gray.

The woman closed the door behind them quickly. "You must keep him quiet, señora, and confined to the room when he awakens. His life depends upon it. The man who shot him frequents the cantina with his friends—and they have powerful allies here in Santa Fe."

Bettany ran to Logan's side and took his hand in hers. His skin was clammy, and he didn't awaken when she called his name, but his fingers curled around hers and didn't let go. Bettany was terrified for him. "What happened? Who shot him?"

There was no answer. She heard the sound of the door

closing, and when she looked over her shoulder the room empty.

Bettany kept a lonely bedside vigil, remembering with fear the long hours she had stayed with Axel the night before he'd died. The small room with its long shutters became her whole reality as she tended Logan and saw to the needs of her son. With only the change in light and shadow to mark the passing time and only her fears for company, the hours seemed like purgatory.

Logan roused on the second day as Bettany was dressing his wound. His voice was a hoarse croak. "Rosalia?"

Bettany's brief pang of jealousy vanished when he opened his eyes and saw her instead. "Bettany . . . Thank God!" That was all.

His hand curled around hers once more, and he fell into a deep, refreshing sleep. She sat beside him until her arms was numb and Grayson began to fuss. When Logan awakened again his fever was gone, but he grew increasingly restless. The enclosed space was a trial for Bettany after the openness she'd grown used to. For Logan it was hell. The walls closed in and the ceiling grew lower hour by hour. He was ready to jump out of his skin.

Bettany smoothed the hair from his brow. "Are you in pain again?"

"No." He sat up, clenching his jaw against the onslaught of resulting agony. When it passed he felt limp and weak. Bettany hadn't badgered him with questions, but he knew he owed her some explanations. "I spent some time in jail. I can't stand to be confined."

She looked at him thoughtfully. "Does that have anything to do with your getting shot?"

"In a way, it has everything to do with it. To begin with I was just in the wrong place at the wrong time. I was in Missouri and fell in with some men headed for Dirrim. What I didn't know was that my companions had robbed a party of traders of their hard-earned profits. Twenty thousand dollars in gold and silver. They were caught when I was with them. I told them I could prove I was in St. Louis at the time, and they sent for confirmation."

His voice was calm, but she sensed the agitation beneath as the whole story came out. "My cellmate was one of the gang, a young cowboy who'd been lured into it. He was dying of the lung disease, and he meant to give the money to his wife so she could go back east with their daughter when he died."

Bettany folded the bandages and bound them to his shoulder, but most of her attention was focused on Logan's words.

"He was riddled with disease and knew he'd never make it out of that cell—so he told me where they'd buried the gold. He asked me to look up his family when I got out. To tell Cassie what had happened to him and to give her his share."

Logan's eyes darkened in remembrance. "There was to be no getting out for any of us. One of the traders had been shot during the robbery. He died of his wounds, and a lynch mob was assembling in the streets. They were going to hang us without waiting for the trial. Halsey's brother broke us out in the nick of time. We escaped together and split up."

Bettany knotted her fingers together. "And the man at the *fonda* was one of them?"

"Eugene, Halsey's brother. He helped plan the robbery but wasn't along when Halsey hid the gold. I knew the country better than any of them—and I got to the gold first."

"What did you do with it?"

"I was going to return it at first. But then I realized that if I went to the authorities, they would have been sure I was part of the gang. I didn't want my neck stretched. So . . ." His eyes gleamed like gold dust. "I took my cellmate's share to his family. Later I brought the rest to Santa Fe and gave it to the mission."

He'd felt good about that, laughing as he rode away. Cassie could go back east if she wanted with her share, and the rest she'd felt would buy forgiveness for her husband

for having stolen it and for herself, for having kept enough
to get her home again. But the farther he'd gone into the
Sangre de Cristo Mountains, the more uneasy he'd felt.

When he'd reached the cabin Cassie and Anna were
dead.

Logan's eyes were shadowed and his mouth was grim.
Bettany thought it was exhaustion. "I shouldn't have let
you talk so much. You'd better rest."

Logan closed his eyes and pretended to sleep; but he
knew he couldn't really rest until he'd settled his business
with Eugene, once and for all.

A week later, with Bettany's tender nursing and the help
of Rosalia, Logan was healing well and itching to be let
out. Bettany wondered at his past relationship with the
Mexican woman. The interest appeared to be all on Rosalia's side, but Bettany was wise enough to ask no questions.
There were some things it was better not to know. Like
what went on in the other rooms above the cantina by day
and by night.

She'd guessed soon after arrival that the place was also
a brothel. Once, back in Pennsylvania, she'd overheard the
one in Clarksville referred to as a "house of joy." There
seemed to be little of that here; except for occasional laughter the sounds audible in the dim corridor were groans,
grunts, drunken curses, and piteous weeping. Even down
below, the music and gaiety gave way to quarrels and fights.
She would be glad when they were finally able to leave the
place. At least she had seen the face of Logan's enemy now
and could avoid him. Rosalia had pointed Eugene out to
her on two occasions. His companion had seemed familiar,
but his face had been in profile to her and she wasn't sure.

She ducked down the back staircase in search of Rosalia.
There was a small private room across from the kitchen
where the woman sometimes entertained special guests. It
was empty, the shutters still drawn against the heat of the
day. Bettany took a seat on the wooden settle and waited.

Logan was getting too impatient. She needed to talk with Rosalia about their plans.

There was a soft knock, and the door opened inward. A man ducked beneath the low lintel, but not quite far enough. He banged his head against it.

"Jesus Christ, Rosalia! Let a little light into the place. It's dark as a tomb in here."

He looked around, rubbing his head, and realized the woman on the settle was not the one he'd sought. "Excuse me, señorita!" he said in fluent Spanish. "I was looking for Rosalia."

Bettany's eyes had adjusted to the faint light, and she had a distinct advantage over him. What she saw took her breath away, literally. She couldn't even speak as she gazed upon the face that she knew so well—that beloved face that she still saw in her dreams. His voice, his features, were unchanged, and any lines that time had engraved there were smoothed away by the dimness.

Bettany found her voice. "Papa? . . . Oh, Papa! Don't you know me?"

Sam Howard had frozen on the threshold in shock, thinking he was seeing the ghost of his long-dead wife. He stepped forward and drew her into the light, unable to believe his eyes. "Button? . . ."

Bettany burst into tears and flung herself into her father's arms.

Twenty-nine

THE REUNION WAS EVERYTHING THAT BETTANY had ever dreamed of, and for Sam it was a miracle. "By God, you're the image of your mother," he said for the tenth time in as many minutes.

He'd been given a second chance after all. "Last spring," he explained, "I went back to Pennsylvania. After knocking about from pillar to post, I'd finally made my fortune and settled down. I was going to make it all up to you."

He squeezed her hand so hard that Bettany winced, but she didn't withdraw it. Sam told her about his arrival at the orphanage. "I wanted to come riding up at dusk, the way I'd promised, and surprise you. The surprise was mine, when Miss Olmstead said you'd gone west and that you were married. I followed the trail and found your name carved at Scott's Bluff, and I was the happiest man in the world. Then I arrived at Fort Laramie and learned about the McGrew massacre."

The light died in his eyes, remembering. "It was the darkest day in my life since your mother died."

Bettany leaned her head against his shoulder. "It's all over, Papa. We've found each other. And if I hadn't set out . . ." I wouldn't have met Logan, and I wouldn't have Grayson, she thought. But it was too early to tell her father everything at once.

She sketched Sam a highly abridged story of her life since leaving the Susquehanna orphanage. As the tale unfolded Sam found it hard to forgive himself. His darling Bettany,

351

married to a clodhopper with two children, forced to accompany him on the rigorous overland journey and to witness the grisly McGrew massacre. He had left behind an innocent child who adored him in order to follow his whim and fortune. Now he would have to answer for it to the adult woman she had become.

He tried to explain, haltingly, that somehow he'd never thought of time passing for her as it had for him—in his mind she had been preserved in crystal, like an enchanted princess, dreaming away the years until he chose to awaken her.

"My life—and my company, to be honest—were rough. It was no life for a child, and there was no woman to look after you." At least not the proper kind of woman. "And your mother had always made me promise that you'd be educated, like she was. As a traveling man I knew I couldn't see to that until I was settled down somewhere, permanently."

He'd found one excuse after another over the years, excusing his failures toward her, but it was impossible to do with Bettany sitting right beside him. They sounded as hollow in his own ears as they must to her.

"My dear, I've missed a great portion of your life and the joys that went with it. They were hard years, often without a roof over my head. My little girl has become a woman, and I wasn't around to watch the transformation. I don't know if I can ever forgive myself for that, but I hope, in time, that you might grow to do so."

Bettany had no stones to cast. Life with Small Eagle's people had made a philosopher of her. The past was gone, the future uncertain. The present might be all they had, and only a fool would waste such precious time on recriminations.

"It's behind us now, Papa. And I think I understand. If ever I returned to Pennsylvania, I suppose I would expect to find the orphanage just as I left it, with Hildy and Maud overseeing the younger girls and Miss Olmstead reading from her Bible at bedtime."

"Good." He patted her hand. "Then we'll pick up where we left off. Why, as Sam Howard's daughter, you'll have the best of everything that money can buy. I hope some handsome young swain doesn't sweep you off your feet and carry you away."

He began making plans of all sorts until she gently interrupted him. Bettany looked down at her hands. "Don't go making too many plans for me, Papa. I haven't told you quite everything." She lifted her head with the same proud gesture he remembered her mother using. "I have my own family now."

She told him about her stay among the Cheyenne. About Small Eagle and Grayson. And Logan. A long silence followed. Sam's thoughts churned in chaos. Bettany's claim that she had been kindly treated as Small Eagle's wife did nothing to assuage his guilt. He could hardly bear to think of it at all, and to accept it would take a major adjustment on his part. In his wildest dreams he had never expected to have a half-Cheyenne grandchild. He shifted to a more immediate problem.

"This Logan . . . is that his first name or his last?"

"Either or both," She laughed.

Her father didn't share her humor. "There's something I need to get straight in my own mind. Just what exactly is this Logan fellow to you?"

"I thought I'd made it plain enough. He is my husband."

Sam's jaw tensed. "By law—or common law?"

Bettany faced him squarely. "Our vows are to each other, but they were made before God. I consider myself his true and legal wife."

"Is that how he considers you?"

She didn't pull her hand away, although the temptation was strong. "That is my concern, Papa. You forfeited all right to ask me such questions many years ago."

It was the first real test of their new relationship. It took all of Sam's willpower to quell his spurt of anger. Their new bond thinned, wavered, finally held firm. "I guess I had that coming. I was a poor father to you. But I never stopped loving you, and I want to make up for it now, if you'll let me."

She frowned slightly. It hurt Sam to see that faint trace of doubt, yet how could he blame her? He'd made a hundred promises and kept none of them; but that was in the past, and they were starting anew. "Honey, I know I haven't given you much reason to believe me, but you can trust this—I'll never turn my back on you again. I'll always be there if you need me. I swear it on my life."

The years rolled away. Bettany knew this was a promise Sam would keep. Long ago she had trusted in him with all her heart and soul. She did again. "Come upstairs with me, Papa. I'll introduce you to Logan—and to your grandson."

He followed her up the back stairs, using the time to master the outward signs of his inner turmoil. Grayson Howard. He had nothing against the boy—how could he, when Grayson was his own flesh and blood? But the very idea of it was as strange as meeting a man from the moon. Did Bettany realize how difficult life would be for her child of mixed blood—or for herself?

When he thought of their future it filled him with foreboding. It would not be easy for any of them. But he could smooth the way with his wealth and power. There was, in his mind, little that couldn't be bought in one way or another. And when he found the mother lode and started mining all that gold, why, he could even buy respectability for Bettany. The rest would be a bit harder.

Bettany tapped on the door and went in. Logan was up and dressed, with his gunbelt buckled across his hips. When he spied Sam behind her, his hand went for his gun and rested on the butt. Years of swift assessment came to the fore, and he relaxed. The radiant look on Bettany's face told him there was no threat here.

"Oh, Logan! It's my father! Papa, this is Logan."

The two men eyed each other warily, poised like bobcats for attack or defense: Bettany's father, Bettany's lover. Sam felt a sharp twinge of jealousy. Once upon a time he had been the center of her universe, but he'd removed himself from it voluntarily. Now another man was her moon and sun. He'd just found her, and he'd already lost her.

Sam's chin jutted aggressively. "Get one thing straight. Any man who hurts my daughter, will be a dead man."

Danger glowed in Logan's eyes. "Then you should have been a dead man twice over."

Bettany ran forward as Sam's hand hovered near his Colt. Logan stared him down. Grudgingly Sam recognized the justice of the accusation. "I had that coming. But I'll tell you this—I wouldn't take that from any other man. Bettany told me how you rescued her from the Cheyenne."

A muscle worked in Logan's jaw. "You're laboring under a misapprehension. I rescued her from a flood. Among the Cheyenne she was my brother's wife."

"Goddamn it, don't make it any harder on me!"

Logan shrugged. "White men play with words. I speak truth."

"Don't speak too damn much of it around Santa Fe. Not if you care a particle for Bettany."

Again the outcome weighed in the balance. Bettany stepped between them. "I won't have you snapping at each other's heels like this. Neither one of you can change my feelings for the other. What is, is. Accept it, because you can't change it."

They did, but only outwardly. Sam still felt chagrin toward the man he considered an interloper. As for Logan, he was reserving judgment. He'd met Sam Howard's kind before: a good man to have behind you in a fight—if he was on your side.

Despite Bettany's protests, Sam hired a carriage to take them out to his partner's hacienda. He climbed up to Rosalia's room to tell her it was all set.

"I assure you, Papa, I can ride all day with Grayson on my back in his cradleboard, without tiring."

Sam slapped his coiled whip against his thigh and appealed to Logan. "Talk some sense into her. I'll bring the carriage round."

When he was gone Logan put his hand on Bettany's shoulder. "Do as he asks. For Grayson's sake as well as yours."

She leaned her cheek against his hand, taking comfort in the warmth and reassurance of his touch. "I would feel better about it if you were coming with us."

He cupped her face between his hands. "It's safer for you this way. And I have business to take care of here."

Logan's eyes darkened to polished amber. He'd been down in the cantina, where wild rumors were flying about, whipping up fears of Indian insurrections. Three years before, Governor Perez had been killed outside the town in the bloody revolt, and Alarid, his secretary of state, had been hauled out of his own home and stabbed to death with lances. Don Santiago Abrue, a former governor, had suffered an even worse fate, tortured and mutilated before delivered by merciful death. Hatred ran high, and there were hints of private armies gathering to strike first, before the Indians did. Logan wanted to keep his ear to the ground. Small Eagle was out there somewhere. And there was the unfinished business with Eugene.

He kissed Bettany so tenderly, so deeply, that her heart froze. He kissed her as if he thought he might never see her again. She shivered against him. "Be careful, my love."

"And you." He slipped the medallion from his medicine pouch. "Take this. For good luck. Keep it for me until we meet again."

Her fingers closed over the medallion, warm from his hand. "Until we meet again. Until tomorrow night."

She kissed him again and went out.

Shortly after she left, Rosalia came in. "The hombre called Eugene. He is back." She nibbled her lower lip. "Do you wish me to lure him up to the room?"

"I've never shot a man in the back, Rosalia, and I don't intend to start now. What I want is to have someone follow him, see where he goes and who his friends are. Can you arrange that?"

She grinned. "For you, I can arrange anything." Rosalia snapped her fingers. "As easy as that."

They'd had a late start out of Santa Fe. By the time Sam and Bettany crested the last rise between them and the hacienda, dusk had crowded out the colors of sunset. The wide valley below was spread out beneath the emerging stars, and the mountains seemed ghostly and insubstantial.

Sam pointed. "Do you see that rounded peak against the sky? Just beyond is our own valley—Howard Valley—and a whole new life. You've been through hard times, Bettany, but they're all over now. I promise you that."

Bettany didn't answer. The silence was filled with all the promises he'd made before and never kept. He urged the horses into a faster pace so they would reach Don Miguel's gates before true darkness fell. Bettany was unsure of her welcome. "I hope Don Miguel won't be put out at having an uninvited guest thrust upon him."

Sam had no qualms. "For all intents and purposes, the old man's estates belong to me. Don Miguel put up his land as loan collateral and failed, time and again, to make the payments. It's only out of courtesy that I let him pretend otherwise. Don Miguel will live out his last days in his accustomed role as *patrón.*"

She was touched by her father's act of kindness. "That is very good of you, Papa. From what you've told me of him, it seems a strange comedown for a man of his background and lineage."

"Yes. He's been a king in his own kingdom all his life. The original de Medina lands, some hundred thousand acres, were from grants dating back to 1650, created by the viceroyalty of New Spain. But I'll tell you the truth. I'll be damn glad to settle in our own place the moment it's habitable. There's something strange—very strange—about the Hacienda Dolorosa and the old man, clinging to the dust and cobwebs of the grandeur he once knew in Mexico. The place is like a damned museum."

A short time later Bettany could see the proof of his

claims. From their approach to it, the hacienda looked both serene and exotic, its smooth exterior walls covered in places with falls of colorful vines. Inside, Don Miguel's home was more like the great vault of a family mausoleum— dark, dank, and filled with the gloom of decay. The mustiness of the place was more than physical, the moldering one of the spirit as much as the house and outbuildings.

Sam ushered her into the *sala*. It was just as he had described. The room was in decent repair, and the walls were covered with calico to shoulder height, to prevent the whitewash from rubbing off on the occupants' clothing; but it was obvious that the calico had not been renewed in many years. The leather of the chairs was cracked and worn and the elaborate carvings of the chests and tables dull with lack of polishing. Whatever Don Miguel had done with the money from mortgaging his estates, he had not invested any in the upkeep of the house.

Only a single candle burned, but Sam lifted it to light the ones in a candelabra of heavily chased silver. "Make yourself comfortable, Button. I'll have a servant prepare a room for you."

Bettany stopped, arrested by the two portraits on the wall. Sam followed her gaze. "Don Miguel's daughter, Ysabella, and his sister—Estrellita, I think he called her."

"They're beautiful."

"They're both dead. Some kind of tragedy, but I don't know the details. He doesn't speak of them often, but I imagine he thinks of them a good deal. I've found him brooding before their portraits more than once. He's the last of his line, you know." Bettany was moved.

The ride in fresh air had made her pleasantly sleepy after so many days cooped up over the cantina. When her father left the *sala*, she settled Grayson and took a chair, yawning. "Are you as ready for a good night's rest as I am, little one?"

Bettany smiled wryly to herself. She was, for the first time in her life, bored. If she had an antelope to skin or dried berries to pound with fat into pemmican cakes, she could certainly keep boredom at bay. Evidently her time among the Cheyenne had spoiled her for more civilized pursuits. Minutes passed in utter silence.

Something fell outside the *sala,* and Bettany jumped in reaction. Since the moment of arrival she'd been fighting the tendency to whisper, the urge to glance over her shoulder. There was something about this joyless dwelling that made her afraid to laugh aloud. Her shoulders prickled and she had the uncanny feeling she was being watched; but when she jumped up there was nothing behind but a patch of shadow and the two portraits hanging in their thick gold-leaf frames.

When she'd first seen the paintings, it had struck her that their off-center position on the wall looked strange. She realized now that they were placed where Don Miguel could see them most readily from a chair beside the fireplace. As she crossed toward them, a candle guttered out. Bettany was startled by the change in the portraits. Upon her first sight of them, the women—one dark-eyed and raven-haired, the other fair—had seemed to smile in soft anticipation of the futures they were destined never to know. Close up, with shadows flitting across their painted faces, their mouths seemed shrewd and mocking.

How different they looked suddenly! Yet it was the eyes that caught Bettany and held her in their spell. They were so alive, so alight with intelligence. She was compelled to go closer, to stand beneath the heavy frames where she could see every detail more clearly. Her father had told her their names: Ysabella in yellow satin trimmed with red—soft, pouty, with a sensual innocence that was forever trapped on canvas between childhood and maturity; Estrellita in green silk with an ivory shawl—a woman of character, with eyes that were haunted . . . by what?

The intensity of the two faces startled her. In the candlelight they burned with passion and urgency, until their presence grew to fill the room. Bettany fancied that if she turned quickly, she might see them beside her, forming out of the shadows of the room. It was impossible to shake off the sensation.

She suddenly felt as if the women were trying to communicate with her. Somehow she knew it was vital that she understand their unspoken message. "What is it? What are you trying to tell me?" Bettany whispered. "What is it that you want me to know . . . or do?"

The noise repeated outside the open window. Bettany was astounded by the sudden change in the portraits. All the animation had drained out of them in a twinkling. They were nothing but two flat images painted upon canvas and forever imprisoned in gold-leaf frames. As lifeless as the two women who had once posed for the artist in all their finery.

Bettany was half-asleep when Sam returned. "Don Miguel is still closeted with a visitor—one of General Armijo's deputies. I had Consuela air out one of the spare rooms for you. She's set out some clothes for you for tomorrow."

Once in the room, however, Bettany was unable to sleep. She was hemmed in by the walls of the house. It seemed a strange way to live now. The cabin had been different, for it had not been four walls protecting her from the world beyond, but four walls protecting the special universe inside them. She wondered if she would ever be able to live inside a house again without feeling stifled and breathless.

She noticed another door beside a chest and explored. It opened to a small side court filled with inky shadows and a star-strewn sky above. Once, long ago, she had watched for that first evening star, waiting for her father. When she had finally given up watching, she had found him at last. Life seemed to go in circles, and things happened when least expected.

Bettany went once around the court, lifting her face to the breeze. A soft cry startled her. Thinking it was Grayson, she went along the wall toward her doorway. Ten feet away she was stopped dead in her tracks by a fearful sight. In the starry light a man's face floated eerily a few feet off the ground. The disembodied features were horribly, shockingly familiar.

Then she realized that it was only a trick of light, distorting a beloved face into a mask that had seemed twisted by age and pain. She peered into the darkness. "Logan?"

He didn't answer. She ran forward lightly and found herself in an obliquely angled hallway. Her fingers touched the metal frame and the cool glass inside. The distorted vision had been a bizarre illusion, created by moonlight striking the mirror.

Or perhaps an actual reflection, distorted by the mottled silver backing. No, that was ridiculous.

As Bettany pivoted around, there was the soft sound of a door closing. Puzzled and thoughtful, she returned to her assigned chamber. Grayson was fast asleep, his hands beside his cheek. She climbed between the sheets beside him and within minutes was sleeping just as soundly. Logan came to her in her dreams, but when she opened her arms to embrace him, his image shattered into a thousand shards of glass.

Long after he'd personally escorted General Armijo's deputy to his guest room, Don Miguel went to his own chamber. In his old age he needed little sleep, and he was glad of that; he feared to dream. Too often he would find himself back in Monterrey, young and vigorous, and see Ysabella and Estrellita dance into the room. Then Julianna would come. The flesh would wither on her skeletal bones, and the others would flee, leaving him to face his accuser. He would awaken, clammy and afraid, to the erratic rhythm of his heart.

No, sleep was not a friend to him.

He poured a glass of the potent brandy distilled from the native cactus and downed it in one gulp. He poured another and carried it out into the private court and across to the other side. The door was unlocked, as always, and a small oil lamp burned in a wall niche. A servant, deaf and mute, slept on a truckle bed. The room's chief occupant sat in the shadows. Don Miguel smiled.

"You are still awake. A guilty conscience, they say, is like a stone for one's pillow."

The man in the chair didn't answer. What he had to say had been said years ago.

"So silent? Perhaps you will have more to say tomorrow. We have guests, you know. I shall give a dinner party." Don Miguel turned back toward the door. "You will join us, of course."

The man stared at him with hatred. "What new torture have you designed for me, you Devil's spawn?"

"You, to call me such a name?" Don Miguel leaned down until they were eye to eye. "You, who in a lifetime of deceit have betrayed every trust and violated the laws of God and man?"

The candlelight flickered over the silver statue in the wall niche, where it had stood for many years, the hands of the Virgin crossed over her sword-pierced red heart. It cast the old man's shadow on the walls in a grotesque humpbacked shape.

"There is no punishment on earth great enough for you. I drink to your good health, Luis." Don Miguel lifted his glass high in a mocking salute.

"May you live a hundred years!"

Thirty

Mexico: 1811

Bishop Delgado, cousin to Don Miguel, blessed the small
congregation in the Church of San Felipe and said the words
of ritual: "Go in peace, the mass is ended."

The voices of the choir soared like angels as the bride
rose from the altar steps and turned to face the congregation. Her face was not radiant, but the sunlight streaming
through the high window over the altar created that effect.
Slowly, hands clasped over her rosary, she began the long
walk down the aisle.

The air was heavy with incense, and little motes of dust
hung suspended in a shaft of light. When Ysabella passed
through it in her plain white robe, a sunbeam winked from
the gold band on her left hand. Voices drifted in from the
plaza. Sounds of life and laughter and all the things she
was leaving behind her. To a chorus of alleluias the rest
filed out after her, solemn and unsmiling as befitted such a
holy occasion.

Portly Don Enrique, one of the last to leave the church,
understood at last why Ysabella had refused to wed him.
His pride was assuaged, his honor sustained. Don Miguel's
beautiful young daughter had not refused him because of
another man, but because she had chosen a heavenly
spouse: today she had taken the first step to becoming a
bride of Christ. After a few years of prayer, study, and
proven dedication, she would take her vows as a sister of
the Order of Saint Margarita of Seville.

Don Miguel had invited him, along with a few others, to witness the ceremony. To stop any rumors before they might arise. Out in the *placita* Don Miguel accepted the puzzled congratulations of his friends and relatives. Everyone had predicted a brilliant marriage for his lovely—and well dowered—daughter. That a girl of Ysabella's spirit and beauty would choose to enter a convent instead was more than a seven days' wonder, but her father offered no explanation, and no one was impolite enough to ask.

Estrella also greeted the guests with outward calm. If she could just get through this day without anyone guessing the strain beneath her cool facade! When Ysabella rode away in the closed carriage, accompanied by two older nuns, she sighed in relief. It lasted only as long as it took to see Quinn Logan crossing the plaza toward her.

His face crinkled in a brilliant smile. "Dona Estrella! I didn't expect to meet you in town. In fact, I'm on my way south and thought I'd swing by the hacienda and pay my respects." He hesitated just a second, then plunged in boldly. "I am planning to speak to your father on a matter of . . . of mutual interest."

So soon! Estrella's heart plummeted. She hadn't expected him to make a declaration yet; but his expression and words made it plain that a formal proposal of marriage was imminent. In all her years, Estrella had never felt such exaltation—to be followed almost immediately by such crushing despair.

Her eyes flickered shut. When they opened they were cold and aloof. "I do not think that would be wise, señor."

Her change in demeanor took him aback. As she tried to brush past him, he clamped a hand on her arm and escorted her, willy-nilly, into an empty court between two buildings.

"What's happened? Why have you changed toward me like this?"

Estrella drew herself up haughtily. "I? Changed toward you? Surely, Señor Logan, you presume too much."

Anger flared in his eyes. "I don't think I misread those

warm looks you were sending my way on my last two visits. What is it? Have I offended you in some way?"

She jerked her arm away. "Perhaps you do not know that I am betrothed. The marriage is to take place after the Feast of the Assumption."

Estrella watched his anger be replaced by shock, then pain. Quinn's hand dropped to his side. "Tell me this is what you want, *alanna.* That you're not being forced in any way."

"Forced? There is no question of such a ridiculous notion." It took all her effort and training to keep up the stream of lies. "I have chosen my husband-to-be myself."

He moved back, his face stony. She turned and went out into plaza that was filled with the bustle of life, dying inside with every step.

Upon returning to the hacienda, Estrella went to the walled garden that was her special retreat. Luis had already threatened to tell Quinn everything. Estrella couldn't have borne watching the love in the Quinn's mossy gold eyes change to loathing. How foolish she had been to hope, to dream. . . .

At least Ysabella was safe. In the aftermath of discovery, Ysabella had succumbed to a storm of hysterical tears and prayers. It had taken Manuela's help and repeated doses of poppy extract to keep Ysabella from crying out her shame to all who would listen. For Estrella the knowledge that she had failed her beloved niece was more terrible than what Luis had done. She would never forgive herself.

Much later, when the weeping ceased, the vivacious Ysabella was gone forever, leaving a stern-faced stranger in her place. She would never marry and let a husband guess her terrible secret. Instead she would spend her days in prayer. The change in her was permanent.

It had not been as difficult to persuade Miguel of their plans as Estrella had feared. Ysabella's frenzied weeping, a few words about their own grandmother, who had become insane in her youth, were all it had taken.

Boots scraped on the walkway, and Estrella stiffened. Luis came through the archway, more handsome than ever. As if his charm grew along with his iniquity. Once, the sight of his dark eyes, lean face, and sensual mouth had made her heart skip a beat. Once, the mere touch of his hand would have melted her from within. Now she recoiled sharply in disgust.

"Leave me. I have nothing to say to you, now or ever."

"You are still angry, Estrellita, but in time you will forget. And then you will remember that you love me."

"I did." Her voice was calm and final. "But no longer. I was young and too bedazzled to see beyond your handsome face and strong arms to what you really are."

"I will make you love me again."

"You cannot raise the dead. I despise you."

Luis's fingers dug into her arm. "You look down upon me because you know my family's shame, but there is not a Creole who does not have a mestizo hidden in the leaves of his family tree." His face twisted in anger. "I know Miguel's grandmother was raped during the uprising, that his own father was sired by an *indio*!"

She pulled away. "Perhaps that is why he is obsessed with it. But that is not what I mean. It is not your lineage, Luis, but your wickedness that sickens me."

"I hunger for you. And your body lusts for mine as strongly. If I am wicked, then you are wicked also. We belong together."

Estrella stared out over the hot summer garden. The scent of roses, sensual and heavy, filled the place. "Yes, I have lusted for you, Luis. And I will burn in hell for it. But although I pray every day to be freed from your curse, I have never harmed anyone else because of it."

She was rigid beneath his touch, but Luis had no doubt he could soften her with the right words, a sensual caress. "You blame me for Ysabella, but I tell you that she threw herself at me—more than once. If not me, it would have been some other man, and terrible scandal in its wake. It is better this way."

His hand came up to cup Estrella's breast, and he heard her breathing quicken. "Ah, *querida*," he murmured into her ear, "if you had not denied me, it would never have happened. A man has strong passions that must have an outlet. It is your fault as much as mine."

"No. *You* were the secret lover who seduced Julianna."

He laughed in surprise. "Ah, no. You have the story backward. Headstrong, passionate Julianna seduced *me*. A family tradition you might say."

Estrella began to tremble in his embrace. He thought it was the shiver of anticipation. *"Estrellita, mi amada..."*

She leaned her head against his shoulder, and triumph flowed through Luis. The crisis was passed. She was his again. Then he realized she was weeping, quietly. Hopelessly.

He lifted her chin in his hand. "Is it so bad, to love me? To experience and to quench the desire that some poor souls never know? You come alive in my arms, *querida*. And I live for the moments we are alone together. We can neither of us escape our destiny."

She looked up at him, her face swollen and tear-streaked, eyes forlorn and remote as the star for which she was named. "Ysabella escaped, but I cannot. It is too late for me."

"It is only the beginning, *querida*." Luis tried to kiss her, but she averted her face.

"No! Listen to me. I have nowhere to turn but to you, Luis. You must help me." Estrella's voice shook. "I am carrying your child."

For once his facile words failed him. He stared at her openmouthed. Estrella laughed bitterly. The laughter ended in a sob. Years ago, in a moment of weakness, she had let him lead her on a crooked path, and they had followed it to this point in time.

Who knew where it would end?

Thirty-one

In the morning Bettany left Grayson asleep in her room and went to the *placita*, where, in fine weather, breakfast was served. Sam put down his cup of coffee and greeted her, adding that he didn't know if Don Miguel would join them. "Took one of his bad turns last night. His heart."

Before Bettany could respond there was a sharp voice from the house. "You are not a fool, you are worse than a fool!"

An old man came out into the sunlight, leaning heavily on the arm of his manservant. He was dressed impeccably in black with gold-and-silver buttons. His face was lined with effort and accumulated decades; but he was plainly irked at having to submit to any assistance at all.

Bettany felt pity for him, an obviously proud man brought low by the ravages of time and infirmity—until he lashed out with his silver-and-ebony walking stick and caught the manservant painfully in the groin. It was a purposeful blow, consciously vicious. The servant grunted in pain, but his expression hardly flickered. Evidently such random strikes were not unexpected.

When Don Miguel saw Bettany he straightened as much as possible and met her gaze, stare for stare, as if the ugly episode had never happened. So this was her father's business partner and her host. Bettany was taken aback. As he came out of the shadows he looked like a black spider emerging from his tattered web—attenuated with age, but still potentially deadly.

He shook off his attendant. "I am not an invalid, imbecile!" The smile he gave Bettany was as gracious as his bow, but she was not deceived. The mask of the aristocrat hid the face of an autocrat, and a very unpleasant one at that. She hoped her stay under his roof would be a short one. And she was glad she'd changed her clothes.

Don Miguel seemed to think otherwise. "It is pleasant to have so beautiful a lady as my guest, señora. I hope your visit will be an extended one."

She made all the proper replies, and the old man nodded. "It is good to have young people among us. It has been many years since I lived in Mexico with my own family, you see. I hope you will bring your son to the *sala* this afternoon so I might see him."

He cast a speculative look at her, his gaze lingering on her silvery hair, his eyes alive with intelligence and bright with malice. "The boy does not resemble you, I am told."

Bettany felt a thrill of danger, as if she were stumbling once more through the quicksand along the shallows of the Platte River. Her only chance was to get over the ground swiftly and step carefully. She smiled with outward calm. "Grayson takes after his father."

Don Miguel seemed satisfied with her reply, or at least with the way she'd handled it. Sam showed no reaction at all, yet Bettany was sure her father had felt that same flicker of danger.

"Well," Don Miguel said, "I shall look forward to meeting your husband, Señora Howard. . . . No, of course that is not the correct name."

Sam was afraid of what Bettany might say and jumped in. "Logan. Her husband's name is Logan."

All the color drained from Don Miguel's face. "Logan." His hand clenched into a fist. "I once knew a man by that name." He recovered himself almost immediately. "But that was long, long ago."

The manservant hovered nearby and came at his master's

signal. Don Miguel made his excuses to Bettany and Sam. "I find I have no appetite this morning. I will rest awhile, since Colonel Armstrong is coming to make his report to me in person."

Sam polished off the last of his eggs and beans. "I'll be away, but tell him I've another little job in mind for him." He turned to Bettany. "Colonel Armstrong is Don Miguel's right arm. He's worked for us since leaving the army a few years back. A sound man, Button. I think you'll like him."

Bettany wanted to escape awhile from the hacienda. The oppressive atmosphere was beginning to infect her. Fresh air would provide the antidote. A servant had given her a wide-handled basket to use as a cradle for Grayson. She didn't want to leave him alone in Don Miguel's house of shadows and brought him along, basket and all.

She took a wrong turning and found herself in an older section of the casa. An empty room led out to a walled garden, and she hoped to find a shortcut to the other side of the house. A pair of small black birds with iridescent wings darted away at her approach and flew out over the walls, feathers glistening purple and blue.

Suddenly she felt the odd prickling between her shoulder blades that she had experienced in the *sala* the night of her arrival. She had the same feeling of being watched, but when she turned around the garden was deserted. Despite its neglected air, there was something peaceful about the little court that appealed to her. She only needed Logan with her to make it perfect.

Settling herself with her back against the sun-warmed adobe with Grayson beside her, she wove hazy plans for the future. They turned from daydreams into real dreams, where golden-eyed boys and silver-eyed girls picked wildflowers outside a mountain cabin. She awakened groggily a short time later to the sound of voices floating through a half-shuttered window.

"C'mon, Ludo! Get a move on!"

"First I gotta find that little black-eyed bitch I had the last time I was here. I need me a woman."

The hairs stood up on the back of Bettany's neck. She thought she was caught up in a nightmare, that she was back on the Oregon Trail, that Axel lay desperately ill in their wagon while the wagon party was being attacked. Then her mind cleared. She was at Don Miguel's hacienda, waiting for Logan.

"*C'mon, Ludo! Get a move on!*" She knew where and when she'd heard that voice saying those same words before. Memories came flooding back. All the blood! The echo of gunfire, the frightened bellow of the cattle. Screams and shrieks fading to moans. The smell of gunpowder, burning wood, and violent death. The men in war paint, carrying Nils and Hannah away. . . .

"*C'mon, Ludo! Get a move on!*"

Panic rolled over her in great, smothering waves. She fought it back and won. There were murderers in Don Miguel's house—and she intended to find out why. But first she had to find her father. Moving as quietly as a Cheyenne, she picked up the baby's basket and made her way back to the *sala*.

She stopped short when she heard familiar names, spoken with scorn: ". . . Small Eagle and the one they call Fog or some such thing. Bad hombres, both of them."

"Then they must be killed." Don Miguel's voice carried clearly. "I must protect my interests, Colonel Armstrong. I have not come so far in the game now only to lose. And there is enough to make us all wealthy beyond belief."

"But if those damned Indians keep finding gold nuggets and trading them for supplies, it won't be long until someone wises up. That's still Mexican land, and Governor Armijo will move right in and take it for himself."

"It is the Devil's own coil! Without the gold I cannot hope to buy the land legally. Colonel Armstrong, those *indios* must be driven away from the gold site as soon as possible." Don Miguel's voice cut like a sword of fine Toledo

steel: "Do whatever is necessary. I will leave the details up
to you."

"The trap is already set. I've got a small army assembling
near Crooked Neck Creek. By this time tomorrow there
won't be one of those goddamned redskins left alive."

Armstrong rose and came into Bettany's view. She
stepped back into an alcove where she was hidden from
sight until he went out into the *placita*. Bettany slipped
away and began searching for her father, without success.
If she didn't find him, she would have to go after Logan
herself—she prayed that he had left the cantina and was
already on his way from Santa Fe to the hacienda.

The house was composed of rooms making squares around
open courts, now and then connected by hallways but more
often by a series of rooms opening into one another. Once
again Bettany lost her way and ended up in the same neglected court. From the position of the sun, she realized
that this court was near the chamber she'd been assigned.
As she was turning she heard a moan. It was faint and low
and scraped along the nerves of her spine like a piece of
broken glass.

Another moan, followed by a crash of wood and glass,
sent her racing across the *placita*. It came from the room
on the end. She ran toward it without hesitation. The
interior was dim, and she tripped over a servant lying just
inside the doorway. The pungent odor of alcohol and the
man's raspy snores told the story—but the sounds of pain
hadn't come from him. They had come from the man on
the high bed.

For a split second Bettany's heart stopped. Then it picked
up its rhythm, banging against her ribs. It couldn't be. . . .
She edged closer. "Logan?"

Her eyes adjusted to the change in light. No, it wasn't
Logan. It was an old man, wearing Logan's face. His eyes
were closed, his cheeks thin and sunken. His hands clutched
the linen sheet across his chest as if it represented the life
he clung to so desperately. The room was filthy, the floor
littered with debris. It seemed at odds with one polished

silver statue in the wall niche opposite the bed that was so different from the carved and colorfully painted *santos* she had seen in Santa Fe. This was exquisite, a work of art from the hands of some long-dead Spanish silversmith.

Broken glass crunched beneath her boot. The man on the bed moaned again. Bettany didn't want to frighten him if he had his senses about him. She put her hand on his. The skin was hot and as dry as sand. "Señor?"

The wrinkled eyelids raised up, and the eyes that had been hidden behind them were like dark coals, burning in his ashen sockets. He struggled to pull himself up to a more dignified position. Only then did she realize that he was partially paralyzed.

"Who . . . who are you?" he whispered.

"More to the point, señor, who are you—and why are you here?"

His fingers curled around her wrist. "I am Luis Francisco Iago Allende. And I am Don Miguel's prisoner."

Thirty-two

New Mexico: 1812

A rough *carreta* drawn by an ox pulled up before the gates of the convent. The wrought iron and carved oak were of splendid workmanship and as fine as anything sent from Spain. In the very center of each, in raised relief, was a heart pierced by seven swords.

The driver climbed down and pulled the bell-chain. A stout nun came out of the hut just inside the wall and eyed him disapprovingly. "Who disturbs the peace of the Lord's Day?"

"I do," a clear voice said, and a woman got painfully down from the cart. Her garments were sober but of exquisite make and her hands were those of a well-born lady unused to physical labor; but her shoes were shabby and caked with dust, as if she had come a long way on foot.

The nun goggled as a second woman clambered down, younger and dressed in the garb of a lay sister from the same order to which she herself belonged, but not of this particular convent. The lay sister helped the other woman hobble up to the gate.

"We come seeking sanctuary," she said quietly.

The portress was startled. Sanctuary, the ancient law of the Church providing asylum for fugitives. She pondered a moment. "Sanctuary," she asked at last, "of the spirit or the flesh?"

"Of both."

"Enter, then, in the peace of Jesus Christ."

As she heaved the post back and swung the gate open, the lay sister turned back to the driver and pressed a bag of coins into the man's work-roughened hand. "For the love of God and for fear of His wrath, remember your promise to me."

"*Si, señora.* No one will ever know that I brought you here." He turned away, chuckling to himself. Her secret was safe—who would even think to ask a mestizo if a fine lady and a convent woman had ridden north in his ox cart? He clucked to his ox and the cart lumbered away.

The portress let the women enter the courtyard, then carefully locked the gates again. She ushered the women inside the convent lobby and to a small room at one side. "You may be seated. Sister Fernanda will be with you presently."

Beeswax and the faint odor of incense perfumed the simple room, familiar, welcome scents. Estrella threw off her wet cloak, wearily. "You should have stayed behind in Mexico City, Ysabella. I should never have run to you for help."

Ysabella shrugged out of her own wrap. "Do you think I fear my father? What can he do to me, protected as I am by my order? He would not dare to lift his hand against me now." She took her aunt's hand in hers. "And how could I turn my back on you, knowing you are in this state because you tried to protect me from Luis? Because you offered yourself to him, in order to keep him from me, until I was safely away in the convent?"

A startled look came over Estrella's face as she shuddered in remembrance. Her niece smiled gently. "Did you think I did not guess what sacrifice you made in those last few months for my sake?"

"I failed you, *mi corazon.* I, who should have protected you."

"It is over now, and I am where I belong. I only hope that you will know the peace and happiness that I have found within the convent's walls. Meanwhile, I swear on the Holy Cross that I will do whatever I can to help you."

A nun entered and there was no time for more. The
newcomer took stock of her visitors. "I was told that you
have come seeking sanctuary, yet I cannot think either of
you has broken any laws."

"Not the laws of man, but of God," Estrella said. "But
it is a man I fear." She let her cloak fall open and pressed
her hand over her abdomen, where her pregnancy was just
hugely visible. "I do not care for myself, but I fear for the
life of my unborn child."

The bells were ringing for Angelus when an ancient priest
arrived at the convent of the Seven Sorrows. Sister Fernanda met him at the gate herself. "I do not know her
name, only that she is sorely distressed."

"A lady?"

"Most unquestionably."

"I will see her."

Sister Fernanda seemed relieved. "She is in the chapel
with a lay sister of our order, who accompanied her on the
journey."

Sister Fernanda left him in the hall outside the tiny
chapel. The room was no more than six feet by eight with
a single window near the high ceiling set with mica panes.
Candles flickered before the statue of Our Lady of Sorrows
to one side of the wooden crucifix. It was not one of the
lively *santos* carved by native artisans, but the work of an
old-world artist, covered with a layer of white gold.

She was kneeling before the small altar, completely
swathed in a dark cloak, her arms outstretched in prayer.
At the sound of his footsteps her whole body jerked. She
turned a frightened face over her shoulder and rose clumsily.
He saw that she was in a very late stage of pregnancy.

He was puzzled. "Señora, I do not understand what circumstances would bring a lady such as you to seek sanctuary
within these walls."

"Perhaps that is just as well."

She came into the light, and he noticed her tear-streaked
face and the bare finger where a wedding band should have

been. To him she was no longer the elegant aristocrat, only a soul in trouble.

"My child, what is this? What has happened to bring you here alone when your time is near? Have you no husband or father or brother to give you shelter?"

"Do not ask me to reveal my sins, Father. They are not mine alone—as you see! But I am in need of your assistance."

"I know nothing of midwifery. Surely the good sisters will be of better use to you than I."

She almost smiled at that. The ghost of one flitted over her face, then changed to a rictus of pain. Her eyes looked huge and sunken. When the contraction eased her forehead was damp. "Sister Fernanda has brought in an old *curandera* for the birth. It is for another task that I have asked for your help. There is no one else I can turn to in my hour of need."

Another contraction came on the heels of the last. She gripped her abdomen and closed her eyes against it. The priest's heart was wrung. "My poor child, I will do whatever I am free to do within my holy vows."

"There is an American staying at the home of Esteban Calijo. A Señor Quinn Logan—pray God he has not left yet! Ask him to come to me here, *por favor.*"

"Is he the father of your unborn child?" The priest was startled. He knew the American. "I am saddened to learn he has treated you so shamefully, getting you with child and refusing you the protection his name. And I had thought him an honorable man." A thought struck him. "Or is it that he is already wed to another?"

Estrella put an imploring hand on his arm. "He is indeed a man of honor. This child is none of his." The pain came back, and she gasped against it. "Do not ask me any questions. The less you know the better for all. To tell you too much might put your life in jeopardy."

The priest helped her to a wooden bench outside the chapel. "Surely not. But perhaps the men of your family are angered. I will not let them harm you."

Estrella's voice dropped as if she were speaking to herself.

"If I had known then, would it have made a difference? He is mad, I think. How else to explain his behavior? I should.have known when they told me Julianna ran away with her lover. I should have guessed."

She snapped out of it abruptly as the pain tore at her again. "For the love of God, go to Señor Logan before it is too late. I have been followed—at any moment they may come riding up to the gates."

Her fear was real. The priest raised his hand and gave her his blessing, then signaled to Sister Fernanda, waiting discreetly at the end of the corridor. "I will do what I can to help you."

Ysabella came out of the shadows. "I will go with you, father. Señor Logan knows me."

"No, stay with me, Ysabella. Please." Estrella handed her a square of embroidered linen. "Give him this. He will recognize it.

Quinn Logan had been hoisting a tankard of potent brew with Esteban Calijo when the priest had come for him, the crumpled piece of fabric in hand. Quinn smoothed out the soft linen on the table. The scent of roses and spice brought back memories, and he knew it belonged to Estrella even before he saw her monogram in the corner. He stood up so quickly that he knocked the stool over. "Take me to her!"

Less than an hour later Quinn rode up to the convent gates and was escorted to Estrella's room. He knocked softly and Sister Fernanda opened the door. "Come in, señor."

Quinn was glad to comply. The air was bone-chillingly cold, and a few flakes of snow sparkled on his shoulders. There'd be one hell of a storm before long.

He felt very out of place in the convent; he hadn't been in a church in ten years. Even his shadow seemed too large, looming against the walls. The nun ushered him in. When he saw Estrella his mouth went dry. So white, so fragile, against the sheets. Her hair was damp and her cheeks hollow, but her eyes held a glow to rival the sun. "I knew you'd come."

He knelt beside the low bed and brushed a finger against her skin. "*Alanna,* how I wish I'd never listened when you sent me away."

Her smile was tremulous. "I knew then, you see. It was too late for us. From that first day, it was already too late."

The baby made a soft squeaking sound. "My son," she said.

Quinn examined the wizened face of the swaddled infant, looking for resemblances beneath the dark thatch of hair. "He has your chin. I hope he has even half your courage."

An awkward pause ensued. Estrella's skin seemed almost translucent. She wished the moment could go on, the three of them together just like this. But soon *he* would arrive. There was no time at all. She took a deep breath and plunged in.

"I have no right to ask this of you—but there is no one else I can turn to." Her fingers curled around his. "No one else to whom I would entrust my child. I have been followed. My son is in danger. I want you to take him."

"What!"

"You must get him safely away from here. There must be some woman you know who can help. He will need a wet nurse and someone to watch over him." Her eyes brimmed with unshed tears. "Someone who will love him until I can come for him."

Quinn's mind was racing. "There is a daughter of Esteban who has just had a child. She might agree. I will speak to her."

"No, you do not understand. You must take him with you tonight. They will be here within the hour."

Knowing he was a fool, still loving the woman he realized he'd never understand, Quinn agreed. There wasn't time to say all the things he wanted to tell her, and now was not the time to do it—but one day, when they were safe somewhere . . .

Estrella took his hand in hers and kissed it. "You are a

good man, Quinn Logan. May God bless you and keep you."

Taking the medal from around her neck, a miniature of the statue in the chapel, she began to pray: "*Mater Dolorosa*—Mother of Sorrows, who stood at the foot of the cross, you who know the pain of giving up a beloved son, intercede for me at the throne of heaven . . . intercede for my son. And for my only friend, Quinn Logan."

Estrella pressed it into his hand. "To keep you safe. Go now. Quickly!"

She turned her head away, and the tears ran down from the corners of her eyes to the damp pillow. "Holy Mary, Mother of God, pray for us sinners . . ."

Quinn picked up the baby, wondering how he'd gotten himself in this predicament, knowing he could not have done otherwise. It had been twenty years or more since he'd held his youngest brother in his arms like this. He'd forgotten how light a baby was, how fragile the newest bits of human life seemed.

The child looked back at him with wise old eyes that seemed to penetrate his soul. "You're a find lad, you are. And you'll see your mother soon."

He pulled the heavy blanket around the baby, with the oilskin over it.

"What do you call him?"

Estrella smiled. "His name . . . his name is Logan."

Don Miguel was weary. The ride had been long and tiring, the bitter wind a true penance. It would be worse in the northern mountains, where the snow had been falling since the previous day; but even here the chill got into a man's marrow. If this first snow was any indication, it would be a hard winter.

Luis rode beside him, his lips curved in a sardonic smile. If Miguel even suspected that he was the man responsible for Estrella's condition, he would not have asked him to join the search.

He would have killed him.

They had wasted time looking for Estrella in Mexico. Only a stroke of luck seven days ago had sent them north into New Mexico. Luis was angry with Estrella. He had figured it all out. His wife had agreed to an annulment, and the application was on its way to Rome. With his wealth and Don Miguel's influence there was no question that the Church would grant one. Then he would marry Estrella, and this time Don Miguel would raise no objections. Scandal would be averted and he would be legal father to his own son, with Miguel none the wiser. The cleverness of the plan amused him. And if Estrella had not panicked and fled when her pregnancy became noticeable, it would all be settled.

Beside him, Don Miguel's back was stiff with pride and anger. He sat his horse like a latter-day El Cid, storming this citadel of God; but instead of the bastions of Zamora or Valencia there was only a high stuccoed wall in need of repair and the heavy wooden gates.

"Announce our coming," he said, and one of his men dismounted to hammer on the wood with his gloved fist. He waited impatiently, but no one came in answer to the summons.

"They are hiding," Luis said to him. "They think if they do not come, we will go away and leave them in peace."

Don Miguel clenched his fist. In San Felipe no one would dare ignore his command—*no one!* Frustration gave way to cold fury. These women thought they were above the laws of man, that he would not dare force his way into a holy place. They would learn their error.

He turned to one of his men. "Look, Rivera. The wall is poorly maintained. The slightest push might send the gate crashing to the ground."

Rivera didn't need a stronger hint. He dismounted and examined the place where the hinges were attached. "The adobe is crumbly," he announced, casually drawing his dagger. "As soft as cheese, *patrón.*"

With his steel point and great strength it was only a short time before he'd worked away the matrix. The heavy post wobbled with the unbalanced weight of the loose gate. Rivera leaned his bulk against it, and the wood creaked and groaned. He threw a glance at his *patrón*, as if seeking further orders. Don Miguel nodded.

Rivera threw his bulk at the weakened spot, and the wood shrieked. A moment later the door opened, but from the inside. A small woman in a nun's habit and a woolen cloak stood inside. "You would disturb this house of God, señor?"

Don Miguel ignored her and sent his horse bounding into the snowy courtyard, with Luis right behind. The cavalcade followed, iron hooves striking sparks from the frost-hardened ground. He rode up to the church steps. "Come out, Dona Estrella. You can hide no longer. You must face me now."

The door that opened was not of the convent, but of the small church. A second woman stood framed in the doorway. Her air of inviolable authority identified her as the Mother Superior. "Who calls Dona Estrella?"

"I, Don Miguel Rodrigez Alvarez de Medina. I have come to claim my sister and take her home."

"Take her, then."

The nun stepped back as the church doors opened wider to the candle lit interior. The sound was obliterated by the sudden tolling of the tower bell. To its doleful rhythm a funeral procession came down the shadowed nave toward them. As the mourners filed out, the horses snorted and the riders covered themselves with hasty signs of the cross.

Luis drew in a sharp breath, and his face, already stiff with cold, became as lifeless as a stone effigy.

Don Miguel eyes narrowed. Did they think to fool him with such a ridiculous trick? He flicked his glove in Rivera's direction. "Open the coffin."

"You would desecrate the dead, Don Miguel?" the Mother Superior asked sternly.

"I wish only to gaze upon my sister one last time." He directed an impatient gesture toward his henchman. Rivera moved to do as he was told. He had no fear of the dead, but his fear of Don Miguel was very real and demanded instant obedience.

After working up one corner with his knife, Rivera ripped open the lid with his bare hands. The nails parted from the wood with a sound like muffled shots. Don Miguel stared impassively down at his sister's face. His jaw clenched. So, it was true. She had escaped his justice, leaving only her shell behind in the plain wooden box. Instead of her brother's wrath, it was her God she was facing now. "Cover her."

Rivera started to replace the lid, but Luis had dismounted. He knelt beside the coffin, disbelieving. She had sworn she would never be his, and she had kept her word. "Estrellita!" How peaceful her face looked in death. How beautiful. His hand touched hers, folded so neatly across her chest. The warmth had already left her, as it was leaving his bones now. He rose slowly. "Where is the child? I will take the child with me."

The Mother Superior folded her hands in the wide sleeves of her cloak. "There is no child here."

Don Miguel looked grim. If Estrella's baby had died with her, the nun would have said so forthrightly; he guessed that the only proof of his sister's shame still lived. "Search the convent."

Rivera hurried to obey, but the nun barred his way. "No good will come of this. You will answer for your actions."

"I think not," Miguel said curtly. "I am well known to the archbishop."

"It was a Higher Authority I had in mind. Turn back. This no longer concerns you."

Luis pushed his way forward, his voice choked with emotion. "It concerns me. The child is mine."

Don Miguel stared at Luis. There was a great roaring in his ears like the sound of a violent wind, yet the air was still. The other men looked at each other and then away.

Don Miguel put his hand on the butt of his gun. "Enough of talking. Find the child!"

Ysabella, praying inside for Estrella's soul and the life of the baby, was startled by the sound of gunfire from the courtyard.

Thirty-three

New Mexico: 1841

"Señor Howard rode out after breakfast, señora. He will not be back until nightfall."

"Thank you, Marisa." Bettany was barely able to hide her dismay. The problem of Don Miguel's prisoner could wait a few more hours after so many years, but there was no time to spare in warning the Cheyenne of the attack. It was to take place at Crooked Neck Creek—and she had no idea where to find it. The only thing to do was to ride to Santa Fe in search of Logan.

. She was trying to saddle a horse, over the objections of a groom, when Logan came up the approach road. Bettany flew out to meet him and was in his arms the minute he dismounted. "I'll have to stay away more often," he said before realizing there was more to her greeting than he'd suspected. "What is it? What's wrong?"

"Oh, thank God you're here! There's no time to be lost."

It took her only a few minutes to pour out the story. "And the man who shot you—Eugene—was one of the men who attacked the wagon party disguised as renegade Indians. So was the one he called Ludo."

Logan wasn't nearly as surprised to hear her strange tale as she had expected. Among the Cheyenne he had learned the hidden meanings of things. Buffalo Heart had taught him that the world was like a great circle, with every event connected in some way with all the others. There were omens and signs, inevitable patterns and designs. Coincidence did not exist.

"I'll need a fresh horse. A fast one." Logan caught Bettany up in his arms. "Don't worry. I'll get there in time. Meanwhile you'll be safe here, since Armstrong and his henchmen are already on their way."

"I'm coming with you. Have you forgotten that Small Eagle vowed to shoot you on sight?"

Gray eyes met gold. Logan touched her cheek with the backs of his fingers. "You have Grayson to consider. And the two of you would slow me down."

He was right. Bettany reached up to kiss his mouth once, quickly. "Godspeed, my love."

She watched him set out once more with tears in her eyes and fear in her heart.

Bettany paced the *sala*. Since Logan's leavetaking the day had passed like a waking nightmare. The fact that Don Miguel had recovered enough to ride out on his lands was the only thing that made the waiting bearable. She would not have been able to keep up a polite facade in front of him and might have given everything away. It was difficult enough to hide her concern from the servants.

She walked over to the portraits and stood staring up at one. Estrella's mouth seemed curved in a secret smile. It was strange how her painted expression appeared to alter with every change in light. The resemblance was there, if one looked for it, in the shape of the mouth and eyes. There was strength there and just a hint of sensual weakness, but Bettany knew that Don Miguel's sister had none of the true evil that dwelled inside him.

And her father was Don Miguel's partner—was he part of it, too? Did Sam Howard know about the pathetic man who claimed he was a prisoner here? Was he part of Don Miguel's plans to massacre the Indians, all in the name of gold?

She was ill with worrying. Would Logan reach the Cheyenne too late to warn them? Or would he become a victim of Don Miguel's mercenaries along with the others? Her imagination supplied horrible pictures, and the reality of the hacienda was almost as bad. Was Luis Allende truly a prisoner, or was he mad?

She heard an approaching rider and ran out toward the main *placita*. Her disappointment was keen when she saw only a tall, thin figure in the robes of a priest, as wan as a man newly recovered from severe illness. He favored her with his sad, gentle smile.

"*Buenas tardes, señora.* I am Father Ignazio, come to see Don Miguel. I have reason to believe he is expecting me."

"Don Miguel is away from the hacienda. I don't know when he will be back."

Father Ignazio was untroubled. "No matter. I will wait until he returns."

Bettany scrutinized the priest. Here was a potential ally. "There is a man here, ill and in need of assistance. His name is Don Luis Allende, and he claims he is held prisoner here."

"Don Luis! How true is the saying that the Lord moves in mysterious ways." A beatific smile illumined the priest's face. His faith had been justified, just as he had always known it would be.

It was morning when Logan found the joint encampment at Crooked Neck. In the past the first sight of the Cheyenne lodges had filled his heart with joy and a sense of home-coming. Now he was a stranger, forever an outsider in the only world he really knew. He called out a greeting in Cheyenne as he rode in and was recognized.

Antelope Chaser put his hand upon his foster son's shoulder. "He does not know you, Setanta. You are safe with me."

Nils stood tall. "I do not fear Wolf Star."

Red Paint Woman was leaving her lodge at the moment and froze in recognition. What was *he* doing here, coming back to stir up the angers she had worked so hard to soothe? A little girl with rippling fair hair peeked out through the entrance flap. Red Paint Woman ducked back inside, taking Hannah with her. "Stay inside," she told the girl sharply. "Here."

She took off one of her necklaces and handed it to Hannah, knowing the bright beads and ornaments would keep the girl quiet for hours. Small Eagle had heard the tension in her voice and was already on his feet. Although he had the rifle Bettany had left behind and the newer one he'd traded for, his hand reached instinctively for his bow. He had a range of well over three hundred yards and could fire off eight arrows in the time it took a man to reload his gun. "What is it?"

Red Paint Woman sighed. "It is Wolf Star, returning."

Small Eagle's face was harsh. Pushing his way past his Arapaho wife, he went out to see with his own eyes. They narrowed at Logan's bold approach. It was like the day on the mountain when he'd called the antelope, and instead Wolf Star had come in response.

He acted out of instinct and anger. The arrow was nocked and ready, the bowstring bent back to send it flying in an instant. The words of his old chant echoed in his head: *Come to me, Wolf Star, my antelope brother. Come to me and give up your life that I might live.*

His hands were steady, the lines of the metal arrowhead sharp and gleaming with fatal grace. *Come, my brother. Let my arrow fly straight and true. Let it pierce your strong heart, your brave heart. . . .*

Logan dodged past the eager children and the string of ponies a young brave was leading. He knew the instant Small Eagle's arrow was pointed at his heart, felt the intensity of the emotions focused upon him, but never slowed his pace. There was no other choice.

Tomorrow Colonel Armstrong would come in force with his mercenary troops on an ostensible mission of peace that would turn into nothing less than a death trap. And he was the only one who could address the council of leaders. He was the only one they would believe.

Silence fell over the entire camp. Not even a dog barked.

A path cleared before him, leaving clusters of Cheyenne and Arapaho on one side, Comanche and Apache on the other. It led straight to the lodge where Small Eagle pulled and held the twisted sinew bowstring back from the curve of his polished bow. The air crackled with tension. Every second, every foot he traveled forward, Logan expected to see the arrow soar, to feel the jolt of it knocking him backward, the hot-poker thrust of it through his flesh.

Still he never wavered. Though he was outcast now, these Tsistsistas were, and would always be, the family of his heart.

Small Eagle's nerves were stretched like his bowstring. His hands, so steady in war or the hunt, trembled as his brother came on. Suddenly the bowstring twanged. The arrow hissed through the air, to impale itself in the ground a dozen yards before Logan.

Red Paint Woman sighed out her pent-up breath. Too much had weighed in the balance: a Tsistsistas who killed another of the tribe was exiled forever from his band. That would have been terrible indeed, yet not as horrifying as the result that would have come about if Small Eagle had loosed his arrow against Wolf Star. The bond between them was too strong. It would have destroyed him. It would have destroyed all their peace and happiness.

Logan's eyes were no longer sharp and wary. His risk had paid off. He dismounted at the lodge as night fell around them. "My brother, I bring evil tidings. Smoke Along the Ground must hear of them, and the others as well."

"You are no brother to me. I told you when we parted in the mountains that I would kill you if ever we met again. Do not be misled because I let you live. We meet as strangers. The day my father brought you to be raised within his lodge was an evil one. It would have been far better if he had left you to die in the snow."

The arrows of the Cheyenne's bitterness pierced Logan to the heart. He had not expected to feel such pain. For a moment his eyes dimmed from rich gold to dull copper. He steadied himself. This was the price of his love for Bettany.

"Call a council of the leaders," he said quietly. "And I will tell them my news."

Morning broke over the grassy plain in bloody splendor. Before the lingering red had faded from the eastern sky, a group of horsemen rode toward the site where the Indians had gathered for their parlay. Eugene was pleased with the Colonel's idea. It would all go according to plan. They would ride in from the front, full of smiles and bearing gifts. Halfway there his group would swing into the shelter of the rocks and begin firing. The rest of the mercenaries would fire from behind, trapping the redskins between them.

When word of the massacre got around, the other tribes would hesitate to push out in this direction; the ones who escaped would instead go on the warpath against the stream of emigrant wagons that had already begun to pour out along the trails. Then the way would be clear, Armstrong had vowed, to get rid of Don Miguel and find the source of that goddamned gold themselves.

Eugene lifted his hand as if in greeting, then dropped it swiftly and turned his horse aside, toward the protection of the rocks. At his signal rifle fire cracked from the rocks where his men were hidden. A volley came from behind them, sending his men and horses scattering. The Indian delegation was only a decoy. They'd guessed his plan somehow, turning his ambush into a bloody rout.

Logan had taken the lead position, drawing the mercenaries away. There would be no cover for him for a good six hundred yards, but it was his plan and he'd taken the dangerous duty as his role. Ludo and Kearns came at him in a pincer movement. There would only be time to get one or the other, Logan knew—and whichever man he didn't get, would get him.

He rode at Kearns, singing his death song. An echo of song seemed to follow him. Logan fired, and Kearns fell from his horse to be trampled by the terrified beast. Ludo almost had him in range, and Logan waited to feel the slam of the bullet through his chest. Suddenly Ludo wheeled his horse. "Goddamn son of a—" He was caught in midcurse by an arrow through his heart. Logan had a glimpse of Small Eagle flashing by and then was swallowed up in the melee. The brother he'd wronged had saved him.

In less than ten minutes it was all over, the sound of the gunfire echoing like a volley of thunder from the distant hills. Armstrong's men lay dead upon the plain, the lone exception galloping desperately away. Smoke Along the Ground had been unhorsed. Logan helped him stanch the blood from a wound along his ribs. "Where is Small Eagle?"

"He was with Spotted Bull in the charge. I have not seen him since."

Numbness crept into Logan's heart. He finished binding the Cheyenne's injury and went in search of his brother. He found him a short time later, lying in a gully. The sides of it were thick with red berries, but the crimson smears across Small Eagle's chest were not from their juice.

Logan knelt beside him. "My brother . . ."

His hand came away wet and warm with blood. "Ah, no! Small Eagle . . ." Bending down, he listened for the sound of breath or the feel of it upon his cheek. It was there, so faint he was afraid he'd imagined it. Then he examined the wounds. Two bullets had passed through Small Eagle's chest and out his back, ripping a path of destruction. A bubble of blood glistened at the corner of his mouth. Pain ripped through Logan.

He lifted Small Eagle's shoulders across his arm to ease his labored breathing. The Cheyenne's eyes opened. A beatific smile illuminated his face. "Wolf Star. The woman . . . she was meant to be yours. She was the Silver Woman of your dreams. I knew this from the first. . . . I took her because . . . because I knew you would want her. Just once, I wanted to best you. I wanted to give you pain. . . ."

The last spark of jealousy died with the admission, leaving a deep tranquillity in its place. "We have walked different paths, Wolf Star, and turned our backs to one another. But no matter what words we have thrown, we are still brothers."

Logan bowed his head. He had known jealousy, too. Now it was over. "We are still brothers."

Small Eagle coughed and grimaced against the onslaught of pain. "How many others are slain?"

"All of the enemy but one. Among the Tsistsistas only three wounded, two dead of Antelope Chaser's Comanche band. Our countertrap was successful."

"It is good." The silence was filled with Small Eagle's light, gasping breaths. "Buffalo Heart . . . he said you would save our people. He spoke truth."

Small Eagle's fingers wrapped more tightly around Logan's wrist, as if that contact were all that kept him from drifting away. "My son . . . my son will be a great warrior. He must know his people."

"He will."

Small Eagle's pallor increased. "*Ipewa.* Tell my son," he said, "of the time we routed the Pawnee at Cottonwood Creek, and of our raid upon the Comanche band when I stole a hundred horses. . . ."

Logan felt as if an iron band were wrapped around his chest. His voice came out small and tight. "You will tell your son of these things yourself. He will hear the tale of Cottonwood Creek from his father's lips."

"No. It is well for a warrior to die in battle. I have counted many coup."

"You have." A shudder ran through Logan, but there was no more dissembling, no false words of encouragement. They were both warriors. They knew.

For Small Eagle the moment was one of revelation. His jealousy of Wolf Star had been one of the driving forces of his existence. It was reduced to insignificance now with death hovering near. He must let Wolf Star know this. His fingers closed over Logan's convulsively.

"Do you remember when we were boys, wanting to be men—when we tried to catch the ponies up in the Medicine Bow Mountains, and fell down the cliff into the mud hole? And the day we were chased by the bees all the way to the river? Tell him that, also, my brother. See that he grows to manhood in the right path. And tell my son—"

Suddenly the coughing overwhelmed him. Then he was very still. For a few seconds he closed his eyes and was a boy again, sitting in the sun beside Buffalo Heart. The old warrior held up a smooth white stone, polished by ages in the river and round as a berry.

"Where does this begin?" he asked Small Eagle. "Where does it end?"

Small Eagle let him place the stone into his palm. "I do not know, Uncle. I cannot answer you this."

Buffalo Heart took the stone again. "No man knows such things. They cannot be understood with the mind, but only through the spirit. But there is a pattern to all things in nature. And who can say where one thing begins and another ends?"

Suddenly Small Eagle was back in the ravine again, looking up through the screen of trees with Wolf Star bending over him. "How dim the sun is . . . how smooth and round. Like . . . like a polished white stone. If I reach out, I can hold it in the palm of my hand . . ."

He never finished what he had been about to say.

Logan sat beside Small Eagle while the sun rose high in the sky and held his brother's hand for a long, long time.

Thirty-four

LOGAN DUCKED INTO SMOKE ALONG THE Ground's lodge, where Hannah cowered. The wailing of Red Paint Woman and the others frightened her, and she had withdrawn into her mind where it was safe and warm. Her eyes snapped open when she saw him and went round with surprise. He was inordinately pleased that she remembered him at all. In the flicker of an eye her attention was caught and held by the bracelet on his wright wrist, a wide silver cuff inlaid with bits of polished, deep blue stone.

Hannah always felt safer with things than with people, and she focused her attention on the bracelet. Her little fingertips explored its shape, the texture of its design, and the smooth, cool feel of the stones in the center. She liked the way the shapes went round and round and round. She ran her finger along the edge in a continuous circle, blotting out all the details outside the bracelet that confused her senses or threatened to overpower them. Contentment welled up inside her as she concentrated. Round, round, round. Smooth, smooth, smooth. Smooth and round and blue . . . falling into blue. Safe inside the smooth, round blue. . . .

The entrance flap was open, and Antelope Chaser and his white son, Setanta, entered. A medallion hung about the youngster's neck, suspended from a leather thong. The last time Logan had seen the medallion it had adorned Eugene's belt buckle. The edges were freshly scored where it had been pried away.

Antelope Chaser paused to speak to another brave, and his new son glanced around the lodge with pride. His gaze reached Hannah, hesitated briefly when he spied her fair hair, then swept on without a hint of recognition. Logan watched intently. Whether the boy's memories of his former identity were buried too deep to reach or whether it was deliberate, it was clear that Nils Vandergroot was gone forever.

Only Setanta remained.

But at least, Logan decided, he could bring Hannah back. He'd already talked to Red Paint Woman. Small Eagle's widow was young and desirable. She would go back to her uncle's lodge and in time take another husband. It would be far easier for her to do so unencumbered by a strange *ve-ho-e* child.

Logan touched her cheek. "Hannah? Do you remember me?"

She didn't respond. Hannah was deep in her private universe, where only now and the bracelet existed, and where everything was smooth and round and blue.

Logan straightened up, wondering what thoughts went through her mind and if they were pleasant. He almost envied her. In her interior world, whatever else it held, he was sure that there was no pain, no loss, no death. "I'll be back for you, Hannah. I'll return and take you to your mother."

But first he had some business to settle with Don Miguel.

Dusk cloaked Don Miguel's hacienda when Logan swung down from his horse, weary and hollow-eyed. There was only one enemy left to face, and he had no fear of one sick, old man and a handful of servants. He threw his reins to a groom and strode across the court and into the *sala*.

"Logan!" Bettany ran across the room to him, stopping when she saw the emptiness in his eyes. "Oh, Logan, no!" She put her arms about him, giving and taking strength.

Logan was grateful he didn't have to put it into words. To speak aloud of Small Eagle's death would make his loss

even more unbearable. A part of him had died. The man
the Cheyenne called Wolf Star was gone forever, left on a
funeral scaffold with Small Eagle's remains, somewhere beneath the blue New Mexico sky.

He took her face between his hands and stared down at
her without speaking. Then he gathered her against his
chest and held her until her scent, her warmth, enveloped
him, easing the chill that had settled in his heart since the
battle at Crooked Neck Creek. He told of the battle.

They mourned Small Eagle's passing together, without
words. Bettany was surprised at how his death affected her
and realized that she had loved Small Eagle, not as a lover
but as a friend. He had been a man of strength and courage.
He had treated her kindly and had fathered Grayson—and
she had come between him and Logan, who was his brother.
The pain she felt was real, but nothing, she knew, to Logan's agony.

He held her so tightly that she feared her ribs might
crack. When he released her, his eyes were as gold as she
remembered, yet they were somehow different. He took her
hands and held them between his. "Grayson must know
his father's people. I gave Small Eagle my pledge."

"He will. I swear it."

Logan closed his eyes and filled himself with the life and
love she radiated. He could have held her forever, but they
were no longer alone.

Bettany saw him first. "Don Miguel!"

Logan put her aside and faced the man whose greed was
directly responsible for Small Eagle's death. His face was
still and terrible as he turned to face his adversary. It was
a look Halsey and his men would have recognized.

Don Miguel stood on the threshold, hand clutched to
his chest and his face a death's-head. His voice shook.
"Luis! How did you get up from your bed! Or have you
died, then? Are you a ghost, come for me. . . ."

He gave a violent shudder and fell backward against the
wall. Silently he slid down, as if his old bones had crumbled
to powder, and folded into a heap. Bettany ran to his side,

and he whispered something. "Estrella," he gasped, so faintly she could hardly hear him. "I hear Estrella laughing. . . ."

She leaned closer. Don Miguel's eyes were sightless and fixed in horror. In the shocked silence that followed his collapse, Bettany thought she heard it, too. A faint, silvery sound that ended in a sigh.

"He's dead!"

Logan knelt and put his hand over the old man's heart. It had ceased its chaotic beating forever. He looked at Bettany. "What the hell was that all about? He seemed to think I was someone else."

"He thought you were your father."

"My father?" Logan stared at her as if she'd gone mad.

Bettany took his hands in hers. "It would have been worse for him if he'd died knowing who you really are. There is no easy way to say this: Don Miguel was your mother's brother—and you are his only surviving heir."

Father Ignazio came to the door of Luis's room to meet Bettany and Logan some time later, smiling his gentle smile. "He has made his confession and received absolution for his sins. Now he seeks to make his peace with Don Miguel."

Logan's voice was harsh. "Then he will have to wait. Don Miguel has gone to meet his God . . . or, more likely, the Devil. His black heart failed him."

The priest turned Bettany. "I see that you have told him everything."

"Not everything." She caught Logan's hand in hers. "I thought Señor Logan would want to read the diaries himself." The priest stepped back and Bettany led Logan to the room where his father had been kept prisoner so many years.

Logan went in alone. At the foot of the bed was a wall niche with a silver statue gleaming in it—not the familiar Madonna of Guadalupe, but a haloed woman whose heart was pierced by seven swords. The Silver Woman of his dreams.

A strange peace came over him. Raised as a Cheyenne,

he'd learned the hidden meanings of signs and omens and understood the very real power of visions and dreams. His journey through the years had brought him, full circle, to this time and place. He knew his place in the universe at last. He had come home.

He moved to the bed. Staring down at the ravaged face on the pillow, Logan saw his own mortality. Whatever this man had done, he had suffered for it. Pity filled him, untinged by sentiment. Logan sat on the chair beside the bed.

Luis groaned and roused from his troubled dreams. It was difficult. The dreams were more real now than this existence in limbo. Twilight had fallen and the lamp had not been lit, yet he knew immediately he was not alone. Perhaps it was Estrella. Sometimes she came to him in a rustle of silks.

Miguel didn't believe that Estrella visited him. *You are mad, Luis, and you dream a madman's dreams.*

But Luis knew it was Estrella. He saw her more clearly each time. With every visit the feather-light touch of her hand upon his forehead became more substantial—or else as his body failed his other senses sharpened. Yes. Perhaps it was necessary to loosen the bonds of earth somewhat in order to see things as they really were. And every night he saw her waiting for him, as young, as intense, as he remembered her. All the passion between them had been burned away, but their bond remained strong. Suddenly the room was filled with the subtle scent of her perfume, a dark note of spice with a scattering of flowers. *Estrellita!* His mouth twisted in a half smile. She had forgiven him, even if he could not forgive himself.

He heard the sound of breathing in the darkness. Estrella made no sound at all. Someone lit the lamp on the table, and its brief orange flare dazzled him momentarily. Luis tried to rise up on his elbows. "Who is it? Who is there?"

Logan stepped out of the shadows. "Your son."

Much later Logan sat on the hard chair beside Luis's bed, pondering the mysteries of fate and his own family history. This frail, pathetic man had seduced his mother and fathered him. The old proverbs ran through Logan's mind. "'Take what you want,' the Devil says—and pay for it!" Don Luis Allende had paid.

He'd been younger than Logan was now when he'd been shot through the spine by Don Miguel in punishment for his sins—and after he survived the initial injury, Estrella's brother had seen to it that his victim's suffering continued over the years. Logan could only imagine what he must have endured as the helpless prisoner of a man who had admitted to murdering his unfaithful wife in the heat of anger—and tried to murder his sister's child in cold calculation. The kind of man who could condone the massacre of a wagon party or a peaceful camp of Cheyenne to further his greed.

It is well, Logan thought, that Don Miguel died before I returned.

He felt no animosity toward his father, only a tired and impersonal compassion. At the moment Luis was drifting in and out of dreams. Only his pride, and the determination to outlive his old enemy, had kept him alive. Now that Miguel was gone, the need was gone also. Logan thought it would not be long, perhaps a matter of mere days or weeks. He hoped there would be time to learn more about the woman who had borne him. Whatever good there was in him had come from her.

Bettany came back with the priest. Father Ignazio had the diary for Logan. "This will answer many questions that you have. There was another, but I never found it."

Luis had roused at the sound of their voices as they discussed the missing diary. His thin hand caught at Logan's wrist. "You must look inside the statue. It was Estrella's. Miguel put it in the niche opposite my pillow so it would be the first and last thing that I saw, waking and sleeping."

Logan went to the niche and lifted the statue, prying it away from its wooden base. Inside the hollow was another small diary like the one Father Ignazio had found before. He frowned at Luis. "How did you know it was there?"

"I did not know." The smile Luis gave his son was

crooked. "But I knew Estrella, and how she thought. You see, I loved her, in my way."

Bettany felt a hand tighten around her heart. For just a moment he looked young and so like Logan that it took her breath away; but she had read the other diary, and she knew Logan as well as she knew herself. Where Luis was weak, Logan was strong. He had escaped his father's taint.

Luis fixed his burning gaze upon his son. "When you have read this book, and the other, I hope you will come back. If you do not . . . well, I will understand."

Logan took the diaries out into the walled garden, where he could still see in the dying light, and opened one at random. The pages were blank except for the first three. He went to the beginning but was almost to afraid to start. These thin slanted letters held the final answers that he had sought for so long. He touched his fingertips to the faded lines, as if they were a link to the mother he had never known.

He stopped Bettany as she went past. "I'll be down by the river. I need to get away from these enclosing walls. I'll wait for you there."

She watched him go, hoping her love would be enough to sustain him through all the changes he was going through. None of it would be easy for him—or for her. She had taken over the reins of the household, keeping the servants from panic in the same calm way she'd looked after the younger girls at the Susquehanna orphanage. Everything was soon in order, with a room prepared for Father Ignazio and supper cooking in the kitchen. Don Miguel had been laid out upon the bed in his room instead of in the *sala* as the priest thought was proper. Bettany was about to go in search of Logan by the river when Sam returned at last.

He came into the *sala*, swinging his hat in his hand. "What, no kiss for your old father?"

Her eyes were like quicksilver, shining and opaque. "I have a few questions first. About Colonel Armstrong engineering the massacre of Angus McGrew's wagon party.

About the men called Eugene and Ludo. And just what your partnership with Don Miguel entails and about his treacherous plans to attack a peaceful encampment of Indians to keep them from discovering the gold he wanted for himself."

"What the hell . . . ?" Sam's surprise was patent. "Button, I don't know what in tarnation you're talking about. My 'partnership' with the old man is a polite way of saying that I bought up the mortgages to half his lands. Bad investments had Don Miguel on his knees. Without me he would have lost everything."

"And what's in it for you, Papa?" She swallowed painfully. She had to know.

"Influence with the New Mexican government, especially Governor Armijo. I made my fortune these past two years with a train of supply wagons running to and from Santa Fe along the trails and even down into Mexico under the Mexican flag, with his protection." He saw the expression on her face "Don't look at me like that, Button. I'm a trader, damn it, not a diplomat. Now, what's all this stuff about the massacre and Indians?"

Bettany filled him in. Sam whistled. "That secretive old devil. Well, I'll be a son-of-a-bitch!"

Her revelations had quickly squashed any emotions he might previously have felt for Don Miguel's death. "I don't spend much time at the hacienda, honey. I didn't know, Button. Not any of it. I swear it on your mother's grave and my own immortal soul. But I don't know how to make you believe me."

There was no way he could have feigned his shock and dismay. Bettany sighed with relief. Her instincts had been right. Whatever Sam Howard might be, he was no murderer. She held out her hands to him. "I believe you, Papa."

He took them and held them. "You'll never have reason to regret it, I promise you that. I don't deserve your trust, Button—or your love. But I'll never let you down again."

For just a moment the air was thick with echoes of all the promises he had made to her in the past and never kept. Then Bettany banished them. It was a time for new beginnings. He drew her into his arms and hugged her, just as he had so many hears before. Bettany realized he even had the same comforting smell of leather and tobacco that she remembered. As she reached up to hug him back, she looked past his shoulder and saw the sky through he open doorway. Smiling, she turned him toward the door. Sam stared up at the sky and grinned.

The evening star hung suspended over the hacienda, burning like a pure white flame.

Later Bettany went in search of Logan. She found him sitting by the river in moonlight so bright that it dimmed the stars. The diaries were in his hand. "Have you read them?"

"I decided to wait until morning. And I wanted you with me."

He took her hand and they walked along the riverbank, talking as much in silence as with words. Don Miguel's death had been the bizarre ending to an even stranger story. Now they could start again, free from the shadows of the past. Bettany found it ironic that the lands he had schemed and killed to save were now owned by his partner, Sam Howard, and by Logan—the grandson he had tried to destroy.

Logan didn't want any part of it. Perhaps he'd change his mind in time, or perhaps they'd sell out to her father and start anew somewhere else. At least now that he knew the truth, his old, open wounds could close and heal. And so could hers.

The breeze caught strands of her hair and blew them across her face. Without speaking, Logan pulled the pins from her hair until it rippled free. He led her closer to the river, where the water sighed over the pebbles. "I have so much to tell you," he said.

She smoothed the hair for his temples. "Not now. Not yet . . ." Time stood still. It was an enchanted place, untouched by responsibilities or painful memories. The willow looked like clouds of silver lace in the moonlight, and they made love beneath them.

In the morning they went back to the willows, Logan with the diaries and Bettany with Grayson in his cradleboard. Her feet walked on clouds of joy. "I can't believe that Hannah and Nils are both alive—won't until I have them in my arms again."

"We can set out tomorrow. Red Paint Woman won't be a problem." He sent a worried glance at Bettany. "But don't get your hopes up about the boy. He doesn't remember anything of his past. He doesn't want to. And he's happy with Antelope Chaser."

"Yes..." She knew that Logan didn't quite understand why she would want to take Nils away from his Comanche family. She would have to see Nils first. Then she would decide. In her heart she didn't think she could ever separate him from his new family. But for a few more days, she could dream.

Bettany sat a little apart, tickling her son's chin with a wildflower, giving Logan the strength of her presence and the privacy he needed. Logan ran his fingertips over the lines of writing. It was strange to sit in the warm sun and read his mother's words, written by a hand long cold. Estrella's handwriting filled the early pages with neat, even script. The last page was little more than a scrawl.

My beloved son,
    If you read this it means that I am no longer on this Earth to tell my story to you face to face. There is so much to say and perhaps so little time to say it. Know this—I have loved you from the moment I first discovered that you were growing inside my womb. You are a part of me, not my shame—Never my shame, but my greatest glory.
    I have made an offering to the convent so that the good sisters will pray for you morning and night. I must write quickly. Miguel has followed me. He

was very angry when he found out. So angry that I
feared for my life. Now I fear for yours. He has
vowed that it would be better that you be left in the
snow for the wolves, than to survive to taint his
name—and I know that he means this.

I cannot bear the thought of being parted from
you, even for a few days, but you will be safe with
Quinn Logan. I have given you into the care of a
good man. The best man I have ever known. Perhaps, if my life had followed another pattern, he
might have been your father. He may still, at least
in name. If all goes well, we shall all be together in
three weeks' time in Santa Fe. Then, if he still is
insane enough to want me, I will gladly be his
bride. I wish I had told him that before he left. God
keep him safe. . . .

There was more. Logan read it through twice, gleaning
clues about the woman who had been his mother. Wishing
he had known her. He'd grown to manhood nursing his
hurt for nothing. He had never been abandoned purposely.
He had been loved.

Now he knew the answers to the questions that had
tormented him all his life. And by the time he'd found
them, they no longer mattered. It was not the past that
was important, but the present and the future. His future
with Bettany and Grayson. His promise to his brother.

*I will remember, Small Eagle. Your son will know your people.
I will tell him of the battle at Pawnee Creek and of the many
coup you counted. And I will tell him of the mud hole and the
time we were chased by the bees. . . .*

Without speaking, he put the diaries into Bettany's hands
and played with Grayson while she read them. When she
had turned the last page there were tears in her eyes. "Oh,
Logan. This Quinn she named you for—she loved him.
She loved him and she never told him."

He smiled. "I think he knew."

"But what happened to him afterward—and to you?"

Logan picked up a pebble and tossed it into the river. "He meant to. I've got it all worked out. Quinn Logan got away at first. But eventually Don Miguel and his men tracked him down through the snow and shot him. He was a resourceful man. Although hurt, he somehow managed to escape under cover of the howling storm and tried to make his way to safety. When he heard Notched Arrow and the others, he must have thought they were Don Miguel's men."

"And they found him . . . "

Logan's face was grave. "No. He left me in the shelter of the trees and crawled off to die, hoping they'd follow his tracks and that—by some miracle—I might still escape. I think that somewhere near the place where Notched Arrow found me, there is a pile of bones that belong to a man named Quinn Logan."

"Oh! How terrible."

"He was brave man. He deserved a better death." Logan's jaw tightened. "My mother gave him her medallion to keep him safe. He gave it to me, sewing it into my clothes. He died—and I lived."

Bettany tucked her arm through his and leaned her head against his shoulder. "That's what he intended. He loved you because you were a part of Estrella. I wish we could have known them."

It was some time before Logan spoke again. "I'm going to go and find those bones and bring them back. We can have them buried in the churchyard at the convent. They'll finally be together."

"I would like to go with you."

Logan raised her hand to his lips and kissed her fingers. He wanted Bettany with him always. She was half of his own soul, and if not for the ancient tragedies, his path and hers would never have crossed. He brought out his medicine pouch, thinking of the man who had given him his name and the woman whose diaries had given him back his past. The medal sparkled against his callused palm, the Silver Woman standing out in sharp relief.

He felt as if he'd made contact with his mother, as if
Estrella had reached out across the years to touch him. The
air was suddenly scented with a touch of spice, a whisper
of flowers. Then it was gone. The shadows of the past had
been laid to rest.

Logan slipped him arm around Bettany's waist, and she
smiled up at him with so much love that he was blinded
by it. The world seemed ablaze with light. Logan's fingers
curled over the medal. He had meant to keep the medallion
with him but decided suddenly to have it buried with Quinn
and Estrella. It was part of the past. It belonged with them.
And he no longer needed it for his talisman.

He had a Silver Woman of his own.

Award-winning author Marianne Willman is a direct descendant of William Clark, of the famed Lewis-Clark expedition, and shares the same fascination with the American West. Although she loves her home state of Michigan, in the very heart of the Great Lakes, she has a special attachment to the Southwest and its many cultures.

■ HarperPaperbacks *By Mail*

"Full of passion and adventure—an exciting book."
—**ROBERT GELLIS**

"Enchanting, luminous...a stunning, sensual love story that will make your heart soar."
—*ROMANTIC TIMES*

THE LILY AND THE LEOPARD

by Susan Wiggs

Lianna of France, mistress of a great castle in Normandy in the year 1414. Rand of England, King Henry's most fearless and trusted warrior. Their turbulent yet triumphant love story symbolized the clash of two mighty nations poised for war. A sweeping, passionate romance novel set in medieval Europe.

**MAIL TO: HarperPaperbacks,
10 East 53rd Street, New York, NY 10022
Attn: Mail Order Division**

Yes, please send me THE LILY AND THE LEOPARD (0-06-104017-7) at $4.95 plus $1 postage and handling. My payment is enclosed (NY, NJ, PA residents add applicable sales tax).

(Remit in U.S. funds, do not send cash)

Name_____

Address_____

City_____

State_____ Zip_____
Allow up to 6 weeks for delivery. Prices subject to change.

56789 10 11 12—HP-21

♚ HarperPaperbacks *By Mail*
BLAZING PASSIONS
IN FIVE HISTORICAL ROMANCES

QUIET FIRES by Ginna Gray ISBN: 0-06-104037-1 $4.50

In the black dirt and red rage of war-torn Texas, Elizabeth Stanton and Conn Cavanaugh discover the passion so long denied them. But would the turmoil of Texas' fight for independence sweep them apart?

EAGLE KNIGHT by Suzanne Ellison ISBN: 0-06-104035-5 $4.50

Forced to flee her dangerous Spanish homeland, Elena de la Rosa prepares for her new life in primitive Mexico. But she is not prepared to meet Tizoc Santiago, the Aztec prince whose smoldering gaze ignites a hunger in her impossible to deny.

FOOL'S GOLD by Janet Quin-Harkin ISBN: 0-06-104040-1 $4.50

From Boston's decorous drawing rooms, well-bred Libby Grenville travels west to California. En route, she meets riverboat gambler Gabe Foster who laughs off her frosty rebukes until their duel of wits ripens into a heart-hammering passion.

COMANCHE MOON by Catherine Anderson ISBN: 0-06-104010-X $3.95

Hunter, the fierce Comanche warrior, is chosen by his people to cross the western wilderness in search of the elusive maiden who would fulfill their sacred prophecy. He finds and captures Loretta, a proud golden-haired beauty, who swears to defy her captor. What she doesn't realize is that she and Hunter are bound by destiny.

YESTERDAY'S SHADOWS by Marianne Willman ISBN: 0-06-104044-4 $4.50

Destiny decrees that blond, silver-eyed Bettany Howard will meet the Cheyenne brave called Wolf Star. An abandoned white child, Wolf Star was raised as a Cheyenne Indian, but dreams of a pale and lovely Silver Woman. Yet, before the passion promised Bettany and Wolf Star can be seized, many lives much touch and tangle, bleed and blaze in triumph.

MAIL TO: Harper Collins Publishers
P. O. Box 588 Dunmore, PA 18512-0588
OR CALL: (800) 331-3761 (Visa/MasterCard)

Yes, please send me the books I have checked:

☐ QUIET FIRES (0-06-104037-1) $4.50
☐ EAGLE KNIGHT (0-06-104035-5) $4.50
☐ FOOL'S GOLD (0-06-104040-1) $4.50
☐ COMANCHE MOON (0-06-104010-X) $3.95
☐ YESTERDAY'S SHADOWS (0-06-104044-4) $4.50

SUBTOTAL ....$_____
POSTAGE AND HANDLING ....$ 2.00*
SALES TAX (Add applicable sales tax) ....$_____
                                    TOTAL: $_____

* ORDER 4 OR MORE TITLES AND POSTAGE & HANDLING IS FREE!
Remit in US funds, do not send cash.

Name _____

Address _____

City _____

State _____ Zip _____

Allow up to 6 weeks delivery.
Prices subject to change.

(Valid only in US & Canada)   H0031